W9-ADP-579

PAPA TOUSSAINT

PAPA TOUSSAINT

By

C. Richard Gillespie

toExcel

San Jose New York Lincoln Shanghai

PAPA TOUSSAINT

All Rights Reserved. Copyright © 1998 **C. Richard Gillespie**

No part of this book may be reproduced or transmitted in any form or by any means, graphic, electronic, or mechanical, including photocopying, recording, taping, or by any information storage or retrieval system, without permission in writing from the publisher.

For information address:
toExcel
165 West 95th Street, Suite B-N
New York, NY 10025
www.toexcel.com

Published by toExcel, a division of Kaleidoscope Software, Inc.
Marca registrada
toExcel
New York, NY

ISBN: 1-58348-124-9
Library of Congress Catalog Card Number: 98-89853

Printed in the United States of America

0 9 8 7 6 5 4 3 2 1

CONTENTS

CHAPTER 1: It is Finished 1

CHAPTER 2: The New Commissioner from France 7

CHAPTER 3: The Liberation of Port-au-Prince...17

CHAPTER 4: Hédouville's Mission...31

CHAPTER 5: By Diligence North 43

CHAPTER 6: Three Interviews with Hédouville..57

CHAPTER 7: The Secret Covenant...67

CHAPTER 8: Toussaint Resigns 75

CHAPTER 9: Theft at Fort Liberté...87

CHAPTER 10: Attack at Fort Liberté 97

CHAPTER 11: Hédouville Flees...109

CHAPTER 12: He Who Is To Come 119

CHAPTER 13: The War of Knives...127

CHAPTER 14: Disaffection..137

CHAPTER 15: Eighteen Brumaire 149

CHAPTER 16: The New Century 159

CHAPTER 17: The Fall of Jacmel...169

CHAPTER 18: Napoléon's Commissioners 179

CHAPTER 19: Rigaud Surrenders 189

CHAPTER 20: Peace 197

CHAPTER 21: The Island Unified 207

CHAPTER 22: In Paris 215

CHAPTER 23: The Constitution..223

CHAPTER 24: Lions and Jackals 233

CHAPTER 25: Trial and Execution 239

CHAPTER 26: Napoléon 251

CHAPTER 27: Leclerc Arrives..263

CHAPTER 28: Reunion 279

CHAPTER 29: At War with France 295

CHAPTER 30: Ravine-â-Couleuvres..305

CHAPTER 31: Créte-a-Pierrot..315

CHAPTER 32: Capitulation 329

CHAPTER 33: Haïti 351

CHAPTER 34: Death and Dishonor 365

CHAPTER 35: The Abysmal Waters..373

BIBLIOGRAPHICAL NOTES..385

MAP OF HISPANIOLA 389

CHAPTER 1
It Is Finished

Agen, France, April 7, 1816.

It is finished. The book is written.

I have worked day and night for the past nine months in order that I might write on April seven, "It is finished."

Thirteen years ago today, on April seven, 1803, my father died, suffering from the ravages of consumption and exposure, and from the betrayal of those he had served at a price few men would have been willing to pay. It is his story that I write here. It is his memory that sustains me in my task.

It is mid-morning. The sun is risen above the distant hills and shines aslant the river. It will be a bright, cold day. As I think of my father's imprisonment and his death in Fort de Joux, I pull my shawl closer around my shoulders. He who loved the sun died in a dark cell where bitter winds wracked his body in winter and chilled waters soaked his feet in spring.

I know I will never see my father's final habitation. For my supposed crimes I am confined to this small town hidden in the bowels of France, with only the gently flowing Garonne whispering of the freedom beyond. I will never visit in person Toussaint's cell at Fort de Joux, but I will see it always in my mind as Mars Plaisir described it to me.

Much of what I relate in this story I did not experience nor observe directly. But I know it to be true. For thirteen years I have labored to pull together the scattered facts. I have culled them from the memories of my father's friends and enemies, anyone who was willing to pause, if only for seconds, to conjure up a remembrance, pleasant or bitter, of the liberator of the slaves of Saint-Domingue.

I have been helped most particularly by Mars Plaisir, the gentle companion to my father's years of greatness and despair, the man who most clearly read my father's thoughts and who stayed by his side until driven from the final prison cell by Napoléon. And by Louis Duclero, who risked Napoléon's displeasure in his attempts to help my father in his last days of suffering. I must also mention my mother, a woman of strength and compassion who, denied the nurture of her people and her work, is drifting away from her mind and is dying, I fear, from the force of her own will. As I have sat by her bed, I have learned from her, in her moments of rationality, facets of my father's character I could have learned from no one else.

From many sources the story came. But I would mislead the reader if I denied my own contributions. As I have struggled to sift fact from fancy, truth from lie, praise from flattery, fault from calumny, I have depended upon my own knowledge of my father and of the other principals in this story, most of whom I have had the fortune or misfortune of having observed personally. I have also depended heavily upon my own judgments when faced with contradictions of evidence, and upon the inspirations which have come to me in dreams, both sleeping and waking. I acknowledge my mistakes in evaluating the intentions of Napoléon Bonaparte and plead as my defense the naïveté of youth. I confess openly my fears and doubts in moments of crisis. But I also stand proudly behind my loyalty to my adopted father, Toussaint Louverture, when his natural son, Isaac, turned from him.

My natural father was a free mulatto named Séraphin Cleré. He abandoned my mother, Suzanne, who, before I was born, married Toussaint. My mother named me Placide and did everything in her power of love to make my childhood conform to my name. I can to this day remember the comfort I felt engulfed in her ample arms.

Before I was born, Toussaint had been granted the state of liberté de savanne: although technically a slave and employed on the habitation, he was permitted to conduct himself in most matters as a freedman. He enjoyed a position of importance on the Bréda Habitation. He started as a stable boy, then became coachman, and from the time I was old enough to remember he was livestock steward. His master, the Marquis de Noé, trusted him with many responsibilities, as he had Toussaint's father before him. Bayou de Libertas, the habitation manager, treated the slaves with relative kindness, a rare phenomenon in Saint-Dominque.

I, therefore, grew up in an environment that for child of a slave in the West Indies was unusually benevolent. I had learned to read and write before I came to France to study.

Surnames, like family groupings, are confusing among slaves. We often identified ourselves by family names not recognized by the slave owners. It was to their advantage to relate slaves to the habitations on which they resided rather than to family groupings, thus making the trading in slaves less personal for the owners. I was, therefore, Placide of the Bréda Habitation, or, more conveniently, Placide Bréda.

My adopted father was named for two saints: François and Dominque, but was called Toussaint because he was born on All Saints Day. For over forty years of his life he needed no other name than Toussaint. When he became an important leader of his people he adopted a surname in order that he might have credibility with the French. In Saint-Dominque, a single name was the mark of a slave, a double name the mark of a man. My father, therefore, assumed the name Louverture. He became Toussaint Louverture. We in his family were called by the same name. Today, I am, therefore, Placide Louverture.

When my father was twenty-three years old, Napoléon Bonaparte was born on another island. When he became the leader of his people, he dropped his last name and was called by one name, Napoléon. In France, a double name was the mark of a man, a single name the mark of a demigod.

These two men, who never met, form the poles of this story: Papa Toussaint and the Emperor Napoléon. Napoléon destroyed Toussaint and in the process lost his empire. Toussaint liberated his people and in the process lost his life.

I make no claim to be dispassionate in telling this story. I write for one purpose only, to correct the lies that have been written about my father and about the Revolution in Saint-Dominque. It is in France that the story must be heard. It is Frenchmen who must read it, and Napoléon Bonaparte, while he reigned, never would have permitted such a book to be published. I began to write two years ago, after the fall of Paris, but hid the manuscript last spring when the devil escaped from Elba and landed at Cannes with his rabble. I began to write again last June after the British sent Napoléon once more into exile.

Even as I write this last chapter, I fear the story will never be published. Napoléon may be confined to Saint Helena, but there are persons of influence who would wish not to see this book in circulation, most importantly the former Princess Pauline.

I can not leave Agen. It is by the barest mercy of little men in distant offices that I was freed from the prison at Belle île and allowed to join my mother and brothers here. Though the war is years over and the issues resolved, no one has the courage to release us from this confinement. My brother Isaac, with the help of a sympathetic doctor, escapes from time to time to the baths at Luchon or Castéra to relieve the agony of his festering skin. But I can not leave the city even to walk about the neighboring mountains. Isaac committed the crime only of being Toussaint's son. I committed the crime of fighting against the armies of France to preserve the freedom of the blacks of Saint-Domingue.

Agen is a quiet city of farmers, tradesmen and clerics. In the cafés they debate the virtues of the Bourbons and the Bonapartes, the kings and the Emperor. No one mourns the Republic. No one remembers the Revolution. Yet a generation has not passed since the cities and towns of France shuddered under the successive shocks of marching armies, Royalist and Revolutionary, French and foreign, Republican and Imperial. Now the citizens of Agen worry about taxes and trade and stare curiously, but without malice, at the black family that dwells in poverty among them.

We live in poverty, sustained only by a pitiful pension granted by a reluctant government. I would write of our suffering here, but that is only postscript and I would not have it distract from the central text, the story of Toussaint Louverture.

The Republic is no more in France, and France is no more in Saint-Domingue. The debate for king or emperor which fascinates France is echoed in Saint-Domingue. In the North of that war-scarred island, the King Christophe has succeeded the Emperor Dessalines. Only in the South does the Republic hold its ground under the presidency of Alexander Pétion.

In the North under King Christophe, the plantations are worked and the economy flourishes, as it did under Toussaint. But the people my father struggled to free are again in bondage, laboring, much as the slaves of Egypt labored, to build for the tinseled king, Sans-Souci—a palace of pride—and Laferriére—a fortress of fear.

In the South, the people bask in the benevolence of their government, as they once did under Toussaint, but no one works. The people sleep and dance, and soon they will starve.

The dreams are gone: Toussaint's dream for Saint-Domingue and Napoléon's dream for France. The dreams could have been one. Each could have supported the other, and the people of all of France, in the metropole and in the West Indies, could have flourished because of those dreams. But now Toussaint and Napoléon are gone and lesser men of smaller vision rule.

Haïti.

I have resisted writing that name. It was Haïti—land of mountains—that the first inhabitants called the island. They called themselves Arawaks—the good people. In time, the fierce Caribs, who in turn fell victims to the Europeans, subjugated the Arawaks. Columbus called the Arawaks and Caribs Indians, mistaking them for the inhabitants of the Indies. He called the land Hispaniola, the Isle of Spain. The conquistadors who followed, in their lust for wealth killed the Arawaks and Caribs and changed the name of the land to Santo Domingo (Saint-Domingue in French). They and the French who followed brought my people from Africa—brought Toussaint's father from Africa—to wrest the wealth of sugar and coffee from the soil. It was in Saint-Domingue that I was born. It was in Saint-Domingue that Toussaint led the slaves to freedom. It was in Saint-Domingue that Toussaint established a French government respecting the rights of all men. I know King Christophe and President Pétion. I want no part of their Haïti. Like my father, I am French. Despite my country's betrayal of Toussaint and of her people in Saint-Domingue, I remain French. The island will always be Saint-Domingue to me.

Saint-Domingue. Was ever a name more abused? Named for the gentle Dominic Guzman—preacher of poverty, friend of Saint Francis, courageous minister to the wild Albigenses—the island became a land in which the heedless search for earthly riches justified all forms of tyranny and cruelty.

Beautiful Saint-Domingue. No man who has seen it will ever forget its green foliage embracing blue waters, its brilliant flowers mantling the plains and mountains, its clear streams plunging over rocks into misting pools, its perfumes filling the breezes, mixing day and night with the songs of hidden birds. Saint-Domingue is a garden of Eden, but unlike God's Eden, its beauty is deeply scarred by the evil of men.

For thirteen years I have struggled in myself as to where to begin my father's story. With his ancestors in Africa who in their native land were chieftains? His birth as a slave in an alien land? His education under the tutelage of that rare pedagogue Pierre Baptist? His family and stewardship on the Bréda Habitation? The outbreak of the slave rebellion? His rise to command of rebellion forces? His appointment as Governor-General of France's richest colony?

In my fumbling attempts to write the story I have at various times begun at each of these moments. But my final choice is to begin at the height of my father's authority and to trace the events of his betrayal and destruction. I do so not because I seek the morbid nor because I am impelled to describe my father as a figure of tragedy. It is rather that the earlier history of his life often has been chronicled, especially by those well-meaning but short-sighted whites who see in my father the embodiment of their belief in Rousseau's noble savage. Such writers are unable to come to grips with his vigorous employment of authority and his deep devotion to France. They look upon his last years as an unfortunate aberration and seek to rationalize his actions with ridiculous theories, when in fact it was in the last five years of his life that Toussaint faced his most rigorous tests and made his most difficult decisions. In the end, it is not his failure I chronicle here, but the failure of the Republic, of France, of the Revolution.

I have another compelling reason to focus on my father's final years. It is then that he and Napoléon Bonaparte faced each other in enmity across the unfeeling ocean. The true story of that encounter has been repressed by the Emperor with a vigor and purposefulness that will distort it perhaps for all time. I do not believe that my poor efforts will make more than a small ripple in the tide of official histories that flowed in the wake of the arrogant Bonaparte. But I will never rest in the world to come if I do not make what efforts I can in this world to correct the injustices done my father by Napoléon's toadies and sycophants, who have over the years pressed upon a gullible public their distorted histories of the unfortunate occurrences in Saint-Domingue from 1798 to 1803.

CHAPTER 2
The New Commissioner from France

Moïse was less than ten years my senior, but there was a generation between us. I was sixteen when I sailed to France and the life of a pampered scholar. I felt the excitement of the new freedom and the pride of being the son of Toussaint Louverture. But Moïse had fought seven years for freedom and had paid for it with deprivations and injuries. Because of the protected life I had lived as a member of Toussaint's household, the realities of slavery had slipped into the recesses of my mind. For Moïse, the memories of the middle passage, which he had endured as a child, and the struggle for freedom and dignity were ever foremost in his thoughts.

Moïse, like Toussaint and Toussaint's wife Suzanne, was of the Arada tribe. When the boy was bought for the Bréda Habitation, Toussaint and Suzanne welcomed him into their family. He called Toussaint uncle, a word that expressed both affection and the blood kinship of being a fellow tribesmen.

De Libertas had Moïse christened Gilles Bréda, but when Moïse joined the Revolution, Pierre Baptiste gave him the name Moïse—for Moses, the prophet of the tribe of Levi, the liberator of the enslaved Israelites.

Moïse was a thin man, of average height, but he carried himself with a pride that gave the impression of great stature. Early in the Revolution he lost the sight in his left eye. With his good eye he could stare down any man. I never remember seeing mirth or humor in that eye. Compassion, yes; gentleness, yes; but never humor.

Moïse was a restless man, at ease only when engaged in a physical task. He hated idleness in himself and in others. Unlike most of our people, he had no patience with children. Although he never spoke of it, I felt keenly his displeasure at what he considered my unnaturally extended childhood.

I was jealous of Moïse, of my father's affection for him and trust in him. Toussaint had love enough in his heart to share with all, but I felt pain whenever my father openly showered his affection on another. It is only now, in retrospect, that I can see the stature of Moïse.

On the morning of Friday, April twentieth, 1798, Moïse woke before dawn. It was raining. Something in his dreams had disturbed him. He rose and began to dress. His movements alerted the household. Moments later his valet arrived, breathless, carrying the general's newly brushed boots.

The dream had involved Toussaint. But that was not unusual. Moïse had been disturbed with Toussaint for some months, and in his mind he often had long, imaginary arguments with his uncle.

The rain stopped before breakfast. Moïse ate on the veranda overlooking the small, land-locked harbor of Fort Liberté. Three droghers were unloading at the quay. A single sloop stood out in the roads waiting for barges.

Moïse was joined at breakfast by his secretary, Delatte, a former French schoolteacher of no family, who, when the Revolution exploded in Saint-Domingue, elected to survive by his wits. Delatte brought fresh dispatches from Toussaint. Among the papers was a copy of Toussaint's appeal to the French inhabitants of the areas of the colony still occupied by the British.

Delatte read, in his flat, nasal voice, Toussaint's proclamation: "For the third time, I appeal to the citizens of Port-au-Prince to return the city to the Republic."

Moïse knew what would follow, promises of pardon if Toussaint's request was honored, threats of retaliation if it was not.

But why another proclamation, Moïse thought to himself angrily. Toussaint could crush the British forces at Port-au-Prince. There were over a thousand battle-conditioned troops sitting idly here in Fort Liberté who would gladly storm the city, no quarter given, none asked. Then the planters who turned to the English for help in holding to their slaves would know what it was to feel the whip on their backs. And the English, who maimed and tortured black prisoners of war and sold women and children to the slave traders of Jamaica, would get more than a note requesting that they act with honor!

Moïse pushed his dish away in anger. "No more," he said to Delatte.

Moïse got up and started toward the fort.

"You remember you are to meet the new commissioner from France in Dajabón today?" Delatte called after him.

"Yes," responded Moïse. "I remember."

Moïse had no stomach for inspection. He yelled at a soldier who had forgotten his boots, and slapped him when he tried to show the general the blisters on his feet. Moïse understood Toussaint's desire that the soldiers look like soldiers, but for himself, he didn't care how they dressed. He didn't care if the soldiers had boots or not. Drill and discipline, yes, but on a long march or in battle the uniforms soon vanished. Let Christophe parade his hussars at the Cape. Here in Fort Liberté there were, thankfully, few occasions requiring boots and fancy uniforms.

By seven o'clock Moïse had started on the short ride to Dajabón. Behind him rode the thirty mounted soldiers of his personal guard. The Fifth Regiment was infantry. The new commissioner, Hédouville, would have to be content with an honor guard of thirty only.

The sun and the fresh breeze from the northeast dried all traces of the morning rain. The dust stirred by the horses' hooves blew in fine particles onto the vegetation pushing to the edge and falling over into the drainage ditches at the sides of the road.

Moïse was sensitive to the sounds surrounding him: the rustle of the wind in the sugar cane, the groan of leather shifting with the movement of horses, the low chatter of his guard riding at ease behind him, the broken patterns of many hooves striking the hard dirt road, the occasional clink of a metal shoe hitting a small stone.

The inscrutability of Toussaint disturbed Moïse. The older man revealed himself to no one. He spoke always of the need to unify all men on the island, yet he was not blind to the duplicity of the whites, all of them, French, English, Spanish, Americans. The blacks had learned from hard experience not to trust any of them.

It seemed to Moïse that Toussaint conducted himself as if he were preparing a defense for some future court martial, an appeal to the court of history, perhaps. It was a foolish way to proceed. What slave ever trusted a court to defend his rights under the Black Code? And history was the game of the white man.

The Revolution may have granted the blacks of Saint-Domingue their freedom, but only their courage and strength sustained it. The fewer the whites, the less threat of treachery. The fish trusts the water, but it is in the water that the fish is cooked.

Moïse and his troops reached the Dajabón River before noon and crossed the long stone causeway into the Spanish lands.

The governor's carriage was in the town square. At Moïse's orders it had been driven from the Cape to await the convenience of the new commissioner.

Hédouville kept the young black officer waiting. The commissioner had arrived hours earlier and, at the invitation of the Spanish agent in the city, bathed and enjoyed a leisurely meal. Outside in the noon sun, the black soldiers of Moïse and the white soldiers of Hédouville lounged on opposite sides of the square, separated by differences not bridged by the revolutionary blue of their French military uniforms.

Gabreil Marie Theodore Joseph, Compt d'Hédouville, former page to Marie-Antoinette and Marquis and Chevalier de Saint Louis, hero of the Vendée, sailed from Brest on the eighteenth of February with two hundred soldiers on three ships. After an uneventful journey he landed the twenty-seventh of March in Santo Domingo City. Following the advice of Saint-Domingue veterans in Paris, Hédouville landed at the capital of the former Spanish colony to confer with the French commissioner Philippe Rose Roume before confronting Toussaint.

The eastern half of the Island, the former Spanish colony of Santo Domingo, had been ceded to France in the treaty of Bale three years earlier. The Directory specifically limited Toussaint's authority to the western half of the island, the part that for a hundred years—since the treaty of Ryswick—had been the French colony of Saint-Domingue. Roume's instruction as civil commissioner was to insulate Santo Domingo from Toussaint's influence. Roume had repeatedly petitioned the French government for assistance in controlling Toussaint's growing independence. Hédouville was dispatched from Paris to provide that assistance. His orders were simple and clear: create dissension between the chief native leaders in the colony—the black Toussaint in the North and the mulatto Rigaud in the South—and use each to destroy the authority of the other.

Hédouville marveled at the remarkable island to which he had been sent. None of his conversations in Paris had fully prepared him for the beauty and graciousness of the land. On the southern coast he sailed past lush plantations situated on wide beaches. At Santo Domingo City, the oldest city of the new world, he found a deep, well-protected harbor, a warm sun, cooling breezes, gracious streets, beautiful stone houses built around luxuriant gardens, and a proliferation of fruits, seafoods and meats heaped in the market place. Compared to the clutter and poverty of Paris, Santo Domingo was paradise. If one considered the gentleness of the climate and the abundance of food, it could be said that a field laborer lived better in Santo Domingo than an artisan did in Paris, and a proprietor better than a courtier did at Versailles. The biggest complaint he heard from the Spanish planters was the lack of cultural and intellectual stimulation, a complaint that registered poorly with him. For Hédouville would choose a ride on a spirited horse through the Sierra Prieta in lieu of attending the best opera ever penned by man. If the planters who complained, thought Hédouville, had spent one half the time he had at the court of France, they would have had culture enough for a lifetime. Hédouville found the Andalusian ways of the city a relaxing relief from the stresses of Paris, especially the custom of the men and women living segregated lives, meeting only for breakfast.

Hédouville's conversations with Roume were pleasant but not particularly instructive. He learned no more of the nature of his adversaries than he had learned in Paris. All he learned of importance was that Roume possessed the qualities of a successful public servant: little intelligence and less imagination balanced by tenacity and a will to survive.

Hédouville elected to ride to Cape François with half of his entourage while sending the remainder by sea. He sought greater knowledge of the land and its people. His fleet commander, Admiral Fabre, wanted to survey the coast and test the English blockade. They planned to meet at the Cape at the end of April.

On his ride north through the center of the Spanish colony, Hédouville found the land sparsely populated. For much of the way he followed a narrow path between the rain forest on the right and the mountains rising on the left. At Saint Yago he was surprised to find an outpost of civilization, a city almost as large as the Spanish capital in the south. But from Saint Yago to Dajabón on the border of Saint-Domingue, Hédouville plunged back into virgin forests and the task of fording unbridged rivers flooded from recent rains.

On the morning of the twelfth day from Santo Domingo City, Hédouville and his party reached Dajabón. There he was informed that Toussaint was sending an honor guard to escort the new commissioner to Cape François.

After his leisurely meal, Hédouville conducted with Moïse a perfunctory review of the soldiers in the square, Hédouville's one hundred and Moïse's thirty. Hédouville accepted Moïse's offer of the carriage for the ride to the Cape. It was a Berlin, with the customary long chassis, high rear wheels and small front wheels. Hédouville noted with satisfaction the Daleine springs. If the roads in Saint-Domingue were as well maintained as those in the south of Santo Domingo, the carriage would be tolerable and would offer a welcome change from the saddle. He invited Moïse to ride with him, but was relieved when the black officer indicated that his responsibilities required that he ride with the commissioner's escort.

Hédouville pulled the curtains against the sun. The carriage, built as a ceremonial vehicle, with a high roof, ornate carvings and painted panels, rode surprisingly well. Its rhythmic swing was restful. But being opened on four sides it admitted more sun and dust than did a travelling coach.

Hédouville had heard much of the destruction of Saint-Domingue, especially in the Northern Plain, by the armies that had battled for this ground. But he saw little of the destruction now. The fields were in cultivation. The houses, the few he could see from the road, were in repair. Occasionally he noted a stone fence with an unrepaired breach or a gate lying unhinged, but none of the devastation he had imagined. He was struck, also, by the number of able-bodied men he saw laboring in the fields. Remarkable, he thought, for a country supposedly wracked for seven years by the bloodiest of civil wars. How quickly, he thought, the wounds of the earth heal in the tropics.

As he sat in the carriage, alone, slipping occasionally into sleep, Hédouville became aware that he was in a country of black men. In his drowsiness, disconnected images grew into an impression which, until he was able to rouse himself to wakefulness, startled him. Along the road groups of black laborers, dressed in their field clothes of loose fitting white trousers and flowing white shirts, with colorful handkerchiefs around their heads or necks, stopped their work raking or patching the roadway to let the entourage pass. In the fields black workers, men in their white, women in colorful dresses, many with children working or playing around them, stopped to watch the carriage and horsemen. On the road ox carts driven by black men, or black women with burdens piled high upon their heads, paused to let the carriage through. In the small towns the streets and markets were filled with black people buying and selling fruit, chickens, pigs, clothes, baskets. As they recognized Moïse, many rushed to him, touching his horse or reaching for his hand, shouting his name. Others peered curiously into the carriage, wide smiles on their faces.

Hédouville had the sense that he was a prisoner in the carriage, that he passed in peace only at the behest of the silent black general that rode before him. In the journey through Santo Domingo, Hédouville's escort of a hundred soldiers had seemed an army. Here in the Northern Plain, surrounded by thousands of black faces, they seemed an ostentation. Hédouville had seen the communes of Paris, led by men of passion, pull down a city and overturn a country. Here, in this black multitude, he knew he was face to face with the strength of Toussaint Louverture.

One of Hédouville's young officers, on the ride from Saint Domingo City to Dajabón, had joked about going alone into Toussaint's stronghold and pulling the jack-a-napes out by his madras handkerchief. Hédouville wondered if the young man was making his jokes quite as loudly, now.

That night Moïse and Hédouville stopped near Quartier-Morim at the Duclero Habitation. Moïse, Hédouville and their senior officers dined with Louis Duclero and his beautiful mulatto companion, Anacaona. Duclero sat at the head of the table with Hédouville at his right. Anacaona sat at the foot of the table with Moïse at her right. Duclero and Hédouville talked animatedly, mostly about the changing political climate in Paris. Anacaona and Moïse spoke little, but their eyes met frequently.

Hédouville and Moïse were given rooms in the great house. Their officers slept in tents pitched on the lawn. The enlisted men slept where they could under the stars. Most of the black soldiers found bunks with friends or relatives in the servants' cailles.

After dinner, Hédouville and Duclero talked long into the night. Moïse and Anacaona walked in the garden. Occasionally they stopped in the shadows and kissed.

The next day, Hédouville chose to enter the Cape on horseback at the head of his one hundred soldiers. He contemplated having Moïse ride with his thirty mounted guards at the rear of the column, but let discretion govern him and had the young general ride beside him. Moïse agreed, but marked well in his mind that his guard of thirty was placed in the rear.

From Quartier-Morim to Cape François the road ran along the edge of the wastelands by the sea, through fields of scrub grass, trailing vines, brambles and a few stunted trees. Hédouville could see the city across the harbor, snuggling along the water and climbing the lower arms of the embracing Morne Haut-du-Cap. White houses gleamed through breaks in the variegated green of the foliage and the exploding red, orange and yellow clumps of flowering vines and trees. In the harbor, coastal droghers and fishing boats crowded the few large vessels that lay at anchor. Hédouville noted that his three ships had not yet arrived from Santo Domingo.

They crossed the bridge at the mouth of the Haut-du-Cap River, turned right onto the quay and rode seven blocks to Place le Brasseur, across the small square and into Rue Government, then nine blocks to Rue Notre Dame. There they turned left and rode three blocks to the Place d'Arms.

Hédouville was struck by the contrasts of the Cape with Santo Domingo City. The harbor was open to the east, and, unlike Santo Domingo's, it was ringed with deceptive shallows. He observed a group of fishermen, a full half league from the shore, wading about with nets within a few fathoms of the anchored ships. There was a rush of industry here that contrasted with the indolence of the South. Although some people followed the horsemen into the square, most seemed too busy to give more than a moment's notice to Hédouville's arrival. The stevedores stopped their work long enough to doff their hats as he passed, and then returned to their tasks.

The greatest contrast to Hédouville was the state of the buildings. The Cape had not fully recovered from the disastrous fire of 1793 when the French commissioners called in the laborers from the fields to help them deport the Royalist governor. The governor left, but not before the slaves—who had not yet heard that the National Convention in Paris had conferred citizenship upon them—ravaged the city and set fires that burned for four days.

Hédouville observed the construction underway, but he also observed the number of huts and shacks that crowded the central section of the city. He marveled that the city which from a distance appeared whole and luxuriant should, when entered, appear fragmented and grubby. It was as a painted woman might appear, her blemishes hidden with distance. In this case the flowering trees and vines that grew in profusion from the charred ground supplied the cosmetic.

At the Place d'Arms, Colonel Henri Christophe had his hussars from the governor's barracks drawn up awaiting the arrival of the new commissioner. Fifty strong they stood on the north side of the square, facing the partially restored church. At their backs was the low stone structure of the guardhouse, one of the few buildings in the city center to escape the fire.

In another setting Hédouville would have been less startled by the sight of the mounted troops, but in contrast to the disarray of the city their resplendence was striking. The horses they sat astride were among the finest he had seen on the island. The soldiers were unusually tall for Saint-Domingue blacks, and the head pieces they wore—tall black mirliton caps, wound with red silk cloths whipping in the breeze—made them appear as giants. They wore blue dolman jackets with ornate yellow braiding on the chests, and blue trousers with yellow piping tucked into calf-high black leather boots with yellow braided tops and tassels.

In front of the fifty stood the commander of the Cape, Colonel Henri Christophe. He was a tall, barrel-chested black man astride a huge black charger. His uniform was a duplicate of his hussars except where they wore yellow braiding, he wore gold. Under the hot sun and heavy uniform the perspiration rolled profusely down Christophe's round face.

As Hédouville entered the square, a small band, located on a temporary platform erected in front of the church, struck up the "Marseillaise." Christophe and his hussars drew their sabers smartly in salute, and the color guard unfurled the tricolor of the French Republic.

As Hédouville sat quietly upon his horse, his own saber drawn in answering salute, a warmth flooded through him. Monarchy or Republic, France was his country, and even in this exotic setting the rituals of her patriotism moved him deeply.

After informal introductions and greetings, Hédouville took his place on the temporary platform with local dignitaries, including Moïse, commander of the North; Christophe, commander of the Cape; Charles César Télèmaque, the black mayor of the Cape, and Julien Raimond.

Raimond gave the welcoming address to Hédouville.

"Citizen Commissioner," he began, "the Executive Directory will be touched by the attachment of the citizens of the island of Saint-Domingue to their mother country and to her constitutional government...."

As Hédouville listened to Raimond his eye caught the sun glinting from the water in the fountain at the center of the square. It was a simple fountain, circled by a low stone wall which now was crowded by black figures standing to get a better view of the proceedings. The water poured gently from a pipe at the top and fell easily over two circular basins to the pool below.

As he watched the water of the fountain sparkle in the sunlight, Hédouville's mind spun with the confusion of the politics of Saint-Domingue. He was being welcomed by Julien Raimond, a man he had been warned to distrust, and yet a man for whom in other circumstances he would have had the greatest respect.

Hédouville looked closely at Raimond. His shoulders were slightly bent with a scholar's hunch. His brown face showed his fifty-four years. His eyes, behind his wire-framed glasses, seemed timid and uncertain. His voice was light but strongly marked by a self-conscious Parisian dialect. He appeared a tired man, one who had long passed his time of battles.

Yet Hédouville knew that Raimond had been foremost in the struggle for the rights of mulattos, risking his life repeatedly for that cause during the height of the Terror. Raimond's companions in the battle, Ogé and Chavannes, had been brutally tortured and killed—close by the fountain whose sun-lit waters had caught Hédouville's eye—by the outraged whites of the Cape when the two arrived from France with the news that the Convention had granted citizenship to mulattos.

Raimond concluded his speech. "We swear hatred to royalty, hatred to tyranny, and complete devotion to the Republic."

And he led the assembled people in the cheers:

"Long live liberty! Long live the Republic!"

Why, thought Hédouville, is Raimond my enemy? Because, he answered himself, this man—who fought against the emancipation of the slaves—sided with the ex-slave Toussaint Louverture against Raimond's fellow commissioners.

The politics of Saint-Domingue, Hédouville thought wearily, is a never-ending convulsion.

CHAPTER 3
The Liberation of Port-au-Prince

A week after Hédouville arrived at the Cape, fifty leagues south in English occupied Port-au-Prince, the city's white mayor, Bernard Borgella, searched through the night for a British officer.

Borgella found him in the Red Lion on the quay near the aiguade. The inn was housed in a worn wooden building hastily constructed after the fire of 1784 had razed most of Port-au-Prince. The inn since had served as a gathering place for sailors and now catered to the British soldiers. Borgella referred to the inn as the chameleon because it changed its color to match the political circumstances. Its most recent name, Red Lion, was adopted to honor the arrival of the Scotsman, Thomas Maitland, to command the British forces in Port-au-Prince.

As he had been advised he might, Borgella found Robert Gillespie in a room on the second floor regaling a group of young officers and several women of the night with stories of his exploits with gun and knife. It took patient persuasion in the face of good-humored insults for Borgella to get the little major to walk with him to the fountain in the old Place Valliere where they could speak in some privacy.

The evening was warm but not oppressive. The sky was clear. The air still. Hardly a night, thought Borgella, in which to seek news of the end of the world.

Gillespie, like many Scotsmen, spoke French fluently, but the flat pronunciation of his vowels amused Borgella, when it didn't irritate him.

"They say Maitland sent you to negotiate with Toussaint Louverture," began Borgella.

"They say many things," responded the diminutive major with an air of exaggerated mystery.

"Is it true?" insisted Borgella.

"That I negotiated for Maitland with Toussaint Louverture?"

"Yes."

"Yes and no," answered Gillespie, smiling shrewdly.

"Well, did you or didn't you?"

"Yes I did, and no I didn't."

Borgella had a strong urge to push the little major into the fountain, but restrained himself with a skill learned from many years of surviving the politics of Saint-Domingue.

"Did Maitland send you to negotiate with Toussaint?" Borgella began again patiently.

"Yes, he did that."

"Did you go?"

"Aye, I did that."

"Did you talk to Toussaint?"

"No, that I did not."

"What happened?"

"The little black fellow sent along a Frenchman to talk with me. A white fellow. As white as you. A good bit taller, though, and not nearly as fat about the gills."

Borgella refused to be distracted from his errand: "Is Maitland surrendering the city?"

Gillespie laughed. "Now, wouldn't I be the fool to answer that?" suggested the Scotsman in good humor. "Do you think I want my guts scattered about like that silly Peyrade fellow?"

The reference was clear to Borgella. Less than a week had passed since Maitland convicted a mulatto merchant of seditious conduct for publicly declaring that the English were going to desert the city to be sacked by the black savages of Toussaint Louverture. Peyrade was tied across the mouth of one of the big cannons at Fort Royal, and in public execution his insides were splattered onto the parapet by a charge of grapeshot. It was a refined touch of punishment Maitland had picked up in Calcutta. Peyrade's fate had stopped open discussion of British desertion, but not rumors.

"If you want to know Maitland's business," Gillespie continued, "you're going to have to ask King Tom himself."

"I intend to," responded the Frenchman, surprising himself with his bravado.

"If I'd met the little black fellow," Gillespie called after the departing figure of Borgella, "you'd have known it. I'd have tucked him in my pocket and brought him back for everybody to see."

As Borgella walked to his house off the old Place l'Intendance, he fought the despair that threatened to engulf him. He had accepted the post of mayor of Port-au-Prince and its accompanying honoraria as an appropriate recognition of his civic contributions. That was before the Revolution. Now the rapid swings of fortune buffeting his city threatened to send him to a madhouse. He was the proverbial man upon the tiger. He yearned to dismount, but he knew that the moment he weakened he would be devoured.

For eight years he had survived. He had survived the rise of the Jacobins. He had survived the mulatto rebellion. He had survived the slave revolt. He had survived the occupation by the English. He had survived by accommodating. He had addressed himself to one issue: the safety of the city. If the city prevailed, then its mayor survived. Borgella had a genius for the cleverest of political acts, the act of appearing to be without politics.

Borgella paused outside his bedroom. The heavy, even sounds of his wife's breathing told him she was asleep. He decided to spend the night in his son's old room rather than risk waking her. He knew he would toss and turn for most of the night.

Borgella had married Cecile la Mahautiere, the daughter of a white lawyer and his mulatto wife. The Borgella and la Mahautiere families had roots in the Cul-de-Sac that pre-dated the founding of Port-au-Prince in 1750.

Borgella, because of his wife, had sympathized with the desires of mulatto leaders to establish citizenship for free men of color. The initial mulatto rebellion in Port-au-Prince had brought anxiety and fear, but in 1791 the whites and mulattos made their peace rather than risk an uprising of the slaves. Borgella helped in reaching the agreement, he and men from the other long established colonial families who, for several generations, had intermarried with the mulattos.

The fear that had brought the mulattos and whites together in 1791 was again stalking the city in 1798: the triumph of the blacks.

As Borgella lay still in the bed, trying to let his mind slip into sleep, two words haunted him, the Swiss!

In the fighting of 1791 the mulattos were aided by a group of maroons, blacks who fled the plantations to live in the mountains. They had been called the Swiss because of their courage and ferocity. After the concordat had been signed, both the white and mulatto leaders were hesitant to send the Swiss back to the plantations or to allow them to return to the mountains for fear they would arouse all blacks to rebellion. The city leaders decided to ship the Swiss to a deserted beach in Mexico where they would have a chance to live free. Borgella supported the plan, he remembered now with great anxiety, because it seemed at the time a humane solution to a difficult problem. But the ship's captain took the blacks to Jamaica and tried to sell them to the English. The Governor of Jamaica sent them back to Port-au-Prince. He did not want them mixing with the slaves of his island. This time the white dominated Colonial Assembly put the Swiss to death—all but twenty whom they sent back to the mountains in an attempt to keep the enmity alive between black and mulatto.

Borgella's body was soaked with perspiration. The night was not hot, but no wind stirred, and the curtains of the bed blocked all flow of air.

The Swiss. What revenge would Toussaint exact for the Swiss if he took the city? Neither white nor mulatto would be safe. The thought made Borgella's stomach ache.

He sat bolt upright in bed as if propelled by an external force, his body shaking. He could hear again the sound of the gun that smeared Peyrade's body on the ramparts and walls of Fort Royal.

Borgella sat still, his arms wrapped tightly about his body. After a few moments he was able to lessen the trembling, and lowered himself back onto the sheets. He lay shivering, as if in a fever, his thoughts on Maitland.

General Thomas Maitland: King Tom Maitland, as his soldiers called him, part in derision, part in fear. A man who seemed to look upon all the world as his enemy. A man who found virtue in no one, neither in countryman nor stranger, neither in subordinate nor superior. A man who gave the impression of being condemned to dwell as the only man of whole flesh in a world of lepers. Maitland had come, succeeding the gentlemanly but inept English general John Whyte. Maitland put the city under martial law, a law that put all men upon a basis of equality—the equality of the forecastle.

———————◆———————

Borgella drifted through the early morning as if in a trance. He breakfasted, but could not remember upon what. He chatted with Cecile, but could not remember about what. His mind was riveted to the face of the tall clock on the stair landing. At seven, precisely, he left the house.

Borgella walked the six blocks to Government House, now called King House—more in honor of King Tom, he thought bitterly, than of King George.

Despite his sleepless night, Borgella's short, heavy body radiated a nervous energy that was best released in exercise. He walked always, reluctantly agreeing to horse or carriage only upon absolute necessity.

Borgella was directed to a small room off the central hall, and there he waited. He was certain Maitland was in. English officers came and went throughout the morning, but Borgella waited. He waited through the noon hour. He had no appetite and was certain a little fasting would only aid his health.

Borgella was alone in the room and stood for long periods looking out of the window toward the harbor. Government House was on ground not significantly higher than the harbor, but the wide streets—a safety measure adopted after the earthquake of 1770—offered glimpses of the British vessels anchored in the crowded roads.

Borgella preferred to look out on the bustle of the city rather than on the austerity of the room. The Jacobins had removed all the pictures and statues of French royalty that adorned the room before 1789. Now the narrow hall was decorated with only two paintings: at one end of the room there was a faded copy of a portrait of King George the Third of England, and at the other end a painting of an aristocratic lad of twelve or thirteen years, dressed in the red and blue uniform of an officer of the Edinburgh Light Horse, seated upon a spirited pony, saber drawn. The young man had a passing resemblance to Thomas Maitland. The buds of youth, thought Borgella as he looked at the painting, how soon they wither.

Early in the afternoon a carriage pulled up to the front entrance of Government House and several English officers dismounted. Borgella recognized the ranking officer as General Nightingale, chief of staff to Maitland. A naval officer whom Borgella did not recognize accompanied him. The two, while their carriage waited, were ushered directly to see Maitland. Thirty minutes later they hurried out and were driven toward the harbor. A few minutes after, a sergeant major informed Borgella that Maitland would see him.

Brigadier General Thomas Maitland was a tall man given to a softness of body. He did not appear fat, but there was the suspicion of slackness in his jaws and neck and in his midsection under his tightly fitting uniform. Maitland's face was set and his eyes were cold, although they seldom caught the gaze of the person to whom he spoke. His appearance was immaculate, his uniform brushed and pressed, his wig carefully powdered.

After a restrained and formal greeting, Borgella closed his eyes for a brief moment, breathed deeply and challenged the British commander.

"Do you intend to defend this city or do you not?" he inquired.

Maitland smiled. "You should be pleased to hear that the war has ended in Port-au-Prince."

Borgella felt a moment of dizziness. "You are surrendering the city," he asked with disbelief.

"A convention of peace was signed this morning by representatives of his Majesty's government and the Republic of France."

"Toussaint?" Borgella spoke the name more as an accusation than a question.

"General Huin signed for the French government, General Nightingale for his Majesty's."

"This morning...."

"Aboard the 'Abergovenny.'"

Borgella remembered staring at the ships. There...secretly.... He felt the anger swelling up into his throat.

"Do you realize, sir, the fate to which you abandon us?"

"It is my understanding that General Louverture intends to issue an amnesty for the citizens of Port-au-Prince."

"Amnesty?....In Saint-Domingue?" Borgella asked incredulously.

"Yes. The word was his."

Borgella was infuriated by Maitland's patronizing smile. "You are being cynical, sir."

"You are being rude!" Maitland responded vehemently.

"Are you going to evacuate from this city all who are not prepared to trust their lives to that man's...amnesty?"

"His Majesty's government welcomes settlers to Jamaica, but I hardly have the means to transport there the population of Port-au-Prince."

"Whom do you intend to evacuate?"

"My first responsibility is to transport his Majesty's troops with their weapons and military stores to Môle Saint Nicholas."

"Toussaint has agreed to this?" interrupted Borgella.

"He has." Maitland continued. "I shall evacuate also all French citizens who fought under the English flag and who desire to continue their service to the King."

"And the rest?"

"Toussaint's government has promised to embrace them all in the open arms of love and forgiveness."

Borgella made a sound between a snort and a laugh.

The two men stood in silence for a moment.

"Sir." Borgella made a half bow and turned to leave the room.

"One moment, Mr. Borgella."

The Frenchman stopped and turned back.

"I would appreciate your knowing that it is not my decision to abandon the war in Saint-Domingue. I am under orders from his Majesty's government to reduce our commitment here. It would never be my choice to seek terms—not from any enemy, and certainly not from ignorant savages. Upon my arrival I found that through his mismanagement and stupidity, General Whyte had made our position militarily precarious. I cannot commit the resources necessary to reestablish it and still obey my instructions from Whitehall. We are both, I fear, the victims of circumstances beyond our control."

"And while, sir," responded Borgella, "you lick your wounded pride in Môle Saint Nicholas or Jamaica, the blood from our wounded bodies may be beyond stanching."

"May I remind you," replied Maitland, "I did not create the conditions of Saint-Domingue. I fear, Mr. Borgella, we live only to serve, each in the place and manner preordained by God."

For the next two weeks, panic governed the city. Many who previously had strived to maintain a visible neutrality, now, in elaborate petitions addressed to the British commander, tried to prove their unstinting loyalty to the English cause. Others bribed the few merchantmen in port to take them as passengers. Others abandoned all property and fled in small fishing boats and coastal droghers. But most agonized in the conflict of their desire to believe Toussaint's promises, and thus be able to retain their homes and property, and their fear of the ravage and torture they had every reason to believe lay before them. The cathedral was filled day and night with worshipers petitioning God to intercede or, at the very least, to soften the hearts of the black victors.

The convention for peace was signed on Monday, April thirtieth. The following Monday, May seventh, Toussaint's proclamation declaring amnesty for all the citizens of the West under the control of the English was read in Government Square and copies posted throughout the city. The next day news came that Toussaint's troops had peacefully occupied Saint Marc. On Wednesday the news that Toussaint had led the assembled inhabitants of that city in a pledge of fidelity to France. Hope ran high in Port-au-Prince that, miracle of miracles, the city might change commands without the atrocities that historically accompanied victories in Saint-Domingue.

Borgella listened to the declarations of hope by his neighbors, but he reminded himself that the citizens of Saint Marc did not massacre the Swiss.

On Saturday, the Eighth Demi-Brigade under the command of the black general Mornay entered the city from the Cul-de-Sac to the north, and the Ninth Demi-Brigade led by the mulatto general Alexander Pétion entered from Léogane to the south. The citizens of the city feared, and to some extent hoped, that when the two brigades met—one predominately black, the other predominately mulatto—the civil war that had haunted Saint-Domingue for seven years once again would erupt. If the mulatto and black troops fought each other, some reasoned, they might overlook the civilians and the city would be spared the massacre all feared.

The soldiers of both commands filtered quietly through the city and took up pre-determined posts in the barracks and fortifications vacated by the English.

Borgella learned from Mornay that Toussaint planned to enter the city on Monday.

Sunday Borgella attended mass. He joined his voice with those of his neighbors in supplication that the storm of retaliation would not begin on the morrow.

As he knelt upon the prie-Dieu, Borgella knew he must not trust his safety and that of the city solely to the Shield of David. After mass, with the irresistible energy that was his when a course of action became clear to him, he fell upon the leading citizens of Port-au-Prince with a fury of persuasion. They must be willing to give generously of the gifts of peace, he argued, if they would not risk losing everything—including their lives—as spoils of war.

———————————— ✧ ————————————

On Monday, Toussaint Louverture left Arcahaie shortly after dawn. He rode his tall, gray stallion, Bel-Argent. He was accompanied by an honor guard of one hundred horsemen, by his valet and by several secretaries. The long, smooth pacing strides of Bel-Argent soon outdistanced the horses of the entourage.

The road south from Arcahaie followed the narrow plain between the Bay of Port-au-Prince on the right and the steep Mateaux Mountains on the left. Where the sun broke through the barrier of the mountains it inflamed the bright, yellow blossoms of the poui trees that spread up the lower terraces of the hills.

Soon it will rain, Toussaint thought, noting the fallen yellow petals sprinkled through the dark green leaves of the coffee and cacao shrubs planted in the shade of the poui.

Bordering the road and scattered through the irrigated fields of sugar cane stretching down to the bay were clumps of mango trees, their green leaves tinged purple by the ripening fruit. In the sandier stretches there were orchards of papaya trees, their broad green leaves scattering out from the clustered fruit like exploding rockets; and plantations of sisal, thin stems shooting ten feet in the air from nests of leaves huddled at the bases.

Toussaint was pleased. Although the narrow plain of Arcahaie was not one of the great fertile areas of the colony, Toussaint was pleased it had escaped the devastation of war.

Toussaint reigned in Bel-Argent where the road crossed the dry streambed of the Torcelle River. From the gentle rise of Point Boucassin he could see Port-au-Prince nestled at the foot of the towering Charbonniere. In front of him a line of ships, almost motionless in the gentle breeze, stretched from the port up the channel of Saint Marc and out of sight to the north: the English evacuation to the Môle.

In less than an hour Toussaint covered the two leagues from Arcahaie to the village of Boucassin. There, before the church, he addressed the assembled population. As he had done at Saint Marc and Arcahaie, Toussaint assured the people that France welcomed back all who were ready once again to swear allegiance to the Republic.

Toussaint's secretary read to them the "Declaration of the Rights of Man and Citizen." Then Toussaint mounted again his beloved Bel-Argent and from the saddle led the people in shouts of "Long live the Republic! Long live liberty! Long live equality!"

Toussaint rode on toward the Cul-de-Sac. Behind him the people shouted, "Long live Toussaint Louverture!"

As Toussaint followed the road into the Cul-de-Sac, eastward now toward Croix-des-Bouquets, he rode past burned fields and razed houses, memorials to the intensity of the offensive against the British in February and March. Near Bon Repos he passed a house burned almost to the ground, marked now by charred and broken walls. Near the veranda a giant flamboyant tree stood in full bloom, its scarlet blossoms echoes of the devouring flames.

Toussaint loved living things: horses, children, cultivated fields. The sight of death and destruction saddened him. He touched his spurs gently to Bel-Argent's flanks and hurried on.

Toussaint arrived at Croix-des-Bouquets shortly after noon. He was greeted by his brother, Paul, commander of the Tenth Demi-Brigade. When the rest of his entourage caught up with him, Toussaint repeated for the citizens of the city the ritual of swearing fidelity to France. Then he joined his brother in a quiet lunch of chicken vegetable soup, cheese and spring water. The two brothers talked of family matters and a little of their hopes for the future of the colony. Toussaint was pleased to see Paul and to take a few moments from the pressures of command and decision. For his part, Paul treated his older brother with deference, mindful of his indebtedness to Toussaint for his rank and affluence. There was an ease between the two men, but little warmth and no intimacy.

In the afternoon it began to rain, steadily but not with great ferocity. Toussaint left Croix-des-Bouquets at four. At the little village of Cul-de-Sac, where the road crosses the Grand River of the Cul-de-Sac, he was met by the first of the deputations from Port-au-Prince.

The water had begun to run in the river from the rain, but it came only to the knees of the horses as Toussaint's party crossed at the ford. On the south bank, the first to greet Toussaint was Bernard Borgella, seated upon a gentle black mare. Behind him the road to Port-au-Prince, a league's distance, was lined with well wishers: men, women, children of all classes and factions.

Field laborers in happy groups waved their hats enthusiastically, or stood quietly, tears of joy mixing with the rain on their faces. Two white women rode by in a one-horse sociable, the top down, colorful parasols protecting their heads from the rain. The liveried black boy driving the carriage kept as close to Toussaint as he could until shooed away by one of the mounted guards.

From the beginning of the Saint Martin Habitation to the Saint Joseph Battery, the road was strewn with blossoms: crimson, purple, orange and white clusters of the paper flower of trinity, delicate sprays of rose spider-lilies, funnel shaped silver cups, crisp stalks of crimson and blue lobster claws that crackled and popped under the horses' hooves, and piles of hibiscus of every hue. A group of small white children presented the black general with a necklace of delicate sky flowers. Another group of children laid a blanket of orange trumpet vines and violet Liane Saint John over the haunches of Bel-Argent.

Just before the Saint Joseph Battery the road was spanned by a hastily erected wooden arch vaguely in the style of the Triumphal of Septimius Severus. Across the frieze was emblazoned in gold painted letters: PORT REPUBLICAIN, the revolutionary name for Port-au-Prince, and over the three portals: LIBERTY, EQUALITY, FRATERNITY.

The garrison of the Saint Joseph Battery was drawn up in review on the ramparts. As Toussaint entered the small square behind the fort, they raised their rifles and in groups of three fired twenty-one salvos in salute.

Where the square narrows into the Rue Grande, Toussaint was greeted by the few clergy remaining in the city. They displayed the trappings of their office that had not been stolen or hidden. With incense, cross, bell and banner they led the parade down the Rue Grande through the center of the city the ten blocks to Rue de Roaille, then left and the three blocks east to Government Square. As Toussaint entered the square, skyrockets were fired from the corners of the square and from the hills behind the city.

The subject of these adulations, Toussaint Louverture, sat quietly upon Bel-Argent acknowledging the greetings along the route with curt nods of his head. His small body perched upon his great horse, he appeared more a jockey from Longchamps than the Governor-General of the colony. His blue and gold uniform was partially covered by a black rain cape draped over his small shoulders. On his head, in place of the wide cuffed bonnet with cockade and plume of a French officer, he wore a yellow madras handkerchief knotted at the nap of his neck. His face and head were small. His lower jaw was strong and protruding. His eyes were large and wide-set. They seemed to move incessantly, missing nothing.

In the center of the square there was erected a covered dais surmounted by a throne-like chair. Borgella, accompanied by a priest and two acolytes swinging censers, approached Toussaint to lead him to the dais.

Toussaint shock his head. "Incense and a dais belong only to God," he said, the first words he spoke in the city.

Although he was tired, Toussaint agreed to join Borgella and his guests for dinner in the great dinning hall of Government House.

Borgella had arranged dinner for one hundred and fifty. He invited the planters, merchants and professionals who contributed the cost of the dinner, but he also made certain that men and women from all classes were included.

Toussaint ate little, briefly acknowledged the many toasts directed toward him and retired early. The dinner continued long into the night. Outside, revelers drifted from party to party, their way lit by massive torches. The hissing of the rain hitting the flames and the shadows dancing across the broad streets parodied the festivities flowing from the great houses. All of Port-au-Prince celebrated the city's miraculous escape.

On Tuesday afternoon, Borgella led a group of twelve distinguished citizens in calling upon the Governor-General. Toussaint received them in the office where Borgella, two weeks before, had challenged Maitland.

Toussaint stood behind a large table. The delegation stood respectfully before him.

A mulatto lawyer, François Lespinasse, had been selected as spokesman. Borgella felt that the mistake he had made the previous day with the dais argued for him to play a less conspicuous role in this day's proceedings.

"Citizen General-in-Chief," began Lespinasse a little nervously, "understand the sentiments of the inhabitants of this city. We come to fulfill a happy duty in laying in your bosom the expression of our fidelity and love for the French Republic. Being her citizens is our happiness and glory."

A little flowery, thought Borgella, but he had been among those who had argued that flattery was important in dealing with a man of Toussaint's background.

Lespinasse stepped forward with a gold medal on a black ribbon. Engraved on the obverse was a likeness of the Governor-General, and on the reverse the words "After God—He," the words Toussaint spoke in reference to Governor-General Laveaux when Laveaux appointed Toussaint as his assistant. Lespinasse attempted to place the medal around Toussaint's neck, but Toussaint took it from the lawyer and, without looking at it, laid it on the table.

With a start Borgella remembered that Toussaint had spoken the words, "After God—He," after saving Laveaux from a mulatto assassination plot. Had Toussaint taken offense at a mulatto giving him the medal? With relief Borgella realized that Toussaint could not have read the inscription. He had not even looked at the medal.

"As you know, Citizen General," continued Lespinasse, "the city of Port-au-Prince was the birthplace of the Revolution in Saint-Domingue...."

Stupidity, thought Borgella. They were trying to convince Toussaint of their revolutionary zeal, and Lespinasse didn't even use the right name! Port Republicain, not Port-au-Prince!

Lespinasse spoke of the cruelties of the English, the courage of the French resistance, the suffering and destruction of the city.

"Look into our hearts and judge us, Citizen General," he concluded. "Lay down the base for the new government of this important city, and you will see that our trust in you will be equaled only by our loyalty and our submission to the laws under which we will go forward to live in happiness."

Toussaint listened to the speech without visible emotion and at its conclusion stood quietly for a few moments without replying.

Borgella's mind churned. Port-au-Prince instead of Port Republicain. The motto that could only bring to mind past treachery. And the Swiss. Toussaint would not let that pass. The worst was not over; Borgella was certain of it.

"Citizens," Toussaint finally began. "My satisfaction in recovering for the Republic the areas occupied by the English equals that which you feel in once again becoming French citizens. If your conduct justifies your right to that beautiful title, I desire nothing more."

Toussaint spoke about his success in saving the city from destruction and its inhabitants from death. He spoke of their duties as citizens and his willingness to forget the past and forge a new future.

"The pledge you have made to me today cannot be made with lips alone. Your heart must dictate it! Your conduct must justify it!" Toussaint insisted with vehemence.

He concluded his speech with the announcement that France was sending a new commissioner to the colony: "Citizen Hédouville, whom it has chosen from among its most worthy citizens. Let us aid him in his important mission by absolute obedience!"

Borgella was light-headed as he walked home. The storm had not come. Toussaint was compassionate and conciliatory. But Borgella was not at ease.

Toussaint was a man of dangerous self-importance, Borgella concluded in his mind. Although Toussaint was gentle in manner, he was also arrogant. What evidence, Borgella asked himself. The three secretaries sitting at the end of the room quietly recording Toussaint's every word. In strange ways, Toussaint reminded Borgella of Maitland. The Englishman was overtly arrogant. Toussaint was more subtly so. But both were impatient with the lesser mortals with whom the world was populated.

Despite his misgivings, Borgella sensed some virtue in Toussaint. He seemed a man of peace. He had spoken extemporaneously, with greater facility for language than Borgella had expected. As a lawyer Borgella was impressed by an effective turn of phrase.

A phrase Toussaint used jumped into Borgella's mind. "The age of fanaticism is over. The reign of law has succeeded that of anarchy."

A good phrase, well put, thought Borgella. But of course he would like it. What lawyer wouldn't want the world ruled by laws instead of force, Borgella thought with a laugh. Deep in his heart he yearned for a world of reason, a world free from imminent terror and revenge.

Could Toussaint Louverture tame the passions of this island? He had already done more than any man thought possible.

Borgella thought about Toussaint's praise of the new commissioner, Hédouville. Was it possible for the rupture between Paris and the colony to be repaired?

Borgella found he wanted to put more trust in Toussaint's assurances than common sense told him he should. No man could heal the wounds of Saint-Domingue, and how unlikely a candidate!

"My God," thought Borgella out loud. "How many times in the past two weeks did I envision my death? Yet today I am alive and well."

With a start Borgella realized that Toussaint did not mention the Swiss! Was it an oversight? When he remembers...?

Miserére nobis, mourned Borgella. How difficult a thing is faith.

CHAPTER 4
Hédouville's Mission

Toussaint delayed meeting with Hédouville. His excuse was his preoccupation with the English who still held strongholds at Môle Saint Nicholas in the Northwest and Jérémie and Tiburon in the Southwest. Toussaint's real reason for delay was that he wanted to confront Hédouville from the position of power he would have with a full victory over the English. But Maitland was too well entrenched in the Môle, and the mulatto forces under Rigaud were too hesitant to attack in the South.

At the end of May, with only his victory at Port-au-Prince to support him, Toussaint reluctantly agreed to meet with the new commissioner.

Toussaint arrived at the Cape on Tuesday, May twenty-ninth. Hédouville greeted him with all the pomp due Toussaint's office of Governor-General. The two soldiers: Hédouville tall, thin and pale, looking older than his forty-three years; Toussaint short, thin and black, looking younger than his fifty-four years, rode side by side in review of the troops of the city's garrison. That evening Hédouville hosted Toussaint at a formal dinner. The black general politely refused all food, complaining of a troubled stomach.

Toussaint had the ability to see behind a man's words. As a child I was convinced he could read my mind. I realize now that he was a keen observer. His eyes caught every gesture, every facial expression. His mind registered every indication of nervousness, every change from the ordinary. The blacks who followed him were convinced that Toussaint had the power of second sight as a gift from Papa Légba. Most found it impossible to conceal their feelings from him and learned to trust his capacity to forgive rather than attempt to lie to him. The gift of truth seeing was of great value to Toussaint. It often saved him from falling into ambuscades, both political and military.

Toussaint did not need many hours in the Cape to detect the ill will harbored there for him. Hédouville's staff conducted themselves before him with due formality, but he could see the ridicule hidden in their eyes. He could see the stifled grins, could sense the whispers beyond his hearing, could interpret the sudden laughter after he passed. He could read the messages of warning in the eyes of the black servants.

On Wednesday, May thirtieth, Toussaint and Hédouville met to discuss the political situation in Saint-Domingue. They met in Hédouville's office in Government House. The windows of the office commanded a view of the city. Immediately below were the formal gardens of Government Square and the fountain in the Place de Montarcher. To the right were the gardens planted by the Jesuits before they were banished from the colony for teaching slaves to read and write. Further below were the church and the Place d'Arms where the ceremony greeting Hédouville upon his arrival had been held. Beyond that, at the bottom of the hill, were the quay and the harbor.

The room was decorated with simple elegance. The center of attention was the Louis Quatorze desk Hédouville had brought with him from France. The walls of the room were lined with bookshelves, most of which were filled with books. The open window was framed by heavy maroon drapes. The floor was parquet, constructed of mahogany, cheery and poui-oak segments arranged to form an intricate design of fleurs-de-lis oriented to the corners of double squares. By the open window were two high-backed, carved, wooden chairs and between them a small, round table on which sat a decanter of red wine and two stemmed glasses. Hédouville and Toussaint sat in the high-backed chairs. Hédouville sipped from time to time from his glass. Toussaint left his untouched.

Hédouville was a model of cordiality and respect. He complimented Toussaint on his victories over the English and on his adroit negotiations for the evacuation of Port-au-Prince.

Toussaint remarked on the excellent reputation Hédouville brought with him from France. "Your success in bringing peace to the Vendée," Toussaint praised the Frenchman, "marks you as the very person to knit together the troubled threads of Saint-Domingue."

Hédouville was forthright in presenting the limits of the authority he brought from France.

"My mission is not military," he explained. "I bring the full authority of the government in matters civil, but I am instructed not to interfere in any way with your direction of the war against the English. Specifically, I am charged with promulgating the laws decreed by the Council, with guaranteeing respect for the Constitution, with assuring the tranquility of the island both in its internal government and its relations with other governments, with protecting the liberty of all citizens and with enforcing strictly"—here Hédouville paused to give his words emphasis—"the Council's ruling against the return of emigrés to French soil."

Toussaint made no challenge to Hédouville, but they were both aware of the potential for conflict in the issue of the emigrés. In his amnesty for Port-au-Prince and surrounding districts, Toussaint had not included the French who had borne arms for the English and Royalists who had not lived in the colony before the Revolution. However, he had welcomed back Saint-Domingue proprietors who had fled to the English for protection during the fighting. At the time, Toussaint informed Hédouville of his intentions and the commissioner made no objections, but his emphasis upon the word "strictly" gave Toussaint some concern for the future.

With the formal aspects of the interview concluded, Hédouville sat back comfortably in his chair and sipped easily from his wineglass.

"Before I left Paris," he began casually, "your friend and defender Félicité Sonthonax suggested to me that the greatest threat to harmony in Saint-Domingue is André Rigaud."

Toussaint made no reply. He felt the tension move up his back and into his shoulders and neck. He did not want to believe what he was hearing. Hédouville was playing the incessant theme of the French: black against mulatto, mulatto against black.

"Sonthonax," continued Hédouville, "suggests that there never will be peace between the races while Rigaud is in a position of authority. It is my understanding that when he was commissioner, Sonthonax declared the man an outlaw."

Toussaint stared at the sunlight glinting on the red wine Hédouville swirled in his glass. The tension had passed into Toussaint's stomach. The sight of the wine made him nauseous.

"I have full authority from the Directory for you to arrest Rigaud." Hédouville paused, waiting for a reply from Toussaint. "How do you advise me? I do not want to move precipitously."

"Arrest Rigaud?" Toussaint responded with controlled anger. "I would as soon arrest myself! Do you not know with what zeal Rigaud has defended the cause for which we all fight? I look upon him as I would upon my own son."

"I stand corrected, of course," apologized Hédouville. "Having only the advice of those removed from the scene, I am dependent upon your judgment."

There was a moment of silence as each evaluated the tension between them. Hédouville broke the silence.

"It was a grievous error for me to suggest that you arrest Rigaud. But it was an error of ignorance, not of ill will."

"I understand," replied Toussaint.

"My fear, now," continued Hédouville, "is that my mistake may grow in dimensions larger that it need. I would not have my indiscretion lead to dissensions between us or between you and Rigaud or between Rigaud and myself. If I knew the matter would go no further than this room, I would be more at ease."

"It is ended."

"Thank you."

Hédouville sipped his wine before continuing.

"I deplore government based in secrecy." Hédouville spoke with intimate confidence. "I am embarrassed that our first meeting should have put us in the position of sharing an unfortunate secret. But I am relieved that I share it with a man of your integrity." Hédouville smiled warmly. "I look forward with great interest," he continued, "to meeting with citizen Rigaud."

The meeting with Hédouville troubled Toussaint. He knew from his experiences with Sonthonax that a shared secret could well be the canker that grows into a disease afflicting the body politic. Toussaint wanted to believe that Hédouville had been sincere in his concern for the relations between Toussaint and Rigaud, but Toussaint had learned from bitter experience to trust his first instincts. He could not forget the anxiety that gripped him when Hédouville began his attack upon Rigaud. Toussaint was resolved to give the Commissioner no grounds for criticism, but he was resolved also to maintain his vigil.

At the conclusion of the meeting Toussaint left the Cape. He rode a bay gelding named Acajou. He had left Bel-Argent at Saint Marc. He had horses placed strategically throughout the island. When he wished to travel long distances, he changed mounts frequently. At each of the habitations where he had a horse stabled, its care was a central concern of the proprietor.

Toussaint missed the even pace of Bel-Argent, but he galloped the five leagues to Dondon, and there, without waiting for his entourage to catch up with him, traded Acajou for the sure-footed little black mare, Noire-Sang, and continued on into the mountains toward Guava.

Hédouville knew he had played a clumsy hand with Toussaint. But he knew also that Toussaint was not to be trusted. He had seen the arrogance burning in his eyes. Sonthonax had said that Toussaint intended to establish himself as the king of an independent Saint-Domingue, and Hédouville now was convinced of the truth of Sonthonax's accusation.

There were two sides to Hédouville's equation. If his calculations regarding Toussaint were not balancing, he would address the Rigaud side. Hédouville looked to the mulatto Julien Raimond to find the way to the mulatto Rigaud.

Hédouville had chosen to live in Habitation Bailly, located five hundred fathoms north of the Cape along the road to Fort Picolet. It was a small enclave, fifty by seventy-five fathoms, surrounded by a high hedge of yellow and pink poui trees. The property was nestled in a draw of the Morne Haut-du-Cap that reached to the edge of the quay north of the city.

The week after his interview with Toussaint, Hédouville invited Julien Raimond to dine with him at Habitation Bailly. Hédouville used as a pretext his desire to have Raimond's opinion, as an economist, on changes Hédouville was proposing for the colony.

As the two men talked after dinner, the breeze blowing down the Mouchois and Silver Bank Passages swept the sweet fragrances of the garden into the dining room where they mixed with the pungency of Cognac and cigars.

"Of course, no changes can be implemented until after the defeat of the English," Hédouville assured Raimond.

"What changes do you anticipate?" asked Raimond.

"Two, principally. First, the laborers will be bound to specific habitations for established contractual periods."

"For how long?"

"That is negotiable, but I would suggest three to six years."

"And your second policy change?"

"The standing army would be disbanded."

"You mean the black army?" asked Raimond

"Yes, that is precisely what I mean," replied Hédouville.

Raimond smiled and shook his head with a quick gesture as a horse might flick off a fly. The two men smoked in silence for a moment.

Raimond asked, "Are you telling me what you are going to do, or are you asking me for my opinion?"

"I value highly your opinion, of course."

"Have you asked Toussaint his opinion on these matters?"

"No."

"Why not?"

"It is premature. I will discuss them with him when the English are defeated."

Raimond paused for a moment to collect his thoughts. Then he spoke.

"You can do nothing in this island," he began, "without the agreement and support of Toussaint."

"France has no intention of surrendering the colony to Toussaint Louverture," Hédouville responded sharply.

"I didn't suggest it should," responded Raimond patiently. "I merely stated a political reality."

"Political realities change. No man is indispensable. The Revolution teaches us that, if nothing else."

"With whom would you replace Toussaint?"

"André Rigaud."

Raimond laughed.

Hédouville was annoyed. He paused a moment to allow his temper to cool. "I do not understand your response," he finally replied.

"I beg your pardon, General. It was impolite," Raimond apologized. "But I fear you do not understand the two men to whom you refer."

"I would appreciate your enlightening me."

"Toussaint wins battles. Rigaud endures sieges."

"I am not enlightened."

"Toussaint wins battles because he is tireless," explained Raimond. "He persuades, he exhorts, he threatens, but he is everywhere. His subordinates never know when or where he will appear and act always as if he is watching them. No matter which way his enemies turn they find Toussaint standing before them."

"And Rigaud?"

"He fights for an hour. Then a pretty wench turns his head and the battle must wait. His subordinates curse, or laugh, and are left to their own resources. They act as if he knows nothing of what they do, and when the battle is lost, he flies the field decrying those who betrayed him."

"I do not intend to remove Toussaint until the war is ended," explained Hédouville.

"The war in Saint-Domingue is never ended," replied Raimond.

Hédouville splashed the amber brandy gently in the sniffer. He felt frustration growing within him. At every turn he was faced with insubordination or timidity. He looked curiously at the small brown man across the room from him. Raimond seemed totally absorbed in wiping his eyeglasses with a large linen handkerchief.

"I do not understand you," Hédouville confessed.

"What do you not understand, General?" asked Raimond.

"I know for a fact that when you served in the National Assembly you opposed the emancipation of the slaves. Now you have sold yourself to a black man."

"I opposed emancipation because I feared the horrors of a black uprising. I support Toussaint for the same reason," explained Raimond reasonably.

"Are you suggesting that Toussaint is the only man who can control the blacks?" asked Hédouville.

"I am."

"I find that suggestion naïve."

"Excuse me, General, but I find your opinion uninformed."

Hédouville was about to retort angrily but controlled himself. He finally responded with excessive politeness: "I look to you, then, to inform me."

"Let us examine your proposed policies," began Raimond energetically, ignoring Hédouville's sarcasm. "You wish to bind the laborers to the land for set terms of years. I think Toussaint would support you in that, if the policy protected the laborers from abuse and provided them with adequate wages. Toussaint, I believe, would support you because he works for the restoration of the economy, and he knows as well as you and I that the Saint-Domingue black, given his head, would not choose to labor on the land. I, for one, understand why. The African was brought to Saint-Domingue because the European could not or would not endure the labor necessary to make the land flourish. You could not pay me enough to voluntarily cut cane. Why, then, should I expect a black man to do it for the most meager of wages when he can meet the basic needs of his life by fishing for an hour and plucking the fruit from the nearest tree? Yes, being a reasonable man, Toussaint might well support your first policy. But who is to enforce that policy if you disband the army?"

Raimond paused for a moment to draw upon his cigar.

"Do you ask me that question," inquired Hédouville. "Or do you ask it rhetorically?"

"I ask you."

"How I would enforce the laws after the standing army is disbanded?"

"Yes. How would you?"

"I would disband only the black forces. The European regiments would be intact. And if there is a major difficulty there is always the National Guard."

Raimond laughed again.

"I find your response both annoying and disrespectful," retorted Hédouville.

"I apologize," replied Raimond quickly. "But I find the official French response to Saint-Domingue to be ridiculous. You would take men like Toussaint, Dessalines, Paul Louverture, Christophe, Moïse, Mornay, Clairvaux—and I mention only a few of the brigade commanders. There are hundreds of regimental and company officers. You would take these men and tell them they must give up their arms and return to the toil of the fields."

Hédouville interrupted. "Naturally the blacks who held leadership positions would not return to the fields."

"No?"

"Of course not. They would be offered positions as overseers if they wished, or pensioned. They would keep the property they have. They wouldn't have to work again if they chose not to."

"You believe that men who have experienced the authority these men have would be content with pensions? Would you?"

"I am not a former black slave. They should be pleased to have their liberty. Only France offers them that."

"If the Revolution has taught us anything, General," replied Raimond, deliberately repeating Hédouville's phrase, "it is that force can only be defeated by force. If you dismiss the black generals and disband their armies—and by some miracle they cooperate—with what force will you combat the force of the laborers?"

"With the only force then left on the island, the European regiments and the National Guard."

"I am trying to make you see that the one irresistible force on this island is the black laborers."

"They would have no weapons. How could they prevail in the face of armed cavalry, in the face of cannon?"

"The way they have prevailed to this day," answered Raimond. "Do you think the blacks began their revolt only after they secured modern weapons and drilled in the arts of soldering? I have seen their charges, nothing in their hands except sticks, rocks or scythes, bursting headlong through double ranks of disciplined musket and pike, the first throwing themselves into the mouths of the cannons to protect those who followed. In their wake no living thing moved. They fight with a passion that is foreign to us. They follow their houngans who have convinced them that they are immune to bullets or else that it is better to die and go to their reward in Guinée than to live in shackles in this world. You saw the passion of the communes. It is as nothing compared to that of the black slaves bursting free from their chains. I have seen women rip unborn children from their wombs rather than have them face a life in slavery. I have seen...."

"But slavery is no longer the issue," interrupted Hédouville, "France does not threaten the blacks with slavery. She demands only discipline and subordination."

Raimond sat for a moment studying the halo of smoke drifting past his head toward the shadows of the inner wall of the room. He dispersed it with an impatient wave of his hand.

"I will create for you an apologue," Raimond responded. "One day a black laborer climbs into the lower branches of a calabash tree. He calls his co-workers to come from the field and hear what he has to say. He introduces to them his cousin on his father's side—a fellow tribesman—who works as a stevedore in Port-de-Paix. His cousin has a fearful tale to tell. The cousin climbs onto the first branch of the tree where all may hear him—the listening crowd growing larger by the moment. The cousin explains that there is a mysterious ship anchored in the harbor of Port-de-Paix. It sits low in the water from the weight of its cargo, but no one unloads it. A maternal brother of the cousin—also a fellow tribesman and therefore a man to be believed—swam out to the ship by night, climbed its anchor chain, forced open a hatch and saw the cargo. It was, he said, chains, shackles and instruments of torture.

"If this scene were played today, within hours, if not minutes, Toussaint or his deputy would be on the scene. The two cousins and several leaders selected by the group would accompany him to the harbor. There they would be rowed to the ship and the hatches opened, where they could examine to their satisfaction that the cargo consisted of logging chains and harnesses for oxen. They would be given samples to take back to the habitation, and soldiers would ride throughout the area explaining the situation.

"Now the scene is played when there is no Toussaint, no Moïse, no Christophe. Within hours there are thousands of laborers storming the city, burning and pillaging out of fear."

"I think you overstate your case."

"I do not, General. I do not."

For long moments neither man spoke. Hédouville recalled the uneasiness he felt on the carriage ride across the Northern Plain. Finally he broke the silence.

"What I do not understand is why, regardless of the dangers involved, you choose to desert your own and throw your support so vehemently behind the blacks."

"Desert my own?"

"Yes, Rigaud. It should be clear to you that I have in mind strengthening Rigaud's position in the colony."

"There is a sickness that affects this colony," replied Raimond bitterly. "It is a set of mind that presumes that virtue and ability increase with lightness of skin. I told you that Rigaud has lesser abilities than Toussaint. Your predecessor, Sonthonax, regardless of his resentments of Toussaint, must have told you the same. He certainly tried all in his power to remove Rigaud from office. Yet you persist in the opinion that Rigaud should be elevated over Toussaint. From no reason that I can see other than that his skin is lighter. And you assume that because my skin is brown I would welcome the advancement of another brown man over that of a black.

"Despite this sickness" continued Raimond angrily, "there is a miracle taking place here, but France cannot see it. For the only time in history that I am aware, black men and white men, former slaves and former slave masters, and the mixed race of their illegitimate progeny, stand side by side in liberty and equality with the opportunity to extend the principles of our great Revolution to dimensions never before conceived by man. The new world that had its birth in the barricaded streets of Paris has the potential of finding its fullness of growth in the mountains and plains of this remote island. But I fear that growth will be stunted. Only one man has the vision and ability to bring it to fruition, and he is not immortal. Because of the color of his skin he is surrounded by powerful enemies, such as yourself, and when he falls—and I cry long life to him—when he falls the promise of the Revolution will fall with him."

"I think you have created," responded Hédouville with quiet intensity, "a Rousseauean romance to mask your culpability in supporting Toussaint's treachery against Sonthonax."

"Am I to understand, then," asked Raimond, "that when Toussaint falls I am high on your list of those to be arrested?"

"I have no such list. That is more of your romance."

"When I entered the struggles for the rights of men of color, I did not expect to survive long," continued Raimond excitedly. "It was a coincidence of fate that my friend Ogé, and not I, was executed in the square of this city. I have no skills at arms, but no man has ever intimidated me into saying anything that is not of my conscience. No man. Not Robespierre, not Sonthonax, not Toussaint and not Hédouville."

"I thank you for your candor. I know now where I can turn for an honest opinion," answered Hédouville with controlled politeness.

As Raimond walked back to his small house on Rue Saint Louis, he felt the conflict of emotions rushing through his chest. He felt the pride of his stand against Hédouville, but at the same time he was aware of the ridiculous figure he cut. He often told himself he had survived the Revolution because no one considered him a threat. His gentle manner, his scholarly appearance, his public reserve marked him as more an eccentric than a revolutionary. He knew he had created the illusion of arrest with Hédouville to satisfy his need to appear courageous.

When he was able to get past the rehearsal of his act of bravado, Raimond felt a genuine pain of despair. Would France never leave Toussaint in peace to complete the Revolution in Saint-Domingue? Perhaps he should warn Toussaint of Hédouville's duplicity. But Raimond knew he would do nothing of the sort. What could he tell Toussaint that Toussaint did not already know? Raimond knew he was only an observer. Even when it might appear to others that he was central to events, he knew that he was only an observer of them.

Hédouville sat for several hours on his veranda smoking. He watched the waves break upon the reef on the far side of the channel, the crests and spew white in the moonlight. He listened to the irregular lapping of the harbor ripplets on the rocks below his garden. Raimond had taught him a lesson he would remember. The loyalties on this island were not marked solely by color.

CHAPTER 5
By Diligence North

Throughout the month of June, Toussaint scoured the island for military supplies to send to Rigaud. As the amnesty was peacefully implemented in the West, he was able to send Rigaud additional troops. Toussaint was careful to keep Hédouville informed of each move. Near the end of the month Rigaud's dispatches reflected growing optimism that the English would soon capitulate in the South.

Toussaint rode to Desachaux.

Toussaint knew he must have Desachaux the first time he saw it. It was a league west of Ennery, south of the main road from the Cape to Port-au-Prince. Its rolling fields, surrounded by citron trees, were nestled in a draw of the great Cahos Mountain range. Due south, hovering like a silent sentinel, was the Morne Chapelet, six hundred fathoms high.

To Toussaint, the hills were like fingers of a cupped hand holding the fields in a gentle embrace. The mountains beyond, dividing North from West, were like the twisted and distended backbone of a hunchback—a trial to travelers but a haven to a people in revolt. The mountains at his back gave Toussaint a feeling of security.

Toussaint loved the sharp edges, the deep colors, the bright forms of precious gems. They were to him miniature echoes of the protecting mountains. In rare moments of peace he sought out gems and brought them to Desachaux for safekeeping. He often thought of Desachaux itself as a rare jewel. Most of the tillable land of Saint-Domingue lay in the Northern Plain, the valley of the

Artibonite and its tributaries, or the Cul-de-Sac of the West. Desachaux was a rare and beautiful exception, lying quietly, hidden between hills and mountains. It was at Desachaux that Toussaint dreamed of retiring with his family, his fields, his gems and his horses. It was to Desachaux that Toussaint fled to find respite from war and politics.

At Desachaux, Toussaint supervised the breaking to saddle of a young stallion. He insisted upon riding the animal first himself, much to the consternation of Suzanne.

"You are too old for that," she chided laughingly as they walked from the paddock to the house.

"He is only nervous," Toussaint answered. "Frightened of the unknown. He has no malice in his heart for me." Unlike many I confront outside Desachaux, he thought wearily.

In the evening Suzanne and Toussaint walked hand in hand, dressed in the simple white of the laborer, to inspect her young coffee trees. In their wake a dozen children romped and played, children of the habitation laborers. Toussaint stopped for a moment to watch a boy of ten or twelve working beside an elderly man. The two were chopping the weeds from their private vegetable garden. The old man worked with deceptive ease, economy in each movement. The boy stopped and started, hoeing with great energy, but always racing to keep up with his mentor. Toussaint thought of his own youth, of the years with Suzanne's father, Pierre Baptiste. He remembered his endless questions and Pierre Baptiste's patient answers: the ways of growing things, the secrets of medicinal plants, the language of animals, and at night, the logic of shapes, the magic of numbers, the meaning of letters, the tales of the past, and most important, the respect for the sacred.

On the twenty-fourth of June, Toussaint received word from Rigaud that the English were beaten in the South and soon should ask for terms. Toussaint forwarded the good news to Hédouville and rode to Port-au-Prince to prepare General Huin for the negotiations with Maitland.

On the thirtieth of June, the English frigate "Roman Emperor" came to anchor in the lee of the île à Vache on the south coast of Saint-Domingue. A ship's boat, bearing a flag of truce and a request for an interview with André Rigaud, put ashore at the city of Les Cayes.

The next day, Colonel Georges Harcourt, a French emigré now in the service of the English, came ashore to speak with the mulatto commander. They met at Government House. The initial meeting was short. Harcourt presented Rigaud with a dispatch from Maitland requesting an exchange of prisoners.

"Is that the only dispatch you have for me?" asked Rigaud suspiciously.

"Yes," answered Harcourt.

Later, over a glass of Barbancourt orange rum liquor, they spoke informally of the political and military situation in Saint-Domingue. Harcourt congratulated Rigaud on his recent election to the island's Legislative Assembly, and then spoke of Maitland's intentions in the island.

"He evacuated the West," Harcourt explained, "in order to concentrate on Jerémie. The English believe Jerémie to be indispensable for protecting the approaches to Jamaica."

"The English are beaten here. Maitland knows that," responded Rigaud. "They are going to have to evacuate the entire South."

"Maitland is well aware of the talk to that effect. But he intends to hold Jerémie. He will give up Tiburon and the rest, but not Jerémie."

Rigaud hated the English. He had little use for any whites, but he hated the English. For reasons he could not fathom they marked him as a potential traitor. In the Christmas battle for Léogane in 1794, they tried to corrupt him into abandoning France. He forced the English officer to speak publicly of the British treachery, and then sent the man packing. In July of 1797 the English offered him twenty million francs to defect. They thought he would be ripe for plucking because of the abuse he had suffered from Sonthonax. But Rigaud's loyalty was not for sale.

Rigaud realized how clever Maitland was to send a Frenchman to talk with him. If Maitland had sent an Englishman, Rigaud would have refused to speak to him.

Rigaud was annoyed at Harcourt's casualness. There was no question in Rigaud's mind but that Harcourt was under instructions to drive a wedge between him and Toussaint. But the Frenchman, with his deliberate speech and disarming manner, was annoyingly slow at revealing the bait.

"I think," said Harcourt finally, "that considering Maitland's determination, you would be well advised to seek a suspension of arms with him."

"You may tell Maitland," responded Rigaud firmly, "that the French government does not intend to allow the English to occupy one inch of Saint-

Domingue. As for, myself," he continued, "I intend to pursue the war to the last extremity."

"Pity," sighed Harcourt. "You should know that Maitland and his staff hold you in very high esteem. He is most anxious to come to some understanding with you."

"Is he?" asked Rigaud with some anger. "I have had men shot—had the Curé of Léogane shot—for less complicity with the enemy than you are suggesting."

"Maitland," continued Harcourt with no apparent regard for Rigaud's sharpness, "would surrender his black troops to you. He cannot take them back to Jamaica. The governor won't permit it. Maitland bought them himself, you know, and he would rather see them with you than with Toussaint. The mulatto troops as well." Harcourt paused for a moment and smiled knowingly. "You will need them for your coming war with Toussaint."

Harcourt cut close to the bone, but Rigaud refused to acknowledge the wound. He had fought the English too long and too unsparingly to give into them now. He had fought them for four years. He had fought them from guerrilla bases in the mountains when he had no forces to command and no arms for the few men who followed him. He had fought them when Sonthonax had tried to arrest him and had sent agents to undermine him with his people. He had pushed the English to their last stronghold in the South, and he was not going to let them up now that he had them defeated.

"No separate peace," insisted Rigaud.

"Pity," repeated Harcourt. "I heard Maitland say just a day or so ago that it is an atrocious calumny—his words exactly—that Toussaint has promulgated against you, that he should be rewarded by France while your value goes unmarked. A man like Toussaint whose loyalties blow with the wind and whose treachery can't be measured."

Rigaud rose angrily.

"If I did not respect the white flag which protects you," he shouted, "you would be a dead man!"

Rigaud strode from the room and slammed the door behind him.

On the thirteenth of July, Rigaud arrived in Port-au-Prince on his way to see Hédouville at the Cape. For the first time Toussaint and Rigaud met. They had corresponded with some regularity for over four years. They had cooperated in complex military operations. They had surmounted misunderstandings, political intrigues and conflicting fortunes, but they had never met.

They met in General Mornay's office in Government House, the room in which Toussaint had received the delegation of planters begging for forgiveness after the withdrawal of the British.

The two leaders greeted one another cordially. They were of the same height and small build. They were both dressed in the blue uniforms of French generals. Rigaud was the younger by seventeen years, but the differences in their ages was not strikingly apparent. Rigaud was mahogany brown in complexion, Toussaint coal black. Rigaud wore a straight brown wig in the natural style popular in revolutionary Paris. Toussaint's head was uncovered, his hair of moderate length, his tight black curls pulled back onto his high collar by a leather and ribbon pigtail.

They discussed at some length the military situation. Rigaud elaborated—being careful, however, to leave out the comments about enmity between Toussaint and himself—on the visit from Harcourt, an event which he had described to Toussaint earlier in a dispatch. Rigaud pledged not to be drawn into a separate peace with the English. Toussaint pledged to keep Rigaud informed of all negotiations with Maitland and to seek Rigaud's advice regarding them. They were both determined that Maitland would not snatch away their victory by instigating dissension between them.

Rigaud wished to spend a few days with friends in Port-au-Prince and Toussaint wished to inspect a plantation he had recently leased in the Cul-de-Sac. They agreed to meet in a week to ride together to the Cape.

The habitation southeast of Croix-des-Bouquets was the third that Toussaint had leased under the system established two years earlier by Sonthonax. Under the plan the plantations deserted by their owners during the fighting were claimed by the government and leased to responsible managers. The rent to the government was one third of the gross profits. Another third was paid to the workers. The final third of the profits belonged to the new manager. The manager provided lodging and nursing care for the laborers. The laborers were required by the government to work for the habitation from three a.m. to noon for nine days of each decade (of the Republican calendar) and could quit the habitation only with the permission of the commander of the local military district.

The arrangement was advantageous to all. It provided income for the government. It kept the laborers employed. And it supplied the basis of wealth for the new leadership of the island. All of the black and mulatto generals managed at least one plantation, and most several. Under the system, the prosperity of agriculture and of agricultural trade was of personal concern to all in Saint-Domingue.

Toussaint managed three plantations: Desachaux, where he lived with his family; Bréda, the habitation south of the Cape on which he had been employed as a slave; and since the liberation of Port-au-Prince, Beaumont in the Cul-de-Sac. Only two of the plantations, however, provided him with income. The profits from Bréda he sent to de Libertas, Bréda's former manager, now living in Philadelphia.

Toussaint arrived at Beaumont at mid-morning on Sunday, July fifteenth. He was angered to see the laborers toiling in the fields. He chastised the overseer, a white man named Vernet, and insisted that a priest be sent for from Croix-des-Bouquets, that the laborers come in from the field immediately, and that when the priest arrived, mass be celebrated. Vernet, of course, did what Toussaint requested but complained of being misunderstood.

"I conform precisely to the government regulations," he argued. "I give the laborers time in the evening to work their garden plots, and they have every Decadi free."

"They should have religious instruction and celebrate mass as well," Toussaint insisted.

"I am aware of your feelings in the matter, and despite the government's prohibition, when the Decadi falls on Sunday, as it did last week, I arrange for the mass to be celebrated."

"That is not more that once in two months," retorted Toussaint. "I want mass each Sunday."

"Do you want Sunday as a day of rest for the laborers as well?" asked Vernet.

"Yes."

"And the Decadi?"

"That, too."

"As you wish," agreed Vernet, but he shook his head in frustration as he projected in his mind the leisure days. Today was Sunday. The next Decadi fell on Wednesday. Then Sunday, again, and then the Decadi the following Saturday, and then Sunday.... Vernet did not know how he would be able to maintain the required work hours under such a system. He got the laborers into the fields only by reminding them that they worked on Toussaint's plantation and by threatening them with Toussaint's anger if they were idle. Now Vernet felt his authority undermined. If the plantation fell back into chaos, he thought, Toussaint would have no one but himself to blame.

Toussaint and Rigaud set off for the Cape early on the morning of July nineteenth. Toussaint had thought to ride, but Rigaud insisted that they take his carriage, a sturdy diligence, roomy, set on heavy leaf springs. Rigaud insisted it would give them a better setting in which to continue their talks. Toussaint agreed reluctantly, dreading a slow, tortuous ride confined inside the hot, swaying vehicle.

As they drove out of Port-au-Prince, their traveling parties following, they passed under the arch built to welcome Toussaint to the city two months earlier. The wood was warped by the rain and grayed by the sun. The legend "Port Republicain" was barely visible.

The passion of the Revolution to make all things new amused and annoyed Toussaint. New names, a new calendar, new means of measuring—of measuring space, weight, time even—a new religion. This passion for newness, thought Toussaint, was the mark of the madness of the times. The future could only be built on the sound basis of the past. For Toussaint, the soundness of the past was Rome, where the rights of citizenship protected all, weak and strong, and the arbiter of action was not privilege, but law. In the "Rights of Man and Citizen" France had brought the essence of Roman law to the modern world. But France's foolish passion for newness, especially the rejection of religion, hid the essential in a confusion of trivia.

"Port-au-Prince" or "Port Republicain," it was of no consequence. In Toussaint's mind the city was "Port-au-Crimes" for the atrocities committed there in the past ten years, especially for the senseless massacre of the Swiss.

In the early stages of the journey conversation was easy. The two men reviewed again their estimations of the English positions in the colony and congratulated each other on their victories of the spring and summer. But with the heat and dust of late morning they fell into an ennui and sat for long periods in silence.

Rigaud found it difficult to look at Toussaint. His foolish, ape-like face, the gaping break between his front teeth when he smiled, the ridiculous bandanna wrapped around his head, his hard, cold eyes moved Rigaud to suppressed anger.

What ironic fate, Rigaud thought, plucked this cruelly ambitious coachman from obscurity, dressed him in the uniform of a French general and endowed him with the power of life and death over hundreds of thousands of more deserving people? Sonthonax's watch dog, thought Rigaud bitterly.

The memory of Sonthonax hit Rigaud with such force he could barely prevent himself from calling out in anger. His body twisted on the hard seat from the pain of keeping quiet. He took a long drink of rum from the flask he kept always at hand. His mind filled with a flow of images, hurtful images of the injustices Sonthonax had inflicted upon him.

By noon the heat in the diligence became unbearable. They stopped at Arcahaie for several hours. Toussaint and Rigaud lunched with Dessalines, commander of the district. Afterwards Toussaint and Dessalines closeted themselves in the commander's office. Rigaud sought out friends he had not seen since the English invasion of Port-au-Prince.

At four they resumed the trip. Rigaud spoke of his friends and his delight at finding them well. Toussaint responded politely, but sat most of the time in silence, disgusted with Rigaud's drunkenness. That evening they stopped in Saint Marc and were hosted by General Agé.

At dawn they left Saint Marc, skirted the hill east of the city, and drove north to the town of Artibonite. The bridge was out. The carriage was the first in the party to be ferried across the river. The two generals continued north toward Gonaïves without waiting for the full party to follow. The horsemen would have no trouble overtaking them.

Crossing the delta of the Artibonite the travelers found the discomfort of the heat increased by the persistence of gnats and mosquitoes. At the Ester River they discovered that the ferry had sunk. The coachman forded the carriage, but Toussaint and Rigaud were forced to wait for someone to forage a fisherman's canot to carry them across.

The discomfort of the journey was becoming unendurable to Toussaint. He was acutely aware of Rigaud's distress at being with him and amazed at the mulatto's capacity for alcohol. Crossing the river Toussaint's spirits were not raised by the sight of several large caimans sunning themselves ten fathoms down stream.

In mid-afternoon they stopped at Habitation Rossignal to escape the heat. As they drove up the lane, in the cooling shade of the great Rossignal orchard, Rigaud opened the subject of Hédouville.

"He means to divide us and use us each to ruin the other," Rigaud insisted.

Toussaint understood well enough Hédouville's intentions, but he knew also not to allow himself to be trapped into sharing confidences with André Rigaud. Being confined in the carriage for two days with Rigaud had made Toussaint painfully aware of the mulatto's weakness of character. Toussaint could see it in Rigaud's face: in his thin lips, his soft chin, his flushed complexion; in his ridiculous brown wig hiding his curly black hair. This is the man, Toussaint thought, who denies to children the comfort of believing in God.

"Take care, citizen Rigaud," Toussaint cautioned. "Your remarks border on treason."

"Treason!" The word sliced at Rigaud. "You accuse me of treason?" he retorted angrily.

"I accuse you of nothing," responded Toussaint evenly. "I remind you that Hédouville represents the political authority of France in Saint-Domingue."

The word "treason" battered at Rigaud's mind. He felt his anger so strongly he dared not allow himself to respond. The hypocrite, the opportunist, the chameleon, thought Rigaud, how dare Toussaint accuse him of treason. He, Rigaud, first carried arms in the name of freedom when he was a youth, in the battle for Savannah. He returned to Saint-Domingue to fight against the Royalists in Port-au-Prince. He was imprisoned and beaten for his politics, grievously wounded in battle, but he had never varied from the path of the Revolution. And Toussaint? He had ignored the cries of his fellow blacks until forced into the flow of the Revolution by the irresistible pressure of events. Toussaint, who followed wherever favor led, dared call Rigaud a traitor? Rigaud's head rang from his efforts to control his tongue.

"I despise your treason!" he shouted at Toussaint.

"I only remind you of your duty," replied Toussaint quietly.

The coach hit a hole hidden by the deep shadows of the trees lining the lane. The carriage shook violently. Rigaud leaned forward and pounded on the roof.

"Clumsy fool!" he shouted at the coachman.

Rossignal received the travelers warmly, and in the custom of the country shared with them his limited larder. They lunched upon fruit, mostly unripe, potatoes, fried plantain and coffee thickly sweetened with raw sugar. Rossignal complained bitterly of the condition of his orchard, famed throughout Saint-

Domingue for its dark forest of oranges, sapodilla plums, hog plums, mangoes, coconuts, rose apples, star apples, bananas, plantain and the newly imported bread fruit. He was embarrassed to offer so little to his guests, but he could not prevent the laborers living in the area and travelers passing by from picking his trees bare even before the fruit ripened.

In the late afternoon, Toussaint and Rigaud rode the short distance to Gonaïves where they spent the night as the guests of Madame Desachaux, the woman from whom Toussaint had purchased Habitation Desachaux. Madame Desachaux, as always, was happy to entertain her benefactor. At dinner she regaled Rigaud with stories of how Toussaint had rescued her from the destitution the war had brought her and her family, of how he lent her, without charge, the house in Gonaïves to live in—a house formerly hers but which she sold to Toussaint with Habitation Desachaux—and how each day someone stopped by with gifts, arranged by Toussaint she was certain, of fish, game or fruit for her sustenance.

The next day, after Toussaint attended early morning mass, the two men resumed their journey. The final leg was the longest, but because the road ran through the mountains they did not have to stop for the heat of the afternoon. As they followed the Ennery River into higher land they could feel the growing oppression of the morning sun in the savanna dropping behind them. Their only discomfort now was the jostle of the diligence on the rock-strewn road. In each of the towns through which they passed, Ennery, Plaisance, Limbé, Toussaint's trumpeter rode ahead to announce to the inhabitants that the Governor-General was about to pass.

Although he appreciated the release from the discomfort of the heat, Rigaud felt a growing discomfort from his inability to communicate his anxieties to Toussaint. Rigaud began to fear that perhaps Toussaint already had conspired with Hédouville to overthrow him. He began to fear that this visit to the Cape might hold the promise of arrest and deportation for him.

Rigaud remembered bitterly the former commissioner's deceptions toward him. More than a year had passed since Sonthonax sent agents to Les Cayes to destroy him. In time, Rigaud thought, he might forgive—even forget—their arrogance, their extravagance, their indulgences, their disrespect for him in public, their conspiracies to overthrow him. But until he died he would never erase from his mind the picture of Marie...beautiful Marie...his beautiful Marie....

———————————✧———————————

Rey sent for him. Rey, a ridiculous man with sansculotte clothes and aristocratic airs. It was early afternoon. Rigaud walked across the Place Royale and down Rue du Parapet to the house by the canal where Rey and the others were staying. Rey, dressed in his nightshirt and robe, welcomed Rigaud and led him to the door of a bedroom.

"General," Rey explained, "I am going to introduce you to the most beautiful woman in Les Cayes."

Rigaud had no liking for Rey's games, but humored him and followed him into the bedroom. Rey pulled open the curtains to the bed, and there, sleeping, covered only by a bed sheet was Marie Villeneuve, Rigaud's beautiful mistress.

Enraged, Rigaud knocked Rey to the floor, grabbed him by the throat and would have thrown him from the bedroom balcony if servants of the house had not heard the noise of the struggle and rushed to Rey's assistance.

"You put too much trust in the good will of Frenchmen," Rigaud said suddenly to Toussaint.

"I trust men who are honest and distrust men who are not," responded Toussaint.

"You trusted Sonthonax, but he did all he could to destroy me."

"He believed you were suppressing the blacks."

"You know that to be a lie!" retorted Rigaud angrily.

"I sent Sonthonax back to France," answered Toussaint.

"Six months after he tried to destroy me!" insisted Rigaud.

"I persuaded Sonthonax to keep you in authority."

"Yes," replied Rigaud with only partially disguised sarcasm. "In that, as in all things, you were steadfast. But if you think Hédouville has your good or the good of the blacks in mind, you are a fool."

Toussaint looked Rigaud firmly in the eye. "We are all Frenchmen, Citizen General. We would do well to remember that."

"I am convinced that Hédouville comes to subvert our authority," Rigaud continued, heedless of Toussaint's caution. "To do this he will seek to turn black against mulatto and mulatto against black. I do not wish to see liberty destroyed on this island, nor do I wish to be a pawn in Hédouville's game."

"I believe you to be no man's pawn," answered Toussaint carefully. "As for me, I am governor of all the people, black, white and mulatto. No man will turn me from the people. If Rigaud is faithful to the people, then Toussaint is faithful to Rigaud."

Again the men fell into silence.

Toussaint felt he had gone as far as he dared in assuring Rigaud there would be no conspiracy between himself and Hédouville. Through his actions in the war with the English, Toussaint had given Rigaud ample evidence that he accepted the mulatto general's authority in the South. But Toussaint saw through Rigaud's game. Rigaud wanted a permanent mulatto seigniorage in the South. That Toussaint would not give. No threat from the French would make him accept the inevitability of the island's permanent division into areas of black and mulatto domination. To do so would condemn the island to eternal strife and assure its domination by external forces.

The coach passed through a dry streambed and for several moments the passengers held tightly to the grips on the sides of the carriage.

"When I deported Sonthonax," began Toussaint unexpectedly, in a gentler tone. "I sent my two sons to Paris with him to be educated."

"As I sent mine," Rigaud reminded him.

"I did this," continued Toussaint, "as evidence of my loyalty to France."

"My loyalty to France is known," retorted Rigaud. "I need proffer no hostages to prove it."

"You and I have enemies in France," Toussaint patiently continued, "the old planters who wish to see slavery restored. But thankfully, their day is passed. France sends us today appreciation of our government."

"Do you expect calm judgment from a country that for ten years has been torn apart by the greatest passions the world has witnessed since the crucifixion?" asked Rigaud incredulously.

"The Reign of Terror has ended," replied Toussaint. "Order comes both to France and to Saint-Domingue."

Rigaud knew nothing could be served by continuing the discussion. Toussaint's concern for the safety of his sons in Paris blinded him to his own dangers. Rigaud cursed himself for revealing his feelings so openly.

Rigaud felt a weakness in his body. Through the window in the fading light he could see the outline of Morne-Rouge. Tomorrow he would be face to face with Hédouville. On this ride north he had hoped to forge an ironclad alliance with Toussaint. Instead he had found intransigence, sententiousness and timidity. If Hédouville chose tomorrow to arrest and deport him, he had no reason to believe that Toussaint would lift a finger to help him. Rigaud regretted that he had left the security of Les Cayes.

CHAPTER 6
Three Interviews With Hédouville

"Citizen General," Hédouville began his first interview with Rigaud, "you have many enemies in Paris."

"It is my misfortune to have enemies in Saint-Domingue as well," answered Rigaud. "I hope not to number you among them."

"I trust you will not give me reason," answered Hédouville.

"If to be faithful to the Republic is not to give you reason, then I shall give you none," Rigaud replied.

Hédouville smiled.

Rigaud felt he presented himself well. Despite his vulnerability so far from his military and political base in the South, he had no intentions of crawling before Hédouville. If he was to be arrested, then let him be arrested for what he was and not for what others said about him.

"Tell me," Hédouville changed the subject unexpectedly. "How does it go with the English?"

The rest of the first interview was spent in discussion of the military position of the British in the South and Maitland's peace maneuvers.

In the second interview Hédouville met with both Rigaud and Toussaint. The subject was Hédouville's new laws for the laborers. The three men were in agreement that the chaos on the habitations had to end. Toussaint, however, felt that the discussion was intended as an indictment of his efforts to restore agriculture, but he hid his feelings from the other two men.

It was true that labor discipline and civil order had been swept away with the old slave system. The incessant wars had reduced to ruin much of the cultivated areas, and the confusion of land ownership hampered the rebuilding of the island's economy. Rigorous actions had to be taken, but the three men disagreed on the particulars. They agreed that the laborers must return to the plantations and that the work force had to be supervised. Hédouville argued for his plan that the laborers be bound to a habitation or workshop for an initial term of nine years and subsequent terms of six years. Toussaint preferred the existing plan of indefinite contracts with the laborers free to change places of employment with the approval of the military commanders of the districts. Rigaud supported Hédouville. Toussaint relented.

Toussaint insisted that the work hours continue as mandated: the laborers worked for his employer from 3:00 a.m. until noon and was free the rest of the day to work his garden plot, hunt, fish or undertake other tasks necessary for his well-being. The laborer was to have one day a week free, but there was no discussion as whether the week was to be measured by the Revolutionary calendar—ten days—or by the Christian calendar—seven days. Toussaint preferred the seven-day week, but he did not raise the issue because he knew he would not prevail against the mandate of Paris.

They agreed that the present division of income should continue: one-third to the laborers, one-third to the government and one-third to the manager or owner.

They agreed, also, that the edict against the use of the whip would remain in force.

The greatest disagreement came over the means of enforcing the labor code. Toussaint insisted that enforcement was a military matter and should be in the hands of the district military commander. Hédouville insisted that the enforcement of labor was a civil matter and should be in the hands of the administrative general of the district and that the military commander should enter the matter only if requested by the administrator. Rigaud sided with Toussaint and Hédouville agreed to let matters stand until after the defeat of the English.

They agreed that Hédouville would issue the new laws as soon as they could be printed, by the end of the week at the latest.

Toussaint was disturbed. Hédouville's desire to take power from the military and put it in the hands of the civilian government argued future conflict. Although he appreciated Rigaud's support on the issue, Toussaint was well aware that in Rigaud's prisons one found only blacks and whites, no mulattos. Rigaud would continue to use his military authority to maintain a mulatto hegemony in the South.

When the meeting appeared to be concluding, Hédouville casually announced that the Directory wished the colony to continue the war against the English after they were driven from the island.

"How?" asked Rigaud.

"Privateers should be authorized to ply upon their shipping, and we should consider actions that might be taken against Jamaica, certainly, and perhaps the Bahamas. France is fighting for her life in Europe," Hédouville explained as neither general showed the least enthusiasm for the idea, "and expects the patriots of Saint-Domingue to aid her with all means possible."

Hédouville turned to Toussaint.

"Citizen General," Hédouville said, "the Directory orders us to continue the war against Jamaica. I have advised them that I believe you to be the man to lead the invasion."

Toussaint was caught by surprise and for a moment had no reply.

"The Directory believes the slaves of Jamaica could be incited to revolt and that your army would insure the success of that revolt and the loss of the island to England. Think, General," Hédouville said with a gentle smile, "you would be the means by which France could grant freedom to thousands of unfortunate blacks suffering under the yoke of English slavery."

"I appreciate the Directory's intentions," Toussaint responded. "But I do not believe we are strong enough to undertake so ambitious and risky a venture."

"I am disappointed to hear you say that. But we will speak more of it later," replied Hédouville.

As Toussaint left Government House he found himself startled at Hédouville's cleverness to taunt him with the suffering of the Jamaican slaves. But Toussaint saw the plot behind the plan. He saw an image of himself, isolated in the mountains of Jamaica with a diminishing army, unaided by the French, while in Saint-Domingue Hédouville or his successors established increasingly repressive laws subjecting again to slavery the Saint-Domingue blacks whom Toussaint could no longer protect.

As Toussaint waited for his horse to be brought from the stables the French Admiral Fabre passed him going into Government House. The Frenchman stopped for a few moments to talk with the black general. Fabre complained of being overworked. Many of his officers responded poorly to the climate and he never knew who would be well enough from day to day for duty. Toussaint sympathized with Fabre and remarked that he, also, felt the weight of work and wished for order to be restored to the colony so that he might retire.

"Indeed?" responded Fabre. "It would be a great honor to me, who brought General Hédouville to Saint-Domingue, to have the privilege of carrying you back to France for your retirement!"

Toussaint, suddenly alerted, retorted, "I fear your ship is not big enough to carry me!"

At that moment the stable boy arrived with Toussaint's horse. Fabre watched the general mount and then called after him with some amusement, "Perhaps you will give me the pleasure, General, to dine with me some evening on my ship so that you might test its size?"

Toussaint rode away without replying, but he marked well the admiral's insolence.

The next morning, Wednesday, July twenty-fifth, Toussaint and Rigaud were to meet again with Hédouville.

As he was riding to the meeting, Toussaint was approached by a white planter.

"Citizen General," the Frenchman called. "Do you remember me?"

"You must remind me," responded Toussaint.

"My name is Lachichotte, a relation of Madame Desachaux. You saved me some months ago from being executed by General Michel."

Toussaint remembered the incident. Lachichotte was apprehended fleeing to the British and was sentenced by Michel to be shot. Toussaint happened by and accepted Lachichotte's plea that he was loyal to France and was fleeing only from a plot against his life engineered by his mulatto half-brother. Toussaint freed Lachichotte and instructed him to enlist under Michel for the campaign to free Saint Marc.

"Yes, of course. I remember you well," answered Toussaint. "How do your fortunes go, now?"

"I must call upon you for assistance, again."

"In what way can I aid you?"

Lachichotte explained than when he returned to his habitation he found his half-brother in control of the property. When Lachichotte attempted to dislodge him, his half-brother raised up the laborers against him and forced him once again to flee for his life.

"Does your half-brother have a claim to the land?" asked Toussaint.

"No, My father did not acknowledge him."

"Has he made claim under the agriculture leasing laws?"

"He has not paid the sequester tax."

"Then pay the tax, and, if you have need, call upon General Agé in Saint Marc to aid you in reclaiming your property."

"But, General, sir," Lachichotte complained a little hesitantly, "General Hédouville refuses to accept my claim. He accuses me of aiding the English and insists that the amnesty does not apply to me."

Toussaint paused for a moment before replying. Then he spurred his horse forward and called back over his shoulder, "I cannot help you. General Hédouville is the arbiter of civil law. My authority is restricted to military matters."

On the steps of Government House Toussaint was stopped by another petitioner, a former plantation overseer whose employer had fled the island. The overseer claimed the abandoned habitation. His complaint was that when he paid the sequester tax the clerk of the deeds refused to file his claim until he paid a bribe. The overseer was uncertain he had enough money left to put the plantation into production.

Toussaint had a few moments to spare before his scheduled meeting with Hédouville and agreed to accompany the overseer to the deeds office.

The clerk expressed amazement at the man's complaint. Yes, the claimant had given him eight Portuguese pieces of gold, but the clerk had understood that to be a tip, a desire of the new landowner to share his good fortune with a faithful and dedicated civil servant. Of course the clerk would return it. He never would have accepted it if he had been aware of the overseer's financial difficulties. The clerk was apologetic that the Governor-General had been disturbed.

That morning Rigaud received a note from Hédouville requesting him to appear an hour early for their meeting.

"I asked you to come early," Hédouville explained after Rigaud arrived, "because I wish to discuss with you, in confidence, General Louverture's performance as Governor-General."

Rigaud froze. The past two days the fear he had felt in the carriage approaching the Cape had seeped away. Now, suddenly, it rushed in, again.

"The Directory has some concerns about General Louverture's..."- Hédouville paused, as if searching for a word of sufficient delicacy—"...dependability."

Rigaud made no response.

"You observed yesterday," continued Hédouville, "his unwillingness to lend himself to the Directory's plan for expanding the war in the Caribbean."

"I was under the impression," Rigaud suggested, "that he questioned the practicality of the plan."

"Do you share his doubts?"

"I have given the matter no thought."

"I would be appreciative if you would give it some thought, now."

"Jamaica is vulnerable." Rigaud surprised himself by the directness of his response.

"You think, then, a small force might have a reasonable chance to carry it?"

"England keeps a foot on this island only to protect the sea routes to Jamaica. If those routes could be closed, even temporarily," Rigaud suggested.

"And if," prompted Hédouville, "the invasion were preceded by a general uprising of the slaves."

"Yes," agreed Rigaud. "It could be done. Jamaica could be taken."

"You agree the plan is feasible, but do you agree with the Directory that it is also essential?" asked Hédouville.

"I am in no position to answer that."

"But as a general of army...?" urged Hédouville.

"In war it is always desirable to hit the enemy where you might do the most damage with the least risk," Rigaud offered.

"Exactly." Hédouville smiled, indicating his pleasure with Rigaud's answers.

Rigaud had a sense that he had been tricked into betraying Toussaint, but he dismissed it. He had not agreed to participate in an invasion of Jamaica. He had only spoken theoretically of the possibility of such an undertaking.

"The Directory has a growing concern," explained Hédouville, "that Toussaint's professed loyalty to France is a mask he wears to hide his intentions of creating an independent kingdom in Saint-Domingue."

When Rigaud made no response Hédouville continued. "The Directory fears that Toussaint uses his negotiations with Maitland to secure English assistance for his ambitions."

"I don't believe that," countered Rigaud.

"What don't you believe? That Toussaint seeks to make himself independent of France or that he seeks assistance from the English?" asked Hédouville.

"I don't believe any of it." Even as Rigaud spoke, he felt himself to be a fool. Everyone knew that Toussaint would some day strike for independence. Rigaud had wanted to speak with him on the subject on the drive to the Cape, but

Toussaint had avoided the conversation. Why? Because he was already dealing with Maitland. Rigaud felt a fool. He had refused to let Maitland separate him from Toussaint, but all the while Toussaint was....

Hédouville interrupted Rigaud's train of thought. "I appreciate your loyalty to your commander. France appreciates it. But I would like to review with you Toussaint's history in the Revolution. If I am wrong in the conclusions I draw, please correct me."

Hédouville waited for a response from Rigaud, but got none.

"The Revolution, when it came, brought an end to all unjust privilege," continued Hédouville. "Men of every rank and position who believed in equality and liberty threw themselves into the difficult task of reshaping the world. Yourself among them."

Rigaud knew he was being flattered, but accepted with gratitude the recognition of his republican fervor.

"But where was Toussaint when the new world dawned?" asked Hédouville. "He first threw himself into the cause of the Royalists in their attempt to insulate this island from the Revolution. His support of Blancheland and de Libertas and the other Royalists is well known. Then when the blacks rose up and threw off their chains, where was Toussaint? Fighting for the Spanish, calling his brothers to desert the Republican army of Laveaux and enlist under the King of Spain, France's and freedom's enemy."

Hédouville paused for a moment.

"Am I wrong?" he asked.

"No. You are right." Rigaud heard his own thoughts echoed in Hédouville's words.

"And when did Toussaint enlist under the tricolor? Only when he was certain that he would be given a position of high command, higher than that offered by the Spanish."

"I think you misjudge him, there," suggested Rigaud.

"In what way do I misjudge him?" asked Hédouville pleasantly.

"Toussaint enlisted under the French banner after he heard that the Convention in Paris had passed the act of emancipation. Whatever his personal ambitions, you do Toussaint an injustice if you believe he does not have a genuine concern for the liberty of the blacks."

"I accept what you say, but not without some reservations," replied Hédouville. "I remind you that Sonthonax had arbitrarily freed the blacks of Saint-Domingue before the Convention acted, but Toussaint urged his brothers not to trust Sonthonax. I suggest that the act of emancipation was only the rationalization that Toussaint used to advance himself. After the news of the emancipation, Toussaint's Spanish army was in danger of dissolving. Why should the blacks fight as slaves for Spain when they could fight for France as free men? And if we grant Toussaint the sincerity of his concern for the blacks, why, then, he had no choice but to enlist under the French. France is the only country to have freed the slaves. Do you think Spain or England or the United States will ever free them?"

"Never!"

"Of course not. In the reactionary countries public policy serves the pocketbooks of the rich and of the merchants. Only France puts freedom and the dignity of man above commerce.

"But after he enlisted in the Republican army," continued Hédouville, "then what did he do? That is a question of greater import than the reasons why he enlisted. He initiated a pattern of actions that I fear continues still and threatens my position here. First, he ingratiated himself with Laveaux. Toussaint performed some valuable services for him, that is true."

There was no change in Hédouville's pleasant, forthright manner, but Rigaud suspected that behind Hédouville's apparent openness lay a threat to him. He had not been involved in the mulatto plot against Laveaux which Toussaint had thwarted. In fact, Rigaud had tried to warn Laveaux to be on his guard. But Sonthonax had not believed Rigaud's innocence, and Rigaud suspected that Toussaint did not believe it, either. Rigaud was grateful when Hédouville continued with no mention of the mulatto plot.

"But after Laveaux rewarded him for his services by granting him increased authority, what did Toussaint do?" asked Hédouville. "He persuaded, with some effort, his benefactor to return to France. A coincidence, perhaps. But then he did the same thing with Sonthonax. Being less gullible than the good Laveaux, Sonthonax resisted. What did Toussaint do then? He forced Sonthonax's deportation and justified his actions to the French government with a story no man could believe who has ever known Sonthonax. Even the Negro generals who follow Toussaint had trouble believing it."

Hédouville paused again, smiled mischievously, and continued with some irony.

"I am aware of your differences of opinion with Sonthonax, but I ask you, did you believe Toussaint's story?"

Rigaud paused several moments before answering. Hédouville waited patiently for his response, apparently intending not to continue until he had it.

"My difficulties with Sonthonax," began Rigaud carefully, "do not permit me to evaluate the man with objectivity."

"But did you believe Toussaint's story?" insisted Hédouville.

"I was grateful that Sonthonax was leaving Saint-Domingue. I did not care what story Toussaint invented to justify his deportation."

Hédouville smiled again, and asked more gently, "But did you believe it?"

"No, I did not."

Hédouville leaned back in his chair in a manner of a man relieved of an irksome burden.

"Of course not," Hédouville continued. "There is an interesting fact I have observed about chronic liars. When they accuse others of devious plots, their accusations are often mirrors of their own dark machinations. If nothing else convinced me of Toussaint's ambitions for independence, the lie he told of Sonthonax would. What strikes me as most bizarre is that Toussaint would think that the French government would believe his lies. The incredulity of it! That a man with Sonthonax's dedication to the Revolution would conspire to overthrow the government he represented. And to what purpose? To create a black state of men only three years from slavery and very little more than that from the jungle? Yesterday we spent the better part of the morning devising the best means by which to get these...children...to go back to work. And Sonthonax, with his sense of duty, his revolutionary zeal, would choose to abandon France to lead an island of helpless children? It is fantastic!

"But there is one aspect of Toussaint's lie that causes great alarm for the Directory and for me. If we accept the idea that the lie is a transparent cover for the liar's own ambitions, then what do we make of Toussaint's statement that Sonthonax intended to lead the blacks in a massacre of the whites? Yes. What indeed do we make of that?"

"I do not believe that Toussaint has any intention of leading the blacks in such a massacre," replied Rigaud with conviction.

"You may be right. I hope you are," continued Hédouville. "But I suggest one thing to you. What happened to Laveaux, what happened to Sonthonax, will happen to me if Toussaint has his way. Mark my words. Mark them carefully. Toussaint will maneuver some issue, I do not know what, to my disadvantage. Then he will seek to discredit me with it and force me from the island, as he did Laveaux and Sonthonax. I tell you frankly, I intend to resist him and, if possible, to disarm him before he can create his diversions. I tell you also that if Toussaint has his way with me, to the degree that you stand in the way of his ambitions, you will be in danger. I can retreat to France. I suggest that at the present you are less welcome there than I. I also tell you, frankly, that you have a choice to make. If you wish to be faithful to France, as I think you do, then you must work with me to strengthen France's control of this colony. If you wish to conspire with Toussaint, I cannot stop you, but I warn you that the man who serves as the jackal's bedfellow risks serving as his breakfast as well. If independence is your dish, then you had best hurry if you would have the English help you cook it, for I am certain that Toussaint already is two hands up on you with the Scottish bandits, Dundas and Maitland."

Toussaint hurried from the deeds office. He was now late for his appointment with Hédouville and Rigaud. As he walked past the old Jesuit gardens he was disgusted to see the prostitutes openly plying their trade. Nowhere else in the colony, he thought, were such actions publicly tolerated.

At Government House Toussaint was ushered immediately into the Commissioner's cabinet. As he entered he observed Hédouville's look of satisfaction and Rigaud's nervousness. There was no question in Toussaint's mind. Hédouville had found the string that made the puppet dance.

CHAPTER 7
The Secret Covenant

The rains were late in the summer of 1798. They did not fall throughout July or August nor late into September. The grass on the savannas and the leaves of the shallow rooted plants were burned brown and brittle. The heat of the summer crept up the hills from the low marshes drying the morning mists from the crowns of the mountains and making sleep uncomfortable even in the highlands.

Late in July, Maitland informed Toussaint that he was prepared to negotiate the evacuation of Môle Saint Nicholas. Toussaint agreed to the negotiations even though he was aware that Rigaud, with the approval of Hédouville, was conducting separate, secret, negotiations with Maitland for the evacuation of the British bases in the South.

Toussaint learned on August fifteenth that Hédouville, without informing Toussaint, had sent his chief of staff, Dalton, to the Môle to sign an evacuation agreement with the English colonel Stuart. Toussaint refused to tolerate the affront to his authority. He complained bitterly to Hédouville, reminding him that the negotiation of the treaty was a military matter falling clearly within Toussaint's area of responsibility.

Toussaint wrote to Maitland threatening him with renewal of fighting if the British general did not honor his agreement to negotiate only with him. Maitland responded by quickly disavowing the Dalton-Stuart agreement, completing his withdrawal from the South and sailing to the Môle to personally conclude the negotiations with Toussaint.

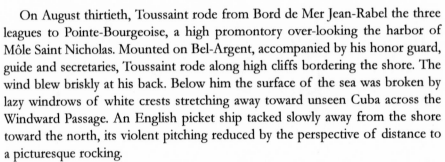

On August thirtieth, Toussaint rode from Bord de Mer Jean-Rabel the three leagues to Pointe-Bourgeoise, a high promontory over-looking the harbor of Môle Saint Nicholas. Mounted on Bel-Argent, accompanied by his honor guard, guide and secretaries, Toussaint rode along high cliffs bordering the shore. The wind blew briskly at his back. Below him the surface of the sea was broken by lazy windrows of white crests stretching away toward unseen Cuba across the Windward Passage. An English picket ship tacked slowly away from the shore toward the north, its violent pitching reduced by the perspective of distance to a picturesque rocking.

The wind blew hot and brought no relief from the discomfort of the dry summer.

By mid-morning Toussaint and his party reached Maitland's camp.

The harbor, fort and town of Môle Saint Nicholas are located in a land-locked bay at the northwestern tip of Saint-Domingue. Pointe-Bourgeoise and the surrounding cliffs shelter the Môle from the prevailing wind. The harbor opens to the afternoon sun. The north arm of the harbor is a marshy peninsula rich in mosquitoes and other insect pests. Maitland chose the open and breezy Point-Bourgeoise for his camp to escape the discomforts of the Môle itself.

Toussaint was met by Maitland, his personal staff and a French priest who fled Port-au-Prince with the British army. Toussaint dismounted and formally greeted the British general. The party walked between two rows of soldiers, weapons at attention, to a large open tent at the center of the camp. The artillery fired a twenty-one gun salute. Toussaint requested of the priest and was granted permission to carry the cleric's cross in the procession.

Toussaint felt the flattery behind Maitland's display of respect. He was greeted not as a general of army but as the monarch of an independent state. At Port-au-Prince Toussaint had disparaged such a show of pomp. He had been concerned with maintaining civil order and protecting the positions of Hédouville and Rigaud. Here he felt no such restraints. No deference on his part would heal the growing breach between himself and the other leaders. Toussaint needed from England firm trade agreements, and if Maitland looked upon him, even hypocritically, as the sovereign of the island, then Toussaint's negotiating position could only be strengthened.

Maitland hosted Toussaint to lunch. In Calcutta, Maitland had learned from painful experience to distrust English cooking in the tropics and employed an

Indian cook when on station between Cancer and Capricorn. On this occasion his cook planned a menu he thought appropriate for a Creole guest. He began with conch pâte marinated in lemon juice and vinegar and cooked in a medium hot masala. The main dish was chicken flavored with cardamom and precious saffron and served with rice, fried plantain, and mango and coconut chutney. The meal was accompanied by a strong Madeira, Maitland's choice, not the cook's.

The table was laid with an heirloom silver service Maitland had as a gift from his mother when he first joined his regiment. It was a mother's legacy to a second son who stood to inherit nothing from his stern father.

Out of sensitivity to his guest, Maitland had the meal served by Indian fusiliers rather than the black Jamaican slaves he employed as his personal servants.

Toussaint, as was his custom, ate lightly, a little rice only, and drank only water.

At the conclusion of the lunch, which lasted throughout the heat of midday, Maitland presented Toussaint with several gifts. The first, in honor of Toussaint's position as General-in-Chief of the French forces in Saint-Domingue, was a bronze culverin, an eighteen-pounder long cannon with handles cast in the shape of serpents; and in honor of his personal valor as a soldier, a cavalryman's double barreled carbine with intricately etched bronze plating.

In presenting the gifts, Maitland toasted his guest.

"Accept these," he said, "as a mark of my esteem and in consideration of the humanity from which you have never departed in treating with British prisoners, and for your generous and frank proceedings during the war and negotiations for peace."

Toussaint was moved. He saw clearly the mask worn by his host, but thought, bitterly, that in the seven years he had fought for liberty in Saint-Domingue, the years he had risked his life in the service of France against her enemies both without and within, he had never been honored with the graciousness shown him this day by a representative of France's chief enemy.

Even as Toussaint indulged in recriminations, a tension gripped his stomach and told him that he lied. He remembered the festival in April two years earlier when Laveaux appointed him to the post of lieutenant governor. Before the army crowded into the Place d'Arms at the Cape, Laveaux had declared before all that Toussaint was "the black Sparticus, foretold by Abbé Raynal, come to revenge the outrages done his people and to lead all, black and white, to a day of freedom and brotherhood."

That was Laveaux, his friend, not France that spoke, thought Toussaint. And the worshiping crowds who welcomed him at Port-au-Prince wanted only to keep their skins intact. And Maitland, Toussaint reminded himself sadly, wanted only to manipulate him to serve England's ends.

Why, Toussaint asked himself, is the praise of men of such importance? He had seen the foolish pomp of shallow men, both white and black. What mattered was not praise but action. What calumny and abuse would he not willingly suffer to destroy once and for all the pestilence of slavery in all its guises throughout the world? Then why was the praise of such a man as Maitland important to him? Et ne nos indúcas in tentatiónem, silently begged Toussaint. That which I do, I would not. That which I would not, I do.

After the presentations of the gifts, the other officers left Maitland and Toussaint alone with their secretaries. Both generals spoke French, but Toussaint's Creole accent and Maitland's Scottish accent made communication difficult. Often the secretaries, who were there to record the conversation, were called upon to translate it.

The early talk concerned the details of the British withdrawal. Tiburon and Jérémie had already been turned over to Rigaud, and the Môle would be surrendered to Toussaint in a month.

After they reviewed the routine details, the two men drifted easily into the chief business of their meeting, that which would be called thereafter, by friend and foe, the secret convenant of the Môle.

"We are in position to mutually aid one another," suggested Maitland. "Saint-Domingue must have trade and England must protect Jamaica." Maitland assured Toussaint that he was fully aware of the Directory's desire to attack Jamaica. "Quite simply," Maitland concluded, "England is offering you trade in exchange for your agreement never to invade Jamaica."

Toussaint complained that the island's trade with the United States had been cut off by Adams' embargo of all trade with France. Because the embargo was in support of England, if England resumed trade with Saint-Domingue would England undertake to persuade the Americans to resume trade, also?

"England would certainly encourage the Americans to do so," agreed Maitland. "In fact, I will request to be sent as emissary to Philadelphia for that purpose. But that will take time. The American Congress never moves precipitously. The fact remains, however, that the day Saint-Domingue declares its independence from France, it is no longer subject to the embargo. Within hours of such a declaration your harbors will be filled with American ships."

Independence. The subject, though unspoken, had been foremost in both men's minds. The details of the British evacuation did not require a meeting between Maitland and Toussaint. Maitland's suggestion that the two men meet, Toussaint's acceptance, the elaborate ceremony of greeting, the discussion of trade and the security of Jamaica were all predicated on one assumption: Toussaint was prepared to declare the colony's independence.

It was a bold concept, and one in which Maitland proceeded without the support of Parker, Admiral of the Jamaica Station, and Lord Balcarres, Governor of Jamaica. Parker and Balcarres argued that it was inhuman to surrender Saint-Domingue to a savage. It would insure the death of every white man on the island and would do no good for England. A guarantee of Jamaica's security from Toussaint was worthless. The word of a black man was not to be trusted.

Parker was concerned for England's honor. When peace came between England and France, England, of course, would do everything possible to restore Saint-Domingue to France and to return the blacks to their slave chains. An independent black state in the middle of the Caribbean was unthinkable. England compromised her honor, then, to encourage the savages now when she had no intention of fulfilling her promises to them after the war.

Maitland privately referred to Parker and Balcarres as pompous asses, but he wrote more discreetly to the war secretary, Lord Dundas. No one force, he argued, should be allowed to become predominant on the island. Toussaint was the most powerful person in Saint-Domingue and his ascendancy threatened France. Encourage him in his desire for independence, but arm Rigaud to prevent Toussaint from securing control of the entire army. Then stand clear when France sent a force to re-establish white control of the colony. Such an effort would cost France dearly in men and money, to England's advantage.

Maitland had one desire in Saint-Domingue. He had been sent to the Caribbean with orders to extract the army from a losing war. It was an assignment which galled him. He wished to turn defeat into victory by the brilliance of his negotiations.

Independence. The word cut at Toussaint's mind. He wished to reach out and embrace the cold-faced white man sitting across from him. He wanted to surrender himself to him. He wanted to shout, Yes! Independence! Let England protect his shores and America supply him trade, and he could deal with the divisions within the island. He could create a nation in which all could prosper.

But Toussaint knew it was illusion. He knew it before he rode the three leagues from Jean-Rabel. He knew it when he marched between the rows of red-coated infantrymen. After meeting Maitland, Toussaint knew without question that it was all illusion.

Toussaint watched Maitland carefully during lunch. He observed his cold eyes, the elaborate way he chewed his food, his nervous fingers constantly moving in an otherwise quiet body. Toussaint noticed how between each bite Maitland picked up his napkin and wiped the corners of his mouth. He noticed Maitland's habit in conversation of holding his hands together as if in prayer, his chin resting lightly on his thumbs, his forefingers touching his lower lip. He noticed that when Maitland spoke he touched the finger tips of his two hands together and opened and closed them gently. Toussaint saw in Maitland's hands two spiders quietly spinning a web.

Toussaint ached to trust Maitland, but he knew he could not.

Toussaint knew also that trust in Maitland was immaterial. Toussaint was not prepared to declare independence. England might promise him protection, but for how long? Until the war with France ended. Then what? And what protection? Its fleet now blockaded the island, but ships sailed daily between France and Saint-Domingue. Sonthonax brought twelve hundred soldiers to the island without difficulty. Hédouville brought three ships across the ocean without incident. Fabre sailed those ships in a circumnavigation of the island without sighting a single British vessel. Even in the Mediterranean, England's bathtub, Napoléon slipped an army into Egypt under the bowsprits of the British fleet. No. England's protection offered no security from French invasion.

"I am not prepared to declare independence at this time," Toussaint answered Maitland.

"It is your intention ultimately, is it not?" asked Maitland.

"It is."

"When?"

"When I am prepared."

"What better time than now? I can assure you of England's protection and America's assistance."

"I am too weak," explained Toussaint. "Let England strengthen me now, and when I have dealt with my enemies, I will be better prepared to stand alone."

Maitland was disappointed. He could not shake Toussaint from his resolve and had to be content with promises of future action.

The conversation turned to the details of the trade agreements. Maitland promised secrecy so as not to compromise Toussaint with the Directory. Toussaint promised to respect Jamaica's security, not to invade the island and not to allow privateers to sail from Saint-Domingue's ports against British shipping. In return, British picket boats would not disturb droghers sailing the north and west coasts of the island, provided they stayed within five leagues of the shore. British merchantmen would be welcome at Port-au-Prince and Cape François. A British agent would be stationed at Port-au-Prince, and ships sailing between Saint-Domingue ports would need passports signed by the agent and a representative of Toussaint.

The conditions of the covenant were to go into effect immediately, but Maitland would have to return to England to secure governmental approval. When he returned the covenant would be formally signed.

The secretaries would draw up copies of the covenant in English and French, and the following morning the two generals would sign a memo of agreement.

Before the interview adjourned, Toussaint raised another issue, the Saint George's Regiment.

The Saint George's Regiment was made up of slaves trained as soldiers and used by the English in the war in Saint-Domingue. Six thousand of the original sixteen thousand survived. These were the black soldiers Maitland had offered to Rigaud.

Toussaint requested that the regiment be allowed to remain in Saint-Domingue, for, he argued, if they returned to Jamaica they would be sold as field slaves. Maitland was reluctant to agree. The blacks were the property of the King, he explained, and he did not have the authority to dispense with Crown property.

"I was under the impression they were your property," Toussaint countered.

"They are Crown property," replied Maitland.

"André Rigaud is persuaded that they belong to you," insisted Toussaint.

"I will give them to you," Maitland agreed without further discussion.

Toussaint requested that the black soldiers be given six months severance pay to assist their integration into the Saint-Domingue economy.

Maitland demurred. He argued he had no authority to make such a gift.

"It would come to far less than twenty million francs," Toussaint replied pointedly.

Maitland understood the reference to the bribe he earlier had offered Rigaud. He requested the evening to consider the matter.

The next morning, Friday, August thirty-first, Toussaint and Maitland met again. The documents were ready. Maitland signed. Toussaint hesitated. He put down the pen and asked Maitland if he had given further consideration to the matter of the pay for the Saint George's Regiment. Maitland, with some weariness, agreed to the request. Toussaint signed.

The next morning, Saturday, September first, Maitland sailed from the Môle on the "Grantham" for England to present his covenant to a skeptical Prime Minister and an irritated King.

CHAPTER 8
Toussaint Resigns

From Pointe-Bourgeoise Toussaint rode to Desachaux. Bel-Argent brought him there by Saturday evening.

Sunday, Toussaint rode to Saint Marc to participate in a church service welcoming back planters who had previously fled with the English. The ceremony also marked the reestablishment of the Church in Saint Marc.

The service was held in the evening, after the heat of the day. Most of the population of the city and proprietors from the Artibonite and as far south as Arcahaie attended. The crowd of worshippers flowed from the church out into the square. The mass was conducted by Bishop Lecun, himself a recently returned emigré. At the conclusion of the service Toussaint led the newly returned emigrés, including Bishop Lecun, in the oath of fidelity to France.

On Wednesday, Toussaint received a stinging rebuke from Hédouville for allowing the emigrés, some of whom had been Royalists, to return and for giving the oath of fidelity at a church service.

Toussaint received the letter at his headquarters in Gonaïves. He dismissed his secretary and sat alone for some moments contemplating his response.

Hédouville was determined to create a confrontation, that was clear to Toussaint. It was not to be avoided. But Toussaint had no intention of allowing Hédouville to select the field of battle.

Patience bat la force, Toussaint reminded himself. Patience overcomes strength.

Toussaint had many secretaries. He was constantly composing letters. He could tolerate no delay in having them transcribed, and he wanted a secretary available to him at every moment. Also, he did not want one man to know all the details of his command. He employed his secretaries in such a way as to have each familiar with limited particulars.

Toussaint summoned Guybre to him and dictated his response to Hédouville. In it Toussaint reviewed his respect for and support of the Republic and the Constitution, and he recognized Hédouville's authority to dismiss him.

"My conduct for some time," he complained, "above all since your interview with General Rigaud, has been in your eyes a continual infraction of the law. Having honorably served my country, having snatched it from the hands of powerful enemies, having extinguished the fires of intestinal war, having too long forgotten a cherished family to which I have become a stranger, having neglected my own interests, sacrificed my time and my years in the triumph of liberty, I wish now to save my old age from insult.

"Men in general are inclined to envy the glory of others," Toussaint continued, "and are jealous of the good which they themselves have not accomplished. A man thus often makes himself enemies by the simple fact that he has rendered great service. The Revolution furnishes many examples of this terrible truth.

"It would be imprudent for me to remain any longer exposed to the shafts of calumny and malevolence," Toussaint concluded. "An honorable and peaceful retreat in the bosom of my family is my sole ambition. I have learned too much of the heart of man not to be certain that it is only there that I shall find happiness."

Hédouville wants to govern, thought Toussaint as he signed the letter, then let Hédouville govern.

Hédouville was uncertain what to make of Toussaint's letter. He did not believe the black general was surrendering.

"He doesn't say he is resigning," suggested Admiral Fabre. "He only says he would like to resign."

Hédouville decided to continue with his campaign to discredit Toussaint and wait for a less ambiguous statement from him before reacting.

If Hédouville moved cautiously, the planters of the Northern Plain, when they heard the news, were far less restrained. In the Cape and its environs the rumor that Toussaint had resigned was greeted with relief. The English were gone. The mulattos were quiet. And now the blacks were once again under France's subjugation. Except for the abolition of slavery, the damage wrecked on Saint-Domingue by the Revolution was being repaired.

Everywhere Hédouville went in the city he was greeted by well wishers. People went out of their way to find him and to congratulate him. Hédouville noted, however, that he received no response from Raimond or Christophe.

One French planter did not find joy in the rumored news of Toussaint's resignation. Louis Duclero, the proprietor at whose habitation Moïse stopped when escorting Hédouville to the Cape, found the news disconcerting.

Unlike most of the proprietors near the Cape, Duclero lived year round on his plantation, eschewing the tradition of maintaining a city residence in order to participate more freely in the social life of the capital.

Duclero accepted an invitation to dine at the Cape on Saturday night, September eighth. He accepted with misgivings. His every instinct told him to make his excuse and miss the engagement. But he rode to the Cape to see for himself the reaction to the news.

At dinner, Duclero was as uncomfortable as he had feared. He found the high spirits of his countrymen intolerable. In celebration of Toussaint's fall, everyone drank to excess. The talk went to slavery. By the third glass, eight years of revolution had shrunken to the dimensions of a bad dream. Anecdotes and stories long unrehearsed came to mind as if they had happened the day before.

"It was a ritual with her," one drunken planter explained. "Examined every buck on the block. She'd weigh his balls, measure his dick, lick his sweat and smack him across the side of the head with her riding crop. I never saw her once buy one. She came to the auctions only to play with the bucks."

"After what Toussaint's done to them," another complained, "France will have to send us an army to get them back in line."

"It will never be done," opinioned a third. "Toussaint's ruined them. We'll have to shoot them all and start over."

"Sell them to the British. They deserve each other."

"They'll come back to work," suggested another. "Shoot a few of the clowns parading around in fancy uniforms, and the rest will beg to go back to work."

"Shoot them, hell. Shoot one and the rest won't know what happened to him. Burn a little powder up the ass of a nigger and the rest will shape up," argued a fifth. "For every one you blow up, twenty will come begging to have their chains put back on."

"You've got to make them yell in pain if you want to affect the others. I used to bury mine in an ant hill...."

The anecdotes continued interminably.

Duclero excused himself from the table and slipped away into the night.

Duclero lived in Saint-Domingue by choice. Many planters waited only until they could return to Paris, wealthy enough to live in ease. Duclero could tear himself away from Saint-Domingue only at the insistence of his wife. As he grew older his visits to France became less frequent. He was disappointed when his wife stayed in Paris to supervise the education of their sons, but he consoled himself with his mulatto mistress.

Duclero had survived the violent changes in Saint-Domingue by treading a careful path of non-involvement. He was a gentle man by nature. As a slave master he had conscientiously adhered to the Black Code even though he was ridiculed by his neighbors for pampering his blacks. He had been derisively dubbed a "nigger lover," but he took no umbrage at the charge. He found blacks to be simple, sometimes dishonest, but genuinely affectionate people.

From no efforts of his own, Duclero lacked the racial bias of his peers. He found the new wage system morally superior to slavery, and he experienced no serious difficulties getting his laborers to work. He had faith, as well, that in the long run the new system would be economically superior to slavery. It was Duclero's conviction that slavery was of more benefit to the slave trader than to the planter, and he found the slave trade distasteful in the extreme.

Although he gave it little thought, Duclero found security in black rule. There was less chance of rebellion when the blacks were policed by blacks, especially enlightened ones like Toussaint. There were difficulties, certainly, with incompetence, graft and confusion. But conditions were no better under Royalist rule. It was just that before the Revolution the wealth to be extracted from the soil made administrative bungling inconsequential. There were riches enough for all, and no one minded sharing with the greedy and the incompetent.

The economic problems facing the island, now, were not of Toussaint's doing. Under Toussaint the laborers returned to the fields. The habitations were restored. The chief problem facing the planters was the failure of trade. The American embargo was devastating and becoming worse by the week. When the war in Europe ended Saint-Domingue would again prosper. Duclero was content to survive and wait.

Duclero had not seen Hédouville since Moïse brought him to visit on his way to the Cape. Duclero had heard rumors that the commissioner sought to crush black rule on the island. He hoped the rumors were false. He had sensed nothing in his one visit with Hédouville to suggest that the he held any animosity for the blacks. Duclero remembered that when he had spoken highly of Toussaint, Hédouville had joined in his praise. But Duclero knew well enough the racial poison that flowed in the white society of Cape François.

Duclero was of a mind to ride back to the Cape and seek an audience with Hédouville, but he made no move to reign in his horse. It was indecently late. The gentleness of the night, the scent of the moonflowers on the stillness of the air, the thought of Anacaona waiting for him, sapped all resolution from him.

Duclero felt a moment of inner pleasure as he glimpsed the white clad form of Anacaona sitting quietly in the dark shadows of the veranda. He spurred his horse into a canter.

As he walked from the stable, his arm around Anacaona's thin waist, Duclero felt a deep sense of contentment. His life was rich in pleasures: his lands, his horses, his wines, and his mistress.

"Did you hear the drums tonight?" Anacaona spoke with quiet excitement.

"Do they speak of resisting Hédouville?" asked Duclero a little apprehensively.

"Tonight they beat for Erzulie Fréda!"

Duclero stood still for a moment and listened. From the Morne Haut-du-Cap he could hear faintly in the still air the soft lilting sounds of what Anacaona called the Rada drums. He was startled. The drums had beat while he rode from the city, but deep in his thought he had not heard them. For many years, it seemed to him, the drums had beat only in anger and outrage, what Anacaona called the drums of Don Pétro.

"Erzulie?" he repeated the name.

"Yes."

Duclero sensed the excitement in Anacaona's body as she clung tightly to him. She wanted to bear him a child. Perhaps tonight.

As they walked into the house, Duclero felt his spirits rise. If the blacks could play the Rada drums then perhaps all would be well. Perhaps the time of the small-minded men of the Cape had passed.

Anacaona pulled Duclero into her bedroom with a passion he had not felt from her in several years. She slipped quickly from her gown and petticoats and lay upon the bed. She held out her hand to him impatiently as he struggled with the buttons of his breeches.

The sight of her thin brown body silhouetted in the moonlight made his fingers tremble in his eagerness. He felt like a schoolboy stealing his first favor rather than a man of forty-five, experienced in the ways of pleasure, the father of grown children.

As Duclero lay quietly upon the bed, his fingers barely touching the moist warm skin of his mistress, he felt himself transported by the soft undulations of the distant drums. The soft rhythms calling to Erzulie lifted and held him in a trance. As in a dream he took Anacaona. They lay quietly, barely moving, their spirits drifting together in the moonlight, in the scent of moonflowers, in the soft beating of the drums. Gently their pleasure warmed and lifted them.

On the Morne Haut-de-Cap behind the Cape, black laborers from many plantations gathered in holy celebration of the advent of peace. The celebrants knew Erzulie Fréda Dahomey had appeared in response to the entreaty of the drums when a heavyset woman in her forties stumbled and fell backward. Two men caught her and held her until the soft soprano voice of Erzulie came from her mouth demanding gifts and jewelry.

The houngan stepped forward to greet the newly arrived loa.

"You are welcome, Mistress Erzulie," he said as he grasped her hand.

"Where are my jewels?" insisted the goddess.

"First, my lady, would you not like to bathe after so arduous a journey?" asked the houngan entreatingly.

The houngan's assistant handed her a bar of scented soap and held in readiness an embroidered towel. A woman brought her a carefully preserved lace dress stolen some years previously from the closet of a proprietor's wife. Several other women erected a tent of white muslin around the loa as she bathed and with much assistance changed her dress.

"The water is too cold." Erzulie spoke in disappointment rather than anger.

"Bring hot water for the beautiful Erzulie!"

An assistant rushed over with a pot that had been heating over an open fire.

"Too hot! Too hot! You have made it too hot," Erzulie complained.

"Cold water for the beautiful Erzulie!"

Another assistant rushed from the spring with a leaking calabash gourd.

"Something for my hair."

A woman offered the loa a white silk handkerchief.

"You have only white?"

Another woman proffered a rose-colored silk scarf. For long moments Erzulie stood in indecision. Finally she pointed to the white handkerchief. Its giver gratefully stepped behind the loa and began to bind-up her hair.

"Tighter.... Now it is too tight...."

Some of the celebrants sat outside of the tent listening to the conversation; expressions of pleasant expectation marked their faces. Some laughed with joy when Erzulie made a new demand or hesitated in indecision. As the celebrants patiently waited for the languid goddess to make her entrance from the tent, a cool breeze began to blow and lifted the oppressive heat from the night.

Erzulie carefully chose her jewelry from the tray offered her. She chose two gold and one pearl necklace, pearl earrings, two gold bracelets for her left arm and two silver and one gold bracelet for her right. She chose three wedding rings, for her marriages to Damballah the snake, Agwé the ocean, and Ogoun the warrior. She examined each item offered, rejecting first one, then another, then returning to the one previously rejected. The process of selection was not burdensome to her. She often expressed disappointment in the quality, color or design of particular items, but never anger or impatience.

After attiring herself in jewelry, she requested powder and perfume.

Finally she stepped from the tent. Eight or nine men rushed forward to escort her. After careful consideration, she indicated that she would accept three, all young and handsome. In the company of her escorts she walked slowly around the clearing. She greeted men with a smile or a touch. The women she examined with coldness, extending the little finger of each hand in greeting.

Erzulie gave a sudden laugh of joy as she sighted flowers—giant red hibiscus, red and white paper flowers, pink amaryllis—piled in great bouquets on the altar. She ran to them, plucked the most beautiful blooms and wove them into her hair. Turning suddenly to the houngan she cried:

"A song. A song of love, monsieur!"

Without hesitation the houngan, in a strong baritone voice, began. The drums and flutes quickly followed. Erzulie, with the gaiety of a child, joined in the dance.

Erzulie Oh! Erzulie Oh!
Grandmother Maiden
The women complain. They bear no children.
Erzulie Oh! Erzulie Oh!
Grandmother Maiden

Erzulie Oh! Erzulie Oh!
Grandmother Maiden
The men sow their seeds upon the moon.
Erzulie Oh! Erzulie Oh!
Grandmother Maiden

Erzulie Oh! Erzulie Oh!
The women dance. The men more slowly.
Erzulie Oh! Erzulie Oh!
Grandmother Maiden

At the song's conclusion, Erzulie separated herself from her joyful, whirling worshipers and, pleading exhaustion, called for a chair. She sat a few moments, a child-queen, her hair in disarray, a wistful smile on her lips, observing her expectant worshipers.

"Is there nothing to eat?" she suddenly cried, as she regained her breath.

In obedience, men brought, one by one, dishes of food from her altar.

The first brought a bowl of callaloo, delicate green in color with bits of red peppers floating on top. Erzulie found the soup pleasing and gave its bearer a golden bracelet as a gift.

The second brought a delicate dish of fish in lime juice with bay rum berries. His gift was a golden necklace.

The third offered a roasted poulard stuffed with bananas seasoned with brown sugar, garlic, rum, lime and nutmeg. His gift was the pearl necklace.

The fourth brought gateau de papate seasoned with vanilla, nutmeg, cinnamon and raisins. The fifth, rum cake seasoned with limes. The sixth, seventh, eighth brought other cakes and delicate pastries, for Erzulie was fond of sweets. Each bearer received a piece of jewelry when the loa found his gift pleasing.

After Erzulie had tasted each delight and there were no more to be offered, she sat for a moment in absolute stillness.

"I am going to sneeze. There is too much dust."

"Quickly, bring water," commanded the houngan.

Several men sprinkled the dance-stirred ground with water from the spring.

"No. Have you no perfume?" demanded Erzulie.

"Yes, my lady." The houngan sprinkled on the ground around her the perfume he had offered her during her toilette.

A quiet fell on the celebrants as they waited expectantly for the loa's changing mood.

"No one loves me." Her voice was under control, but tears glistened in her eyes.

"Everyone loves you," insisted the houngan. "You are the most beloved of all the loa."

"Why have you given me no gifts?"

"We gave you the richest we possessed."

"I have no bracelets, no necklace."

"You gave them as gifts to the young men who served you."

A young man to whom she gave a silver bracelet rushed to her and knelt by her chair. "Please, my lady," he said, "take this as a gift of my love."

"No. I want you to have it." Erzulie smiled as she spoke. "I want those who love me to have beautiful things."

Suddenly, without prologue, Erzulie began to weep, great sobs of despair welling up in her chest.

"MadeMoïselle Erzulie, do not weep. We love you," pleaded the young man.

A woman offered her a cup of liquor made from the hibiscus flower. Erzulie shook her head and stood up to escape the attending press of concerned worshippers. She put her arms around the necks of two of the young men who first escorted her.

"Damballah has abandoned me," she sobbed quietly to the man on her right.

"I cannot believe it," the man answered.

"And Ogoun and Agwé," she insisted to the man on her left.

"No, it is not so," he replied. "Ogoun loves you. He has told us so."

"No. No. He has abandoned me." The tears flowed freely down Erzulie's cheeks; her soft soprano voice turned harsh.

"He loves you," insisted the man on her left.

"He neglects me."

"He is distracted by the duties of war, but he loves you."

Overwhelmed by feelings of rejection, Erzulie slipped again into great sobs of despair. Finally her voice failed and she began to tremble. Her arms and legs lost all strength. She was prevented from falling only by the efforts of the two men on whose shoulders she clung. Her neck went limp, her head fell back, and she passed into unconsciousness. For a few moments the two attendants held her, her arms across their shoulders, her body pendant between them. Then the attendant on her left picked her up in his arms and carried her into the tent. He laid her gently on a blanket spread on the ground. He left her and joined the others outside in the dance as the drums continued their rhythmically lilting paean to the Ancient Queen of Heaven.

Toussaint could see them in the clearing above him, but couldn't reach them. His feet were held fast to the earth where he stood.

"Stop the drums! Stop the drums! We want no more blood!" He screamed his commands. But the sounds of his voice were carried away by the wind swirling from the spinning dancers.

A huge, half-naked black man appeared in the center of the clearing and in a thunderous voice shouted, "Honor Don Pétro! Honor Don Pétro!"

The celebrants whirled more wildly as if in a frenzy, chanting at the tops of their voices. Several men rushed to bring the giant food, a whole roasting pig. He tore at the meat with fingers and teeth, devouring it hungrily. Suddenly he turned toward Toussaint. Don Pétro's face swelled, filling Toussaint's vision. The giant's eyes glowed red, the strips of meat hanging from his lips and teeth were in the shapes of the limbs of men.

"No more!" screamed Toussaint. "No more killing! No more blood!"

Toussaint was helpless. His voice would not leave his mouth. His shouting only served to fill his head and ears with pain.

"Honor Zandor!" a reedy voice behind the giant shouted. It was a white man in a French officer's uniform.

The celebrants near him fell to their knees shouting "Zandor! Zandor! Congo Zandor!"

Zandor grabbed the food prepared for Don Pétro and shoved it into his mouth. Between mouthfuls he continued to shout "Honor Zandor! Honor Zandor!"

"Honor Don Pétro!" The bass voice of the giant black threatened to blow away the smaller man, but Zandor continued eating, unperturbed.

"Pétro!"

"Zandor!"

"Pétro!"

"Zandor!"

The celebrants shouted support for first one then the other, anticipating with both delight and apprehension the expected battle.

Zandor, rising slowly from his feasting, seized a celebrant near him and lifted him above his head, holding him aloft effortlessly with one hand.

"Zandor! Zandor!" The celebrants shouted and danced in a frenzy of appreciation.

The drums grew louder in Toussaint's ears.

Don Pétro picked up a knife lying near the food and slowly, deliberately, pushed the blade into his own stomach, pulling it in and out several times without drawing blood and without sign of pain. The drums and dancers mounted to new levels of frenzy.

Zandor ripped the skin from his left arm and with a show of disdain devoured his own flesh. The celebrants shouted their appreciation.

Don Pétro produced from the air a burning torch and threw it to the ground. Instantly the flames lapped at the dust and filled the clearing. The celebrants fell back, fleeing in panic. Don Pétro stood in the center of the flames laughing at the discomfort of the others.

"No more! No more!" Toussaint shouted, helpless as the fire raced down the hill toward where he stood fixed to the earth.

"Toussaint!" Suzanne shook her husband, trying to wake him.

"No more! No more!" Toussaint opened his eyes, trying to focus on his surroundings.

"Wake up, Toussaint."

"Suzanne?"

"You were crying out in your sleep again."

"Did I waken you?"

"I was afraid you were not well."

"I was dreaming."

"The same as before?"

"The island was in flames."

For a few moments the two lay quietly together on the bed, the night disturbed only by the distant drums, barely audible in the still air.

"Let me send for my father," Suzanne suggested gently. "He will know of herbs to help you sleep."

"Just rub my head, here."

Suzanne stroked Toussaint's temples. Her short, strong fingers eased somewhat the trembling of his body. She could feel the turmoil deep within him. She let her fingers brush the rough scar on the left side of his head where the cannon shot had grazed him. The wound, she was certain, was the cause of his nightmares. She thought of the other scars on his thin body, the musket shot in his hip.

No more fighting, Suzanne prayed. Toussaint's luck could not continue forever. If there were more fighting he surely would be killed.

"You must rest," she urged.

"I cannot while the drums beat."

"It is only the people worshiping."

"The houngan prepare them for war."

Suzanne lay back on the bed and was quiet for a few moments.

"Toussaint." Suzanne's voice was gentle but firm. "Send for Placide and Isaac."

"They have much to learn in France. When they are ready they will return."

"If war comes again it will be with France. The boys are not safe in Paris."

"There will be no war with France!"

Toussaint got up from the bed and walked out onto the veranda and into the shadows of the lawn. Suzanne did not follow him.

CHAPTER 9
Theft at Fort Liberté

Throughout most of September, Toussaint stayed at Desachaux or at his headquarters in Gonaïves. He kept informed of activities throughout the island but took active leadership only in those matters concerning the British evacuation. On the sixteenth of the month he sent his secretary, Guybre, to France with letters to Toussaint's old friend Laveaux and dispatches to the Colonial Minister and to the Directory warning that Hédouville's actions against the blacks of Saint-Domingue were endangering the internal peace of the colony.

Upon his arrival in Paris, Guybre visited with Isaac and me, bringing us letters from our family and news of the island. Throughout the time we were studying in Paris our father sent letters to us by every traveler he found sailing for France, and we in turn sent letters back to him and to our mother by every ship we found bound for Saint-Domingue.

In September, the unrest among the laborers increased. They questioned Hédouville's laws binding them to the habitations, and no one appeared from Toussaint to explain the laws.

The laborers on the habitations could always find food in the forests, in the streams and the ocean. The workers in the cities, however, faced possible starvation from the failure of trade.

Hardest hit of all were the black soldiers. In an effort to force the disband-
ing of the army, Hédouville, despite Toussaint's protests, delayed the distribution
of food and supplies and held up the soldiers' pay. The officers struggled with
falling morale and failing discipline.

On the eighteenth of September the rains began in the Northern Plain, and
on the nineteenth in the Artibonite. On September twenty-first, Revolutionary
Day—the anniversary of the Republic and the first day of the year in the
Republican calendar—Hédouville hosted a day of celebration at Cape François.

Toussaint did not attend the celebration. He sent his regrets, contending that
the rains had made the rivers unpassable. He also sent assurances to Hédouville
of his continuing loyalty to the commissioner and to France.

On the twenty-second, Toussaint received a copy of Hédouville's speech. In
the middle of it Toussaint found the veiled warning he had expected.

"Too often," Hédouville had spoken, "in the middle of the shock of passions
which mark the sudden and revolutionary passage from despotism to liberty,
men profoundly ambitious or greedy for riches, either to establish their personal domination or to perpetuate the abuses by which they live, smother the voice
of reason with violence and seize every occasion to mislead a credulous people
into slandering their government and undermining their trust in liberty. The
national interest is clear. He who dresses himself in a false virtue to work only
for his own interest will quickly be unmasked."

It lacked only my name, Toussaint thought angrily. But he knew Hédouville
did not feel himself secure enough to accuse by more than innuendo.

With the speech was an urgent note from Hédouville requesting Toussaint to
aid in the repression of the unrest among the laborers and the army. Hédouville
wrote that he was convinced there was a plot for the black laborers to rise up
and slaughter the whites living in the colony, and Toussaint must take an active
hand in preventing such a tragedy.

In dispatches to Toussaint from Port-au-Prince was a report that there had
been an uprising of laborers south of that city. The disturbance had been suppressed by Rigaud. The cause of the uprising was discontent with the nine and
six year terms of the new labor laws.

Toussaint sat alone for some time evaluating his position. He had sympathy
with the laborers in the South. He knew how effectively Rigaud could suppress
blacks. But Toussaint knew he must not let himself be distracted from the main
action.

Doucement allée loin, thought Toussaint. Easy does it. Hédouville had one foot in the grave and was kicking at the ground with the other one.

Toussaint addressed himself to Hédouville's request. He wrote a sharp note to Hédouville reminding him that over Toussaint's protests the commissioner had demoralized the army, the chief agency of order in the colony.

Toussaint denied that the laborers had murderous intentions. "I must disassociate myself from the malicious slander," he wrote, "that the black citizens of Saint-Domingue await only the opportunity to assassinate the white citizens." But Toussaint acknowledged his responsibility "as a faithful citizen of the colony" and agreed to address a proclamation to the commanders of the districts.

"The malicious suggestion that the blacks wish to kill the whites," he wrote to the commanders, "brings injustice to a good people and accuses you of not preventing an imagined evil. Although fully convinced that the blacks of Saint-Domingue have no injurious intentions, my duties require that I renew your responsibility to protect the tranquility of the area under your command."

When Toussaint sent the proclamation to his officers, he did not, as he was accustomed, send private letters to each defining specific duties.

When he finished dictating the proclamation, Toussaint left his headquarters in Gonaïves and rode back to Desachaux. The following week he contented himself with answering Hédouville's daily letters and letting matters in the island take their course.

At Fort Liberté, Moïse's frustration had reached the level of exasperation. He had written daily to Hédouville deploring the conditions of his troops, requesting money to pay them, food to feed them and uniforms to clothe them. From Hédouville he had received only empty promises and bureaucratic excuses.

Moïse received the proclamation from Toussaint on Monday, September twenty-fourth. That same day an American schooner flying the Spanish flag slipped into Fort Liberté. The next day Herbin, a quartermaster officer from Cape François, arrived and attempted to off load from the schooner thirty barrels of salt provisions and fifty bags of wheat for shipment to the capital. The harbormaster insisted that the provisions stay in Fort Liberté. After a heated argument Herbin retired, empty-handed.

Hédouville was furious. It was clearly a case of insubordination.

Admiral Fabre laughed. "If you try to starve them," he said, "you've got to expect them, from time to time, to steal from you."

Hédouville had asked Fabre and two of his staff officers, Dalton and Watrin, to confer with him on the deteriorating conditions in the colony.

"I think you should proceed cautiously," advised Watrin.

"You should arrest Moïse for stealing," argued Dalton hotly.

"I don't think you have grounds, yet," countered Watrin.

"It was stealing, and if you can't make that stick, you certainly can break him from command for insubordination," insisted Dalton.

"Excuse me," said Watrin. "But the criminal act was committed by the harbormaster, not Moïse. You can arrest the master, but Moïse can deny all knowledge of it."

"He's right," agreed Admiral Fabre. "You don't want to lose your fish by pulling in your line before you have him hooked."

Hédouville threw himself into a chair, put his hands behind his neck, took a deep breath and closed his eyes. He had to keep his animosity for Moïse as a person from effecting his judgment.

"I'll put the disciplining of the harbormaster to Moïse," he said calmly, "and see where that leads us."

"I think your biggest problem is finding the right people to replace the black generals," said Watrin softly.

Hédouville was annoyed with Watrin. Like a bulldog, he thought, once he sets his teeth he won't let go. But he had a way of going straight for the jugular vein. A stubborn peasant, thought Hédouville, round face, heavy body and a mind as practical as a fishwife's.

Hédouville intended to put an officer in command of each of the major districts, North, Northwest, West and South. For the time being Rigaud was acceptable in the South. The three areas under Toussaint's control were the problem. Hédouville knew Watrin's argument. He had heard it often. To replace the blacks with Hédouville's own officers would cause instant alarm. There had to be a transitional process, Watrin argued.

"I don't think you have to replace that many," insisted Dalton.

Hédouville had heard Dalton's arguments before, also. To Dalton, Toussaint was the key. Arrest and deport Toussaint, Dalton insisted. Once Toussaint was out of the colony there would be no difficulty in governing the island.

Hédouville looked at Fabre.

Fabre took a long pull on his pipe, a pipe with a hinged cover. His pirate's pipe, Fabre called it. It made no glow in the dark. "You can sneak about at night, don't you see," Fabre always explained to the curious, "and do your dastardly deeds without giving up your bodily comforts."

"Well?" Hédouville asked the doughty little admiral.

"All you can do is set your sail for the wind that's blowing. You've got to change it with the changing weather no matter what you do now."

Hédouville laughed. He didn't know why Fabre with his sarcastic and irrelevant advice amused him so much.

"Let's examine the particulars," insisted Dalton. "In the South there is Rigaud. We are all agreed that he will stand with us."

"With me," said Hédouville quietly but firmly. He had no intention of proceeding without advice, but he did not want his advisors to lose their perspective.

"Of course," agreed Dalton, properly rebuked.

"In the South there is Rigaud," prompted Hédouville.

"In Port-au-Prince there is Huin. He will certainly stand with you."

"I am not sure," responded Hédouville.

"But he is white!" insisted Dalton.

"And in Léogane there is Laplume. He is mulatto and he is in the South, but he will most certainly support Toussaint," replied Hédouville.

"And the black Mornay in Port-au-Prince will support Rigaud," added Watrin to help Hédouville make his point.

"If we are to trust Rigaud's opinion," agreed Hédouville.

"In Saint Marc you have Agé," continued Dalton trying to regain some credibility. "He will most certainly stay faithful to France."

"Because he is white?" asked Fabre, a little sarcastically.

"No. Because he is a patriot," responded Dalton testily.

"In your journey up the west coast you skipped Arcahaie," said Hédouville pointedly.

"Dessalines is caught between Huin and Agé. He can be contained until the colony is secure," suggested Dalton.

"You are talking about the most dangerous man on the island," said Watrin quietly.

"Perhaps Toussaint would say Huin and Agé are contained because Dessalines has a hand on each," suggested Hédouville.

"I'd be willing to wager," added Fabre, "that Dessalines is the one man in Saint-Domingue that Toussaint fears."

The four men were quiet for a moment.

"My God!" Dalton suddenly exploded. "Are we going to sit here and surrender the colony because of one savage sitting forty leagues on the other side of a mountain?"

"No one is surrendering the colony," answered Hédouville. "But Dessalines is one 'particular' that we cannot ignore."

"It is absolutely essential," said Watrin, "when you move against Toussaint that Rigaud is persuaded to move instantly north against Dessalines and keep him engaged."

No one responded to Watrin.

"I cannot emphasize the point strongly enough," Watrin continued.

"He is right," agreed Fabre. "When you are disarming the burglar, you do poorly to take your eye off his watch dog."

"Go on with your list," Hédouville said suddenly to Dalton.

"Well, Gonaïves must be given to Toussaint. He has a sanctuary there in which he is impregnable. But in the North he has little support on which he can rely. Bellegarde at the Môle, Golart at Jean-Rabel, Michel at Limbé, Barthélemy at the Haut-du-Cap, Dalban at Fort Liberté, Grandet at Monti Christi, all will stay with France.

"If it is seen clearly that Toussaint is a rebel," added Fabre.

"I don't want to sound overconfident," continued Dalton, "but I would not want to be in Toussaint's position."

"Don't be naïve," retorted Watrin. "You are talking about the coastal cities. In the interior Toussaint is the only authority. You didn't mention Paul Louverture or Moïse Louverture...."

"Even on the coast there is Maurepas at Port-de-Paix and Clervaux...," added Fabre.

"But they are both mulattos!" argued Dalton.

"Only a fool judges a man's patriotism by his skin on this island," countered Fabre.

"This argument is of no help to me," said Hédouville suddenly. "If Toussaint can be made to show his true ambition, his desire to rip this colony away from France, there will be leaders enough to combat him. My concern is with the laborers. They follow him as if he were God. They are like a great keg of black gunpowder. It is my duty to hold this land for France. To do that I must frustrate Toussaint's ambitions. But if to unseat Toussaint is to ignite that keg of powder, we will have won nothing."

"Excuse me, sir," said Fabre. "No ship slips its moorings but that the captain has a healthy fear of the tempest."

"We have not mentioned the Cape," Hédouville said changing the subject. "What is your evaluation of Henri Christophe?" he asked Dalton.

There was a momentary pause; then Watrin and Fabre laughed. Despite his better judgment, Hédouville found their laughter infectious.

"You are mistaken, gentlemen," said Hédouville after he gained control of himself, "if you think Christophe is all show and no substance."

"Christophe can be led to the gibbet," averred Fabre, "and persuaded to put his head in the noose with a bribe of a little wine and the promise of an abundance of white whores in heaven."

"I do not agree," said Hédouville emphatically. "He drinks constantly, but I have never seen him drunk. And he has always a smirk upon his lips."

"Christophe is an enigma," agreed Watrin. "But I believe that if he is not personally threatened he will stay with France. You may not agree, but I think he is your best choice for the commander of the North."

Hédouville said nothing but nodded his head thoughtfully.

"And what of Toussaint's nephew," Hédouville asked Dalton somewhat sarcastically, "General Moïse Louverture?"

"Dangerous and unstable," Dalton answered confidently.

Watrin nodded in agreement. "I think he is Toussaint's weak link. The old man has a great affection for him and could be goaded into a rash act to defend him."

"Toussaint could be tricked into an act of civil disobedience, or even treason," quickly agreed Fabre.

"He might have to show his hand with England and the United States," agreed Watrin. "Then you would be assured of the support of the officers that still waiver."

"Why don't you openly accuse Toussaint of treason?" asked Dalton impetuously. "You know full well he conspired with Maitland to create an independent kingdom here."

"We know nothing of the sort," responded Hédouville sharply.

"But we do," insisted Dalton.

"Sonthonax could not catch him in that net. His acts must convict him, not our suspicions," replied Hédouville.

"They are not suspicions," persisted Dalton. "We know the treachery of the English. If from nothing else, from my dealings with Stuart. My God, they are willing to...." Dalton stopped in the middle of his sentence. He looked at Hédouville, then down at the floor.

Everyone in the room knew the content of Dalton's incomplete sentence, but no one commented. Stuart had suggested a secret agreement between Maitland and Hédouville for English assistance to reestablish slavery in Saint-Domingue at the conclusion of the war in Europe. Hédouville had been horrified by Dalton's report. The one invincible weapon in Toussaint's hands was the blacks' fear of slavery. Hédouville was determined not to give Toussaint ammunition for that weapon. He had sworn Dalton to secrecy regarding the conversation with Stuart. Even so, and despite Hédouville's efforts to calm the population with his speech on Revolutionary Day, the rumors persisted that he had signed such an agreement with Maitland.

Hédouville stood abruptly and thanked his friends for their time and advice. As the three men prepared to leave, Hédouville asked Watrin to stay a few moments.

When they were alone, Hédouville explained to Watrin that Toussaint had sent Guybre to Paris to argue his position before the ministers and Directory. Hédouville wanted Watrin to undertake such a journey for him, immediately, to explain his plan for reorganizing the civil and military commands under himself, and his evaluations of Rigaud and Toussaint. Watrin agreed and promised to be ready within two days.

When he was alone, Hédouville stood for a few moments absently watching through the window the flow of people crossing the square before Government House.

Hédouville respected Toussaint's power, but knew—beyond question—that Toussaint was preparing to treasonably create an independent state in Saint-Domingue. Hédouville felt confident that he had sufficient loyalty among

Toussaint's officers to frustrate his efforts. But Hédouville feared an attack upon Toussaint might ignite a violence beyond anyone's control, even Toussaint's.

Hédouville shook the vagueness from his head. He focused his eyes on the pen, ink and paper lying on his desk. There was no question but that the theft of provisions at Fort Liberté was a tempting opening through which to thrust at Moïse. The question was, how best to exploit the opportunity.

CHAPTER 10
Attack at Fort Liberté

During the last days of September and the first days of October, Hédouville and Moïse exchanged heated letters on the subject of the stolen stores at Fort Liberté. Hédouville accused Moïse of ordering the insubordination of the harbormaster and demanded that the stores be sent to the Cape.

Moïse denied pre-knowledge of the act but refused to allow the supplies to leave Fort Liberté.

"I have written you continuously of our destitution," he wrote. "I will not send food to the Cape when I am forced to feed my soldiers on half a dried cassava root a day."

Moïse had two maternal brothers serving under him in the Fifth Colonial Regiment. The younger of these, Charles Zamor, was known for his quick temper. On the second of October, while attending a celebration at Laxavon, Zamor was provoked to a quarrel and in defending himself wounded several would-be peacemakers.

Moïse was informed of his brother's actions and as punishment confined him to quarters for three days. When the confinement ended Zamor was again provoked by the same officer, Captain Marteau. Moïse arrested and imprisoned both officers.

Moïse had at first assumed that the quarrel was the result of his brother's quick temper. But despite the impartial arrest of both officers, unrest in the Fifth Regiment mounted. There were frequent outbreaks of quarrelling and rumors that Moïse intended to execute both his brother and Marteau.

Before Moïse could unearth the causes of the unrest he received an urgent note from Toussaint to come to Desachaux.

On October third, Toussaint took possession of Môle Saint Nicholas from the British. On the fifth he left the Môle to ride to the Cape to report to Hédouville. As was his custom he outdistanced his guards and arrived at Habitation Hericourt, close to the Cape, accompanied only by his guide. At Hericourt he was met by Raimond's white secretary, Pascal.

"Do not enter Cape François," Pascal warned Toussaint. "There are plots against your safety there."

Toussaint immediately rode south to Gonaïves. In crossing the rain-swollen Ennery River he suffered a sad mishap. He lost the sword that his friend Laveaux had presented to him in gratitude for Toussaint rescuing him from the mulatto plot.

The loss of the sword disturbed Toussaint. He regretted to lose a gift from a dear friend, but more, the loss disturbed him as an omen. The sword was a symbol of France's recognition of his authority. Toussaint feared the sword's loss presaged his fall from power. He began to think that he had waited too long. He no longer knew which officers he could trust. How otherwise could he have ridden from the Môle to the very gates of the Cape with no word of the plot against him? Ridden through Jean-Rabel, Port-de-Paix, Limbé, with no word to warn him?

Toussaint waited for the laborers to grow restive under Hédouville's rule, and while he waited, Hédouville corrupted the officers of his army.

Toussaint knew there were two officers he could trust implicitly, not only because of their loyalty to him, but because of their hatred for the French. Hédouville used lies about Toussaint's ambitions to undermine him. Moïse and Dessalines were immune to such lies. They would have long since declared the island's independence, except for Toussaint's restraint of them.

On Monday, October eighth, Moïse and Dessalines arrived at Desachaux. Toussaint explained to them his fears of Hédouville. He intended to move against the commissioner, but he had to wait for a provocative incident to justify his actions. When Toussaint made his move, Dessalines was to cut off all routes from the South, preventing Rigaud from coming to Hédouville's aid. Moïse, on his return North, was to spread the word that Hédouville was conspiring with the English to reestablish slavery. The laborers were to arm themselves, and, when Toussaint called, they were to march upon the Cape. After alerting the laborers, Moïse was to hurry back to Fort Liberté, maintain a vigilance for possible treachery from Hédouville against the Fifth Regiment, and on Toussaint's command, put his regiment at the head of the laborers advancing against the Cape.

On his journey across the Northern Plain delivering Toussaint's message the last area Moïse visited was Quartier-Morin. There his path took him to the habitation of Louis Duclero.

Anacaona slipped from her bed, dressed quickly and quietly descended the stairs and out into the night. In his room Duclero heard her. He had been awakened by the drums of the voudoun worshipers. Anacaona often slipped away to join in the strange ceremonies.

On this night, however, Duclero also had heard the plaintive notes of a wood pigeon whistling sharply against the low thumping of the drums.

Moïse.

Duclero turned his back to the window and tried to lose himself in sleep. He slept fitfully but would not let himself get up from bed until daylight.

While he waited for the dawn, Duclero counted in his mind. It was twelve years since he first saw Anacaona, in a line of chained women being led to the auction. She was a defiant, sullen wisp of a girl; he guessed about fifteen years old. He bought her on the spot and after paying the slaver, he marched her to Government House and filed the papers for her freedom.

"You may go where you please," he responded to her startled eyes when he explained that she was free.

She did not answer him, but he was not surprised that she followed him to his horse. He understood the looks directed towards her from the men they passed on the street. Even then her beauty was remarkable.

Duclero put her to work in the house, first in the kitchen, but then, as she proved exceptionally intelligent, as his wife's personal maid. Although he thought the little girl most attractive, he had no designs sexually upon her until his wife's absences in Paris grew longer, and finally permanent. By then Anacaona was a young woman and his need for her grew from their daily proximity. He worried that she accepted him only from gratitude, but as the years passed he had come to believe that she loved him.

She had from the beginning come and gone as she pleased. Although he never escaped from his feelings of anger and jealousy, he came to accept her absences and always welcomed her back.

The power of love to enslave puzzled Duclero.

They had been lovers for several years before she spoke to him of her past. She explained that she was able to do so only when she felt strong enough to leave him if he rejected her.

She was born in the mountains south of Port-au-Prince. She did not know her father. He was killed when she was a baby. Her mother told her her father was a Songhai, a descendant of the Pharaohs of Egypt. Her mother claimed to be the daughter of a white French father and Carib mother. She, too, was named Anacaona.

Duclero believed that Anacaona's memories of her early childhood were mostly fantasy, dreams she held, perhaps, to compensate for the pains of her adolescence.

When Anacaona was nine, she and her mother were captured in a raid against the mountain maroons, and despite her mother's pleas that she was a freedwoman, were sold to a bordello in Port-au-Prince. Anacaona's mother died within the first year. Anacaona became defiant and despite beatings refused to obey her master. He was reluctant to damage her beauty and lessen her value, and chose to send her to the market in the Cape where she was not known. It was there that Duclero bought her.

When he got up from bed, Duclero did not call for his servant but washed and dressed himself. He caught a glimpse of his image in the mirror and stopped to examine it. His body was tall, his shoulders broad. For his years and his love of wine, his flesh was firm. His gaze lingered on his receding hairline—on formal occasions hidden by a wig—and the unfashionable beard, now graying, that he wore to conceal the pockmarks on his face.

He knew that when Anacaona returned he would make no complaint of her absence.

Hédouville was prepared to act. The Fifth Regiment was close to mutiny. He had reason enough now to disarm them. He had at hand officers and soldiers ready to undertake the task.

But Hédouville delayed. He could not persuade Toussaint to come to the Cape, and he did not know where Moïse was. Hédouville was hesitant to spring his trap without the promise of ensnaring his two chief quarries.

Most recently Hédouville sent Henri Christophe to fetch Toussaint. But the good-natured black commander of the garrison forces at the Cape returned without his friend and mentor. "He fears for his life in Cape François," Christophe explained to Hédouville.

On Monday, October fifteenth, in Fort Liberté, Charles Zamor and Captain Marteau were released from prison and immediately resumed their quarrel. They were joined by partisans on each side. The quarrel grew into a brawl which engulfed the barracks, the brawl into a riot which spread out into the city.

Hédouville knew he could delay no longer. He issued a proclamation accusing the Fifth Regiment of disobeying the orders of the established authorities and destroying the peace of the colony. He ordered the regiment disarmed and placed under arrest.

Immediately Grandet, the white commander of Monte Cristi and Laxavon, where Charles Zamor first had been prodded into quarrelling, marched on Fort Liberté at the head of the Spanish cavalry. The two European regiments quartered in Fort Liberté were alerted, and the police and National Guard were readied under the command of Quayer Lariviere, a mulatto known for his hatred of blacks. By nightfall Hédouville had three thousand men ready to face the seven hundred soldiers of the Fifth, who were without ammunition, quarrelling among themselves, without their commander and unaware of their danger.

When he read Hédouville's proclamation calling for the arrest of the Fifth Regiment, Delatte, Moïse's secretary, was alarmed. He approached the adjutant major of the Fifth, Fringnat. But Fringnat, who had been won over by Hédouville's agents, assured Delatte that there was no danger. As the evening progressed and Delatte saw the preparations by the two European regiments and the National Guard and the continuing disorder of the Fifth, he decided to seek out Moïse and alert him to the conditions in the city.

Delatte rode first to Duclero's habitation. It was past midnight when he arrived. Duclero was not pleased to receive him. At first Delatte thought it was the hour, but when he explained his mission, Duclero complained angrily that Moïse had passed by two days earlier and he had not seen him since.

Aware of the embarrassment he was bringing to the planter, Delatte nevertheless urged the importance of his mission and pressed for intelligence of where he might find Moïse. Reluctantly, Duclero suggested that when Moïse wished to be unavailable he often visited the Bréda Habitation.

At two in the morning Delatte found Moïse and Anacaona at Bréda.

On the morning of October sixteenth, Hédouville's forces, supported by five cannon loaded with grapeshot, were armed and drawn up in the city square. Manigat, a black magistrate selected by Hédouville for the task, ordered the Fifth Regiment to leave its barracks and fall in before Moïse's house by the square. The regiment, sleepy and disorganized, obeyed. It appeared at first that they were responding to a general mobilization of all forces in the city. It was only when they were ordered by Manigat to stack their weapons while the other soldiers stood before them with arms at the ready that the officers of the Fifth realized their danger.

"I defy your order," shouted chief of brigade Adrien Zamor, brother to Charles and half-brother to Moïse. "I take orders only from General Moïse," he cried and forbade his soldiers to obey Manigat.

Manigat repeated his order, but other officers stood with Adrien. A deep-chested Socos, only a few years from the Gold Coast and known only as the African, snatched back his sword from where he had thoughtlessly placed it on

the ground and with it prodded his soldiers to reclaim their weapons already
dropped.

At this moment Moïse and Delatte, having ridden all night, arrived at the
gates of the city.

Moïse raced to the city square and rode up to the balcony of Government
House from which Manigat directed the disarming of the Fifth Regiment.

"Take care, Citizen Manigat!" Moïse shouted. "You cannot make war as I
can!"

When Moïse appeared in the square, his soldiers gave a cheer of relief. Any
who still wavered jumped to reclaim his weapon and closed ranks defiantly
behind the two chiefs of brigade, Adrien Zamor and The African.

Alarmed by the change of events, the traitor Fringnat grabbed a match from
one of the cannoneers, touched the fire to a primer and sent a blast of grapeshot
ripping into the closed ranks of the Fifth. Thinking the command to fire had
been given, the other four cannoneers quickly followed.

At the first cannon blast the soldiers of the Fifth still on their feet fled in
every direction seeking cover. The blasts that followed tore mostly into the stone
walls of Moïse's house. But the carnage was intense. Hundreds of dead and
dying men lay strewn across the edge of the square, the wounded crying out in
pain.

Moïse shouted for the survivors to follow him.

In the confusion of the massacre and the conflicting orders of the many
commanders of Hédouville's forces, Moïse and several hundred of his soldiers
raced to the powder magazine. It was unguarded. Before they could break in the
heavy door, Grandet's Spanish cavalry and Lariviere's mounted units of the
National Guard were upon them.

The Fifth Regiment fought valiantly with sword and knife, but when the
infantry of the European regiments reached the scene it was clear that resistance
was futile.

Moïse saw his brother Charles pierced through the chest by a saber stroke and
Adrien and The African fall beneath the press of numbers. Desperately Moïse
slashed at the bayonets thrust toward him. For an instant he broke free and ran
to the mangrove forest behind the magazine. There he threw himself into the
maze of rushes and twisted roots that choked the shallows of the west bay.

Moïse lay buried to his neck in the mud and water, his head thrust beneath a
tangle of debris. On the bank above him he heard the sounds of men searching
through the trees, of sticks and bayonets thrust into holes and crannies, of men

shouting. From the city behind him Moïse heard an occasional shot and shouts
of discovery, and—as the hours passed—quiet, broken only by the strident
shrieks of quarrelling palm birds, the gentle splash of a cormorant fishing and
the indistinct murmur of voices in the distance.

Moïse waited until dark. His mind seethed with anguish and accusation. He
cursed himself for dallying with Anacaona when his duty called him to Fort
Liberté. He cursed her. But in the next thought he reached for her with his arms
to hold her tightly to him. She had urged him to return to his regiment. He had
refused to leave her.

Moïse cursed himself. But his body trembled with his need for revenge.
Those who had wronged him would feel his anger.

For hours, waiting for dark, Moïse lay still, but his mind surged with the
images of his revenge. Vengeance. He formed the word silently with his lips.
Vengeance. He would fall like the tempest upon his enemies.

Within hours the news of the debacle reached the Cape. Hédouville was dismayed. He had thought to avoid bloodshed by a large show of force. He knew
the slaughter of many unarmed men would cry for revenge, and Moïse was free
to raise the alarm.

Hédouville immediately posted Moïse as an outlaw and sent dispatches to
Toussaint ordering him to march upon Fort Liberté to restore order and to aid
in the apprehension of Moïse. Hédouville also sent emissaries by land and by sea
to Rigaud alerting him to the situation and requesting that he march north to the
aid of the garrison at the Cape.

The activity did not lessen Hédouville's feeling of dismay. His worse fears
were realized. The black powder keg was lit.

At nightfall, Moïse pulled himself from his hiding place and made his way
through the thick woods west of the city. Stripped to the waist, bootless, mud
smeared, trousers clinging wet, his fury clear in his every gesture, Moïse was not
to be crossed. The steward at the Croiseuil Habitation gave him no trouble, and
Moïse was soon mounted and riding south. By dawn he had roused the garrisons

at La Martelliere and Terrior-Rouge and blocked all roads leading to Fort Liberté. Soon after, messengers were on their way to Toussaint at Gonaïves.

Duclero woke with a pounding headache. For a moment he was suspended in a web of déjà vu. He was living again in August, 1791. The room was filled with the sounds of beating drums, shouting men and the sickly sweet smell of burning sugar cane.

He jumped from his bed and rushed to the window. In the distance he could see black smoke rising in scattered columns in the east and southeast.

The dream and the heart-stopping terror that accompanied it were pushed from his mind by the realities before him. The prevailing breeze carried the sounds of distant drums and the smell of distant fires. Behind the house he could hear loud but indistinct voices, occasionally shouts.

Was the Terror starting again?

Anacaona. Duclero remembered Anacaona. She had returned the previous day from her assignation with Moïse. She had made no explanation of her absence. Duclero had asked for none. They had eaten dinner in silence. Afterwards he had drunk too much and had gone to bed with a deep anger buried within him.

Duclero rushed from the room, into the hall, and pushed open the door to Anacaona's room. The bed was empty.

His chest tightened. He took a deep breath, walked back to his room, pulled off his nightshirt and quickly dressed.

Duclero found no one in the house. He walked toward the house servants' cailles. Before he reached the compound Guillaume, his black steward, rushed to meet him.

"Master," Guillaume shouted. "Go quickly." He pointed toward the Cape. "They are burning all the plain."

"Who is?" demanded Duclero impatiently.

"They are," answered Guillaume. He gestured vaguely toward the servants' compound.

"Why?" Duclero felt his head about to burst.

"France wants to put them in slavery again."

"That is nonsense!" Duclero's vision was blurred from the pain throbbing in his temples and at the nape of his neck. The stupidity of the situation was beyond his endurance. The thought of the habitations of the Northern Plain again razed, the white proprietors threatened once more with death and devastation, and all because of a rumor, a lie! Duclero kicked savagely at the trunk of one of the plantain trees lining the path.

"It is a lie!" he screamed.

"No, sir," Guillaume insisted. "Toussaint says it is so."

"You heard him say it? With your own ears?"

"No, sir. But there are those who heard him."

Duclero knew argument was of no use. If the blacks believed Toussaint said it, then no one could convince them to the contrary. Duclero turned and looked at his house. His stomach churned with the thought of having again to rebuild his beautiful home.

"You should go to the Cape." Guillaume spoke softly behind him. "I will stay with your house. If you are not here I can stop them from burning it."

Guillaume paused for a moment.

"They would not burn it." He gestured toward the servants' compound. "They would." He gestured toward the southeast.

Duclero turned suddenly to Guillaume.

"Anacaona! Where is she?"

Guillaume gestured vaguely toward the east. "They came for her early this morning."

Duclero took with him only the currency he had on hand and the most negotiable of bullion and jewels. If his habitation was burned again, nothing could be saved. If the blacks responded to his fairness by respecting his property, then nothing would be lost.

The road was crowded with proprietors and their families riding toward Cape François, some on horseback, others in carriages, many with wagons filled with heirlooms and family treasures. Tempers were short. A few threatened or complained. Most rode in silence, occasionally glancing back at the plumes of smoke in the distance.

All of Duclero's anger fell upon Anacaona. He did not know why. He had accepted her liaison with Moïse. He had agreed that she was free to come and go as she wished. She certainly was in no way to blame for the destruction of this day. His anger, he thought after some searching among his feelings, was because she was free to come and go, to move in and out of the many worlds of this island, and he was not. She was free. He was trapped, trapped in the world of the landed white.

What insanity, Duclero thought, to feel trapped in a world of wealth, power and privilege. But it was a way of life threatened not only in Saint-Domingue but also in France, perhaps in all the world. Faced with the threats to his world, it seemed Duclero had no choice but to defend it. He was envious, angry, that Anacaona, a half-illiterate, mulatto girl, could slip unhindered through the nets of necessity while he was caught in them, frozen in time and circumstances. When we build, he thought, we think to build civilizations, but all we construct are ornate tombs.

The bridge over the Haut-du-Cap river was crowded with refugees. There was a line waiting to cross and join the stream of those flooding the city from the south and west.

As he waited his turn to cross, Duclero's mind played with a phrase from the American Revolution. When he finally negotiated the bridge, the phrase had become, "If we do not burn alone, then we shall all burn together."

Moïse met Toussaint at Habitation Hericourt. Moïse wore no shirt, had a broken straw hat pushed low on his head and his sweat streaked black body was smeared with the brown dust of the road and the gray ashes of burned cane.

The meeting between the two men was short. When it was over Moïse rode east toward the Cape, Toussaint south to Gonaïves.

Toussaint found the long strides of a fine horse put him into a reverie. His anger, his fear, his frustration melted. He was unconcerned for the roughness of the road. He endured without complaint the jolts of rocky trails, the lashes of low tree limbs, the discomforts of rain and flooded rivers. He found that the feel of the horse's muscles working beneath his thighs, the sounds of the horse's labored breathing and occasional snorts, the working of the leather tackle, the sense of distance falling behind, lulled him from the pains of conflict and carried him to a state of mind in which he could pass with equanimity through the issues of life and death with which he was constantly confronted.

Toussaint ached at the thought of the rich Northern Plain falling once more to fire and knife. He had worked hard, took great pride in the restoration of cultivation. To see the habitations once more razed brought him the deep pain of loss. The thought of the proprietors faced once more with the terrors of torture and death made him cry out with a sympathetic concern for his own dear family safe at Desachaux, and for Isaac and me in distant Paris.

It must be. Hédouville must go. If Toussaint surrendered to him, slavery would come again, if not by Hédouville's hand, then soon after by the hands of those who followed.

From Gonaïves Toussaint sent orders for Dessalines to take command of the Fourth Colonial Battalion at Arcahaie and to move it north. Toussaint also reminded Dessalines that all communication between the Cape and Rigaud in the South must be intercepted.

On Saturday, October twentieth, Toussaint was met at Ennery by emissaries from Hédouville, two men Toussaint knew well and trusted: Colonel Charles Vincent and the Abbé Antheaume. Vincent, an army engineer, was one of the architects of the rental plan by which the habitations were being restored. Antheaume was a churchman of high character renown for his charitable works.

"All that we have built in the North," the always phlegmatic Vincent stated simply, "will be lost if the laborers are not calmed. Only you can do that."

Toussaint needed no one to define for him the precipice upon which he walked, and in moments of crisis he shared his thoughts with no one. He was angry that Vincent and Antheaume consented to serve as lackeys for Hédouville, but at the same time he knew they proceeded from sincere concern for the well being of the colony.

Toussaint was angry because only hours earlier he had heard of the needless deaths of three of Hédouville's officers killed south of Saint Marc for refusing to surrender their dispatch cases to Dessalines' pickets. Toussaint knew he must move quickly to control events in the North, and the presence of friends like Vincent and Antheaume speaking for his enemy annoyed him sharply.

"How does General Hédouville respond to General Moïse?" Toussaint asked Vincent.

Vincent knew the love Toussaint had for Moïse and saw the threat behind the question, but he answered without hesitation: "Hédouville has declared Moïse a traitor and has ordered him hunted down and shot on sight."

Toussaint turned to Caze, his aid-de-camp.

"Place these men under arrest."

Then Toussaint walked abruptly from the room.

CHAPTER 11
Hédouville Flees

In Cape François on Sunday, October twenty-first, masses were held throughout the day for the safety of the city.

Most of Sunday night Hédouville met with Dalton and Fabre planning the city's defense. Early Monday morning Hédouville, in the attempt to allay the fears of the citizens by a show of strength, ordered the city garrison, the militia, the garrisons of the surrounding forts and his personal guard to be drawn up in review in the Champ de Mars.

Before Hédouville could address the assembled forces, panicked civilians from all quarters of the city swarmed onto the field. The general's personal guard held firmly, forming a barrier before the trees to the east of the square. Christophe's hussars sat easily on their horses in front of their barracks on the west side. The militia, the few that had appeared in uniform, melted into the crowd of civilians. The artillerymen from the forts were pushed in disarray into the streets and neighboring barracks.

Hédouville surveyed the scene in dismay. Only the day before the city had been tense but orderly. He was not long in discovering the cause of the panic. News had reached Cape François that morning that Dessalines was in the Northern Plain. He was reported in Marmelade—in Dondon—in Grande Rivière—in Le Trou. He was everywhere. And he was marching inextricably toward the Cape, pausing only to burn and pillage and to gather up the rampaging field workers into his swelling army.

Hédouville made several attempts to establish order on the field, but his efforts were without conviction. He knew that if he ordered Christophe to sweep the square with his hussars, within minutes order would be restored. But Hédouville could not bear to witness the sight of sabers in black hands slicing into the white flesh of his countrymen.

Hédouville had heard enough of the horrors of the massacre of 1791 to know he could not submit the city to such a fate again. Not at the hands of Christophe in the name of order, and not at the hands of Dessalines in the name of pride.

Toussaint had won.

Hédouville extracted himself from the confusion and under the protection of his personal guard marched the two blocks to Government House.

He found Raimond waiting in his office.

"Send for Toussaint," the mulatto urged.

"Toussaint is well aware of his responsibilities," Hédouville responded with rancor. "I have reminded him of them often. His answer is to arrest my messengers."

"I will go to him."

"Go. I do not stop you!"

"I will tell him that you recognize his authority, that the attack upon Moïse and the Fifth Regiment was a mistake and that in permitting it, you interfered in military matters."

"You will tell him nothing of the sort!" interrupted Hédouville angrily. "I will not bow and scrape to that traitor! He means to steal this island from France and fools like you are aiding him!"

"If you will not submit to him, then the Cape will burn," replied Raimond evenly.

"No," answered Hédouville. "I intend to sail for France today. Toussaint wants me gone. I am going. You can tell him that. When I am gone he will have no need to destroy the city."

"I will see that he is informed of your intentions"

Raimond turned to leave the office.

"I thank you," said Hédouville sarcastically. "But I do not think he needs either of us to inform him of what is happening here."

Raimond paused. "That may be. But I do not wish to leave the safety of the city to chance."

Raimond continued toward the door.

"My god!" Hédouville exploded. "When are you going to wake up?"

Raimond paused, his hand on the door latch.

"You are supposed to represent France in the colony," Hédouville continued angrily. "And you connive and plot for your country's overthrow here. What will you do when the last vestiges of French rule are gone? Who then will protect you from his machinations? Do you think the services you have done him will keep you from the massacre?"

Raimond exited and closed the door quietly behind him.

From his office, Hédouville organized his withdrawal from the city. He ordered the three large ships in the harbor to be ready to sail upon the tide. He established a priority list of people to sail with him, including those who came with him and those whom he felt had the most to fear from Toussaint. Hédouville sent messengers to the chosen, instructing them to board the ships with only their most valued possessions.

He then dictated a letter to Rigaud describing the state of affairs at the Cape and his choice to evacuate rather than risk the city's destruction. In the letter, Hédouville appointed Rigaud, in the name of the Directory, sole commander of the South and equal in rank with Toussaint. Hédouville had several copies of the letter transcribed and sent by several channels. He included a copy in a dispatch to Roume in Santo Domingo City, informing the French commissioner there of the situation in the Cape, of Toussaint's treachery and of Raimond's complicity.

In the confusion of the city, Hédouville managed to locate the deputy director of the port artillery, Gassonville, and ordered him to spike the cannons of Forts Aux-Dames, Saint-Joseph and Picolet. Hédouville did not wish to have his ships blown from the water as they negotiated the narrow channel from the harbor to the sea.

News of Hédouville's pending departure spread rapidly, and the French commissioner was deluged with pleas from those who wished to sail with him. Before he could board the ship himself he had been pressed into issuing over two thousand passports, dangerously over-crowding the three vessels of his fleet.

In the afternoon, after he had taken up quarters on his flagship, Hédouville prepared one final salvo to fire at Toussaint, a proclamation to the citizens of Saint-Domingue denouncing Toussaint for conspiring with the governments of

Great Britain and the United States to establish an independent kingdom on the island with Toussaint as ruler.

As Hédouville read over the copy before it went to the printer his eye caught the heading his secretary had provided: "1st Brumaire year VII, aboard the Bravoure." Hédouville quickly struck out "aboard the Bravoure" and wrote in its place, "Government House, Cape François." He did not wish the irony of his fleeing aboard a ship named the "Bravoure" immortalized in a printed proclamation.

Admiral Fabre was ready to sail on the afternoon tide, but Hédouville delayed one more day. He wished to see his proclamation printed and distributed to the citizens of the city. To have sailed before that, he reasoned, would have made his flight seem more cowardice than discretion. It was not easy for him to retreat from a battle, and he wanted the people of the Cape to know that he did so only to preserve them from harm.

Hédouville was awakened at dawn on the twenty-third with the news that during the night Dessalines had slipped across the Morne Haut-du-Cap into the rear of the city. His soldiers occupied Fort Belair guarding the roads into the city and Fort Picolet guarding the mouth of the channel to the sea. His forces also had moved into the barracks in the Providence area of the city by the Champ de Mars. Nowhere had he met with resistance.

Hédouville ordered Fabre to sail at once.

"Can't," replied the admiral. "It's flood tide, and the winds are too light to move against it."

Hédouville knew that even if Gassonville had spiked the guns at Picolet, as ordered, before the tide turned Dessalines would have them repaired or replaced. Hédouville was trapped, the victim not only of Toussaint's treachery but of the elements and the crush of frightened refugees crowded into the overladen ships.

Hédouville retired to his cabin and did not come out, not even for relief from the oven-like noonday temperatures of his restricted quarters.

For two days the stalemate held. Dessalines did not attack, but Hédouville dared not sail past the harbor forts without assurances of safety. Dessalines granted none.

On Thursday, October twenty-fifth, Toussaint entered the city. He was greeted by the citizens as the city's liberator. He went first to the church where he joined in a mass of celebration with the people who had gathered there for protection. Toussaint led the singing of the te deum of thanksgiving. He then sent an officer to the print shop to burn the bundles of Hédouville's still uncirculated proclamation.

At two o'clock in the afternoon, Raimond was rowed to Hédouville's ship and ushered into his cabin. Hédouville greeted him dressed, because of the heat, only in a loose fitting pair of cotton under-trousers. Raimond handed Hédouville a list of names, Manigat, Fringnat and other persons involved in the overthrow of the Fifth Regiment at Fort Liberté, men to whom Hédouville had granted asylum aboard the ships.

"When these men are delivered to Toussaint," Raimond explained, "you will be permitted to sail without resistance."

"These men are under my protection," Hédouville responded angrily.

"Toussaint insists they be tried for their crimes against the government."

"Crimes," Hédouville scoffed. "He wants them because they had the courage to serve the government loyally. Now Toussaint demands that I betray them or be held prisoner myself. As France's representative, is this the government you support?"

"They will be fairly tried," Raimond responded coldly.

Hédouville made a sound of derision.

"I think they will not be harmed," Raimond continued. "Toussaint, I think, will use the trial as an opportunity to show that his justice is well tempered with mercy."

"And his justice for me...and for France?" asked Hédouville sternly.

"You have several hours still of ebb tide. Everyone would be served best if you acceded to Toussaint's request and withdrew," replied Raimond.

Hédouville, the sweat flowing freely down his arms and chest, sat at the writing desk and scribbled his assent upon the page of names. The ink, where he touched the paper with his sweating hands, was smeared and blurred. Without looking up he handed the paper to Raimond.

"Give this to Admiral Fabre. He will see to your needs.... And Raimond!" Hédouville looked directly at the enigmatic mulatto he had grown to despise. "I hold you personally responsible for the well being of these men."

Raimond exited without pausing or replying.

Within the hour the three ships slipped their anchors and drifted slowly out of the harbor, past the silent guns of the forts. In the vanguard was Hédouville's flagship, the "Bravoure.

————————◆————————

The day before Hédouville sailed, Duclero left the Cape. He passed by Dessalines' pickets without challenge.

On the short ride to his habitation he observed that the destruction of property had been selective, mostly on the plantations where the proprietors were known to treat their blacks cruelly. Duclero was relieved to discover that his property had survived intact. His field hands and most of his house servants were absent, but Duclero was confident that when Toussaint arrived in the Cape and the conflict with Hédouville was resolved, his workers would return.

In the living room Duclero found Anacaona working on her embroidery. When he saw her he walked quickly to her, put his arms around her shoulders, leaned over and kissed her fully on the mouth. She returned his kiss with the warmth that always drew from him all anger at her absences. He asked her nothing about her activities of the past days.

Duclero looked with his usual puzzlement at the design of Anacaona's needlework: a confusion of bright flowers intertwined with incomprehensible graphic patterns. Each figure had a specific meaning to Anacaona, but Duclero was bewildered by the complicated profusion of symbols.

"Erzulie?" asked Duclero, pointing to an ornate heart divided vertically by a staff crowned with several wreath-like figures.

"Yes," replied Anacaona, smiling with pleasure at his efforts to understand her work.

But he could go no further. The rest of the forms and lines confused and annoyed him. He felt sharply the chasm that lay between his thoughts and the mind of the woman he loved.

Duclero attended none of the celebrations for Toussaint in Cape François, but because of her friendship for Moïse, Anacaona wished to attend the ceremony reestablishing his command in Fort Liberté.

On Thursday, after the heat of noon, Duclero and Anacaona rode to Fort Liberté. They arrived after dark and spent the night as guests of Moïse. To avoid the heat of the day, the ceremonies began at five in the morning.

Compared to Cape François, Fort Liberté is a small city, no larger than one of the Cape's seven administrative districts. Whereas in the Cape there are a number of open spaces, each district having at least one, in Fort Liberté there is only the town square. It was there, in the same square in which ten days earlier the Fifth Regiment had been decimated by Hédouville's cannon, that Toussaint addressed the assembled citizens.

Toussaint, his officers and the local authorities stood on a platform on the southwest side of the square, before the entrance of the church of Saint Joseph. Before them, on the ground in chains, flanked by armed guards, stood those responsible for the massacre. Behind the prisoners, the surviving soldiers of the Fifth Regiment stood at attention. Behind the Fifth Regiment, the civilians gathered to hear Toussaint speak. On the steps of the church a regimental band played the "Marseillaise."

Anacaona, eager to hear Toussaint, pushed her way to the center of the square where she stood on one corner of the four sided fountain, balancing herself with a hand on one of the granite faces from whose now dry lips water had once flowed.

Duclero stood on the ground beside Anacaona, his right hand raised and resting on her hip as she stood on the fountain ledge. She did not need his support, but in the press of people he felt the need to hold on to her.

From where he stood Duclero could see little of the proceedings. The music irritated him. He had adjusted to a plethora of changes since the Revolution, but he could not, without discomfort, listen to de Lisle's childishly chauvinistic song, sung or played ad nauseam, at every affair of state.

The "Marseillaise" finished, Toussaint rose to speak. Duclero could catch but a glimpse of him, but the Governor-General's reed-like voice cut through the restless noise of the crowd and the rattle of the wind in the acacia trees beside the church.

"Citizen's of Fort Liberté," Toussaint began, "once again our troubled land is divided and shaken by intestine struggles."

He spoke deliberately, allowing each idea to be digested by his audience before proceeding to the next.

"General Hédouville says that Toussaint and the brave soldiers who follow him are traitors. Hédouville says that I am against liberty, that I want to surrender to the English, that I wish to make myself independent.

"Who ought to love liberty more? Toussaint Louverture, slave of Bréda, or General Hédouville, former Marquis and Chevalier de Saint Louis?

"If I wished to surrender to the English, would I have driven them from the land? If I were disloyal to France would I have sent there my sons to study at the wellsprings of freedom and wisdom?

"At the very moment I brought peace and serenity to this colony, General Hédouville chooses a Negro to destroy the brave General Moïse and the Fifth

Regiment—soldiers renown for their efforts in driving out the English and securing the peace of our homes."

It was clear to Duclero that Toussaint was not speaking to his troops arrayed before him, but rather to the civilians crowded into the square behind the Fifth Regiment.

"Do you not know," continued Toussaint, "that there are thousands of blacks behind you who would have taken revenge for the courageous Moïse and his faithful soldiers? Is this what France demands?

"I reinstate General Moïse in his former functions. Let all men give him the obedience due his rank.

"Remember! In all of Saint-Domingue there is only one Toussaint Louverture! At his name all men must tremble!"

At the end of Toussaint's speech, Anacaona was ready to leave. Duclero was surprised. He had expected her to stay for the afternoon and evening celebrations, or at least to say goodbye to Moïse.

As they rode home through the rising heat, Duclero had some thoughts as to why Anacaona left Fort Liberté abruptly. She must have considered herself an embarrassment to Moïse before his uncle. Toussaint's insistence that his generals practice a strict code of personal ethics was well known. Moïse joked often of his uncle's displeasure that he never married. Duclero did not understand why Moïse remained single, but the Frenchman was content so long as Moïse did not marry Anacaona. Duclero could live with the tensions and disappointments of the present arrangement, but he could not envision living without her. He dreaded the thought that she might someday choose to leave him and marry the younger man.

Duclero and Anacaona rode for a long period in silence. His mind was on Toussaint's speech, and he was troubled.

Duclero did not understand what Toussaint wanted to say. He had the wealth and influence of the Northern Plain assembled to hear him and he had only one message: the whites must chose, Toussaint or massacre.

In Duclero's mind the choices were without substance.

Choose Toussaint for what? To assume full political as well as military authority? That was for the Directory to decide, not the residents of Saint-Domingue. For months the rumors had persisted that Toussaint would declare for independence when the British were defeated. There were certainly valid arguments in support of such a move, but in his speech Toussaint specifically denied such intentions. What did he mean, then, they must choose him? If he did not intend to move for independence then, to Duclero, the choice was without substance.

The second choice was equally hollow. Duclero knew of the hysterical fear of blacks expressed by many planters. But he did not believe the blacks posed a threat to the whites. There would be no massacre even if Toussaint or another black declared the island independent. The attack against the Cape after the massacre of the Fifth Regiment was a sham, a carefully orchestrated charade. Duclero was confident of that. Of course, there were the few who had sought to lead the blacks against the whites, the legendary Mackandal, the vicious Boukman, but that was before the abolition of slavery. Today the fear of another general uprising of the blacks was not justified—unless Toussaint led it.

Why, then, did Toussaint play upon the terrors of the whites? "There is only one Toussaint and all men must tremble at his name." Duclero had never before known Toussaint to stoop to demagoguery.

The facts were simple. Hédouville proved treacherous and Toussaint replaced him. He had replaced others before, men more competent and deserving than Hédouville, and Toussaint had done it without demagoguery.

The more he thought about it, the angrier Duclero became. The difficulty at Fort Liberté, Duclero reasoned, was not caused by Hédouville's perfidy as much as by Toussaint's irresponsibility. Six months ago the whites had accepted the inevitability of Toussaint's rule. By resigning his office he had played into the hands of the Royalists, and they in turn had urged Hédouville to rashness. When Toussaint was forced to reassert himself, he had to bluster and threaten in order to cover his own culpability. A sorry spectacle. The more Duclero thought about it, the more doubts he had regarding Toussaint's abilities. Perhaps he had overrated the man. He had looked for a Mirabeau in Toussaint, where in fact there might be only a Robespierre.

Despite it all, Toussaint was the best the island had to offer, of that Duclero was certain. But he could not shake the feeling of alarm Toussaint's demagoguery raised in him. In an effort to break his growing mood of pessimism, Duclero turned to Anacaona.

"Have you met our Governor-General before?" he asked, uncertain as to where she might go on her absences.

Anacaona shook her head.

"What do you think of him," Duclero asked.

"He is the great horse."

"Duclero was surprised by the intensity in her voice and her exotic image.

"You mean he is possessed?" he asked, referring to the voudoun belief that leaders are possessed by the loa or native gods.

"Yes. Maît' tête. The spirit in his head."

"You believe the loa work through him?"

"I have never seen the charge so great. I believe it is the loa."

"Then you believe he is the great houngan? Many, black and white, say he is."

"I do not know if he is the great houngan. I do know he is possessed, and he carries a great charge of whoever rides him."

"How do you know?"

"I saw it in his eyes."

"But we were so far away."

"I saw it."

"Who do you think possesses him?"

"I think it is Papa Légba."

"Papa Légba is the guardian of crossroads and entryways, is he not?" Duclero asked, with some pride in his knowledge.

"Yes," Anacaona agreed. "Toussaint is l'Ouverture," she explained.

The two rode on in silence. Duclero became conscious of the rhythm of the horses' hooves striking the soft dust of the road. Like drums, he thought. In Saint-Domingue everything echoes the drums.

"I hope it is Papa Légba." Anacaona spoke with concern in her voice. "I hope it is not a bacalou."

"Bacalou? I do not recall what a bacalou is."

"It is the malevolent spirit who impersonates the loa."

Duclero found amusement in Anacaona's interpreting every event through the black superstitions of the island, but he had the sensitivity not to disparage her beliefs.

"The bacalou feeds on human flesh," Anacaona continued quietly, after a moment's silence.

"For all our sakes," Duclero answered sincerely, "I hope Toussaint is possessed by Papa Légba and not a bacalou."

CHAPTER 12
He Who Is To Come

That evening Toussaint dined with Moïse. During dinner Toussaint was more agitated than Moïse had ever remembered seeing him. Toussaint ate little and was impatient at the slow progress of the meal. Several times he burst into tirades against Hédouville.

"Hédouville," he shouted to no one in particular, "threatens to gather a force in France and return to defeat me. Does he think such threats frighten me? I have defeated three nations. The English lost twenty-two thousand men fighting against me. I do not fear what forces Hédouville can raise. I do not wish war with France. We are part of France. But if France attacks me, I will defend myself."

Toussaint paused. His mood was not one to encourage the others at the table to offer rebuttal or to engage in idle conversation.

Moïse noted that his secretary, Delatte, was writing down Toussaint's comments. Moïse was about to order his secretary to put down his pen when Toussaint began again to speak.

Toussaint described Hédouville's treachery in trying to send him to Jamaica and abandon him there without support. He spoke of Hédouville's interference in the military government of the island, of his interference in the negotiations with the English.

Between each outburst Toussaint paused. Moïse realized that his uncle was waiting each time for Delatte to record his words. Moïse shook his head in amazement. No doubt, he thought, Toussaint expected Delatte to secretly send the notes to someone in authority in France. Another opportunity, Moïse thought, for Toussaint to play to the politics of Paris, or to the court of history, perhaps.

"I did what I had to do," Toussaint concluded. "I have nothing with which to reproach myself. I reject what Hédouville says, but let him be assured that he is free to return whenever he wishes."

After dinner, Toussaint indicated his desire to retire early. Moïse and his friends sat with their wine, fruit and cheese for several hours discussing the events of the past weeks.

As Moïse prepared to retire, a servant informed him that Toussaint wished to see him in his room.

"I thought you were asleep," Moïse said as he entered the guestroom at the front of the second floor of the house.

"In dismissing Hédouville I did only what I had to do," began Toussaint abruptly.

"Of course, Uncle," Moïse replied. The younger man was startled at the intensity of feeling that the recent events had stirred in the older man. Moïse was sorrowed by the losses his regiment suffered, but he had come to expect treachery from the French. He had long accepted the fact that there would be no safety for the blacks in Saint-Domingue until all white rule had been broken. Toussaint's discomfort with the dismissal of Hédouville surprised and troubled Moïse.

"France grants us our liberty and then sends us men who lack the wisdom to preserve it," mourned Toussaint.

"Or wish to destroy it," suggested Moïse.

Toussaint lay in the large bed dressed only in a nightshirt and cap. Moïse was struck by the frailty of the man when stripped of his uniform. In embarrassment he glanced out of the window. His eye caught the pattern of moonlight and shadow on the church across the square. In the silence he could hear the masons working below by torch light on the damaged walls of his house.

"Uncle," Moïse was surprised to hear himself say, "we will never be free until we are independent of France."

"There is no surer way to lose our liberty," responded Toussaint, more gently than before. "Sit down. There are things I need to tell you."

Moïse pulled the chair from the desk over to the bed and sat beside his uncle.

"France is our mother," Toussaint continued in the patronizing manner that irritated Moïse. "We are not strong enough to be free of her. If we cast ourselves adrift, all of our enemies will return to drink our blood and pick our bones. We cannot stand alone."

A trace of frustration crept into Toussaint's voice. "Moïse, as God is my witness, I have tried to share authority with the representatives of France, but they betray her and me."

Moïse had heard these complaints before and listening to them again made him feel weary.

Uncle," he broke into Toussaint's thought, "we must be independent and only you can lead us there."

Toussaint gave a great sigh, as if the last breath was leaving his body. After a moment he spoke very quietly.

"Moïse, you must listen to me. I am an old man. I may not live much longer."

"Nonsense," replied Moïse good-naturedly. "You are as strong as I am."

"I am fifty-three years old."

"You are younger than most men are at thirty."

"Listen to me," insisted Toussaint. "I have many enemies. At any moment I could die."

Moïse said nothing. The thought of Toussaint dying struck him as a blow to his solar plexus.

"You must understand the precariousness of our position," continued Toussaint. "If we act rashly, with unbridled passion, we will fall once more into slavery. We must not talk idly of independence. Those who urge us to, do so for their own purposes, not our well being."

Moïse was silent. Toussaint could see the troubled look on his face.

"You are an intelligent man," Toussaint continued. "But you do not always allow your intelligence to guide you. You lash out too quickly against those you think wish you harm."

"If we turn the other cheek," countered Moïse, "it will be branded with the slaver's mark. I showed tolerance to Hédouville and it cost me the lives of Charles and Adrien and hundreds of my soldiers and friends, almost my own."

"Listen to me," Toussaint repeated. "If I die there is no one else capable of leading our people through the trials that lie ahead of us."

"I will listen," Moïse replied respectfully, restraining the anger he felt at the memory of Hédouville's attack.

"We are in a precarious position. The English dally with us. They want us to weaken France in Europe. They want us to declare our independence in order that France will have to take soldiers from the war in Europe to fight against us here. Maitland promises us aid, but his promises are the lures of a fisherman. For his promises he is condemned before his king by Admiral Parker.

"How do you know this, about Parker and the king?"

Toussaint always spoke as if he possessed the knowledge of men's minds, even men half way around the globe. Moïse had no means of refuting his uncle's assertions, but he found their absoluteness irritating.

Toussaint thought for a moment. How did he know about Parker's feud with Maitland? A letter from an abolitionist in London. A conversation with a black sailor from Jamaica. Maitland's hands when he talked. A word, a gesture, a flash of inner knowledge. Each added to the other.

"I cannot say how I know, but I know," Toussaint answered.

"What does it matter?" Moïse asked irritatedly. "We have as much a chance against them as we have with them. Let them come, all of them. We defeated them before, we can do it again."

"No!" insisted Toussaint. "Where is our freedom if we are always at war?"

The two men were quiet for a moment, each fighting within himself to control the vehemence of his feelings, for each loved the other and wanted no schism between them.

"If the European nations stop fighting among themselves," continued Toussaint in a more reasonable manner, "long enough to turn en masse against us—and they will do that because of their fear of what their slaves may do in emulation of us—where will we find the resources to wage war? We must secure our safety before we can be independent."

"How, Uncle? How? We can never be secure. I think we must survive as the maroons have. Hold our bit of mountain by minding our own business and making it too costly to others for it to be worth their efforts to drive us out."

"Perhaps we can be nothing more than a nation of maroons," answered Toussaint sadly. "But I dream of more than that. I dream of a cultured nation where all races live together in peace. Where a man is judged for his value to his fellow man and not for the color of his skin. Where children are born and grow with the knowledge that opportunity is equal for all."

"I don't disparage your dream, Uncle," Moïse replied impatiently. "But how is it to have time to grow when we are beset by enemies?"

"We must move slowly, throwing nothing away that is of use to us and examining carefully all gifts offered us."

"How can we move at all, when our enemies will not leave us in peace?"

"That is why we must keep the French with us as long as we can," Toussaint explained. "Dismissing Hédouville was a defeat, not a victory. We must do all we can to justify our actions to Paris and to remedy things here."

"What things?" Moïse encouraged his uncle to speak, but deep in his body he felt the helplessness of Toussaint's dreams. How, he thought, does one divine between dreams and illusions?

"I shall send emissaries to Paris to argue our case," Toussaint continued. "Whites who are loyal to me. Then I shall invite Roume to move from Santo Domingo to the Cape to serve as the French civil commissioner here."

Moïse smiled. "You won't have any plots from Roume. He is too cautious to choose sides at a cock fight!"

"But it will show the Directory," Toussaint continued, "that my dismissal of Hédouville was not an attempt to remove all metropolitan authority from the colony. But that is covering the past. We must not stop moving toward the future. Our best hope right now is the Americans. They have a passion for freedom and independence."

"They also hold slaves," Moïse interjected.

"Yes," Toussaint agreed.

"And they walk lock step with the English."

"Yes," Toussaint again agreed. "But there is a passion there for our Revolution. They do not forget that many men from Saint-Domingue fought in their Revolution."

"Free mulattos, not black slaves."

"Yes," Toussaint again agreed. "But they are a new nation. I have faith that there is a passion there for us. The task is to build trade with them, and friendship, without breaking from France."

"They are at war with France. They will not trade with us while we are French,

"No. They are not at war with France."

"Uncle," Moïse persisted, "we have faced starvation here in Fort Liberté these past three months because the Americans refuse to trade with us because we are French. If we declare our independence they will trade with us. But not as long as we are French."

"We must appeal to them to make exceptions for us, to be aware of our dilemma. Our uniqueness. We have friends in Philadelphia."

"We have enemies there as well," Moïse contended, "emigré Royalists who work for our defeat."

"Yes," Toussaint again agreed. "But we have powerful friends there who work on our behalf. They will persuade Adams to support us. With American trade and American arms we will grow strong enough to dissuade England and France from reaching out together to pluck us. But that will take time, much time. Until then we must not break from France."

"Uncle," responded Moïse with some frustration, "it seems to me that we are in danger of falling into the sea like a man who tries to keep one foot on the boat and one on the wharf."

"Listen to me." Toussaint sat up in the bed, leaned over and grasped Moïse's hand. "You must go beyond the narrowness of your vision. You must see the complexities of our path. America may be the way to economic and military stability, but that is not the way of our soul. France is more to us than an ill-natured overseer. We do not speak English. We speak French. We are not Anglican. We are Catholic. The French Revolution freed us. The vision of the French Revolution is our vision. We must find our way through the political entanglements before us, but not at the expense of cutting ourselves off from the source of our culture. We cannot prosper without technology, without science, without education. To live as maroons in the mountains offers us no more freedom than slavery. We only serve different masters, the elements and our ignorance rather than white proprietors. Moïse, we must build a modern nation, not a transplanted African village."

Moïse did not answer. Toussaint let go of Moïse's hand and laid back in the bed again.

"I do not see only our freedom here," he continued. "I see the freedom of slaves everywhere. I see the political freedom of Africa. If we fail here, I do not know how long our people everywhere will have to wait for another chance to be free. We are the hope of the black race."

Toussaint paused again, and then continued with some reluctance.

"I have an account in a bank in Philadelphia. In it I put what money I can divert from the needs here. The money is to purchase, some day, our brothers from the English and American slavers. With them we will build an army, an army to liberate all the Antilles and then return to Africa and free our people there. Free black people will be a force in this world to be reckoned with. But we will not offer slavery to our enemies, but friendship, equality, a vision of the races living and working together."

Moïse listened silently to his uncle. He respected the older man's vision. His heart reached out for it, but his mind screamed its impracticality.

"Moïse...." Toussaint paused for a reply.

"Yes?"

"There are those who say that I am the black Spartacus foretold to lead his people to freedom. I am not. I lead only for this time on this island. I am Louverture, he who opens the way. I am the voice crying in the wilderness. I prepare the way for he who is to come. You are Moïse. You are Moses who will lead his people to the promised land.

The two men talked long into the night. Toussaint made no more references to his successor. Moïse said nothing on the subject. He understood Toussaint's hope for him. He felt pride that Toussaint held so high an opinion of his abilities, but Moïse knew he could not do what Toussaint wanted.

Pierre Baptiste, in the wisdom of his second sight, gave Moïse his name. Moïse knew why. He knew that he, like Moses, would not enter the promised land, because he, like Moses, was too filled with doubt.

When Moïse finally retired to bed, his head hummed with a confusion of images and emotions. He tried to concentrate on the three tasks that Toussaint had outlined. First they must work for the improvement of the economy. The key to that was trade with England and America. Second, they must work for the unification of the island under Toussaint's rule. The keys to that were the dismantling of the mulatto oligarchy in the South and the annexation of Spanish Santo Domingo. And third, they must work at maintaining the colony's relations with its mother, France.

To Moïse, Toussaint's plans were unnecessarily complex.

Moïse remembered little of his early life in Africa, but the memories which survived the nightmare of the middle passage were of a simple time, of days filled with warmth and love. There were none of the material riches of Saint-Domingue, but Moïse would trade the riches of all the world for the peace of mind he thought he must have known as a child. Deep in his heart, Moïse was not sure that life in an African village, even though transplanted to the West Indies, was not a more desirable end than Toussaint's dream of a modern nation.

CHAPTER 13
The War of Knives

Usually any motion of a boat made Toussaint anxious, if not sick. But on the short row from the anchored "Camilla" to the dock at Arcahaie, Toussaint felt nothing. The day was still and the bay calm, but if a tempest had been blowing, it would not have broken into the storm swirling in Toussaint's head.

At last. After how long? Toussaint found himself measuring the months in his head. Today was June thirteenth. His meeting with Maitland at the Môle had been on August thirteenth, Monday, the thirteenth, he remembered, the twenty-sixth of Thermidor. Even the Revolutionary date was fixed in his mind.

Toussaint always dated things with the Gregorian calendar and let his secretaries translate the date into the Revolutionary one. A stupid calendar, thought Toussaint. The names of the months in the Revolutionary calendar may be fitting for the seasons of France, but not for tropical Saint-Domingue. Toussaint preferred the old Roman names. Everyone used them anyway, except in official correspondence.

September thirteenth to June thirteenth. Ten months. The ten months had been difficult. They had been time wasted, time in which Rigaud grew more arrogant, the British more weaseled, the Americans more greedy, and Commissioner Roume more demanding. During the past months, Toussaint felt as though he were a wild pig, jerked about by a score of restraining lassoes. But now he had his trade agreement; he had the means to make war on Rigaud. Now the Americans would bring him the British Brown Besses stacked in American storerooms, rusting remnants of the American War of Independence. He could put guns in the hands of his soldiers and provide his army with stores and ammunition. Toussaint had his trade agreement.

Maitland had guaranteed that the trade agreement would remain secret. He had sailed for England in September, shortly after his conversation with Toussaint at the Môle. Maitland said he needed only to get King George's approval. But before Christmas, before there was any word from Maitland, Toussaint heard that the SUN and the TIMES in London had heralded the secret agreements and reported, with some accuracy, the conditions of the covenant. Toussaint was certain that Maitland released the stories deliberately in the attempt to force Toussaint to break with France.

Toussaint glanced over his right shoulder at the British frigate anchored behind him. It sat motionless in the still bay, its gun ports shuddered, like two rows of eyes closed in sleep. What would he not give for a fighting ship, even a small frigate like that.

"I trust you are pleased with the agreement." The slight man perched next to Toussaint on the longboat's thwart spoke.

"I am well pleased," Toussaint answered, aroused from his reverie.

Dr. Edward Stevens had arrived at the Cape on April eighteenth. He had been sent from the United States to serve as its commercial agent in Saint-Domingue. He replaced Jacob Mayer, a common thief whom Toussaint could not endure. Stevens was sent, Toussaint was certain, because of his appeals to President Adams for responsible American representation in the island.

Stevens had been helpful. He had arrived at the Cape in Toussaint's absence, but had refused to meet with Roume, the French commissioner. Stevens understood that the power in Saint-Domingue was Toussaint, not the French government. In the negotiations of the past weeks, Stevens had operated always from the position that Toussaint, and only Toussaint, spoke for the island. In the short time he had been in Saint-Domingue, Stevens had proved himself trustworthy and honest. He was a welcome relief for Toussaint from the deception of the English, the conspiracy of Rigaud and the distrust of Paris.

Toussaint had moved Roume from Santo Domingo City to the Cape to serve as civil commissioner. Roume was quiet and malleable. Toussaint expected no difficulty with him, but by January he was urging Toussaint to invade Jamaica and the southern states of the United States. It was the same game as Hédouville played.

When Maitland first arrived in the "Camilla" early in June, he cruised the north and west coasts of the island and sailed his little frigate into whichever harbors he pleased, throwing the inhabitants into fear.

Roume had demanded, and Toussaint refused, that the harbor forts fire upon the ship. When Maitland finally came to anchor off Arcahaie, Roume ordered Toussaint to arrange for Maitland's capture. It was Edward Stevens who helped Toussaint calm Roume's histrionics and persuade Maitland to cease his posturing.

"I am indeed grateful for your help," Toussaint told the gentle, introspective man sitting beside him. So different, Toussaint thought, than the hard swearing, distrusting American sea captains who Toussaint prayed would soon again be thronging into his ports seeking to make a profit with every puff of wind.

The coxswain ordered the oars shipped and steered the longboat to a gentle bump at the dock. Toussaint and Stevens were helped out of the boat by members of Toussaint's entourage waiting nervously for his return.

Toussaint bade Stevens farewell, walked briskly to where his guard, already mounted, waited his orders, pulled himself easily onto Bel-Argent, and struck out in a canter south for Port-au-Prince.

Toussaint's troops in the West and South out-numbered Rigaud's slightly, three thousand to perhaps twenty-five hundred. Toussaint had twenty thousand more in the North, including the National Guard and inactive regiments. He ordered Moïse immediately south with ten thousand and Dessalines to gather up another ten thousand and march south within the week.

Toussaint knew he must strike quickly.

During the past six months, when he could not act for fear that he would exhaust his supplies with no source for replacing them, he had suffered many defections from his army. The pattern of defections angered him.

Toussaint could understand the mulattos flocking to Rigaud, especially the undisciplined, greedy plantation owners who had found in the Revolution not a passion for freedom but rather a means to wealth.

What Toussaint could not understand is why the blacks of the South did not denounce Rigaud and why some blacks of the North followed their mulatto brothers in defecting to the South. Rigaud was an unpleasant, pleasure-loving, unpredictable and undisciplined braggart. Toussaint could not understand why any man would choose to risk his life to follow such a fool.

Toussaint's problem was he did not know which of his officers he could depend upon.

On June fourteenth, the day after Toussaint had his trade agreement, the troops of Toussaint and Rigaud were in open battle. The attack began on both sides. The heaviest fighting was in the small ports on the Gonave Channel, west of Port-au-Prince. The fighting was fierce, and Rigaud's forces prevailed.

Toussaint rushed to Léogane to rally his army. He placed Moïse, who had arrived with his reinforcements, in command.

In the midst of reorganizing his faltering army, Toussaint received word that the people of Port-au-Prince had danced in the streets when they heard of Rigaud's victory and were preparing for his triumphal entry into the city.

Toussaint was furious.

He marched his guard, reinforced with infantry units which should have been at the front, back to the city.

In the early afternoon Toussaint's soldiers moved methodically through Port-au-Prince rounding up all male mulattos. They were pulled from their homes, from their shops, from the docks and herded at bayonet point into the cathedral. Those who could not be stuffed into the sweltering church were crowded onto the steps by the open doors.

Waiting for them was Toussaint, standing in the pulpit, before him a row of soldiers, shoulder to shoulder, bayonets fixed. The perspiration flowed freely down Toussaint's face and soaked through his uniform.

"What do you rejoice at?" he shouted at his fearful audience. "Is it that you want to be masters in the island? Now that I have driven out the English do you wish to kill all the whites that remain and enslave again the blacks? I am France's legal authority here. Why do you not follow my orders?" he asked them. And then answered for them: "It is because I am black, and your history with blacks is well known! When the Swiss helped you win your freedom, how did you reward them? By sacrificing them. And why did you sacrifice them? Because they were black! Why does Rigaud not follow my orders? It is because I am black!

"Men of color, you have already lost your political influence in this government. Rigaud is lost. In my eyes he is at the bottom of an abyss. He is a rebel and a traitor to his country. He will be destroyed by the troops of liberty.

"Mulattos," Toussaint concluded, "I see to the bottom of your souls. You would betray me. My army may not be always in this place. But I have here always my eye and my hand. My eye watches you. My hand holds you."

Still agitated, Toussaint descended from the pulpit and prostrated himself before the high altar. His voice audible only to those nearest him, he prayed for forgiveness and guidance from God. Then, his anger still not assuaged, he rose and exited hastily through the sacristy door.

Outside, Toussaint mounted his horse and rode toward Government House. The startled congregation sat unspeaking for several moments. Then Toussaint's soldiers withdrew from the church, fell into formation on the square and marched off. Realizing that they were no longer under restraint, the mulattos hurriedly exited.

Borgella had tried to suppress the city's ardor at the news of Rigaud's victory, but no one listened to him anymore. He no longer had authority. Only Toussaint's generals had authority in Saint-Domingue.

Borgella knew Toussaint would punish the city. When the soldiers were rounding up all mulattos, Borgella knew that at last Toussaint was going to exact his revenge for the city's treatment of blacks. Many of the white planters, remembering how well Borgella had dealt with Toussaint's first entrance into the city, rushed to the mayor for leadership. He urged them to gather at Government House where he was certain Toussaint would come.

When Toussaint arrived at Government House he was calm. He greeted the whites graciously, speaking to those he knew by name and asking after friends and family. The atmosphere was strained, but no one dared ask the question on everyone's mind: What was Toussaint going to do with the mulattos?

Reports reached Government House of Toussaint's actions at the cathedral. It appeared that at present he was going to do no more than threaten.

Just as Borgella was confident that once more a crisis had been weathered, a tall, handsome mulatto officer strode into the gathering and confronted Toussaint.

"What you say about the Swiss is false," the officer addressed Toussaint without preamble. The officer's demeanor was firm, but not insolent.

"General Louverture," Borgella interrupted, attempting to maintain the civility of the occasion. "Do you know General Beauvais?"

"By reputation," Toussaint answered.

Toussaint was startled by the authority in Beauvais's presence. He knew of him, of course. Everyone on the island knew of Beauvais. He was second in fame only to Toussaint. Beauvais had been the chief military leader of the mulatto drive for citizenship early in the Revolution. He was now commander of the Jacmel district of the South and served under Rigaud, his former lieutenant. Toussaint had corresponded with Beauvais many times, especially in the war against the British. The men had not met because Beauvais did not venture to the North nor Toussaint to the South. Their paths had crossed in Port-au-Prince, which had become a border town between the two armed camps of Saint-Domingue, but at such times each had avoided a meeting with the other.

Now that Toussaint stood in Beauvais's presence he understood why they had not met.

Louis Jacques Beauvais was tall and carried his height with authority and grace. His voice was resonant, his manner reserved. He was a man comfortable with himself and with his authority.

Toussaint measured men when he met them. Even in the strong he saw veins of weakness: vanity, greed, fear. He found no such faults in Beauvais. Toussaint knew he stood in the presence of a man of strength and honor. Beauvais was no Rigaud. Given the choice, Toussaint would not choose Beauvais for an enemy.

"You misinterpret the Swiss incident for your own purposes," continued Beauvais. "It had nothing to do with race or caste. It was an unfortunate political decision made at a time when we did not yet understand what the Revolution was about."

"After those brave black men helped you to your freedom you killed them. That is genocide, not politics!" Toussaint answered angrily.

"You are wrong in every particular," Beauvais responded. "No man helped me to my freedom. I have always been free, as were my father before me and his before him. I fought to free others, not to free myself. You say I killed the Swiss. I knew and loved those men. You know them only as a cause. If I had been born in bondage, I would have been one of them. I would not have waited for the Revolution to free me, I would have fled to the mountains as they did."

Borgella, sensing the accusation against Toussaint in Beauvais's words and fearing Toussaint's retaliation, attempted to intervene: "Gentlemen, please. The matter is history. It is not germane."

"It is germane," insisted Beauvais. "I will not have the truth distorted."

"And I will not have the guilty hide from their guilt," countered Toussaint.

"I hide from no man," answered Beauvais. "My actions are an open book for any to read."

"You exiled the Swiss to Mexico."

"I agreed they should go."

"And you executed them when they were returned."

"I had no authority then. You want to see their executors? Then turn and look around you."

Borgella felt his stomach churn. He, as had many of the whites in the room, voted for the execution of the Swiss. He had felt relief that Toussaint blamed the mulattos for the act. Borgella felt the silence of the people standing behind him.

"You see only the death of black men," Beauvais continued his argument with Toussaint. "The Swiss weren't all black. Fully a third of them were mulatto. It wasn't a mulatto who urged their deportation. It was Lambert, a black. We agreed to it for the safety of the Swiss, to prevent what happened when they returned. It was the whites who killed the Swiss, the whites with whom you surround yourself today, and not the mulattos whom you defame and persecute."

Toussaint felt his anger rising to his face and prickling his skin.

"When Sonthonax liberated the slaves," Toussaint shouted, "you, yourself, tricked them back into their bonds!"

"I prevented a massacre!"

"You protected your property!"

"I dealt with realities. There was no Toussaint in the South to lead the blacks. He was serving the King of Spain."

Toussaint wanted to strike out at the tall man standing before him. For a moment they stood, two fighters of uneven size about to fall to blows. The people surrounding them were quiet, uncertain.

Beauvais continued, with more control: "What we did then we did with limited knowledge. Today it is not the blacks who are persecuted. It is the mulattos."

Toussaint, with effort, controlled his anger: "I do not persecute mulattos..." he began quietly.

"I was at the cathedral," Beauvais interrupted.

"It is Rigaud!" Toussaint felt his self-control breaking. "It is Rigaud who is the traitor! It is Rigaud who will not obey his commander! It is Rigaud who is disloyal to France! I will not have people singing and dancing to celebrate his treachery!"

"I see no treachery," Beauvais responded. "The Revolution lives in the South."

"For the mulattos," Toussaint countered. "Not for the blacks jailed and murdered in Corail."

"I know nothing of Corail. All are free in Jacmel."

"I do not question your administration. I question whether the people of this island will keep their liberty if Rigaud plays the pawn to Hédouville. It is a time in which patriots must choose. Whom do you serve?" Toussaint demanded.

"I serve the Revolution," Beauvais replied.

"Whom do you choose, Rigaud or Toussaint?"

"I choose France."

Toussaint looked carefully at Beauvais for a moment. "This is the open book for all to read?" he asked sarcastically.

"Toussaint is the Governor-General and commander of the North. Rigaud is the commander of the South. I serve under Rigaud," answered Beauvais easily.

"And Rigaud serves under Toussaint," Toussaint prompted.

Beauvais did not reply.

"Rigaud," continued Toussaint, "says that Hédouville appointed him Governor-General of the colony with secret orders to displace Toussaint. Do you accept that?"

"Hédouville does not speak for France in Saint-Domingue. Citizen Roume does."

"Then if Roume says Toussaint is Governor-General, do you accept that?" Toussaint asked.

"I serve France," was all that Beauvais would answer.

That evening, after the confrontation in Government House, Beauvais returned to Jacmel. Toussaint stayed on in the city to coordinate the war.

The next day, June twentieth, Toussaint had arrested and sent to Gonaïves, General Mornay, the black military commander of Port-au-Prince who had not suppressed the mulatto celebration of Rigaud's victory.

That day it began to rain and rained for three days.

On June twenty-second, Toussaint published a proclamation praising Beauvais and damning Rigaud.

At 6:00 p.m. that evening news came that the army of the North was at the gate of Saint Joseph and would pass through the city to the battle in the South. An officer preceded by twelve drummers walked the route the army would follow announcing that all citizens would provide illumination throughout the night for the march.

Obediently, Borgella placed a bowl with pine tar before his steps, lit it, and listened for a few moments to the hiss of rain hitting the flames before he returned to the protection of his house.

The march began at dusk. All night the wet streets were filled with the noises and smells of ten thousand men and their beasts and equipments of war passing through the city.

Borgella could not sleep. He sat in the window of his sitting room, the rain running in streams down the windowpanes, and watched the parade. He had never seen such a mass of soldiers, not even with the British. And this, he thought, was only half. The other half of the army was already with Moïse at Léogane.

At dawn the commanding officer entered the city with the last of his troops. Borgella knew Colonel Dessalines. He had been with Toussaint's troops when they liberated Port-au-Prince from the British. Borgella had had no conversation with him, and, in fact, had avoided him because of his reputation. Now Dessalines marched to join Moïse in the war against Rigaud.

Although all dreaded the war, many whites looked to the conflict between black and mulatto as a good sign for whites. If they destroyed each other, they argued, the whites might again gain control of the island, and, as some whispered—although Borgella avoided all such conversations—again restore slavery.

Borgella was too much of a realist in politics to dream such an outcome from the war. Those who did only created the conditions of more suffering later. Borgella knew that Rigaud, despite his early success, could not defeat Toussaint. The black commander had too much strength and too much determination. What Borgella feared was that Moïse and Dessalines, who were outspoken in their hatred of whites, would rise in influence through their victories. Then, with those two in power, and Rigaud and the mulatto oligarchy crushed, all that would stand between the whites and annihilation was Toussaint.

With Dessalines came the news that Mornay had been executed by bayonet in Gonaïves.

The War of Knives had begun.

CHAPTER 14
Disaffection

Suzanne tried to keep Toussaint at Desachaux. She could see he was exhausted. He appeared in the morning, ate a little lunch, napped for a few hours and was ready to leave by evening.

Suzanne begged him to stay at least for the night, but he insisted he had to be at the Môle by morning.

"But you cannot go forever without sleep," she insisted.

"I will take the carriage and sleep in it," Toussaint answered.

Suzanne knew he would get no sleep in the carriage, but she knew, also, that she could not stop him from leaving.

Toussaint did not, at first, realize that the sounds were shots. He had dozed fitfully, his head bouncing against the back of the seat with each lurch of the coach. He had been dreaming of war and he could not separate the sounds in his dreams from the sounds in the night. He woke from the sudden lunge of the carriage when the coachman whipped the horses.

No one in Toussaint's entourage was hit, and in the darkness pursuit of the assassins was fruitless.

Moïse was not surprised by the attempt on his uncle's life. Toussaint created enemies. He saw conspiracies everywhere. The more he attempted to ferret out the conspirators and destroy them, the more enemies he created. Toussaint was told that the mulattos in Arcahaie conspired against him, and on one man's word he arrested and executed all he could find. He did the same in Port-au-Prince. It was no wonder the mulattos in the North rose in rebellion, Moïse reasoned. They feared for their lives.

Moïse hurried North with the Fifth Regiment. His assignment was to put down the mulatto rebellions in Port-de-Paix, Jean-Rabel and the Môle. But Moïse was not surprised Toussaint had pulled him from the fighting in the South.

Moïse had no heart for the war. He had been soundly defeated at Thozin, although he had ten times the number of troops Rigaud was able to field. Moïse's own Fifth Regiment had behaved abominably, leaving the Ninth to hold the field alone. Moïse had been ashamed of his troops, but he could not punish them. They had brothers, half brothers and cousins with Rigaud. They shared Moïse's hatred of the war. They knew, as he knew, that the army they battled was not the enemy.

Moïse had no heart for the battle for the South. It was Rigaud's territory. Let him keep it. But the North belonged to Moïse. There would be no rebellion there, by anyone. He had the heart to suppress rebellion in the North.

As Moïse marched, he gathered into his regiment cultivators from the field. He loved haranguing the laborers, moving them to a passion. He loved the enthusiasm with which they left the fields and pressed on behind his troops. With the workers massed behind him, Moïse felt invincible.

Port-de-Paix had been under siege for a week. It fell to Moïse in a day. Moïse moved on to Jean-Rabel. Behind him the commander of Port-de-Paix put captured rebels to death, tying them to the mouths of cannons.

Moïse drove the rebels at Jean-Rabel into the mountains, and then he moved toward the largest stronghold, Môle Saint Nicholas.

The Môle was well fortified. It withstood a week of siege, Moïse by land and two of Toussaint's dispatch boats by sea.

Finally, the leaders of the rebellion escaped by canoe in the darkness of night, carrying with them to the South the treasury of the city. The next morning, Moïse's soldiers entered the town, executed all the rebels remaining, and freed from the prison those who had been imprisoned for their faithfulness to Toussaint.

Commissioner Roume would not be hurried. He lay back in the chair and let the warmth from the towels wrapped around his face soothe his nerves.

Roume knew Toussaint was in a passion. The first messenger had come at dawn. Two more had followed. Roume would attend upon the Governor-General at a reasonable hour, after breakfast and a shave and not before. Crises came and crises went. He had been through too many to be hurried by them.

While he slipped into a half-sleep under the ministrations of the barber, Roume allowed himself a few moments of self-pity.

It was difficult enough dealing with the conflicts in this island without Paris playing secret games, Roume commiserated to himself. He had not liked Hédouville when the general came through Santo Domingo City. Roume would have resigned his post and gone home then if had known Hédouville's true mission. Paris sent Hédouville to stir up trouble and then expected him to put everything back together again.

Paris didn't ask his opinion, Roume complained to himself. It seemed to him that the way to become an expert on the politics of Saint-Domingue was to make a fool of oneself in the island: first there was Sonthonax and then Hédouville, both now the darlings of Paris.

Roume did what he could. He knew he was criticized in Paris, but he did what he could with the mess Hédouville had left. He knew he was criticized for allowing Toussaint to sign trade agreements with Maitland and Stevens, but the purists in Paris did not understand. They expected the people of Saint-Domingue to starve rather than trade with enemies. But the war with England was in Europe, not the West Indies. The enemy in the West Indies was hunger.

His chief problem, Roume decided, was that he was too gullible. He had taken Hédouville at his word. Toussaint told him what Hédouville was up to, but Roume believed Hédouville's argument that Toussaint's complaints were smoke screens covering his culpability. Roume distrusted Toussaint when he drove Hédouville out. Although there was nothing he could do to stop it, Roume was sure it was the prologue to Toussaint's declaring independence. Then Rigaud published Hédouville's letters. Toussaint had been right again, and he, Roume, had been the fool again.

Clearly, Roume thought, the collective left hands of the Directory do not know what the collective right hands do. Every dispatch from Paris he received confirmed Toussaint in authority. Apparently every dispatch from Paris Rigaud received confirmed Rigaud in authority.

What did Paris want, Roume mused, to give the colony to England? The Directory, as far as he could see, was doing its best to do just that.

When Roume reached Government House, Toussaint was in a foul mood. Roume preferred Toussaint's attitude of gracious concern. But no matter the pose, Toussaint always got what he wanted. It was just that life was more pleasant when the Governor-General was polite.

"Beauvais will not break with Rigaud," Toussaint complained

"But he does not declare for him, either," Roume replied, carefully modulating his voice in the attempt to keep the discussion civil.

"You have declared Rigaud an outlaw."

"Yes, as you requested."

"Rigaud is not an outlaw because I requested him to be. He is an outlaw because he puts himself outside the law," Toussaint replied angrily.

"Of course."

"You issued the proclamation because it was a fact, did you not? Not because I requested it."

Roume did not respond.

Is that not so?" Toussaint questioned.

"It is so," Roume answered with some reluctance.

"Is not then Beauvais also outside the law?" Toussaint asked.

"He has not sided with Rigaud."

"He holds a major district of the colony for Rigaud," Toussaint countered.

"He commands at Jacmel, but he does not necessarily hold it for Rigaud," argued Roume.

"They are in daily communication. Beauvais receives supplies and materials from Rigaud. The garrison is officered by men known to support Rigaud, many who have defected from their posts in the West and North. Do you think I could march soldiers into Jacmel without their being fired upon?" Toussaint asked.

"No, I don't think this is the time to take possession of the city," Roume replied.

"Then Jacmel is not under French authority. It is under the control of rebels," Toussaint pressed.

"Beauvais needs more time," Roume began.

"Time for what?" Toussaint interrupted. "Time to strengthen the forts, to reinforce the garrison, to prepare for a siege?"

"No, time to work things out. If you give him time, a way to preserve his honor...."

"I can not afford his honor. The longer I delay taking the city, the greater my loses will be."

"General Toussaint," Roume said quietly, "you push people into becoming your enemies. They are afraid of you."

"No, Commissioner, Beauvais is not afraid of me. I have heard enough of this argument," he continued in a controlled voice. "I do not create enemies. I have them without effort. I have made no attempt on Rigaud's life. His life is safe in my hands. If he surrenders today, tomorrow, next year, I have no plans for his death. But he has for mine."

"I understand," Roume replied in an attempt to prevent the tirade he feared was coming. "You have written to me of the attempt on your life."

"You do not understand," Toussaint continued with some agitation. "All the world looks at this island and sees one thing only. Slaves."

Roume looked away for a moment, his face revealing his impatience.

"You do not understand," Toussaint continued with some anger, aware of Roume's discomfort. "Only I understand. You did not understand Hédouville's mission. I told you, but you did not believe me. I tell you now, Rigaud works for the return of slavery."

"I do not believe that," Roume interrupted. "You may need to say that to motivate your army, but you know it is not true."

Toussaint stared for a moment at Roume, and then shook his head in disgust.

"Beauvais is outside the law," he continued after a moment. "He must be declared a traitor."

"Very well," Roume agreed reluctantly. "I will declare him outside the law."

Edward Stevens had written to Toussaint every day trying to get the problems of passports resolved. The few answers he received were inconclusive. He had written to Toussaint because he got conflicting answers from Christophe, Roume and the port officials at the Cape. Stevens did not know whose authority to accept. One thing was certain, the military and civil arms of the government

seldom agreed on any issue. Roume insisted on his authority in matters of commerce, but Christophe advised that Stevens do nothing without Toussaint's
approval. Stevens had no difficulty with Christophe's suggestion. Stevens understood the delicacy of his position. The United States supported the English
blockade of French ports. He was in Saint-Domingue not to negotiate with the
French government, but to encourage Toussaint to break from France and
declare for independence. It was a difficult path to walk when he found himself
almost never with Toussaint and in daily contact with Roume, with whom
Stevens was uneasy. It must be how a mistress feels, Stevens mused, who must
live with the wife she is trying to displace.

Stevens was in the habit of walking in the late afternoon, after the heat of the
day. He returned from one of his constitutionals and found his house surrounded by mounted soldiers. Stevens was fearful at first. He had heard many
tales of unexplained arrests and murders in the island, and he was apprehensive
that his turn had come. To Steven's relief, Toussaint's adjutant came forward to
greet the doctor and escort him into the house where Toussaint waited for him.

"I did not mean to keep you waiting," Stevens apologized.

"You had no way of knowing I was here," Toussaint responded.

"May I get you something to drink?" Stevens asked, preparing to call his servant.

"I need nothing," Toussaint answered. "Please, have what you wish."

"I do not desire anything," Stevens answered.

There was a pause in the conversation which Toussaint apparently enjoyed.

"I hope you are comfortable here," Toussaint inquired.

"Yes, quite."

"Is the house to your satisfaction?"

"It could not be better."

"It was owned by Commissioner Hédouville," Toussaint explained. "When
he left quickly for France, I purchased it from him. It captures the breeze well. I
thought you might enjoy it."

"It is very pleasant, indeed."

There was another silence.

"May I talk business with you?" Stevens asked. "Or would you prefer to wait
for a more appropriate time?"

Toussaint smiled. "All times are appropriate for me to do business. I came
because you wrote you needed to see me."

With some embarrassment because of the setting, Stevens presented his list of concerns.

He and Cathcart, the British agent in Port-au-Prince, wanted Toussaint to sign blank passports and leave them in each city with a trusted representative. Toussaint should not make each ship wait for someone to find him, get his signature on the passport and then return the passport to the ship before it could sail. Ships were delayed days, sometimes weeks. The captains were unhappy. They were losing money. It was not the way to encourage trade.

Toussaint agreed to the change.

Stevens argued for the British assistant agent, Douglas, to come to the Cape. There was no need for an American presence in Port-au-Prince, Stevens explained, because most American shipping entered through the North. But British ships destined for the North had to sail past their ports and enter at Port-au-Prince in order to register with the British agent. Then the ships had to sail back to the North to load or unload their cargoes. It was inefficient.

"Why can you not work with the British and enter their ships here?" Toussaint asked.

"I do," Stevens replied. "But it is not efficient. It would be helpful to have a British presence here at the Cape."

"Would not two Americans serve? Could you not ask Jacob Mayer to assist you?" Toussaint inquired.

Stevens breathed deeply. "I would prefer to keep my problems with Mr. Mayer separate from my dealings with you," he replied. "He is a scoundrel. Giving him authority would be of no assistance to you or me."

Toussaint laughed. "Scoundrels are the burdens of honest men. I fear we shall never escape them."

Stevens enjoyed Toussaint's pleasantry. He was always delighted with the general's good humor. He wondered how Toussaint persevered under the provocations he faced each day. A lesser man would break from the weight.

"I will take the matter of Douglas under advisement," Toussaint continued. "But I make no promise."

"Thank you, General," Stevens replied. "I hesitate to ask this last question," he continued. "But I pledged Mr. Cathcart that I would."

"No," Toussaint answered before Stevens was able to frame the question. "Colonel Grant is not welcome in the colony"

"I do not mean to press you, sir," Stevens persisted. "But I understand he has been in Jamaica some weeks and that you assured General Maitland that Colonel Grant would be accepted."

"General Maitland assured me the that the trade agreement would be secret. Thanks to the London papers the entire world now knows. France and England are at war. I can not accept a military officer as a trade commissioner. It would be seen as an act of independence."

"But General Maitland had your pledge."

"And I had his for secrecy. I am not Maitland's fool, Dr. Stevens. I will accept Grant when I can. Not before."

"I understand," Stevens acquiesced.

Toussaint got up from the chair in which he been sitting and walked to the open door overlooking the harbor. "I need you to help me, Dr. Stevens," he said.

"Whatever I can do."

"I need you to persuade your government to blockade the ports of the South."

"I think you must write to President Adams yourself. I do not have ambassador status. I am only a commercial agent," Stevens replied diplomatically.

Toussaint turned away from the door and looked back at Stevens. He gazed at the American for a moment, and then turned back to the view of the harbor.

"Every one here plays games," he continued, "with each player writing his own rules. England plays the game of the donkey and the carrot. I am the donkey and trade is the carrot. They promise everything, and deliver nothing. Where do they try to lead me with the carrot? To a break with France. Not because they want an independent black republic in Saint-Domingue. They most certainly do not. It would be an unacceptable threat to Jamaica and the Bahamas. They promise to stop all trade with Rigaud. The trade goes on, protected by the British fleet. They promise to blockade the South. Instead, they harass shipping in the North. Games, Dr. Stevens, games."

Toussaint waved to his adjutant outside the door. The officer brought him a packet of papers.

"Here." Toussaint handed the packet to Stevens.

"What are these, sir?" Stevens asked, uncertain as to whether or not he should open the packet.

"Dispatches from Paris to Rigaud. They order him to prepare to invade Jamaica, Cuba and the southern states of America. He is to send agitators to persuade the slaves to rise in rebellion when his forces arrive."

"I have heard of these orders. Mr. Cathcart tells me that you are under the same instructions."

"I ignore them. If you examine the papers in your hand you will see that Rigaud has already sent agitators to Jamaica. They are in the fields working at this moment. They are the forerunners of what the Directory calls the "flying artillery." I believe Mr. Cathcart might find this information of some interest."

Stevens opened the packet and began to examine the documents.

"Dr. Stevens, it is in the interest of your country to aid me in my war with Rigaud. When you send Mr. Adams these papers I hope you will urge him to consider my request to blockade the South."

"I will, sir," Stevens replied sincerely. "You may be assured I will."

Toussaint was tired. The war in the South was mired. His generals fought without intelligence. Rigaud's forces, though out numbered, fought with brilliance, moving rapidly, hitting and running, retreating in order when faced with superior numbers. Toussaint's troops were demoralized, Rigaud's inspired.

Toussaint knew he must rest. He would return to Desachaux, only for a few days.

Toussaint was in his coach, half-dozing. He was riding from Port-de-Paix south, across the Gros Morne. At a place where the road narrows between two abutments and the guard had to ride before and after the coach, the party was fired upon by a body of men hidden on the top of each of the escarpments. The barrage of fire was intense. Bullets pierced the carriage and rained down on the guard.

Toussaint instinctively thrust his head from the carriage. A bullet carried away the plume on his hat.

Toussaint pulled back. As he turned he saw his doctor, who was riding in the seat beside him, lying on the floor, blood pouring from his body.

Within seconds, half his guard was driving their horses up the incline in pursuit of the attackers. The others surrounded the coach and protected it the best they could until they gained safe cover.

Toussaint was furious. His doctor and friend was dead. Three of his guards were killed and five wounded. Ten horses had to be destroyed.

It was several hours before Toussaint was prepared to continue his journey. He had his friend's body returned to Port-de-Paix for shipment to the doctor's

home, Port-au-Prince. He insisted on having the few assassins who were captured brought before him. They answered his questions without dissembling so
great was their fear of him. What they told him confirmed what he already knew.
Toussaint sent messengers to the cities of the North with orders for the commanders to hunt down and execute the mulatto leaders of the plot.

When Toussaint continued his journey, he would not ride in the coach. It had
been cleaned, but the doctor's blood could not be scrubbed away. He rode a
horse offered him by one of his officers. It was a good horse, sound of wind
and swift, but it was not Bel-Argent. His beautiful silver was quartered at
Desachaux waiting his arrival.

As was his want, Toussaint out distanced most of his guard who rode with
the coach. When the party reached the spring at Habitation Aubry, Toussaint dismounted and rested. He allowed the coach and its guard to catch up to him and
then to proceed before him. He knew he would have no difficulty catching them.

As Toussaint and the few officers with him prepared to mount, they heard
gun shots ahead. Toussaint could not believe the rebels would try twice in one
day.

Despite the warnings of his companions, Toussaint raced toward the sounds.
When he arrived he found his coachman dead and his guard in pursuit of the
assassins.

Suzanne put her arm across Toussaint's shoulders. He lay on his stomach, his
head away from her. She could feel his body tremble.

"I do not know why," Toussaint said in a quiet voice, "I am frightened."

Suzanne did not reply. She held him gently.

"I am not afraid of death," Toussaint continued after a moment. "I believe in
God and the ascension of the soul. I have never entered battle without knowing
I might die."

Suzanne hummed quietly and gently rubbed his back.

"It is the way of death that causes me despair," Toussaint continued after a
moment. "To be shot in a cowardly way by cowardly men." He was quiet for
another moment, then continued. "Let me die in battle. Let me be shot by men
I can see, not shot in the back by men afraid to face me."

Suzanne raised the volume of her humming and began to rub his temples.

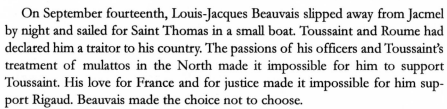

On September fourteenth, Louis-Jacques Beauvais slipped away from Jacmel by night and sailed for Saint Thomas in a small boat. Toussaint and Roume had declared him a traitor to his country. The passions of his officers and Toussaint's treatment of mulattos in the North made it impossible for him to support Toussaint. His love for France and for justice made it impossible for him support Rigaud. Beauvais made the choice not to choose.

The fate of Louis-Jacques Beauvais is not important to the story of my father. But I find myself compelled to relate it. I never met Beauvais. I knew him only by reputation. But I never met a man, including Toussaint, who did not speak well of him. The one exception was André Rigaud's son who studied with Isaac and me and the other young scholars from the West Indies at the College de la Marche in Paris. Young Rigaud shared his father's jealousy of the greater man.

The English captured Beauvais before he reached Saint Thomas and took him to Jamaica. His captors found him of no danger to British interests and allowed him to join his wife, Veuve, and two daughters, Caroline and Marcillette, in Curaçao. The four of them sailed for France on the French frigate "Vengeance" on August twenty-second, 1800. The English captured the ship. Beauvais and his family were again sent to Jamaica, and, because he had broken his parole by sailing on a French warship, he and his family were sent to England. A storm hit the ship carrying them. The captain ordered the ship abandoned and drew lots for seats in the lifeboats. Beauvais won in the draw, but gave his place to his wife and daughters. He disappeared beneath the waves of the Atlantic on October twenty-eight, 1800.

CHAPTER 15
Eighteen Brumaire

Dessalines was disgusted that he could not move the Southern defenders from the channel ports of Grand and Petit Goave. He had won back Léogane but could push no farther west.

He felt that the invisibles kept him from success. It was the only explanation. Every time he attacked, Rigaud anticipated the move and countered it and then counterattacked in the places Dessalines least anticipated.

The invisibles had turned against him, Dessalines was certain. He could guess the cause: Toussaint's purge of innocent people.

Dessalines sought help. The houngan to whom he turned denied that Toussaint disturbed the invisibles. Toussaint was the great houngan who had the loa at his command. The problem was that Rigaud had employed a strong houngan to bless his army. Dessalines's houngan promised he could counteract Rigaud's magic—for a price.

Dessalines gladly paid, and then waited for the results. He did not have long to wait.

That very day, he heard later, Rigaud was wounded in his hand and retired from the war, returning to his headquarters in Les Cayes, far to the southwest.

A few days following, Dessalines learned that he had been promoted to general of brigade by Toussaint and made commander of all the forces fighting the war against the South. Dessalines's former commander, Moïse, was reassigned as commander of the North and stationed at the Cape. Commissioner Roume supported Dessalines's appointment. The war was Dessalines's to win or loose.

Dessalines had barely began to congratulate himself on his changing fortune when the most remarkable event of all occurred.

He attended a dinner for his officers given by the city council of Léogane in thanksgiving for their deliverance from Rigaud. Dessalines was seated beside a woman, a widow of his own age, a black woman of incomparable beauty, graciousness, intelligence and charm. Dessalines was stunned. He found himself tongue-tied in his efforts to make conversation.

That night and the day following he could think of nothing but her. It was not a situation which Dessalines found familiar. He was past forty. He had known many women, but despite Toussaint's insistence that his generals marry, Dessalines had seen no woman with whom he wished to enter into an alliance—until Marie Félicitè Claire Heureuse.

The second day after the dinner, Dessalines called upon Claire. By then he had found his voice. He had quieted his fear of her by reasoning that she was part of the rewards for his offering to the loa, and everyone knew it was poor sense to reject a gift from the invisibles. She was his. He needed only to take her.

Claire was cordial, but greeted Dessalines's confession of love with amazement. She said she was pleased that a man of such handsome appearance and renown found her of interest. But she had not thought to marry again. And, she confessed with some apprehension, Dessalines frightened her.

He could not imagine why she should be frightened of him. He was the most caring of men and would treat her always with gentleness.

Claire said she believed him, but stood in awe of his fierce reputation. She agreed to accept him as a suitor, but made no promise as to the outcome of his suit. Above all, she insisted they wait until the war ended before they had any further discussion of marriage. She did not want to distract him. He might become careless and expose himself to unnecessary danger.

When he pressed her, she agreed to answer his letters.

Toussaint ordered the army away from the port cities. He was reluctant to commit the forces necessary to dislodge the Southerners from their fortifications while he had the threat of Jacmel on his flank.

He had hoped that Beauvais, under the pressure of censure, would deliver the fortified port on the south coast to Toussaint's forces. With Beauvais gone, officers sympathetic to Rigaud were in control.

Toussaint made one more attempt to secure Jacmel without combat. He had Dessalines issue an appeal for the residents of the city to recognize Toussaint's authority. Dessalines promised amnesty for all.

The officer who succeeded Beauvais in command, a black man, gathered his staff to discuss the offer. They refused the amnesty and informed Dessalines that Jacmel stood with Rigaud.

Dessalines knew his soldiers were demoralized from their early defeats and were not prepared for an attack against the forts of Jacmel. In the attempt to bolster their spirits he mustered his entire army in a large field in the coastal flats northwest of Léogane.

Dessalines inspected each unit and spoke encouragingly to each soldier. He saw that each received ten cartridges and provisions for the march to Jacmel. The inspection was long and went into the night, but Dessalines did not let the troops break ranks.

Shortly before midnight, the sky was filled with a shower of meteorites. The unexpected and startling sight caused panic among the soldiers, already fearful for the battle to come. Many ran terrified from the field. Others fell upon their knees, their arms raised above their heads to ward off the fire, and prayed to God to forgive them the blood they had shed.

Dessalines felt fear rush into his belly, but he did not move. If God was to take him now, then he would go without cringing. But in the recesses of his mind he was certain that it was a sign that the All Powerful One had taken Toussaint's life for shedding innocent blood. The thought came to him that Toussaint's death was another gift from the invisibles. In his mind he begged them to withdraw the blessing. He was not prepared for such greatness.

The shower subsided after an hour. Dessalines had not moved nor spoken, but now he called his men back to their ranks. He did not yell at them. He calmly reminded them that the fire had injured no one. He argued that fire in the sky was an omen of good fortune. It was a sign that God blessed their efforts to come. They could begin the campaign with confidence.

The soldiers wanted to believe their commander, but many saw in the sky the omen of their deaths.

Whatever worries Dessalines had of Toussaint's death were relieved when he received detailed orders from the Governor-General for the siege of Jacmel.

By the final days of November, Dessalines had moved a thousand cavalry and nearly twenty-thousand infantry the twelve leagues from Léogane to Jacmel. On the way he swept the area clear of Southern sympathizers, summarily executing all rebels. Rigaud's forces held the peninsula from Grand Goave west, but Toussaint's forces were free to move from Port-au-Prince south to the Caribbean. Even the maroons of the imposing mountains of the South, called the Saddle, traditional allies of Beauvais, had withdrawn to their mountain sanctuaries before Dessalines's overwhelming power.

Henri Christophe was pleased Toussaint had honored his request that he be allowed to participate in the war in the South. Christophe had been stuck in an administrative position at the Cape for too long. He had done all that was requested of him. He had stood firm to Hédouville. He had purged the mulattos from the area. He had maintained the security of the capital. But Christophe knew promotion was won on the battlefield.

Christophe had done well for himself at the Cape. He had acquired several plantations and made them profitable. He had a comfortable import business in the city. As military administer of the capital he had many opportunities to profit from people desiring administrative favors. His life since Toussaint's ascendancy had been comfortable. But Christophe was not yet a general. Dessalines was. Moïse was. Christophe knew he was every bit as talented and deserving as they.

If Christophe was going to war, he was going in the style to which he was accustomed. Dessalines and Moïse spent their money on land. Toussaint spent his money on gems. Christophe spent his money on war.

His one thousand regular cavalry and his two thousand infantry marched the eighty leagues across mountains and rivers from the Cape to Port-au-Prince, but Christophe and his fifty hussars sailed on the American brig "Rebecca" which he had leased with the help of Dr. Stevens.

Christophe bathed in the attention he received as he disembarked at Port-au-Prince. His fifty hussars in full dress leading their horses were the first off the ship. Mounted they stood guard at rigid attention as the infantrymen, who had arrived earlier, and the dock stevedores, working to the rhythms of their work chants, unloaded his five hundred barrels of flour, his two hundred barrels of salt pork, his two cannons on carriages with one hundred balls each, his supplies of powder, shot, spare uniforms and other accouterments of war. The bustle and discipline of his troops pleased Christophe, and he knew he created a spectacle worthy of admiration.

Christophe dallied for several days in Port-au-Prince before moving to his post at Dessalines's side. It was Christophe's first visit to the city, and he enjoyed the social whirl. He enjoyed impressing new acquaintances and greeting old friends. Christophe had all the social graces, and although he was illiterate, he was fluent in speaking both French and English, skills he acquired as a waiter in his youth. He especially enjoyed meeting with the British agents in the city and goading them with his views of the politics of Saint-Domingue.

Yes, of course, he assured Cathcart, Commissioner Roume was plotting with Rigaud to overthrow Toussaint. And, yes, Roume was serious about invading Jamaica. In fact, Rigaud had a massive force ready for the invasion. And it was true, as Cathcart had heard, Toussaint intended to execute all mulattos. Those who served with him were safe only until the fall of Rigaud.

Christophe smiled to himself when he thought of poor, gullible Cathcart sending all that information to Whitehall. He laughed out loud when he imagined the consternation his opinions would create in Kingston and London.

Toussaint felt that Jacmel would fall quickly to Dessalines and Christophe. When Jacmel fell, the way to Les Cayes would be open and Rigaud would have to capitulate. It was time now for Toussaint to prepare for his next project, the annexation of Spanish Santo Domingo.

When Roume received Toussaint's request for approval for the annexation of the Spanish territory, he was, at first, infuriated. He prepared a torrid reply. But as was his want, he took a few days to contemplate the problem before sending his answer.

With time, Roume decided his first response was emotional. He felt pressured by Toussaint. He felt himself used in the way Toussaint used Sonthonax, Laveaux and Hédouville.

Roume tried to get beyond his feelings and to look at the issues. There were, he could see, valid arguments on both sides.

In opposition to Toussaint's request was the fact that the Directory had specifically prohibited such an action. For what reason? Distrust of Toussaint's motivations, the fear that he would use his power to create an independent state. If Toussaint stole Saint-Domingue, France would need Santo Domingo from which to launch a military campaign against him.

On the other side, Toussaint's argument was at least partially valid. He argued that in Santo Domingo the slaves were not free, which he considered a violation of French law and an affront to justice and morality. Roume agreed. Toussaint also argued that blacks from Saint-Domingue were captured and sold into slavery in Santo Domingo. Roume was certain there was some such trade, but hardly significant. On the other hand, he could appreciate Toussaint's offense at any such actions.

Toussaint's last argument troubled and angered Roume. Toussaint argued that Santo Domingo was a haven for his enemies. For good reason, Roume felt. Roume dreaded to think that the mulattos who sought refuge there might be endangered again. And he dreaded to think what might happen to the Spanish proprietors if Toussaint took it upon himself to punish them for holding slaves.

Roume wrote a new, more reasoned reply to Toussaint: he was sorry, but his instructions from France specifically prohibited Toussaint from annexing Santo Domingo. He could not acquiesce to the Governor-General's request.

Roume knew he was avoiding the issues in a bureaucratic response, but such was often the safest course.

When Toussaint increased the pressures on Roume, Roume held fast, but he asked Toussaint's friend Colonel Charles Vincent to sail to France and request the Directory to send a commission to aide him. Roume was finding the pressure of containing Toussaint too difficult.

When he learned of Roume's action, Toussaint asked Julien Raimond to sail with Vincent and to represent Toussaint's position in Paris. Toussaint felt that the mulatto Raimond could diffuse the rumor that Toussaint was prejudiced against mulattos and intended to execute all of them on the island after Rigaud's defeat.

Ironically, Vincent and Raimond departed the Cape for France on November ninth, 1799. On that date—eighteen Brumaire by the Revolutionary calendar—at Saint Cloud near Paris, Napoléon's soldiers surrounded the Royal Palace and would not let the legislators out until they had established a new government, the Consulate, with Napoléon Bonaparte as First Consul.

Toussaint's frustration with the British was already high. But in mid-November, there occurred an incident that proved to him beyond the slightest doubt that the English wished only for his failure.

On Sunday, November seventeenth, Toussaint dispatched four ships from Léogane to blockade Jacmel.

Toussaint had gotten his little fleet by commandeering three French merchantmen and a schooner from the French navy. The captains and the cargoes of the merchantmen were deposited on the cay at the Cape while the ships were armed for war.

The ships were small. The largest, the schooner "Le Vangeur," was only three hundred and fifty tons. The ship "L'Egiptien" was two hundred and fifty tons; the ship "L'Elan" and the brig "Le Levrier" were even smaller. None was a match for the British men-of-war patrolling the coast.

The trading covenant Toussaint had with the British provided for him to sail droghers within five leagues of the coast. The size of the vessels was limited, and the larger two ships of his small fleet were outside those limits. He noted that fact when he requested passports for his little fleet from Hugh Cathcart. Toussaint made clear to Cathcart that the ships sailed to blockade Jacmel and were no threat to Jamaica.

For three days the ships were becalmed off Cape Dame Marie at the southwest point of the island, the point closest to Jamaica. On Thursday, the wind picked up and the fleet doubled the Cape and started east along the south coast. At noon the ships were approached by the British frigate "Solbay," boarded and ordered to sail to Jamaica.

In Jamaica the ships were condemned by the Admiral's Court as spoils of war and sold at auction. The black and mulatto crews, four hundred and twenty-three men, were sold as slaves.

By the end of November, Toussaint heard that France had a new government, at the head of which was the Corsican general, Napoléon Bonaparte.

The news from France confused Toussaint. His first impression was that the change would not be detrimental to his welfare. Toussaint had restored to Napoléon's wife her mother's plantation near Léogane and sent the profits to Josephine in France.

Josephine showed her gratitude by giving special attention to Isaac and me in Paris. We were several times guests in her house and found her concern for us comforting.

But Toussaint's first impressions were eroded by the reports from Paris. He heard rumors from travelers that Napoléon intended changes in the government of Saint-Domingue. All Toussaint could glean were rumors, but any threat of change suggested to him the restoration of slavery.

Toussaint wrote to Napoléon, congratulated him on his good fortune and pledged loyalty to his government. Toussaint waited for Napoléon's response.

Edward Stevens received notice from Moïse that Toussaint would be at the Cape and wished to see him. Stevens was delighted. He had not seen the Governor-General for several months and looked forward to the visit.

Stevens was surprised by Toussaint's appearance. He looked tired and received Stevens with much formality.

"I need, sir," Toussaint began, after the formal greetings, "your country to sell me a frigate."

"I can speak only provisionally for my country, General, but I think my government will not do so," Stevens responded.

"Parker," Toussaint continued, "has pirated my ships and enslaved their crews. I must have a ship to blockade Jacmel."

"The British seized your ships because the were larger than allowed by the covenant. They would never permit you to sail a frigate. They would see it as a threat to Jamaica," Stevens explained.

"A frigate could defend itself," Toussaint countered.

Stevens smiled to himself, but did not respond.

"Will you sell me a frigate?" Toussaint implored.

"I can only notify my country of your request," Stevens repeated.

Toussaint moved to the window, his back to Stevens and for a few moments did not speak. Stevens was uncertain if the interview was over. He was about to ask if he was excused when Toussaint's spoke again.

"I need six thousand muskets, two thousand breastplates, six thousand pouches and belts, fifty-six thousand flints, four thousand pistols, three hundred carbines, thirty thousand pounds of lead, one hundred thousand pounds of gun powder...." Toussaint recited his shopping list in an agitated voice.

"You have requested these things from the British," Stevens interrupted.

"They say they do not have them. They say I do not need them. Then they sell them in Jamaica on the open market. Maitland and Parker pocket the money, and I can not press my war against Rigaud."

"I know nothing of these things," Stevens responded. "I will advertise your needs. But you will need cash."

Toussaint waved his hand in a gesture which Stevens interpreted to indicate agreement. Stevens continued no more with the point, but he was not at all certain Toussaint had the money to pay for the goods. He knew the American captains would not unload weapons for credit or barter.

To change the subject, Stevens asked Toussaint his opinion of the new government in Paris.

"I have no concerns," Toussaint replied.

"How will you receive the new commission?" Stevens asked. Stevens was testing Toussaint's readiness for independence. He had heard rumors that Toussaint was prepared to embark Roume for France and wondered if the new circumstances would delay or speed Toussaint's decision.

"New commission? I know nothing of a new commission," Toussaint replied with some anxiety.

"It is reported here," Stevens explained. He reached into his waistcoat and removed a folded newspaper and handed it to Toussaint.

"What is it?" Toussaint asked, ignoring the paper.

"A copy of the CHARLESTON CITY GAZETTE of a fortnight past."

"What does it say?" Toussaint demanded irritably.

"That Napoléon is sending a commission to Saint-Domingue to strengthen French rule here."

Stevens saw disbelief on Toussaint's face

Toussaint grabbed the paper from Stevens and perused the printing. Stevens knew Toussaint did not read English and marveled at the gesture.

"Will you receive the commission?" Stevens asked.

"No!" Toussaint responded angrily.

"You will reject the government of France?"

"Toussaint governs in Saint-Domingue."

"And Roume?" Stevens asked, suggesting that now Toussaint would dismiss Roume and create a de facto independence.

"Commissioner Roume represents France in the island," Toussaint replied.

CHAPTER 16
The New Century

By early December, Toussaint knew he could not starve Jacmel into submission. The Americans blockaded the port for him, but supplies still trickled into the city. He could not storm the forts guarding Jacmel: they were too strongly defended. The only choice open to him was to move heavy siege guns from the fortifications at Port-au-Prince.

Although there were no mountains between Port-au-Prince and Jacmel, the terrain was hilly and the roads were damaged from years of neglect.

Toussaint went to Port-au-Prince to personally direct the operation. He sent press-gangs throughout the city and the Cul-de-Sac rounding up able-bodied men from all classes. The sons of the white and mulatto proprietors were not excepted.

The one disconcerting element of the maneuver was that the maroons from the Saddle struck at the labor gangs and Toussaint had to pull troops from before Jacmel to chase the guerrillas back into the mountains.

The eighteenth century ended and the nineteenth began.

Toussaint was too weary and too harassed to mark the event. He had earlier in the decade thought that the moment would be significant. He had hoped that the new century would mark the establishment of the first black republic in the new world, the first country in history created and led by men brought to its shores as slaves. It would be a country, he dreamed, to serve as an inspiration for enslaved peoples everywhere, an inspiration for centuries to come.

Now, Toussaint marveled that the blacks of Saint-Domingue had sustained their freedom for as long as they had. Nine years of war had passed since the blacks declared themselves free, six years since France recognized that freedom, two years since they drove out the last foreign invaders. But still the struggle continued. Toussaint felt too strongly the pain of each day to indulge in dreams of grandeur to come.

Early in January of the new century, Toussaint set up temporary headquarters in the great house of the Gast sugar refinery north of Jacmel where the Gosseline River flowed into the Grande River of Jacmel. The refinery was inactive. The proprietor had chosen to join the defenders in Jacmel.

Toussaint could not stay long at Jacmel, only long enough to encourage his army and organize one more effort to dislodge the defenders from the city.

Toussaint always had trouble sleeping, especially when he was away from Desachaux. Some years previously a voudoun houngan had set a curse upon him which closed his nose. The condition made his speech sound nasal, but more troublesome, it prevented him from breathing freely. At night he sometimes woke gasping for breath. The problem was aggravated if he ate before going to bed. Often he woke choking, unable to get his breath, his throat filled with bile.

That evening Toussaint ate little, but he slept poorly. He fell to sleep a few hours before dawn, but woke, choking. When he got his breath, he thought he heard the sounds of drums.

He called a secretary to attend him and dictated a decree forbidding the voudoun dances and all other African fetishes, practices and superstitions. The penalty for violations was death.

Toussaint knew that if he did not break the power of the houngan he would not be able to rule. The maroon chiefs used the fear generated by the African rituals to control the countryside near their mountain strongholds. Toussaint knew well the techniques. He had used them to unify the blacks after the initial slave uprising, when they were fighting each other in the service of various European factions.

But now the voudoun divided the island, inspired indolence and licentiousness in the workers and prevented the blacks from civilizing themselves.

Toussaint was most disgusted by the dissolute parodies of Christian sacraments indulged in by the followers of the African cults. In the holy seasons when Christians solemnly celebrated the most sacred of mysteries, the cultists engaged in raucous dances and public lewdness. No country could prosper with such impiety at its core. Most importantly, Toussaint knew the voudoun kept him from preparing the people for the great struggle still to come.

When the secretary left to copy the decree, Toussaint lay down again on the large bed in the master bedroom. Although the night was not oppressive, he was sweating. He was not choking, but he felt a weight pushing on his chest. He felt fearful and for a moment thought to call back his secretary and cancel the decree. Toussaint fought the fear. He knew well enough the power of the voudoun on the imagination, but he was a Christian. He would not, must not, fall to the threat of the Devil.

Toussaint climbed from the bed and fell to his knees. He prayed for strength. He stayed on his knees until Mars Plaisir came to dress him. Toussaint dressed and prepared for the day, but he could not shake the anxiety he felt.

During the day and through the night into the next day Toussaint directed a major assault against Jacmel. Christophe, at the head of the Second Demi-Brigade from the Cape, attacked the Blockhouse of Jacmel and Fort Tavlavigne. By night the forts fell to him, but at dawn the Southern forces counterattacked and won back the positions.

Toussaint could not understand the resistance of the defenders. He knew that they were without food and had been reduced to eating cats and rats.

The next day, his attack failed, his body racked with discomforts—his head in pain, his stomach distraught, his old wounds inflamed—Toussaint left the siege to Dessalines and returned to Port-au-Prince to deal with the latest problems with Roume.

In Les Cayes, Rigaud sat in his headquarters and waited. He waited for his hand to heal. He waited for help from Paris. With every ship that slipped into the harbor he expected to hear that France was sending an army to assist him in subduing Toussaint.

The messengers from Jacmel, who filtered through Toussaint's forces or past the American warships off the coast, brought appeals for relief. But still Rigaud delayed. He feared Jacmel would fall before relief reached it, and the relief forces would be lost as well. With each report of the courage of Jacmel's defense, Rigaud slipped deeper into his depression. After the city had held for four months, and it appeared France had forgotten its loyal son, Rigaud roused himself and marched with five hundred men to raise the siege.

Rigaud reached the coast of the Bay of Jacmel several days after Toussaint's unsuccessful assault on the city. He divided his small force into three columns. He sent two columns of one hundred men each into the hills to attack from the rear Dessalines's army of twenty thousand. With the remaining column, three hundred men, Rigaud launched a frontal assault.

Dessalines quickly routed Rigaud's forces and sent them running.

Rigaud rode with the cavalry at the rear of his three hundred. When his soldiers raced past him in retreat, he fell into a fury, leaped from his horse and grabbed at the men fleeing past him.

"Stop!" he shouted to his soldiers. "Turn and fight! Cowards run. The honorable do not fear death."

Several of his officers tried to persuade him to leave the field and come with them. He refused.

"No!" he cried. "I will die before I run." He threw himself down and beat the ground with his fists.

Several of his officers dismounted and lifted him back on his horse and led him away.

Rigaud returned to Les Cayes and spent the next two months lamenting that he had not died at Jacmel.

Roume traveled from the Cape to Port-au-Prince, arriving on January twelfth. His first action was to order the release of prisoners, including Manigat and the other conspirators from Hédouville's attack on Fort Liberté.

Toussaint arrived at the city from Jacmel on January thirteenth and berated the commissioner for over-stepping his authority. Roume rejected Toussaint's accusations and argued that Toussaint had failed to honor his promise of amnesty to the conspirators. Roume refused to allow the men to rot in prison any longer.

The argument became vehement. Toussaint attacked Roume for trying to undermine trade with England and the United States. Roume countered with the charge that Toussaint gave succor to France's enemies. Toussaint demanded that

Roume support the annexation of the Spanish half of the Island. Roume refused, absolutely.

On January fourteenth at dusk, the British brig "Alert" anchored in the harbor of Port-au-Prince. On board were Edward Robinson, the British trade commissioner for Jamaica, and Hugh Cathcart, the British agent in Port-au-Prince, who had boarded the "Alert" at Arcahaie.

On January fifteenth, the two Englishmen requested an interview with Toussaint.

Toussaint agreed, reluctantly.

When Roume heard, he denounced the meeting and insisted that Toussaint arrest the Englishmen: they had arrived unauthorized in an enemy warship.

"The ship sails under a cartel flag," Toussaint answered wearily.

"Only because you are willing to bend to the English. Do you dare sail a ship to Jamaica, cartel or no?" Roume persisted.

"Despite your suspicions of me, I have no love of the British. Do I not bar their warships from the Cape?"

You allow in the American warships, and they are the allies of the British."

"Commissioner Roume," Toussaint began patiently, "we are becoming enemies for no purpose. I know France is at war with England...."

"...And the United States," Roume interrupted.

"No," Toussaint corrected. "Dr. Stevens assures me the United States is not at war with France."

"American ships serve the British in these waters!" Roume insisted vehemently.

"Whether they are at war with France or not," Toussaint argued, "France cannot succor us here. The Caribbean belongs to the British and Americans. If we do not trade with them, we will starve."

"I think," Roume responded pointedly, carefully controlling his anger, "there must be peace between you and Rigaud before this colony slips entirely away from France."

"I welcome peace with Rigaud," Toussaint replied wearily. "It is Rigaud who must be persuaded."

On the morning of January sixteenth, Toussaint met with Cathcart and Robinson at Government House. The two Englishmen were models of contrast.

Cathcart was a thin, balding, timorous man of forty, Robinson a heavy-set, robust man of fifty.

Cathcart introduced Robinson to Toussaint and then handed the general a packet of letters.

"What is this?" Toussaint asked.

"They are for you from his Majesty's envoy, Mr. John Wigglesworth," Cathcart replied.

Toussaint threw the letters, unopened, onto his desk.

"I have told you, Mr. Cathcart, I will accept nothing from Mr. Wigglesworth."

Cathcart, his exasperation barely concealed, turned to Robinson for help.

"Your Excellency," Robinson began, "His Majesty's ministers have empowered Mr. Wigglesworth to speak for them. You have asked to send an emissary to London. His Grace, the Duke of Portland, has responded by sending Mr. Wigglesworth to you."

"I accept only Mr. Cathcart, no other agents," Toussaint insisted with vehemence.

"You know Mr. Wigglesworth," Robinson continued undeterred. "He is a former resident of this city. He is known both to you and to General Maitland. The ministers thought he would serve admirably as a bridge between you."

"I will receive no other agents than Cathcart until Admiral Parker returns my ships!" Toussaint shouted. "He," Toussaint continued, pointing to Cathcart, "is safe here. He has my word, and my word is sacred. But no one else!"

"General..." Robinson patiently began again, mopping the sweat from his florid face with a large handkerchief.

"No one else," Toussaint interrupted. "My word is sacred. Parker should have returned the vessels on my word. I would have repaid his officers for their value."

"They were contraband," Robinson replied carefully, keeping his voice moderated. "Several of the vessels were former property of his Majesty's government captured by your privateers."

"I have no knowledge of that," Toussaint insisted.

"Even the stores were British, taken from Port Royal," Robinson continued.

"They were given to me by Maitland!"

"The Admiralty Court has no knowledge of that," Robinson responded.

Toussaint felt his anger rising. He understood what the British were doing. He knew well enough how to use the law to dissemble.

"If England truly wished for my welfare," he shouted, "it would have made an exception for me!"

Toussaint waved his right arm at the Englishmen and turned away to the window.

Robinson turned to Cathcart for guidance. Cathcart raised his hands in a gesture of futility. Robinson turned back to Toussaint to speak.

Toussaint's secretary shook his head at Robinson and spoke quietly. "The interview is over."

The Englishmen turned to leave. Before they reached the door, Toussaint spoke.

"I will meet with one of you tomorrow," he said quietly. Then he turned to the desk and indicated the dispatches. "I will read these," he said dispiritedly.

On Friday morning, January seventeenth, Cathcart and Robinson arrived at Government House at seven in the morning, the usual time for Toussaint to begin receiving visitors. They were informed that he had left for Léogane before dawn. They requested a boat to follow him. They were instructed to go to the docks, where they waited until 10:30 before a black boatman with a crew of two boys arrived in a small drogher. They fought light and shifting winds and did not reach Léogane, a voyage of only twelve leagues, until 11:30 at night. Because of the reported activity of Rigaud's armed barges in the area, the Englishmen were apprehensive until they stepped ashore at the small docks near the ancient city, one of the oldest in the new world.

Despite his earlier statement that he would receive only one of the Englishmen, Toussaint met with both on the eighteenth.

Toussaint was less angry but no less vehement in his refusal to receive Wigglesworth.

"Mr. Wigglesworth served as supply agent for Maitland in Port-au-Prince," he explained. "He is considered a belligerent by my country and is not acceptable as a commercial agent."

"He is a civilian," Robinson insisted heatedly. "He did not then, and does not now, hold military rank."

"I will receive no more agents until Parker compensates me for the loss of my vessels," Toussaint repeated angrily. "I have always treated with England with honor," he continued, not permitting Robinson to interrupt. "I was instructed by my government to hold General Maitland when he was at Gonaïves. As a man of honor, I would not do that. I have been instructed by my government to attack Jamaica. Not only have I refused to do so, I informed Parker of

Rigaud's agents in your island. You have arrested them on my information. After Admiral Parker commandeered my ships, my droghers brought a British merchantman into Port-de-Paix. I released it and convoyed it to safety. I sent a letter with the captain to Parker. Parker has not responded to my letter. Commissioner Roume had a British merchantman seized at the Cape, imprisoned the captain, and sold the vessel and cargo. When I heard of this affront I responded with honor. I released the captain, restored his vessel and cargo, compensated him for his loses and permitted him to depart...."

Robinson attempted to interrupt, but Toussaint would not permit him to speak.

"No, sir. You will hear me out!" Toussaint commanded. "What has England done?" he continued. "She seized my vessels sailing under passports signed by her own agent...."

"Your Excellency," Cathcart interrupted anxiously. "I do not represent Admiral Parker...."

Toussaint glanced at Cathcart with contempt, and continued to Robinson. "Before that, when Maitland was under the cartel flag at Gonaïves, a British warship seized a drogher within the bay. Among the passengers were the wives of two of my generals. The captain promised to release the passengers in the morning. Instead he took them to Port Royal. They were released only when Maitland returned to Jamaica. My vessel was never returned. When my cartel boat was returning from Jamaica you fired upon it while it flew the flag of truce. Three men were killed, seven wounded. The ship sought refuge in Cuba, where you took the survivors prisoner. You will not return them, and I fear they, like others, have been sold as slaves."

"I will look into the matter of the prisoners," Robinson promised in a conciliatory manner.

Toussaint shook his head in discouragement. "You allow ships under Spanish flag to sail from Jamaica to supply Rigaud," he continued.

"The ships you cite sail for Santo Domingo or San Juan. If they stop at Les Cayes or Jérémie it is not England's doing," Robinson defended.

"You condemn my ships sailing under British passports, but you will not stop English ships sailing under false colors?" Toussaint asked sarcastically.

"I do not think they are English ships," Cathcart suggested meekly.

Toussaint ignored him.

"You list transgressions committed against you," Robinson interrupted with some vigor, "but neglect to mention the central issues. British aid was predicated on your paying for it—I remind you that you owe his Majesty's government in excess of twenty-five thousand pounds for materials delivered—and on your declaring yourself independent of France. His Majesty's government has seen no indication that you intend to fulfill your promises."

Toussaint laughed.

"You want me to be England's pawn," he answered. "If my friends saw that I was that weak, they would forsake me. The field would be left to Rigaud, and he is not England's friend. You want me to expel Roume. I would be pleased to send him back to France, but in my present state I dare not. You strengthen Rigaud against me. He inspires insurrection in the North, defiance in the South. If I sent Roume packing I would send him into Rigaud's arms, and with England blocking my every move, together they might prove too strong for me. Let England abide by the covenant, and I will."

"His Majesty's government wishes to correct misunderstandings," Robinson responded. "To this end it sends Mr. Wigglesworth to meet with you. What more can his Majesty's government do if you refuse to receive Mr. Wigglesworth?"

"I will accept no agents other than Mr. Cathcart until Parker returns my ships," Toussaint reiterated.

"If you speak with Mr. Wigglesworth, I am certain you will discover that he is authorized to find solutions to your problems," Robinson insisted. "If you do not meet with him, our hands are tied."

"I am certain, Excellency," Cathcart interjected, "that Mr. Wigglesworth will have a resolution to your troubles. If he does not, Excellency, I will consider my honor violated, and I will request to withdraw from Saint-Domingue."

Toussaint nodded his head to Cathcart.

"I will meet with Mr. Wigglesworth in Arcahaie," Toussaint replied wearily. "If he has nothing to offer, instruct him not to come."

Although he considered it ridiculous, Toussaint used Cathcart's bravura as the vehicle for compromise. He knew he could expect only treachery from the British, but he did not want them in open opposition, at least not until Rigaud was defeated.

CHAPTER 17
The Fall of Jacmel

Toussaint was frustrated by the ineffectiveness of his law against the voudoun. The gatherings and dances on the habitations continued, but with the rites concealed. The workers moved from place to place to participate in the celebrations, often leaving the fields untended. The proprietors complained to the district commanders that they could not control the workers. On the other hand, Toussaint heard from his district commanders that the workers complained of being mistreated and unpaid by the proprietors. Agriculture and commerce were suffering. Toussaint was finding it difficult to pay for his imports, especially his military supplies. He was forced to issue scrip with promise of payment when the treasury received funds.

In an effort to control the unrest among the laborers, Toussaint established a registration policy. All employers were required to register with the district commanders the names, ages, professions and salaries of all employees. District commanders were required to issue registration cards to all employees identifying place and type of employment. All laborers leaving employment were required to relinquish their cards and secure new ones from their new employers. All without cards would be considered vagabonds and placed on habitations. Those who refused would be put to work for the state, building roads and fortifications.

✦

Late in January, Roume met in a search for peace with several hundred citizens at Port-au-Prince. After the meeting he published a national appeal for the fighting to stop. He assured all Southerners that they would be granted amnesty. He begged Rigaud to give up the rebellion and accept Toussaint's authority.

After he issued his plea for peace, Roume returned to the Cape. Upon his return, Moïse placed him under house arrest.

In Port-au-Prince, Toussaint summoned Cathcart to Government House.

"Mr. Wigglesworth does not meet with me. I have agreed to meet with him, but I have heard nothing from him," Toussaint complained.

"He is ill, your Excellency," Cathcart explained apologetically. "He has had a recurrence of his fever. I have forwarded to him your dispatches"

"I have arrested Roume," Toussaint reported matter-of-factly.

"Yes, your Excellency," Cathcart replied. "Douglas informed me from the Cape."

Toussaint corresponded with Wigglesworth through Cathcart. He learned only that Parker remained adamant. Early in March, Wigglesworth capitulated to Toussaint's pleas to take his case to London, but before he could sail, Wigglesworth died of his fever.

Alexander Pétion begged Rigaud to let him take command of the besieged city of Jacmel.

Pétion, who was destined later to become the first president of the Republic of Haïti, was born in Port-au-Prince in 177O, the son of an elderly white artist and a mulatto mother. His father refused to acknowledge his son and denied him his name. Pétion chose for his surname a pet name given him by a friend of his mother, a derivative of "mon petit."

At a young age Pétion fell in love with war. At six he marched in play beside the soldiers training to help the North Americans in their revolution against England. He studied in Paris at the School for Colonials and at the Military College. He was successful in his studies, but he took offense at the prejudice he experienced because of his color. At eighteen he returned to Port-au-Prince and served in the mounted militia. When the Revolution reached Saint-Domingue Pétion fought for the freedom of both mulattos and blacks and became an artillery officer in Toussaint's army.

Pétion deplored the favoritism Toussaint showed the former Royalist proprietors he welcomed back to the colony. When Toussaint threatened the mulattos in the cathedral at Port-au-Prince, Pétion knew he must join with Rigaud, even if the cause were hopeless. When he found the opportunity, Pétion slipped away from the North to the South.

Rigaud refused Pétion's request to take command of Jacmel. He did not want to sacrifice him to a lost cause. But Pétion persisted, and Rigaud, deep in dejection from his own failure to raise the siege, conceded.

At 10:00 a.m. on Sunday, January nineteenth, Adjutant General Alexander Pétion slipped into Jacmel, past the American warship "General Green" and Toussaint's armed barges, to take command of the besieged city.

Pétion was not prepared for the suffering he found. The city was in ruins. Heavy balls from the siege guns rained down on the city in unpredictable intervals. Everyone, civilians and military, were dressed in rags. What little food was available was carefully rationed, four ounces of bread a day. Children died at the breasts of their mothers who had no milk to feed them. The starving residents ate whatever they could find: horses, donkeys, dogs, cats, rats, harnesses, even grass from the streets. The hospital, located for safety under the cannons of the blockhouse, was filled with the dying.

Daily the city received entreaties from Dessalines to surrender. He promised honors of war to all. Because he felt they might succumb to Dessalines's promises, Pétion had all white officers relieved of command.

In early March, having no other recourse, and with the hope that Dessalines would honor his promises, Pétion sent from the city the sick who could still walk.

When they arrived before his lines, Dessalines wept for their pain. He ordered them feed and clothed. Toussaint, when he heard the news, rushed to Jacmel to direct the rescue.

At 8:00 on the morning of March twelfth, after Toussaint had returned to Port-au-Prince, Pétion brought together all of his garrison, except those manning the blockhouse. He presented a plan for the fourteen hundred soldiers and four hundred civilians remaining in the city to break free and to flee to Rigaud's lines to the west. Any too weak or wounded to march would stay in the hospital and hope for Dessalines' mercy.

A white doctor, angered by Pétion's debasement of whites, slipped away during the night and revealed Pétion's plans to Dessalines.

Before dawn on Thursday, March thirteenth, a clear morning lit by the waning moon, the Jacmelians broke free from their battered city. A small force, making much noise, decoyed to the west, and then retreated quickly back into the city. The main body, with Pétion in the front guard, slipped quietly past the blockhouse to the north.

Christophe, alerted by Dessalines, was ready for them. He attacked, but was driven back by the fire from the small group of defenders manning the blockhouse. Christophe retaliated by firing his cannons into the charging mass. Grapeshot tore into the bodies of soldiers and civilians alike, killing men, women and children. The smoke from the cannon obscured the field.

The Jacmelians were cut into two groups by the charge of Christophe's forces.

One group, under Pétion, fought their way north along the Grand River of Jacmel, where the enemy was the thinnest. About two hundred grenadiers reached the woods and struggled west, against Dessalines's sharpshooters, through the day and into the night.

The larger group was surrounded by Dessalines's troops. The Southerners fired from behind rocks and fallen trees and when attacked fought desperately with sword and bayonet.

Dessalines was struck by their courage and ordered a cease-fire. He was determined to spare their lives. He sent an officer to ask them to put down their arms.

Before the officer reached the field of battle, the Southerners charged at the center of Dessalines' army. They struck with cries of "Viva Jacmel!" and broke through the startled soldiers.

Half of their number fallen, the Jacmelians gained the slope of Cap Rouge north of the city, and broke toward Habitation Gast, Toussaint's now abandoned headquarters.

The two units, each mourning the loss of the other, discovered each other at five on the evening of March fifteenth. The Jacmelians, now reduced from eighteen hundred to less than six hundred in number, retreated in order to Grand Goave, where they were received as heroes.

———————◆———————

As soon as the way was open, Christophe sent his troops into the abandoned city. He felt they should have the profit of spoils as reward for the long siege. He instructed them to take everything of value and to burn what they could not take.

While he was pursuing the Jacmelians, Dessalines heard of Christophe's actions. He left the pursuit and rode into the city to stop Christophe.

Christophe was furious, but he dared not disobey. Dessalines was his commanding officer and Toussaint did not tolerate insubordination.

Christophe retired to his camp and refused to move until the army marched west. But he ordered executed every prisoner who fell to his forces. He spared only the sick and dying in the city hospital.

The prisoners who fell to Dessalines were humanely treated. The able-bodied were recruited into his army. Few refused.

Rigaud received word at Les Cayes of the breakout from Jacmel. He roused himself from his lassitude long enough to issue a proclamation describing the destruction of Jacmel and the summary execution of its defenders. He called upon all citizens of Saint-Domingue to defend their hearths from Toussaint's barbarians.

Toussaint journeyed to Jacmel to inspect the city. From there he issued a proclamation in answer to Rigaud's. Toussaint made no mention of Christophe's actions. He described the miserable condition of the civilians who fled to Dessalines and the welcome they received. He declared that only one man had been executed, a black soldier named Charles who had deserted from Port-au-Prince.

In Saint-Domingue, each person read proclamations according to his own predilection.

With the fall of Jacmel, Toussaint thought he was close to victory in the South, and it was time to prepare for the occupation of Santo Domingo.

Toussaint wrote again to Roume and requested that he approve the annexation of the Spanish part of the island.

Roume again refused.

Toussaint instructed Roume to come to Port-au-Prince.

Roume replied that he could not; he was a prisoner at the Cape.

Before he could persuade Roume that he was not a prisoner, Toussaint received information that a French force had landed on the Island of Guadeloupe to dismantle Victor Hugues's guillotine. If France had turned against the Revolution in Guadeloupe, Toussaint reasoned, how long before reactionary forces would march against Saint-Domingue?

Moïse began the campaign against Roume according to Toussaint's instructions. He had the mayor of Dondon, where Roume had his plantation, write to the mayor of the Cape expressing his loss of confidence in Roume. The National Guard from Dondon marched to the Cape to emphasize the people's displeasure with the commissioner.

Moïse, with the mayor and other city officials, escorted Roume from his house at the Cape to the Bréda Habitation a league south of the city. Moïse explained to Roume that they were taking him to Bréda for his own protection. The people were angry with him

Roume was not alarmed. He had seen Toussaint's maneuvers before. He knew why he had been under house arrest for two and a half months and what the present clamor was about, and he was not going to give in to Toussaint.

The road to Bréda was lined with people, mostly black cultivators, yelling at Roume and threatening to storm the carriage in which he rode. Moïse shouted at the people, asking them to let the commissioner pass, promising them that justice would be done. Riding in the carriage, Roume felt anxious despite his efforts to persuade himself that Moïse was directing a carefully prepared charade.

When the group reached Bréda, they were surrounded by more people, mostly cultivators and soldiers. Moïse had his guard push the people back from the carriage to allow Roume to get out. The people refused to disperse.

"What do you want me to do?" Moïse yelled at the crowd.

"We want Roume!" they answered.

"Let him get out of the carriage, and you can talk to him," Moïse replied.

The people backed away from the carriage, and Roume, valiantly trying to control the trembling of his body, climbed out. Immediately the crowd shouted for his life and pushed against the guards protecting him.

Moïse dismounted from his horse, drew his sword and threatened the crowd. As if responding to a signal, they quieted and formed a circle around Moïse and Roume.

"What do you want to say to the commissioner?" Moïse asked.

Everyone in the crowd shouted at once. Moïse raised his sword, and they were once again quiet.

"The commissioner can not hear you all at once. Let someone speak for you." Moïse pointed his sword at an elderly black man dressed as a cultivator. "You, what do you want to say to the commissioner?"

"We want land," the man said with some hesitation.

"I'm not certain the commissioner heard you," Moïse prompted. "What did you say?"

"We want land!" a number of other men shouted.

"You want land? How can the commissioner give you land?" Moïse asked in pretended naïveté.

"Break up the habitations," a young man shouted.

"Yes," another agreed. "Half for the proprietors, half for the workers."

"You want the commissioner to divide the land and give you half?" Moïse prompted.

"Yes!" the crowd shouted. "Let us have land. We don't want to work for wages anymore!"

Roume looked at Moïse with amazement. "Toussaint would not approve," he said quietly.

Moïse smiled at Roume.

"What else do you want from the commissioner?" Moïse shouted to the crowd.

"Slavery stopped in the East." The old man spoke again.

Right on cue, Roume thought. The situation was so obviously staged that he felt his fear dispersing.

"You want our brothers and sisters in the East freed from their chains?" Moïse asked.

"Yes!" the crowd shouted.

"What will you do if they are not freed?" Moïse asked.

Roume wanted to warn Moïse not to get the crowd too excited. They might get out of hand. Then the fear gripped Roume again as two of the guards grabbed him by the arms.

Moïse placed his saber edge against the side of Roume's neck.

"What will you do?" Moïse again asked the crowd.

"We will kill the whites if they stop us!" a young man shouted.

Moïse spoke to Roume with quiet intensity: "Will you sign the decree?"

Roume did not answer.

"I could cut your throat," Moïse said matter-of-factly.

Roume had no doubt that he could.

"You will sign," Moïse said quietly.

Roume was pushed roughly through the crowd and thrown into a shed used for brooding hens. The door was closed and latched. Through the cracks Roume could see the crowd disperse.

Roume was permitted to leave his rude prison to answer the calls of nature, but always he was returned to the shed. During the days people shouting threats against him often surrounded the shed. During the nights the habitation was surrounded by fires and inundated by the sounds of drums.

Each day Moïse visited Roume. On each visit Moïse presented threats of the consequences of Roume refusing to sign the decree annexing Santo Domingo. Moïse described the unrest sweeping the colony. He warned of the possible massacre of whites because of Roume's intransigence. At one point Moïse presented Roume with a petition signed by over twenty-five hundred leading citizens calling for Roume to surrender all authority to Toussaint.

Roume was angry at his treatment. He was furious at the filth and lice he endured. He was worried about the safety of his wife and daughters in Dondon. Although he hid his feelings from his captors, inside he railed at the attack on his dignity. But what troubled Roume most was that he could not discern between sham and reality. He was frightened that Moïse was losing control of his charade, or worse, was pushing events for his own purposes. Roume wasn't certain Toussaint was still in command, that Moïse was not acting on his own. Roume did not trust Moïse. Everyone knew of Moïse's dislike of whites and that only Toussaint restrained him. If Moïse was out of control, then the events he described or threatened might be realities, and the blacks of the Northern Plain might once again be in insurrection.

Roume was relieved when Toussaint appeared.

Roume complained bitterly to Toussaint of his treatment. Toussaint apologized: he had not been aware of what was happening, but Roume must understand that the passion of the people of Saint-Domingue against slavery in the Spanish lands was reaching uncontrollable heights. Roume would be released immediately and allowed to return to the city.

Toussaint accompanied Roume to the Cape where they met for two hours. Toussaint argued that to keep peace Roume must sign the decree. Roume resisted all of Toussaint's arguments.

"I will not sign for the death of those peaceable people," Roume declared. "If you mean to kill me, then do so. France will avenge me."

If Roume did not sign, Toussaint threatened to enter the territory with a torch in one hand and a sword in the other.

The day after the meeting, after he had time to think, Roume was surprised at how relieved he had been to see Toussaint and how much he dreaded seeing Moïse. He told himself that Moïse acted only on Toussaint's instructions. But he wasn't certain any more. Toussaint's fears might be justified. The cultivators might explode once more into violence if Roume did not relent.

Roume knew that he was being tricked. Like a victim of a mountebank, he knew that he was being duped even while he watched the magician at work. Roume was tired. He did not want to be at the center of conflict. Whether he signed or not, Toussaint would take Santo Domingo when he wanted.

Roume looked for a way out, a way to stall until Napoléon's representatives reached the island, a way to give Toussaint an apparent victory with no substance to it.

Roume told Toussaint he would sign the decree only if Toussaint guaranteed the safety of all, black and white, in the former Spanish colony.

Toussaint agreed. They each would write to the governor of the colony, Don Garcia, and request that Toussaint's agents be received peacefully. General Agé, a European, would lead an invasion of a small force of white troops, would keep all Spanish officers in their grades and functions and would respect the manners and customs of the people.

In a secret letter to Don Garcia, Roume complained of being coerced by Toussaint and suggested that the Spanish governor, if he could, delay compliance to Toussaint's demands until the arrival of Napoléon's commissioners.

CHAPTER 18
Napoléon's Commissioners

After the fall of Jacmel, Dessalines brought a tailor and his shop of fitters, cutters and stitchers from Port-au-Prince and had them make for him a uniform of scarlet velour decorated with gold and precious stones and a hat covered with brilliant plumage. Toussaint in his uniforms might rival the officers of King Louis and Christophe might appear as the richest of hussars, but Dessalines knew that dressed in his scarlet jacket and cloak and mounted on his tall black gelding, he was the match of any emperor in the ancient or modern world.

While Toussaint was engaged at the Cape persuading Roume, Dessalines began his sweep of the South. He promised to turn the Land into a dessert of fire in which even the trees lifted their roots in the air if the Southerners did not surrender. The Southern forces replied by fighting city by city in a stubborn retreat.

Dessalines gave Christophe the honor of leading the attacks. Christophe liked to kill, Dessalines explained to his adjutant. Let him serve where his appetite could be fed. Dessalines rode with his cavalry in the rear, a place fitting to a general, where he could survey the battle and make the decisions necessary for victory, and a place where he would be more likely to survive to marry Claire Heureuse.

By April twenty-eighth, Dessalines had swept the southern coast between Jacmel and Bainet and turned north to renew the attack on Grand and Petit Goave. Crossing the base of the peninsula, his lead column was ambushed and suffered heavy losses. On the twenty-ninth an impassable rain delayed

Dessalines. On the first of May he reached a hill that overlooked Grand Goave. He looked down upon the city, the river before it, the bay beyond.

Dessalines watched his front guard engage the defending force before the river. Christophe repulsed the Southerners and advanced toward the city but was met by a counterattack of the Southern Fifth Regiment. Christophe was driven back and Dessalines sent reinforcements. The battle raged for an hour. With most of their officers killed, the Southern soldiers broke from the fighting and retreated toward the city. Dessalines ordered a cease-fire out of admiration for their courage.

When Dessalines's forces entered the city they found it in flames. Rigaud's forces had retreated toward Petit Goave, burning Grand Goave and surrounding habitations as they went.

André Rigaud met his soldiers at Petit Goave. He wept for the loss of his officers and friends, gave command of the army to Pétion, and retired to Les Cayes, again to await support from France.

When Dessalines reached Petit Goave, he found that city in flames and the Southern army in retreat toward Miragoâne, six leagues farther west on the coast of the Gonave Channel. In the port of Petit Goave Dessalines's forces found and released three American ships captured earlier by Rigaud's forces.

In the middle of May, Toussaint in Port-au-Prince received news that Napoléon's commissioners had arrived at the Cape. He sent orders to Moïse to arrest every passenger on the vessel and to hold them until his arrival. Toussaint sent orders to General Agé at Gonaïves to ride as quickly as possible to Santo Domingo City. He should travel as lightly as possible to avoid causing alarm to the Spanish and should send the troops he needed by ship. Toussaint wanted the annexation settled quickly and without conflict before he was confronted with instructions from Napoléon.

Moïse confined all the passengers to the ship except Napoléon's commissioners. There were three. Two of them were old friends and supporters of Toussaint, Colonel Charles Vincent and Julien Raimond. The third was General Michel, an officer in Napoléon's army. These three Moïse marched under guard through the streets of the Cape to the Place d'Arms where he confined them in the common jail.

When Toussaint arrived at the Cape, he expressed his displeasure to Moïse for the way that he had handled the commissioners.

Moïse smiled. "You said arrest them," he replied.

Toussaint saw the intensity in Moïse's good eye, and decided to treat the matter with humor rather than reprimand his nephew.

Before Toussaint went to the commissioners to apologize for the indignities they had suffered, he had their papers searched. He was not pleased by what he found. Napoléon sent greetings to the people of Saint-Domingue, but sent no letter addressed to Toussaint. Napoléon sent a memorandum confirming Toussaint's position as Governor-General, but he sent also specific instructions ordering Toussaint to employ all weapons in the island against the English only and to make peace immediately with Rigaud. Napoléon sent a memorandum continuing Roume in his position as political commissioner, but he sent Vincent, Raimond and Michel to share the responsibilities with Roume. And, as Toussaint had anticipated, Napoléon sent specific instructions forbidding Toussaint to annex Santo Domingo.

What troubled Toussaint most were Napoléon's references to special laws for the governance of the colony. Nowhere in the documents were these laws described.

Toussaint rode alone before night to the small house on the road to Bréda where Pierre Baptiste resided. Except for the solid walls and shingled roof, the house was little different from the cailles in which Pierre Baptist had lived for ninety years, first in Africa and then on the Bréda habitation.

"Toussaint, my son," Baptiste greeted the Governor-General eagerly as he dismounted from his horse before the door.

"How do you know it is me?" Toussaint asked.

"I know," Baptiste said as he pulled the smaller man into a tight embrace. When they separated the old man traced his fingers gently along Toussaint's face. "You are troubled."

"When am I not?" Toussaint asked. "Are you well?"

"Always when you are with us."

Baptiste took Toussaint's hand and led him into the house and to a simple wooden chair in the front room.

"Mama," Baptiste called. "Something for Toussaint to eat."

An old woman stirred herself from the bed in the back room, rose slowly and shuffled outside toward the cook-fire behind the house where a kettle hung over a pile of cold ashes.

"She doesn't know you," Baptiste explained. "She recognizes no one anymore."

Toussaint nodded. He knew his godmother's mind had failed. Her body and gros-bon-ange lingered, but her ti-bon-age was already with God.

"I am not hungry, Uncle," Toussaint said.

Baptiste held his finger to his lips. "A little soup," he insisted quietly.

Toussaint did not argue with him.

Neither man spoke for several minutes. Baptiste waited for Toussaint to open his heart.

The old woman shuffled back to her bed and returned to her nap. She had forgotten what she was to do. Both men knew she had returned without the soup, but neither spoke if it.

"I have no one to advise me, Uncle," Toussaint began finally.

"Listen to your heart," Baptiste instructed.

Toussaint shook his head. "My heart does not guide me," he replied.

"Then tell me your concern."

As the twilight faded quickly to darkness, Toussaint spoke of his problems to the older man. He sought the comfort he had known as a boy when he turned to Baptiste for answers to a child's curiosity about the order of the sky, the healing nature of plants, the lives of ancient kings and emperors, the laws that govern God and men, and the mysteries of men's hearts.

Toussaint needed to be as a boy again, to be able to surrender to the wisdom of someone wiser. But even as he spoke, he knew the futility of the effort. The old man had no knowledge of politics, no understanding of Napoléon, of Maitland, Parker, Roume, Rigaud, of trade and economics, of the myriad personalities Toussaint placated daily to hold intact the gossamer threads of freedom in the island.

"Whom the loa choose to mount must carry the burden," Pierre Baptiste responded to Toussaint's lament.

Toussaint was startled.

"The loa do not mount me," he replied stiffly. "I am a Christian, Uncle."

"I, too, am a Christian," Baptiste replied. He was hurt that Toussaint might think otherwise. "The battle is larger than Toussaint and Napoléon," Baptiste continued. "I do not know who rides Napoléon, but I know the loa ride Toussaint. Ogoun, perhaps, or Papa Légba."

"I do not believe in the loa," Toussaint said. "I do not believe in superstitions."

"No, of course not," Baptiste agreed. "But I do not speak of superstitions. I speak of powers." Baptiste continued with the gentle insistence of a practiced teacher. "I am a Christian. You know that. Like you, I believe in Christ. But the battle here is more ancient than Christ. The white man has divided the Supreme One into their saints, which, like them are white. The blacks know the saints and loa are kindred. But the whites do not know this. They are frightened of the loa. Their fear makes them enslave the worshipers of the loa because they can not enslave the loa."

Toussaint was not pleased with the old man's defense of voudoun, but out of respect he did not contradict him.

"The power to resist the whites," Baptiste continued, "can come only from the loa. They choose who will do battle for them. They have chosen you. They decide what you do."

When Toussaint rode back to the Cape, he was irritated that he had allowed himself to be weak before Pierre Baptiste. Toussaint remembered him as a man of great wisdom, but now he was lost in superstitions. Toussaint was sad at what had happened to the mentor of his youth.

After Toussaint left, Baptiste sat thoughtfully in the darkness. He knew he had not been eloquent with his godson. There was much he had not been able to explain.

Pierre Baptiste reached for his walking stick. When he found it he drew it to him and traced a design on the floor. The stick made only faint lines in the dust, but the marks Baptist drew were not for his blinded eyes, but for the eyes of his mind.

He sketched two figures. The first was the crossroad; two lines of equal length crossed each in the center of the other. The second was the Christian cross.

Pierre Baptiste spoke as if Toussaint were still in the room, although he knew he was not.

"This," he said, pointing to the symbol of the crossroad, "is the true cross, the crossroad of life where mortals"—Baptiste retraced the horizontal line—"and the loa meet." Pierre Baptiste retraced the vertical line.

"But on the Christian cross"—Baptiste retraced the vertical line—"the dying god is hung above the crossroad where God and man meet." Baptiste retraced the horizontal line above the center of the vertical line.

"The whites do not understand this," he continued. "They think they live now where Christ hangs as a promise of the life to come. Because they do not understand this, in their confusion they look down on the rest of the earth."

Pierre Baptiste contemplated for some minutes the images in his mind. Then with his stick he drew a curve from the top of the Christian cross to the point where the lines crossed, a symbol much like the chi rho.

It is a sword, he thought. He had not seen it before. But he understood its necessity. When one tries to stand superior to nature, one must have a sword to defend oneself.

It would be a great battle, and it was a terrible thing to be ridden by gods at war. Pierre Baptiste feared for Toussaint. He wanted to help his godson, but he knew of no way. Mortals were helpless to change the ways of the immortals.

In the morning, Toussaint went to the barracks to see to the release of Napoléon's agents. He apologized for the treatment they had received from Moïse. Toussaint denied any knowledge of the arrest, and insisted that as soon as he was informed of their plight, he rushed to the Cape to their aid.

Vincent and Raimond accepted Toussaint's explanation without comment. They were accustomed to events in Saint-Domingue. General Michel was incensed. He swore he had never experienced such governmental incompetence. He held Toussaint personally responsible and would accept no apology. Toussaint listened, but said nothing.

While Toussaint at the Cape received Napoléon's commissioners, Dessalines in the South pressed the war against Rigaud. Dessalines allowed his army no moment to rest in Petite Goave. He wanted to rush upon Rigaud's forces while they were in full retreat. He found them at the Miragoâne Bridge, where Alexander Pétion chose to confront Dessalines' army of twenty thousand with his army of one thousand.

One road only led from the ports on the northern shore of the peninsula to the cities in the west, Rigaud's stronghold. The road passed over the Miragoâne Bridge. The bridge was located at the south end of a lake and was surrounded by swamps to the north and mountains to the south. In this narrow pass, like Roland at Roncesvalles and Leonidas at Thermopylae, Pétion chose to meet with his small forces the massive army at his rear.

For three days Dessalines attacked Pétion at the bridge, but saw his soldiers slaughtered on the road by Pétion's cannon and the few that reached the bridge cut down by the brave men who fought beside Pétion.

The price of the frontal attack was too high for Dessalines. He had cannon mounted on the hills overlooking the bridge, pulled back from the attack and settled into a war of artillery.

Like Xerxes at Thermopylae, Dessalines knew he must encircle the enemy. He selected several officers he felt were the most resourceful and sent them with their troops through the mountains to the south and the swamps to the north. Pétion was taken by surprise. He had believed the swamps and mountains impassable and had not defended his rear.

When he heard that Pétion was surrounded, Rigaud rushed to aid him, but was too late. Pétion had spiked his cannon and withdrawn to the gates of Miragoâne. Together Rigaud and Pétion prepared to defend the city. They held for five hours against Dessalines. At dark they withdrew into the city, burned it during the night and abandoned the ruins to Dessalines the next morning.

Dessalines sent his light cavalry south to harass the retreating Rigaud and marched his main forces into Miragoâne to rest.

The inhabitants of Miragoâne fled with the Southern forces before Dessalines. Their fear amused Dessalines. He threatened them with no harm, but their flight made it easier for him to feed his soldiers with the food they abandoned and quarter his army in their houses still standing. Dessalines was pleased, also, that Rigaud was burdened with the care and feeding of the civilians who fled with him.

After Dessalines had settled into one of the houses still intact and prepared to bathe, he was disturbed by an uproar in the street. His adjutant informed him that he was needed. The soldiers wanted to leave the city.

Dessalines dressed and followed his adjutant to a house before which a group of soldiers stood, some angry, some deeply frightened.

"It is a dead girl," a platoon leader informed him. "They left without burying her."

Dessalines entered the house and saw a young girl of about twelve years clothed in her confirmation dress laid out on a funeral bier surrounded by flowers and pictures of the saints. He was furious.

"What woman would leave her child unburied?" he asked the officers who accompanied him. "What mother, even to save her own life, could leave her daughter to wander forever, her spirit never at rest?"

Dessalines ordered the child buried with all proper rituals. His officers protested. There was no one from the family present. Who had washed the body? Whoever washed the body must stay with it. Where could they find a woman willing to wash again the body? And if they forced someone to do it, would not she and they risk retaliation from the family loa?

"We do not know how she died," his adjutant argued. "What if she died from being struck by lightning or from the pox?"

"What foolishness," Dessalines declared. "You can see she did not have the pox. Her face is smooth. You see no burns from lightning."

Dessalines calmed the fears of his officers. He ordered that a woman be found to accompany the body, that children be found to sing and play games in the funeral procession and that a priest be found to read the prayers.

"What if they refuse?" his adjutant asked.

"If any refuse, there will be more than one funeral today," Dessalines declared.

In June, Toussaint heard that the British off the north coast near Porto Plata had captured the schooner carrying the seventy soldiers to support Agé in Santo Domingo City. Because the soldiers were white the British did not take them to Jamaica to sell them into slavery but put them ashore at Monte Cristi. Toussaint dared not send such a small force south to Santo Domingo City by land. The Spanish surely would ambush them. He dared not send a larger force with the war unsettled in the South and Napoléon's commissioners observing his every move.

Toussaint called Vincent to meet him in Port-au-Prince.

Of the three commissioners, Toussaint felt confident of the support of Raimond and Vincent, if he did not flagrantly defy Napoléon's instructions. But he had more trust in Vincent's appraisal of the politics of Paris. Vincent was a native of the metropole, Raimond a mulatto from Saint-Domingue.

Colonel Charles Vincent was a heavy-set Frenchman who carried his forty-eight years with some weariness. He came to Saint-Domingue before the Revolution, in 1786, as a newly promoted captain of engineers. After the Revolution he was appointed chief of brigade in Toussaint's army and then director of fortifications. He, with Christophe and Sonthonax, designed the plan of leasing the plantations by which agriculture was rebuilt. He had, on several occasions, carried Toussaint's story to Paris at the request of the black general.

"Is Napoléon my enemy?" Toussaint asked Vincent when they met.

"I don't know," Vincent answered as honestly as he could. "I do not think so, but he does not understand Saint-Domingue."

"Why did he not write to me?" Toussaint asked.

"He is a close man. It is difficult to read him."

"What did you tell him of me?" Toussaint asked.

"I told him that you are the only man who can keep order in the colony."

"What are the new laws for Saint-Domingue?" Toussaint asked with some irritation.

"Napoléon brings a new order to France, a new Constitution...."

"But the new laws for Saint-Domingue," Toussaint interrupted. "What are they?"

"I do not know what the First Consul intends," Vincent replied.

"You are afraid to tell me!" Toussaint accused.

"No," Vincent responded calmly. "If I knew I would tell you. I think Napoléon does not know specifically what laws he intends. The new Constitution provides for special laws for particular geographic and social situations, but Napoléon has not asked the legislature to enact any specific laws. I believe he intends only that the Constitution allows the nation to respond to contingencies."

Toussaint felt the specter of fear invade his heart. Napoléon prepared France for the reestablishment of slavery!

"I have withdrawn Agé from Santo Domingo City," Toussaint volunteered, changing the subject abruptly.

"That is wise," Vincent agreed.

"Napoléon thinks I want to keep France out of Santo Domingo, but that is not true. I wish only to stop slavery there."

"Raimond and I understand your position, and General Michel is beginning to. On his way to Santo Domingo City he encountered slaves chained and beaten by their Spanish owner. He had never before witnessed such horrors. He was incensed. Michel is not your enemy. He does not understand the island, but he is beginning to. If you are faithful to Napoléon's instructions, I believe that when Michel returns to Paris he will be more supportive of you than he was when he left Paris," Vincent suggested.

Toussaint felt a familiar frustration. Vincent spoke reason and common sense, but Toussaint did not want to hear reason and common sense. He wanted to hear that Rigaud was beaten. He wanted to hear that his command extended throughout the island. He wanted to hear that Napoléon—that France—accepted his government in Saint-Domingue. He wanted to hear that all threats of slavery were ended.

Toussaint suppressed his anger. He would try once more.

"I will halt Dessalines. I will declare an amnesty in the South. I will give Rigaud one more chance," Toussaint said.

"Those are Napoléon's wishes," Vincent reminded Toussaint.

Toussaint wanted to scream that they were not his wishes. He wanted Rigaud dead. He wanted the mulatto threat ended. He wanted peace on his terms, not on Rigaud's, not on Napoléon's. Instead, Toussaint turned his anger to one insufferable order from Napoléon.

"But I will not change the flag!" Toussaint shouted. "There is one flag for France and for Saint-Domingue. We are as French as the metropole."

"I understand," Vincent replied.

After Vincent left, Toussaint could not relieve his anger. He would not be patronized by Napoléon. Napoléon ordered Toussaint to print on all French flags in Saint-Domingue, "Brave blacks, you owe solely to the people of France your liberty and your equal rights."

Toussaint would not accept that lie! He would not publish it. He would not serve under a flag that proclaimed it. The blacks of Saint-Domingue did not owe their freedom to the largess of France. They owed it to their heroism in battle!

CHAPTER 19
Rigaud Surrenders

All through June Toussaint vacillated. He had assured Vincent and the other commissioners that he would declare a truce in the South, but Toussaint waited. Conditions were not right for a truce. If Rigaud and his followers did not know that they were defeated, the truce would solve nothing.

Toussaint intended to halt Dessalines at the gates of Cavaillon or Les Cayes and negotiate with Rigaud when the mulatto chief felt desolation at his doorstep. But Dessalines was not at Cavaillon. It had taken him fifteen days of siege to take Saint Michel. At the fall of Saint Michel, Dessalines had fallen ill. The march of his army stopped before Aquin, his officers feuding, jealous of Dessalines's appointments of command.

Despite Napoléon's instructions and the impatience of the commissioners, Toussaint was not going to act from weakness.

Dessalines had not eaten for days. His stomach accepted no food. His head was on fire, his body torn and twisted with pain. He had no strength in his legs. He was certain he was dying.

The doctor assured Dessalines that he would live. He had breathed too much of the vapors of the swamp at Miragoâne. The vapors had poisoned his blood. The doctor bled Dessalines twice a day to relieve the poison. In time, he told

Dessalines, his blood would throw off the poison and Dessalines would be himself again.

Dessalines knew his sickness was not from the swamp. It was from the loa. They were angry because of the burial of the girl in Miragoâne. From that day he became ill. Why, Dessalines mourned, did the loa create impossible situations for men? Why did they not punish the mother who abandoned her daughter instead of he who tried to help the child and honor the loa?

Dessalines sent for the houngan at Léogane who had persuaded the loa to give him his victories and his promotion. When the houngan heard of the incident of the burial of the child, he shook his head in despair.

"You should not have stepped between the loa and those in the family on whom their wrath should have fallen. It was a brave act, my General, but not wise."

The houngan vowed to do his best. For three days he entreated the loa to release Dessalines. He sacrificed chickens and bathed the general with the blood. He called upon other serviteurs in the area to aid him. They sacrificed a goat and a bull. But Dessalines only grew sicker. Finally the Houngan fled back to Léogane in despair.

Dessalines, convinced he was to die, sent for Claire Heureuse so that he might say goodbye to her. He was afraid she would not come because of fear of his illness or disdain for his weakness.

She came, and brought with her herbs which she prepared in a hot, bitter soup and insisted that Dessalines drink. To his surprise, his stomach did not reject the fluid.

That night, and for a week following, Claire sat by his bed. She bathed his head with wet cloths. She held his hand when he awakened and sang softly to him when he slipped into sleep.

Dessalines felt his strength return. He was able to eat and after the week, able to get up from his bed. He began to recover his strength.

When the loa first gave Claire to him, he knew she was a gift of great value. Now he knew she was an angel. He begged her to marry him that very day. She refused.

"When the war is ended," she reminded him, "I will consider your proposal. Not until then."

With Dessalines well again, Claire returned to Léogane. Dessalines, faith in the promise he heard in her words, was determined to crush Rigaud without delay. Then he would return to Claire a victor and claim her as his prize.

Dessalines joined his army at Vieux Bourg, near Aquin, in time to repulse a cavalry charge led by Rigaud. Bullets pierced the mulatto leader's hat and clothes, but miraculously he was not wounded. He lost his horse, but scrambled to safety and avoided capture.

Rigaud escaped, but his forces could no longer hold Aquin and withdrew. Again he left the fighting to others and returned to Les Cayes.

During the early weeks of July, Dessalines continued his march along the south coast toward Cavaillon and Les Cayes. Rigaud's forces would hold bravely for a few hours, and then, overwhelmed by Dessalines's superior numbers, burn the town they defended and retreat to the next. Only the heat which exhausted men and animals slowed Dessalines.

When Dessalines approached Saint Louis, he received orders from Toussaint to cease-fire. Toussaint had declared a truce and was sending a deputation to Rigaud offering amnesty.

Dessalines did not know whether to laugh or cry. It was Toussaint's way, Dessalines knew, to stop the fighting when victory was within reach.

On the one hand, Dessalines did not mind. His army was tired. They had fought well in the summer heat. They would welcome the rest. He knew that Rigaud would refuse the amnesty and in time Dessalines would sweep through Cavaillon and Les Cayes and on to Jerémie, if necessary. The delay, he knew, would strengthen him more than Rigaud.

On the other hand, Dessalines wanted the war over so that he could return to Claire. He thought to slip back to Léogane and visit her, but rejected the idea. He did not want to face another refusal.

Dessalines would have to wait for Toussaint to placate the French, or whatever it was he did when he played his games. The wait provided unexpected amenities when the mayor of Saint Louis invited the commanding general of the army besieging his city to a dinner in the general's honor.

For the final push against Rigaud, Toussaint moved his headquarters from Gonaïves to Léogane so that he would be closer to the war and better able to make decisions.

Toussaint seldom now visited the areas of battle. He had generals to lead the fighting, but only he could deal with the problems of the colony as a whole, Toussaint told himself. But in moments of stillness, Toussaint knew he feared the battles. He was afraid he would be killed. As many times as he faced danger on a battlefield, he still feared violent death. The fear did not lessen with time; it grew worse: partially, he thought, because of Suzanne's fears, and partially because he knew that any man who faced war as often as he did must die from it. "An eye for an eye, a tooth for a tooth," the prophet said, and a life for a life, Toussaint knew, and he had sent too many men to death in battle not to find his own death there as well.

In the middle of July, when Dessalines was well and again leading the army toward Les Cayes, Toussaint called Vincent to Léogane.

"I want you to take a letter to Rigaud offering him peace," Toussaint told Vincent. Neither man mentioned the weeks of delay since Toussaint had promised the truce.

"I would be most pleased to take your letter," Vincent accepted the assignment with enthusiasm.

Toussaint was gripped by a new fear. He had expected hesitancy from Vincent. The request was not an easy one. Rigaud would not welcome a messenger from Toussaint. Defectors from the South reported that Rigaud was at the point of madness, that he threatened death to anyone who suggested surrender. Rigaud would surely threaten no less to a messenger from Toussaint.

Toussaint could think of only one reason for Vincent to have no hesitation in going to Rigaud: he brought him good news, news that Napoléon supported the mulatto leader, or that aid was coming from France, or that Toussaint was to be arrested.

Toussaint hastily ended the meeting. Vincent would hear from him.

Vincent left the meeting in confusion. Never before had Toussaint seemed uncomfortable in his presence. He vowed to himself to keep the Governor-General informed of each step of his negotiations with Rigaud. Vincent did not wish to fuel Toussaint's anxiety.

The next morning Vincent received Toussaint's instructions. He was to ride overland to Jacmel and from there take ship to Les Cayes. When he met with Rigaud he was to insist that Toussaint's letter offering amnesty be published in all areas of the South. All those who fought under Rigaud would be pardoned except for five men: Rigaud must submit to arrest in recognition of the lawful government of the colony. One of his staff, who was not a citizen of Saint-Domingue, would be deported. Three others, including Pétion, would be confined to prison for a short time for their treason, and then allowed to return to their families. No one else had anything to fear from Toussaint.

Vincent had some concern for the sail from Jacmel to Les Cayes. He faced capture from a British picket ship on the way and arrest, or execution when he landed in Les Cayes if Rigaud wished not to see him.

Vincent and his companions reached Les Cayes safely, and they were not killed when they landed. But they were not welcomed. They were met by André Rigaud's brother, Augustin, who explained that André was not in the city. He gave no further explanation. Vincent and his two companions waited through the day. No one tended to their luggage or any of their needs. At night they were escorted by a body of cavalry to Government House and given rooms in which to sleep.

As Vincent prepared for bed, a small man came to his room. The man was dressed in a green waistcoat with no sign of military grade. He was heavily armed with a saber, a belt of pistols and a dagger up his sleeve, the handle in his hand.

Vincent had never met Rigaud but had heard him described.

"Are you General André Rigaud?" Vincent asked of the strange, silent, agitated man.

Rigaud made no response. He stared at Vincent as if to see into his soul.

"You are Colonel Charles Vincent!" he said as if in accusation.

"Yes," Vincent responded quietly.

"You come to hang me!"

"Hardly. There are only three of us, and we are unarmed," Vincent answered.

"Why do you not bring me aid from Napoléon?"

"Napoléon wants peace. I bring you an offer of peace from Toussaint."

"Toussaint!"

Rigaud spat on the floor. "I want nothing of Toussaint but his head!" He burst into a tirade of the wrongs Toussaint had done him. He raved on for many minutes damning Toussaint, his generals, the French who supported him, the English who conspired with him. Vincent listened without comment.

As Rigaud spoke, he paced the room and shouted from time to time from the door or window. Several of his officers heard the shouting and gathered by the door. Everyone listened. No one interrupted.

Finally, exhausted, Rigaud flung himself into a chair.

"What does he want?" he asked Vincent in a defeated voice.

Vincent began to explain the conditions of Toussaint's amnesty. Before he had gone beyond the demand that Rigaud publish Toussaint's letter, Rigaud was on his feet again.

"No!" he shouted. "I will publish nothing of Toussaint's. None of his lies." Rigaud flipped the knife from his sleeve and held it to his throat. "Toussaint wants me dead. Fine. He may have me dead. Tell him you watched me cut my throat."

Several of Rigaud's officers tried to calm him. They sought to persuade him of his importance to the South, to those who depended on him. They pledged their support to him to the death. They begged him not to kill himself. Better to fight to the death against Toussaint, they urged, than to surrender to despair.

Vincent felt the anger in the room directed at him and his colleagues. It seemed quite likely to him that Rigaud's officers might sacrifice the bearers of the bad news to propitiate their unstable leader.

As abruptly as he put the knife to his throat, Rigaud pulled it away

"You speak for Napoléon," he addressed Vincent. "What does Napoléon want me to do?"

"I am one of four commissioners representing the metropole," Vincent attempted to explain.

"What does Napoléon want me to do?" Rigaud shouted, his eyes filling with tears.

"He wants peace," Vincent answered softly.

"I am loyal to France," Rigaud insisted, barely able to suppress his tears. "I will do what France wants."

Rigaud rushed from the room. His officers following quickly after him

The next morning, Vincent was informed that Rigaud had left the city. He later learned that Rigaud left before dawn for Saint Louis to punish the traitors who had dined with the enemy.

At nine in the morning, the general alarm was sounded in Les Cayes. The citizens were mobilized to defend against an attack from Dessalines. Vincent attempted to persuade Rigaud's brother that Dessalines would not break the truce. Vincent hoped he was correct.

In the midst of the alarm, André Rigaud returned to the city and instructed Vincent to leave.

"I cannot protect your life, here," he warned.

Vincent managed to meet once more with André Rigaud that evening. He told Rigaud that General Michel was returning to France on the American frigate "Boston." Vincent explained that he could arrange for Rigaud to sail with Michel. Rigaud again flew into a rage and repeated his warning that he could no longer protect Vincent's life.

The next morning Vincent and his companions left the city by horseback. They passed safely through both armies and met Toussaint on the road between Saint Louis and Aquin where Vincent reported to Toussaint the failure of his mission.

The next day, July twenty-seventh, Dessalines moved through Saint Louis and occupied Cavaillon, the administrative capital of the South.

In Les Cayes, Rigaud called upon the inhabitants to fall with the city, to burn it down and to be buried under its ruins. He had all the buildings in the city coated with tar.

That night, officers more steady-minded took command of the city and stopped Rigaud's patrols from setting it afire.

The next day, Dessalines was reported three leagues from the city. Rigaud said goodbye to the people thronging Government House and the Place d'Arms, and with his family and twenty-four loyal officers, including Pétion, rode to Tiburon. There the party embarked on two ships for Saint Thomas.

The War of Knives was ended; the accusations, the recriminations and the punishments, not yet.

CHAPTER 20
Peace

Toussaint's entry into Les Cayes was marked with the appropriate triumph. Citizens met him at the bridge by the police barracks and escorted him to the church amid the sounds of cannons firing and bells ringing.

Les Cayes was a small city of no more than seven hundred houses, many built on platforms to keep them above the water of the river and irrigation canals. There was none of the bustle of commerce that marked the Cape and Port-au-Prince. Les Cayes was surrounded by the sources of its former prosperity, straight-edged square and rectangular shaped fields lined with irrigation ditches, most now fallow from neglect.

Les Cayes seemed, to Toussaint, as ridiculous as its most famous citizen. Like Rigaud, the city pretended to an importance beyond its nature. How aptly named, he thought. As Rigaud's seat of power it was indeed a reef threatening the ship of state.

In the square before the church, Toussaint was presented a proclamation signed by fifty-two notables praising the Governor-General and condemning Rigaud.

Toussaint was escorted into the crowded church. Upon his entrance the clergy began a te deum of celebration for the city's deliverance. It was a custom now well established by the defeated in Saint-Domingue to propitiate and flatter the victor. Toussaint climbed into the pulpit and made the speech the citizen's of Les Cayes prayed to hear. He forgave all and promised to forget the past. But Toussaint knew he would neither forgive nor forget.

The hypocrisy of those who followed Rigaud infuriated Toussaint. It made him want to hate all mulattos, but he understood too well the folly of judging a man by the color of his skin. It was one man he hated, André Rigaud, and all the fools who sold themselves to Rigaud's madness.

Rigaud was insane. Vincent testified to it. Toussaint could not comprehend what drove sane men to follow an insane man into war. He could not understand a Pétion deserting to serve under a Caligula, nor Beauvais playing Seneca to Rigaud's Nero. But however little he understood Rigaud's power over men, Toussaint knew that those still loyal to the ridiculous, ostentatious jackanapes formed a canker that threatened Toussaint's life and the stability of the colony.

From Les Cayes Toussaint issued several proclamations to all the citizens of the South. He declared the war ended. He promised peace and prosperity to all faithful to France and to France's government in Saint-Domingue. He called for all to return to their homes and to their work.

When he finished his official duties, Toussaint turned to a personal task.

Toussaint's father—Gaou Guinou—before he was captured in Africa and sold into slavery, married with the daughter of the King of the Aygas, a kindred tribe to the Aradas. He had two children from that union. They were sold into slavery with their father. One of those children survived. Toussaint had never met his half-sister, Genevieve, but he knew of her and that she lived in Les Cayes.

Toussaint rode to the modest house on Rue Traverfiere. His entourage filled the wide street and blocked all other traffic. Concerned that his sister not be frightened, he insisted upon walking to the door alone, despite the misgivings of the commander of his guard. Genevieve opened the door before Toussaint could knock. She paused only a moment before embracing her brother. Then embarrassed, she pulled back.

"Your Excellency," she apologized, her head slightly bowed.

"No," Toussaint said, and embraced her again.

Genevieve was in her early sixties, five years at least older than Toussaint. She was shorter than he, heavier. Her hair, mostly covered by a colorful handkerchief, was gray. She was nervous at meeting her famous half-brother. Toussaint was moved that in her face he saw the broad forehead and alert eyes of his father.

There were only the two of them in the room. Toussaint refused her offers of food. She obeyed, nervously, his request that she sit and talk with him. He wanted to know about her, why she had not written to him, what he could do to make her life more comfortable.

Genevieve was slow to open to her brother, but with his encouragement she explained that she had been frightened to contact him. She had three children by a white merchant named Chancy. He fled with the English and she heard that he had died of fever in Jamaica. She had felt that her life was in danger often: before the Revolution because she lived openly with a white man; when the English invaded because she was Toussaint's half-sister; when the English retreated because Chancy went with them; during the War of Knives because of the hatred in Les Cayes for Toussaint. Now she was frightened for her children because of Toussaint's hatred for mulattos.

Toussaint assured her he did not hate mulattos. He told her of me, that Suzanne had been with child by a mulatto when he married her and that he loved me as well as he did his natural children.

Genevieve cried. Toussaint embraced her. He asked her where her children were and how he might help them. Through her tears she told him that her daughters, Victorine and Louise, had fled Les Cayes. She did not know where they were, or even if they were alive.

"And you have a son," Toussaint reminded her.

"Yes."

"Where is he?" Toussaint asked most gently. He thought perhaps that the son might have been killed in the War of Knives and that she might hold him responsible.

After some moments of crying, she was able to tell Toussaint, hesitantly, that her son, Bernard, was upstairs. Toussaint feared that Bernard might be wounded or crippled.

"Why does he not come down to meet me?" Toussaint asked.

"He is afraid."

"Of me?"

"Yes."

"Why?"

Genevieve did not answer. She began again to cry.

The realization came to Toussaint. "He fought with Rigaud," he said.

"Yes," Genevieve replied hesitantly.

Toussaint smiled, and then laughed. He reached out for his sister and pulled her to him in a bear hug.

"The war is over," he said. "I have forgiven all who fought against me."

"We were afraid," Genevieve tried to explain. "He was your nephew."

"Call him down," Toussaint said with a smile. "Let me see the traitor in my family!"

Genevieve hesitated, not certain that Toussaint was joking.

"Call him down," Toussaint repeated. "I want to see him," he insisted.

Bernard was a slight young man in his late twenties. He was dressed in the white trousers and shirt of a field hand.

Toussaint took him by the hand and then pulled him into an embrace.

"So you are the young man who would have shot me if he could have," Toussaint teased him.

"No, I would never have shot you," Bernard replied earnestly.

"Why are you not in your uniform?" Toussaint asked.

Bernard glanced at his mother.

"Go, put it on," Toussaint directed. "I will wait for you. You will go with me. I will assign you to my headquarters."

While Bernard was changing, Toussaint questioned Genevieve for more information about her daughters. He promised her that he would find them and take them to Desachaux were they would be educated.

On the bright, sunny, Wednesday morning of August twenty-seventh, 1800, Toussaint participated in a celebration of peace in Léogane.

Léogane is a small town, hardly five blocks square. During the War of Knives it had swelled with tents and temporary cailles built to house the soldiers who passed through on their way South. The city was old. As an European settlement it was almost as old as Santo Domingo City. Before the Europeans, it was the royal city of the Xaragua, the home of the Carib chief Behechio and his sister Anacaona.

The service celebrating peace was held in the ancient church of Saint Jacques. It was crowded with the notables of Port-au-Prince, Léogane and the ports of the north shore of the Bay of Gonave. Toussaint and his officers—emblazoned in their colorful uniforms with gold and silver epaulettes and plumed tricorn hats, their every step accented by the jangling of gilded sabers hanging from jewelled sabretaches and silver spurs from high-topped boots—entered in solemn procession behind the clerics. The soft, cool air of the vaulted church was filled with the silver toned quavers of the rattle, the perfume of the spiraling censor and the hoary voice of the chanting priest. Embracing all—celebrants, priests and church—were the deep tremolos of the organ and the grave pealing of the great bells.

After the te deum, Toussaint, as was his custom, climbed into the pulpit and spoke. He exhorted all, soldiers, civilians and clerics to join in a union of hearts in giving praise to God in heaven for bringing peace at last to Saint-Domingue.

At the end of his remarks he called Henri Christophe and Jean-Jacques Dessalines to come forward. When they stood before the pulpit—the short, muscular general and the tall, large-chested colonel—Toussaint announced that in recognition of their courage, loyalty and accomplishments, he was promoting Christophe to general of brigade and Dessalines from general of brigade to general of division.

At the conclusion of the celebration, the priest performed the first reading of the banns announcing the betrothal of Claire Marie Félicitè Heureuse Bonheur of Léogane to Jean Jacques Dessalines of Grande Rivière du Nord.

That night, Dessalines held a celebration of installation to his new rank. Present were the officers of his division, friends—including Claire Heureuse—and Dessalines's mentor, Toussaint Louverture.

At his installation, Dessalines made a speech. He declared that the war just ended was a small war. There were two wars to come that would test the mettle of each of them. The Spanish had insulted the Governor-General and must be punished: Santo Domingo must fall to Toussaint. And the French, after they were freed from their enemies in Europe, would return to put the blacks back into the chains of slavery. Dessalines vowed that every officer and soldier in the army of Saint-Domingue would fight to the death to defend the island, and they would prevail as free men.

Dessalines did not say that he meant only the black and mulatto officers and soldiers. He did not trust the whites to fight against France. He knew there would be no whites in his army at Armageddon.

Toussaint was uneasy about Dessalines's speech. Toussaint had every intention of taking the Spanish colony, but not with Napoléon's commissioners looking over his shoulder. Toussaint knew the battle would come with France, but he did not want the whites in the island alarmed. He still needed them. They were essential to his administration and to the development of the economy.

The morning after Dessalines's installation, Toussaint met with his new general of division. The meeting was strained. Toussaint wanted the Rigaudians purged.

"May not each man be judged on his own merits?" Dessalines asked.

"I want no trials," Toussaint insisted. "I want the threat to my life and to this government ended, and I want it ended quickly and without confusion."

Dessalines had no difficulty killing. But he did not enjoy killing brave men. He admired courage. Throughout the War of Knives he was moved by the courage of the Southerners. He wished such men served him.

When Dessalines left Toussaint that morning, he knew he would obey Toussaint's instructions, but he knew also that he would recruit to his army every Southern officer and soldier willing to serve under him. When the war with France came, he would need those men fighting beside him, not buried in graves of revenge.

Before Dessalines could begin his campaign to save the Southern soldiers, Toussaint gave orders to the local military commanders to execute all military prisoners in the jails of Léogane and Port-au-Prince. Three hundred were killed in Léogane and fifty, mostly officers, were bayoneted in a wood behind the hospital in Port-au-Prince.

Both cities had close family ties with the men in Rigaud's army. The executions personally touched many. Borgella, the mayor of Port-au-Prince whose own son fled with Rigaud, asked for an audience with Toussaint.

"The executions are creating panic," Borgella explained.

"What executions?" Toussaint asked.

"In Léogane and here. The executions of the military prisoners."

Toussaint denied any knowledge of the executions and promised he would find out who committed them and see that they were stopped.

The next day as Toussaint prepared to ride north from Port-au-Prince, a black woman pushed her way past his guards and threw herself at his feet.

"I beg for mercy, Excellency," she cried.

Toussaint stooped and helped the woman to her feet.

"Mercy for whom?" he asked. "Why do you ask mercy from me?"

"It is not for me, Excellency. It is for a soldier."

"What soldier?" he asked

She explained that in the morning before dawn, when she was buying milk for her family, she discovered a mulatto officer. He was lying beside the wood behind the church. Attackers had stabbed him through with a bayonet and left him for dead, but he had crawled to the side of the road where she discovered him.

Toussaint insisted that she bring the man to him and sent soldiers with her to assist. They carried the officer on a chair to Toussaint. The man was stripped to the waist and had a rough bandage wrapped around his chest where he had been pierced through on the left side.

Toussaint was horrified by the man's suffering and ordered his own doctor to tend him. Toussaint praised the woman for her compassion and ordered Bernard Chancy to see that she got money to help her care for the wounded man until he recovered.

On the ride to Saint Marc, Toussaint, as usual, outdistanced most of his entourage. He was troubled by the events in Port-au-Prince. He could not bear to see the suffering of men wounded or dying. He struggled in himself to counterman his order to Dessalines but could not strike from his mind the sounds of the bullets whistling past his head at Gros Morne, or the sight of his friend bleeding in the coach beside him.

When Toussaint reached Saint Marc, a heavy storm darkened the sky. The wind blew the rain in sheets. Toussaint's mood was as foul as the weather. Dessalines had executed none of the six hundred prisoners in the city.

"Do it now!" Toussaint commanded.

For the next three days, the rains continued and each day Dessalines marched units of the prisoners to the beach and executed them by musket and bayonet. He offered to save all who would enlist under him. Many accepted, but many chose death.

Before the executions ended in Saint Marc, Toussaint rode on to Gonaïves. He could not bear to hear the sounds of the muskets.

At Gonaïves he found seventy-two mulattos in the jail, most of whom were from the North or West and had been arrested for plotting against Toussaint's life. He had them marched beyond hearing distance of the city and shot. Eight officers from Rigaud's army were marched to the beach and offered their lives if they would denounce Rigaud. Instead they cursed Toussaint. They were tied to cannons and torn apart by grapeshot.

When he could hide from the executions, Toussaint was exhilarated by peace. Saint-Domingue was his, now. He rode through the colony from Jérémie to Saltrou, from the Môle to Fort Liberté, from Port-de-Paix to Jacmel. All was his.

Toussaint traveled accompanied by his entourage: his German musicians and French secretaries, his notaries and petit administrators, his cooks and valets, and his honor guard of two thousand. He dressed his guard—his royal guard, infantry and cavalry—in the fleur de lis, and white and gold uniforms reminiscent of King Louis.

Toussaint gave short notice of his arrival at a city or district. Heralds rode before him and announced the coming of the Governor-General. Toussaint and his entourage arrived soon after. He set up court, heard complaints, summoned defendants and witnesses, rendered judgments, bestowed rewards, delegated, instructed, cajoled, encouraged, gathered up his entourage and moved to another setting.

Toussaint enjoyed the adulation of his people. He knew they would not follow a leader who did not inspire respect and awe. He knew also that if they did not follow him they would fall back into slavery. He needed their confidence and adulation. They needed his vision and courage.

Toussaint respected strong leaders: Louis XIV, the Roman emperors, the English King George. He distrusted democracy. He witnessed the madness of the people in the French Revolution; he saw the vacillation and bigotry of the Americans. A strong leader guided by law and followed by willing subjects was the only hope for a people threatened by each shift of the wind.

Dessalines, obeying Toussaint's orders, swept through the South identifying officers who served Rigaud.

His path took him to Léogane, where he visited once again with Claire Heureuse.

Claire was distraught. "Why do you do it?" she demanded of Dessalines.

"I am ordered," he replied.

"You cannot kill men because you are ordered," she insisted.

"I am a soldier. I follow orders."

"I did not want to marry you until the war ended..." Claire began.

"Because you were afraid I would be killed," Dessalines reminded her.

"And because I did not want to live with a man whose occupation was killing other men," Claire added angrily.

Dessalines smiled easily. "If I am not prepared to kill, there are those who soon would kill me," he explained.

"I am troubled," Claire replied. "I feel great pain that you kill whomever Toussaint tells you to. That is not war. It is murder."

"I kill no man. I give each the choice to live or die. Those who die choose death. I am not Toussaint's slave. We have a difficult task. Toussaint knows, and I know, that soon we will fight for our lives."

Claire shuddered. Before she could speak, Dessalines pressed his fingers to her lips.

"When the French come," he continued, "we will have difficulty with the whites who now profess loyalty to us. We must not have other enemies behind us, ready to stab us in the back, enemies who persist in the illusion that because they are light-skinned and their fathers were not slaves the French would not enslave them, enemies who hope even to enrich themselves from our misfortune."

"How is Toussaint any better than the French if he kills men because their skin is lighter than his?" Claire persisted.

Dessalines smiled again. "I am not interested in who is morally superior. I am interested only in living—as a free man."

During the end of summer and the beginning of fall in 1800 Toussaint saw his subjects slipping from him. Wherever he traveled he sensed fear in the people.

Toussaint summoned Dessalines.

"The executions must stop," Toussaint instructed his general.

"As you command," Dessalines replied.

"I said to prune the tree," Toussaint explained, "not uproot it."

CHAPTER 21
The Island Unified

At the end of the summer of 1800, the British sent a new agent to serve at Port-au-Prince. The agent informed Toussaint that in the summer Napoléon had dispatched a flotilla of ships for Saint-Domingue, but the British navy had sent them limping back into French ports. Toussaint knew he must secure his power throughout the island before France and England made peace and he would not have the British navy to protect him from Napoléon's army.

Toussaint delayed invading Santo Domingo until he strengthened his position in Saint-Domingue. He exhorted the citizens to renew their efforts, the managers and leaders to organize and plan, the laborers to return to the habitations, the fathers and mothers to raise their children in the fear of God, the military commanders to be vigilant.

Toussaint established new, harsher penalties for disobedience, fines for concealing workers, reduction in grade for military laxness. Women were prohibited from the barracks. Everyone had his assigned task: military, administrator, manager, merchant and worker. The prosperity of all depended on the obedience of each.

In October the island was devastated by a hurricane. Much of the work of the summer was destroyed by the winds and flooding. Factories and refineries were washed away. Workers were drowned. Most of he destruction was centered in the fertile valley of the Artibonite.

Toussaint rushed aid to the stricken areas. He devised means of financially compensating proprietors for their loses. He himself braved the floods and winds to visit the distressed.

Following the disaster, Toussaint concentrated on governmental reform. He reorganized the government to respond more readily to emergencies and to eliminate graft and waste. He did away with the overlapping layers of administration, had an inventory made of the colony's resources, and reformed the monetary system. To improve trade, he reduced import duties and organized a maritime police force to stop smuggling. He removed the names of dishonest merchants from the customhouse list and had dishonest custom officials tried before military tribunals.

To take the people's minds off the executions of the summer and the storms of the fall, Toussaint organized fêtes in the cities. He participated in many. In late November he participated in one at the Cape. The celebration was similar to others, with music, speeches—comparing Toussaint to Bacchus, Hercules, Alexander the Great and Napoléon—and pledges of fidelity to his government.

The next day, Toussaint summoned Julien Raimond to Government House. Toussaint stood when Raimond was ushered into the room and remained standing for the interview. A secretary recorded the conversation.

"I have given instructions to General Moïse to arrest Commissioner Roume," Toussaint began. "Commissioner Roume is to be escorted to Dondon where he will be with his family. He will not be harmed, but he will be under house arrest. I have given General Moïse specific instructions not to injure nor embarrass the commissioner." Toussaint wanted Raimond to understand there would be no repeat of the charade of the past March.

"What do you want from me, your Excellency?" Raimond asked.

"I want you to serve the colony as Administrator of National Estates."

"If you think I have the capability, I will serve where you need me," Raimond replied. "But I do not understand what my appointment has to do with Roume's arrest. Since the two appear to be linked in your mind, I would appreciate understanding your thoughts."

"Many will think I arrested Roume because he will not authorize the annexation of Santo Domingo," Toussaint began.

"I am of that opinion," Raimond responded.

"Partially, perhaps. But when I am ready to move against the Spanish, I will move with or without Roume's permission."

"I have no doubt that you will," Raimond agreed.

"My quarrel with Roume is more serious," Toussaint continued. "An agent of André Rigaud in Cuba writes passports for followers of Rigaud who wish to return to Saint-Domingue. I have asked repeatedly for Roume to deny entry to men with such passports. He defies me. I have asked him to track down Rigaud's agents provocateur who have illegally entered the colony. Roume refuses me. The French desire to divide the rule of this colony continues, and I must believe that Roume is a conspirator in the effort."

Raimond began to understand the connection.

"You want me to serve as Administrator of Estates because I am mulatto," he said.

"Yes," Toussaint responded without pause, "and because you are an able administrator, and an honest one."

There was silence between the two men for a few moments. Raimond evaluated his position. Before he responded, Toussaint continued.

"I intend to hunt down Rigaud's agents. Many will say it is because I hate mulattos. It is not so. Any who know me know I surround myself with able men, whatever their color. My oldest son is mulatto. Many of my generals are mulattos, as are many of my administrators and secretaries. I offer you this appointment because you are able and because—I will not lie to you—I want to show that I do not discriminate against men of color who are loyal."

Raimond did not need time to make his decision.

"I accept, your Excellency. My desire is to serve your government how and where I can."

As Raimond prepared to exit, Toussaint stopped him, and, as if as an afterthought, asked him if he would serve on a special commission.

"I am going to call for a central assembly to write a set of laws for the colony, laws needed for the peace and prosperity of the island. I would be pleased if you would stand for election to the assembly."

"It would be my honor, Excellency."

As Raimond walked to his house he was light headed with elation. Toussaint wanted the assembly to create a constitution, the first step to independence. The issues of independence or colony were moot to him. The thrill was in being a part of history. He saw himself as a Thomas Jefferson, a Jean-Paul Marat or an Emmanuel Sieyes. He might hang for it, but with his mind and his pen, Raimond would leave his mark on history.

———————◆———————

In the middle of December, Toussaint had exhausted his patience with Roume and Don Garcia, the Governor of Santo Domingo, and began his armed annexation of the Spanish half of the island. Toussaint acquiesced to his nephew's entreaties and allowed Moïse to lead the invasion from the north.

At the same time that Moïse marched on Santo Domingo City from the north following in reverse the route Hédouville took two years earlier, Toussaint sent an army led by his brother Paul from Port-au-Prince along the southern coast toward the Spanish capital. Toussaint stayed at the Cape for several weeks from where he sent dispatches to Don Garcia requesting his cooperation. Toussaint hoped his presence at the Cape would conceal from the Spanish the speed of the invasion and allow his armies to occupy Santo Domingo without resistance. Toussaint wanted to avoid casualties on both sides.

Shortly after Christmas, a French man-of-war slipped through the English blockade and landed at the Cape. As was his custom, Toussaint had the vessel quarantined until he understood the nature of its visit. From the quarantine officer, Toussaint learned that the captain of the ship carried dispatches for Toussaint from the Consulate in Paris. Toussaint guessed that the dispatches contained new instructions prohibiting him from taking control of Santo Domingo, and he left the Cape before the dispatches could be delivered to him.

The captain of the ship, when he was released from quarantine, followed after Toussaint for three days, but was unable to find him and deliver his dispatches.

Toussaint put himself at the head of the forces advancing along the southern coast. He wanted the annexation accomplished as quickly as possible.

The major resistance to the occupation was organized by the mulattos who had fled to the east earlier to escape Toussaint's wrath. The Spanish made but one effort to stop him, at the River Nisao southwest of Santo Domingo City. Toussaint easily broke their defense and sent them in disorder back to the capital.

On January nineteenth, 1801, Don Garcia surrendered and requested terms from Toussaint.

On January twenty-sixth, Toussaint arrived in Santo Domingo City on the ship "Cabildo." He landed at the foot of the fortress above which, from the Moorish-looking Tower of Homage, the French tricolor now flew. As Toussaint climbed the stone stairs to the fortress yard, the cannons of the fort exploded in a twenty-two-gun salute which was echoed by the French ships laid-to outside the harbor.

Toussaint was met in the fortress yard by a delegation of military and municipal leaders and escorted through the modern gates of the fort, north on Calle Las Damas—the first European street in the new world—to the royal houses, where in the Sala Capitular of the Royal Court of Appeals, Don Garcia, and his officers waited for him.

Don Garcia invited Toussaint to take the oath to the Holy Trinity, a custom for all governors of Santo Domingo. The oath was to be administered by the rector of the Primate Cathedral of America. Toussaint refused. He represented the Republic of France, he explained, and it would not be appropriate for him to take the oath of a Spanish governor. But he promised, before God, to forget the past and to make the people of Santo Domingo secure and content.

Don Garcia, before Toussaint's arrival in the Sala Capitular, had placed the symbolic keys to the city on a table. Don Garcia now invited Toussaint to take the keys. Toussaint refused.

"Hand them to me," Toussaint instructed. "I do not come as an enemy to steal the city. I come as its rightful governor."

Don Garcia, with great reluctance, obeyed.

Toussaint spent several weeks in Santo Domingo. He oversaw the reorganization of the government to conform to that of Saint-Domingue. He appointed both French and Spanish to administrative posts. He promoted his brother Paul to general of brigade and made him military commander of the district.

Toward the end of February Toussaint left the city and rode through the countryside. He was moved by the misery of the people and angered by the sloth and waste in agriculture. The peasants lived in small villages. They were mostly naked, ill, eating only yams and potatoes. He found the people gentle, religious, strongly moral but without leaders. There was no government administration, no police.

Everywhere in the colony the plantations were in disarray, producing only food for domestic consumption. The sugar refineries were neglected and decaying. The Spanish, seeking all possible profit before Toussaint's annexation, had cut deeply into the mahogany forests, hauling out only the largest logs for market, leaving smaller, but valuable, pieces to rot. In places entire forests had been destroyed.

Toussaint sent instructions to his administrators to alleviate the suffering of the people, to control and encourage the development of agriculture, and to halt the exploitation of the forests. He instructed that each community have a local police force housed, mounted and paid by the community but armed by the central government. He ordered that the Spanish proprietors raise sugar, coffee, cotton and cocoa for export, and cease growing only potatoes, bananas and yams, for which there was no market. He prohibited logging in threatened areas, prohibited entirely the exporting of mahogany and called for reforestation.

Two events in March encouraged Toussaint that he would be able to bring his plans for the island to fruition. The Colonial Assembly met to establish a constitution for the colony, and priests sympathetic to the Revolution arrived from France.

On March twenty-second, the Colonial Assembly met in Port-au-Prince. Toussaint opened the session and then left it to its work.

The ten members of the Assembly, although elected from each district, were chosen to please Toussaint. Among the ten were Julien Raimond and Bernard Borgella, the little Mayor of Port-au-Prince. All but Raimond were white. All were sympathetic to Toussaint's government and some, including Borgella, actively pressed for independence as a solution to the colony's problems.

The major business of the Assembly, writing the Constitution, was completed before the Assembly met. Pascal, Julien Raimond's secretary, wrote a draft. Raimond and Bernard Borgella rewrote the draft.

The Constitution gave Toussaint what he wanted. It accepted his leadership for life with the right to appoint his successor. It gave him authority over all aspects of government, civil as well as military. It established the colony's economic autonomy without declaring the colony's independence from France.

In March, Catholic priests sympathetic to the Revolution arrived in Saint-Domingue. Toussaint greeted them with enthusiasm. His efforts to establish the Catholic Church as the state religion had been frustrated by secular authorities who followed the dictates of the Revolution in suppressing all religions, and by the conservative priests who rejected all secular law and recognized only the authority of Rome.

Toussaint had written to Henri Grégoire in France and begged for his assistance. Grégoire was a priest who supported the Revolution and, as a delegate to the Estates-General and the National Assembly, fought for the emancipation and suffrage of the slaves. Grégoire broke with Rome, took the oath to the Civil Constitution of the Clergy and was appointed the Constitutional Bishop of Blois. Grégoire, after months of delay and confusion, responded to Toussaint's request. He arranged for the Constitutional Church of France to send sympathetic priests to the colony.

Toussaint, for the first time since he had entered into the struggle for freedom, felt the promise of success. The entire island was under his authority. There was no harbor for his enemies and no undefended beach for England or France to land an invading army. Loyal officers and competent administrators served him. He had the law and the means to build a strong economy and a peaceful, God-fearing society respecting people of all races. He had trade with the United States, and support, however quixotic, from England. He would create a society that embodied the best of the Revolution, one that France would have to respect. Under Toussaint's leadership, Saint-Domingue would be economically vital to France. Napoléon would not dare attack him for fear of the economic and military consequences for France.

The structure was built. The plan was clear. Now Toussaint must inspire the people to greatness and lead them to their place in history.

CHAPTER 22
In Paris

I am certain that every man sees a stranger when he looks back upon his youth, but surely there are few who are more estranged from their past than I. It is difficult for me now to remember my state of mind as a boy in Saint-Domingue and as a youth in Paris.

My memory of slavery is dim. I worked hard, but was treated kindly. My father was a person of importance on the habitation and I basked in his reflection. As a young boy I had some sense that momentous events were shaking the world. But I comprehended little of them. De Libertas, the manager of Bréda, was a leader of Royalist resistance to the Jacobins. His house was often filled with angry proprietors and government officials arguing and plotting the defeat of the Revolution. I knew only that the gentle conditions of my life were dependent on the kindness of de Libertas. I was frightened for the dangers to his life and prayed each night for his safety and for that of his master, King Louis.

In the summer of my eleventh year, the slaves of the Northern Plain rose in rebellion led by the giant houngan Boukman. At Bréda we heard the drums at night and in the morning the stories of the wild rituals in the woods and mountains and the bloody reprisals of Boukman's followers on the whites. The most vivid memory of my life in Saint-Domingue was of my fear that summer.

By force of will Toussaint forbade the blacks at Bréda from harming de Libertas and his wife. Many of the slaves on the habitation, including Moïse, fled to join the rebels. De Libertas came and went, joining with groups of Royalists who alternately battled against the slaves and appealed to them to return to the plantations. On Bréda all work stopped. At night small bands of black men slipped into the cailles to urge the slaves who remained to kill their master and mistress and join Boukman. I hid and watched my father confront the threatening strangers, fearful that they would harm him.

A week after Boukman's rebellion, as the ashes of burning cane blew into the streets of the Cape and onto the ships anchored in the harbor, the white Republicans and Royalists joined in an uneasy truce to confront the threat of the slaves. The killing that followed was indiscriminate on both sides.

I remember sitting all night with the few who remained at Bréda watching the fires burning near Quartier-Morin, across the narrow Haut de Cap River. The next morning, Toussaint sent Madame de Libertas to the safety of the Cape with his brother Paul to protect her on the short ride. He then sent my mother, my nine-year old brother Isaac, my four-year old brother Jean, my grandfather Pierre Baptiste, my grandmother and me with three house slaves that had not fled, to Dajabón and on into the mountains of the Spanish half of the island to seek sanctuary with maroons.

On that long walk, as we passed burning houses and fields, as we hid from the marauding bands of blacks and the white soldiers who pursued them, I felt helpless without my father's strength to protect us. I did not think that we would survive without him to stand between us and the violence that threatened to engulf us. How little I understood what lay ahead, and how few days I would share with him.

For five years we hid while the Spanish, English, French and bands of slaves fought for the land. We saw Toussaint for brief moments only until the French freed the slaves and Toussaint became the assistant to the French Governor-General Laveaux. Then Toussaint moved us to the safety of Desachaux. Shortly after, Isaac and I came to Paris to study. I was sixteen; Isaac fourteen

In Paris we were sequestered at the College de la Marche, where the sons of Creoles studied. The College was unique. Nowhere else did the sons of white, mulatto and black men live and study together.

In the beginning, life as a student in Paris was exhilarating. Around us swirled the kaleidoscope of the greatest city in the world. Within our little college we learned of the past, debated the future and fought about the present. The passions of the Revolution and the politics of Saint-Domingue engaged us daily. Our microcosm shifted and twisted with each letter from home. The difference was, we fought with words and occasionally fists, never guns or bayonets.

When Napoléon came to power, Isaac and I were several times invited by Josephine to visit her at Malmasion. She told us that she was grateful for the kindness Toussaint showed her in caring for her mother's property near Léogane, and that she wished to return his kindness by seeing to our well being in Paris. We were flattered by her attention and enjoyed the prestige it gave us among our peers.

Our college master was the Abbé Coison, a man uniquely qualified for the position. He served the Church in Saint-Domingue before the Revolution and returned to Paris an avid Royalist. The Revolution first shook then reaffirmed his faith in God. He never tired of telling his students of his conversion, and each year he adapted his story to the changing fortunes of France. On February fourth, 1801, as was his want, Father Coison lectured to us on the emancipation.

"What happened this day in 1794?" he began.

We answered collectively, "The emancipation!"

Then he launched into his story.

"It happened at a time when I was in the very depths of despair. The wanton destruction of the Revolution had convinced me that Armageddon had come, but Antichrist was in the victory saddle. When the madmen took the life of our dear King Louis and his gracious Queen, I was brought to such despair, that I, like Job, almost cursed God. I resisted even walking abroad in the city because everywhere I saw evidence upon evidence of the defeat of God and His Church.

"Then, on a bitter cold day, while I was hurrying to the cathedral, Abbé Grégoire called to me from across the street. We were not closely acquainted, but we knew one another. He was not a man whose company I sought. He had left his parish and had come to Paris to join with the Jacobins, and as a Jacobin he was elected to the Assembly. I could not understand how a man of God could neglect his Christian duties and join with the enemies of the Church.

"'Father Coison,' Grégoire called to me, 'If you would see the hand of God at work, come with me.'

"As though I were not my own master, I went with him. I was in such despair, if the Devil himself had appeared before me and offered to show me the hand of God, I would have followed.

"Grégoire brought me to the Chamber of Deputies. At his direction I seated myself in the gallery while he took his seat in the raised section of the floor where the Mountain, those fanatical followers of Robespierre and Danton, sat.

"Finally I began to understand the reason for Grégoire's excitement. A new delegation from Saint-Domingue was being accredited by the Convention, and the leader of the delegation was a black man, the first to appear before the Convention. When he appeared the proceedings were interrupted by applause upon applause. Finally the chairman of the committee of decrees, I believe it was, got the president's attention and moved the delegation's admission. Someone else demanded that the delegation receive the president's fraternal embrace, which was done to more applause, thunderous approval, in fact.

"Finally the black man, Bellay was his name, was recognized to speak. What a speaker he was! The gifts of oratory that God bestowed upon Moses's brother Aaron must have descended in our time upon this humble black man, a man, like Aaron, born into slavery. It is not possible for a man to move his listeners to greater rapture than this former slave moved the Convention."

"Do you remember his words?" Isaac asked. Bellay's speech was our favorite part of the story, but we were always disappointed by how little of the speech Father Coison remembered.

"Not totally," Coison answered. "But the words alone are pale echoes of the speech itself. As Bellay rose to speak, tears filled his eyes. He spoke of those tears as being shed both for the kindness of his welcome and the pain he felt for the suffering of his island. He showed us the scars of slavery upon his face and back, but he swore he spoke not in reproach for what had been, but rather in hope of the promise of what must be. He spoke of the glory of the Revolution and of the pride and happiness that the blacks of Saint-Domingue felt as Frenchmen because the Revolution with its promise of liberty, equality and fraternity for all men had come, by the grace of God, from France.

"Then, in the most moving of words, he called upon the Convention to erase the last barrier to man's dignity, to remove the final reminder of man's inhumanity, to abolish for all time that abominable institution which claims both master and chattel as its victims—slavery.

"When he finished speaking, there was silence. Some, especially the delegates from the maritime provinces, no doubt would have liked to have offered rebuttal, but the power of the speaker intimidated all who heard him. Finally, one of Robespierre's followers rose and called for the Convention to recognize without debate the liberty of the blacks. The delegates exploded into a fury of agreement.

"Close to where I was sitting, a black woman watching the proceedings swooned from the excitement. As those of us in the area were looking to her comfort, one of the delegates demanded that she be admitted to the floor. The motion was approved by acclamation. The woman was led to the front of the chamber to sit at the president's left. Other resolutions followed recognizing the freedom of the slaves and instructing the Ministry of Marine to so inform the colonies."

When Father Coison reached this point in his story, we sat in silence, partially in respect for the momentous events of that day, and partly in anticipation of the moral we knew would follow.

"Until that day," Coison continued, "I had accepted politics as being of the things of Caesar and had seen in it nothing of the hand of God. When men spoke to me of the cruelties of slavery, I answered that what happens in this world is of little matter if only our souls are saved in the eternal world to come. The years I spent in Saint-Domingue I labored to save the souls of the slaves and was blind to their carnal misery. I even argued that the slave, through his suffering, was closer to the Kingdom of God than the master who languished in his wealth and ease. But when I heard Bellay speak, I knew Grégoire was correct. The hand of God was touching that place and this nation. The suffering of our dear King, the agonies of the Church, the despair of the people, were all part of our atonement for the cruelties of slavery. The Revolution was truly a foretaste of Armageddon and Christ was to be victorious. 'Suffer no evil to befall the least of these my children.'

"The proof was soon to come. With this, the last act of the Revolution, order was restored. The agents of the Devil, Robespierre and Danton, fell victims to their own infernal machine, and,"—Coison added as his reflections on the new year—"finally today, from the very army of the Revolution, Napoléon Bonaparte arises to bring order and glory to France and restores once again God's Holy Church to its rightful place in the leadership of the nation."

"It is the same with father," Isaac interrupted. He found it necessary to defend our father from every imagined slight.

"Yes," Coison agreed. "In France, Napoléon Bonaparte. In Saint-Domingue, Toussaint Louverture, the black Napoléon. And it is proper where once the white man led by force and torture, Toussaint now leads by precept and example."

Young André Rigaud rose in anger to dispute Coison's allegation, but the Abbé silenced him, and to avoid further dissension quickly ended his lecture. "We are blessed indeed to have lived to see the new century, a century of great promise for France and for all mankind. Truly we move closer to the millennium forecast in Revelation."

Our father wrote several times to Napoléon asking that Isaac and I be allowed to return to Saint-Domingue. We knew of the letters because Josephine told us of them. With each request, we hoped to return to our home and were always disappointed when Napoléon insisted that we remain in France.

In the summer of 1800, Napoléon acquiesced to Toussaint's requests and instructed me to sail with a flotilla of ships for Saint-Domingue. I was led to believe that the ships brought reinforcements to aid Toussaint in his efforts to pacify the island. I was assigned as aide-de-camp to the commanding general, Sahuguet, to serve as liaison between him and my father. I was delighted by the assignment. But on board ship I learned that the British fleet blocked our way to the West Indies. We turned, instead, to Egypt, to raise the siege there. But there, too, the British fleet stopped us, and we returned to France and I to my studies.

In April of 1801, André Rigaud reached Paris, nine months after he left Saint-Domingue. His journey was delayed when an American man-of-war captured his ship and he was imprisoned until after France and the United States signed the Treaty of Morfontaine.

Rigaud sought an interview with Napoléon to tell the First Consul of the disasters in Saint-Domingue. Rigaud complained that he had been betrayed by Toussaint and abandoned by France, that he was not to blame for the massacres in the island.

Napoléon paid little attention to Rigaud's tale of despair. The First Consul lacked patience with men who lost and burdened others with excuses for their own shortcomings. Napoléon's mind was on other things.

Regarding Toussaint Louverture, Napoléon did not lack for advice. Hédouville, Sonthonax, the former planters who fled the island, the merchants of the maritime provinces who wanted the slave trade restored, all argued that Toussaint was the greatest obstacle to France's future in the West Indies. Others, Roume, Raimond, Vincent, argued that Toussaint was devoted to France and that his arrogant behavior was motivated by his fear that France would restore slavery.

The voices of shortsighted hirelings, tradesmen and military factotums did not persuade Napoléon. Not even the voice of Josephine persuaded Napoléon—the voice that flattered Isaac and me with lies of her admiration for our father while it begged Napoléon to restore to her islands the slave culture of her youth. Napoléon's vision was larger, more grand than anyone at the time imagined.

Napoléon knew that France was his. In time he was destined to be its king, its emperor. An emperor needed an empire to support his grandeur. Before 1801 Napoléon looked to the East for his empire, to Egypt and beyond to India. He had failed in his first attempt to take India three years earlier when Junot threw away the French fleet at the Bay of Abukir and left Napoléon's army trapped in its victory. But in the fall of 1800 Czar Paul invited Napoléon to join Russia in taking India. They would divide India and in the process destroy the British fleet. Then the Channel would be unguarded. Then Napoléon could invade England when he wished and take for himself the rest of the British empire. With such riches, Napoléon would have no need for Saint-Domingue. The blacks had destroyed the island's economy. Let them keep it. It would be no loss to France.

But then, only weeks before Rigaud's interview, Czar Paul was murdered by his son and Russia was closed to Napoléon. In Bonaparte's mind, it was an English plot. It was Pitt's doing. Napoléon was not fooled by Pitt's resignation before the assassination. It was part of the plot, to keep suspicion from England.

Napoléon's three-years' dream of possessing India was lost. But even before it was lost, another dream replaced it: the Empire of the Americas.

Napoléon never trusted to one plan only. Less than three months before he signed the treaty with Paul of Russia, Napoléon secretly traded a slice of Italy to Spain for a third of North America: the Floridas and the Louisiana Territory. India was a shorter route to riches, but America would do. The key to the Empire of the Americas, Napoléon knew, was Saint-Domingue. It sat at the center, between France's possessions in South America and the West Indies and the new territories acquired from Spain. In Saint-Domingue were harbors to protect Napoléon's fleet and a ready supply of slaves to work his fields.

Napoléon had no intention of allowing Toussaint Louverture to stand between France and its destiny. When Napoléon had his peace with England, and he would have it. The English grew weary of war and many voices called for accommodation with France. When Napoléon had his peace with England, he would chasten the black rogues of Saint-Domingue.

CHAPTER 23
The Constitution

When Toussaint returned to Saint-Domingue from Santo Domingo, he discovered that unrest was wide spread among the laborers. The unrest was particularly evident in the Northern Plain. Toussaint summoned Moïse to Government House at the Cape.

Toussaint had no patience with Moïse's argument that the life of a laborer was little better now than it had been under slavery.

"Where are the whips?" Toussaint demanded. "Where are the chains? Who now tears families apart, kills with impunity, profits from the trade in human lives?"

Moïse argued that laborers had no freedom to live where they wished, no choice of employment, no freedom from the oppression of white managers.

"What you say," Toussaint retorted, "is that laborers do not wish to work. If they do not work, we will all starve. In Toussaint's Saint-Domingue no man is denied advancement because of the color of his skin. If a laborer wishes to better himself, then let him work harder and persuade his colleagues to work harder. If the habitation owner earns more from the land, then the worker earns more. If the worker wishes to advance himself, then let him learn to read and write. Let him learn his numbers. Let him learn to follow instructions!"

———————◆———————

Toussaint discovered that one cause of discontent was white and mulatto landowners who taunted the laborers that under the black Toussaint they were no freer than they were under the white King Louis. When Toussaint discovered the culprits, he deported them and appropriated their property.

Moïse argued that the appropriated land should be divided among the laborers on the habitation.

"That is madness!" Toussaint insisted. "If each man had a small plot of land he would produce only what he needed. He would produce nothing for export. If we do not have exports, we have no money for guns and ammunition. If we have no guns and ammunition, we will fall once more into slavery."

Toussaint sold the confiscated property to men wealthy enough to purchase it and strong enough to work it.

In April, trouble erupted once more in the South.

Lamour Derance was the leader of a band of maroons who inhabited the Saddle, the band of mountains which parallel the south coast from Port-au-Prince to the border of Santo Domingo, where the mountains are called the Sierra de Bahoruco.

Derance was a small, dark, muscular man with the broad features of the Congo black. His bearing and lithe movements belied his sixty years. He dressed in mixed remnants of uniforms, but when presiding over the governing council of his maroon nation, he wore the red jacket of a British major whom he had killed in battle.

When he was forty, Derance was brought from Africa to Saint-Domingue and sold to a planter in the Cul-de-Sac. He waited patiently for his moment, and when finally he was released from his leg irons, he stole by night into the mountains.

After the Revolution, Derance allied with Beauvais who recognized the independence of the maroons. When Dessalines besieged Jacmel, Derance harassed Dessalines's forces until he learned that Beauvais had fled the island. Then Derance withdrew to his mountain sanctuary and waited. When Rigaud fled, six companies of the Southern army enlisted with Derance.

When Toussaint's harsh regulations created unrest among the black laborers, Derance harassed the habitations near his mountains and recruited from the laborers. The sounds of the African rituals celebrated by the mountain dwellers attracted other workers. In April of 1801, Derance was strong enough to attack. He launched a campaign against Marigot, on the south coast east of Jacmel, and occupied the city.

Infuriated, Dessalines marched on Marigot and retook it. He sent a force to track Derance to his lair. Less than a third of Dessalines' force of three hundred returned—without Derance.

In the North, the established priests considered the new priests sent by Grégoire schismatics and refused to associate with them. Toussaint deported the old priests.

Concerned for the growing debauchery in the island, Toussaint closed all the houses of pleasure in the Cape and Port-au-Prince. Prostitution and gambling were outlawed. Offenders were fined and imprisoned.

As the field laborers felt the restrictions of Toussaint's harsh regulations, they turned to the African rites for solace and release. Toussaint ordered the military commanders of the districts to suppress the rituals and to execute all houngans apprehended in the act of conducting them.

Dessalines was in a quandary. He must obey Toussaint. Dessalines knew that if the voudoun was not stopped, discipline could not be enforced. But Dessalines owed his victories, his promotions and Claire Heureuse to the benefice of the loa. He dared not now offend them.

Seeking guidance, he sent for the houngan in Léogane who had aided him before. Dessalines's messenger returned with the news that when the houngan heard that Dessalines wished to speak with him, he fled.

Dessalines contemplated the omens. Two things stood out in his mind. The houngan had not healed him when he was ill. Claire had. Claire was a Christian and did not believe in the loa. Dessalines sensed that he was at a crossroad. The houngan had fled because he saw in Dessalines's mind things that Dessalines himself had not yet seen.

Dessalines, disciplining his fear, marched against the voudoun wherever he saw it. He struck with ferocity felt only by the converted.

As April ended, Toussaint found it increasingly difficult to meet the costs of his army and to continue to stockpile munitions for the coming war with France. He ordered that a tax of six percent be paid by all on the purchase of food and provisions. He argued that the army was for the protection of all, and everyone should share in its support.

Toussaint exhausted the funds he previously had secreted in Philadelphia buying guns and munitions from the United States. He now squeezed dry the income from customs for the same purpose. The Americans would trade only for hard cash.

Toussaint regretted that Edward Stevens had withdrawn from the island. He had suffered from malaria and a year earlier had returned to the United States. Steven's successor, Tobias Lear, an aristocratic looking, gray-haired gentleman, was all business and had no understanding of Toussaint's circumstances. Perhaps it was because Toussaint had no time to cultivate Lear. Stevens had understood the struggle. Lear understood only dollars.

In May, in an effort to ease the constant discontent he sensed throughout the colony, Toussaint had all the mulatto prisoners from the War of Knives brought to the church at the Cape. He choose the Cape rather than Port-au-Prince for the occasion because he did not wish to summon up memories of his meeting with the mulattos in the cathedral there.

After the te deum, Toussaint spoke warmly to the prisoners and announced, "I pardon you. Return in peace to your families." He had clothes and money distributed to each of them.

In June, Toussaint summed Colonel Vincent to the Cape.

Vincent, having spent most of fifteen years in Saint-Domingue, wished to return to France, but Toussaint delayed him. He was willing to let him go only if Vincent would carry with him to Paris a copy of the new Constitution and explain its necessity to Napoléon.

Vincent agreed. But when he read the Constitution, he tried to persuade Toussaint to proceed with caution so as not to alarm the First Consul.

"I cannot slacken my pace," Toussaint declared. "I am not in control. I am propelled by an occult force which I am helpless to resist." Concerned that Vincent might think he meant he was possessed by the loa, Toussaint quickly added. "I am flying in the realm of angels. I must find my way back to the earth. I must have a rock to stand upon. The Constitution is my rock. With the Constitution I can move again among men. I can govern by law."

When Toussaint announced that the Constitution would be published in July, Vincent was horrified.

"I understand the need for a special set of laws for the colony," Vincent acquiesced. "Napoléon would agree. He foresaw the need in his Constitution for France. But," Vincent argued vehemently, "you must not publish it without approval from France!"

"France does not understand the needs of Saint-Domingue," Toussaint replied.

"Then instruct France," Vincent answered. "But don't defy France."

"I have tried. With Sonthonax, with Hédouville, with Roume, with everyone France has sent, I have tried."

"Publishing the Constitution will not help. Withdraw it from the printer and send a hand written copy to Napoléon for his response."

"The water does not flow back into the spring," Toussaint answered.

"Do you not understand how inflammable your Constitution is?" Vincent continued. "It concentrates all power into your hands. There is no place for France."

"France will send commissioners to speak with me," Toussaint said sarcastically. "They always have. I see no reason for them to stop."

"You mean," Vincent answered with some recklessness, "France is to send you charge d'affaires and ambassadors as the Americans and Spanish will certainly do. And the English!"

"I do not need you to remind me that the English are the most dangerous for me," Toussaint replied angrily. "But they write to me. The King of England sends me messages! The President of the United States sends me letters! Bonaparte does not write to me! Bonaparte does not even acknowledge me! He writes to his enemy, the King of England. But he does not write to Toussaint Louverture, an officer of the French army and the Governor of a French colony!"

Vincent respected Toussaint's anger, but persisted. "As a friend, Excellency. As a friend and servant who has never wavered in loyalty to you, I beg you to withdraw the Constitution."

"You could as well beg me to unanchor this island, sail it across the ocean and grapple it to France," Toussaint replied. "Until France and Saint-Domingue are one land, the Constitution stands."

Toussaint set July seventh as the day of celebration for the new Constitution.

Vincent, desperate to stop Toussaint, turned to Raimond, Moïse and Christophe for help. He tried to persuade them that the Constitution would increase the danger from France.

"When the war with England ends, France must reestablish its authority here," Vincent argued. "If for no other reason, to keep England from snatching it. But Toussaint is wrong to think France desires to reestablish slavery. France can only honor the brave men who fought to keep the colony from England. The mistake," Vincent insisted, "is to give France reason to believe that the blacks intend to create in Saint-Domingue an independent state."

Raimond, already showing signs of the illness which would take his life in a few months, dismissed Vincent's arguments.

"Toussaint is right to suspect Bonaparte," Raimond insisted. "The only problem with the Constitution," he argued, "is that it does not go far enough. In France, the Revolution is dead. Its only hope of survival is in an independent Saint-Domingue."

Moïse no longer knew what his uncle intended. "Toussaint thinks he is already king of Saint-Domingue," Moïse complained. Regarding Vincent's other concerns, Moïse kept his own council. He was pleased that his uncle finally appeared willing to pull free of France, but he found no joy in Toussaint's Constitution.

Christophe was more sympathetic to Vincent's dilemma, but begged ignorance of constitutions.

"I am only a simple soldier," he insisted.

Vincent urged Christophe to persuade Toussaint to withdraw the Constitution.

"The wind does not listen to the trees," Christophe explained.

"As the commander of the Cape," Vincent continued, "you can insure that when the French come they are permitted to land in peace."

"I do not want to see war again in Saint-Domingue," Christophe answered sincerely.

"You will welcome the French?"

"I will do all I can to preserve peace," Christophe agreed. "And now, Colonel, if I may?" Christophe gently pressed the Frenchman away from the curtains to the private dinning room. "I have other matters calling for my attention," he explained, and pushed passed Vincent and into the small alcove where a young white woman waited for him.

Vincent knew he faced an impossible task. He knew that Toussaint was mistaken in publishing the Constitution. He knew that Napoléon would not tolerate the affront to his authority. But Vincent also knew that in Saint-Domingue there was no alternative to Toussaint. Vincent would have to do the impossible: persuade Napoléon to be patient with the black leader. The situation was much like that of a parent and child, Vincent thought. When the child cannot be persuaded to act with wisdom, the parent must exercise wisdom in dealing with the child.

On July seventh, the celebration for the Constitution was held in the Place d'Arms at the Cape. Bernard Borgella was the chief speaker. He praised Toussaint for his strength, piety and wisdom. Other speakers lectured on the various provisions of the Constitution. At noon there was a service of thanksgiving in the church. In the afternoon Toussaint received in state in Government House. In the evening he entertained six hundred for dinner. Throughout the night, revelers danced in the streets and filled the sky with rockets. Toussaint ordered the prisons opened and all prisoners released except those accused of violent crimes.

On July twentieth, Vincent sailed from the Cape. He had delayed as long as he dared hoping Toussaint would change his mind. Vincent delayed again in Philadelphia hoping for a reprieve from his impossible task. In August, Vincent knew he could delay no longer and took passage for France.

In September, Toussaint released Roume from arrest and allowed him and his
family to sail for France. Toussaint had no further use for the French commissioner and saw no reason to detain him.

Moïse held the rank of general of brigade. He was commander of all the
North. Of Toussaint's officers, only Dessalines outranked him. Moïse had
power, wealth, prestige, the loyalty of his soldiers and the homage of the people. But Moïse was deeply disturbed. His uncle had lost the path. Toussaint was
blinded by his love for the French.

Toussaint outlawed the African rituals, and now his Constitution made
Christian Catholics of everyone. It was punishable by imprisonment and fine to
miss church on Sunday. It was punishable by death to worship the loa on any
day. And Moïse was ordered to enforce the laws.

He would not. Christianity was the religion of the white slave masters.
Voudoun was the religion of the blacks, slave or free. Moïse gloried in the rites.
He thrilled at the appearance of the loa. They were the bridge between Africa
and Saint-Domingue. Moïse would not enforce Toussaint's laws. He would not
kill his own for remembering they were African.

Moïse knew when last he felt the great love he once had for his uncle. It was
when Toussaint stayed the night with him in Fort Liberté after the defeat of
Hédouville. Moïse had argued then that a man cannot stand with one foot on
the shore and one on the boat. Now he could see the wisdom of his thought.
Toussaint tried to stand with one foot in each world. No man could, not even
Toussaint. He no longer stood with the people. He was now as white as any
Frenchman.

Moïse knew his power with the laborers. At his word they would rise against
any enemy, even if the enemy were Toussaint.

But Moïse hesitated. He was strong only in the North, and he had few allies
even there. Many of Toussaint's officers groaned under his tyranny and many
grumbled of their discontent, but few were willing to join in open rebellion.
Toussaint had armies and loyal generals to lead them. Moïse had only the black
cultivators weary of their continuing subjugation. Moïse knew he could not prevail against Toussaint's force. But he could not let the people stay in slavery.

Despite what Toussaint said, Moïse knew that the people were still enslaved.
They had no freedom to live where they wished, no freedom to work where they

wished, or starve if they wished, no freedom to worship as they wished. The workers were whipped now with sticks instead of leather thongs. Dessalines disciplined the recalcitrant in his district with lashes across the bare back with a green, knotted limb of the lemon tree. And where that did not produce the desired response, he intimidated with public executions.

The workers were still enslaved. Toussaint's Constitution, written by whites was, under its libertarian language, a replica of the Black Code. The bondage of the blacks under Toussaint lacked only the shackles and scourges of the old order, and those, Moïse knew, in time the French again would supply.

CHAPTER 24
Lions and Jackals

On a bright and gentle morning in the middle of October, Dessalines's long campaign of the heart came to a successful conclusion. He and Claire were married. Theirs was not the passion of youth. They were both forty-three. Claire was six years widowed and had sworn eternal devotion on the grave of her dear Pierre. Dessalines had taken women were he found them with no thought of permanent alliance.

But Dessalines knew from the moment he that first saw Claire in Léogane that he would have her for his wife. Her quiet beauty, her gentle strength, her inner peace infected him with the tranquility that glowed like an aura around her. She, in turn, was frightened by his ferociousness and yet helplessly attracted to him as one might be to a tiger who walked from the jungle and rubbed lovingly against one's leg. For two years she resisted her fascination with his brutishness. But finally, with faith that her wild beast could be safely domesticated, she succumbed to his entreaties and agreed to marry him.

The wedding was a quiet one, performed in the ancient church of Saint Rose. Dessalines chose Saint Rose because it was the parish church to Habitation Cormier, on which he was born and raised as a black field slave to the cruelest of owners, a free black named Duclos. Dessalines relished in the catharsis of returning to the place of his bitter origins as a man to be feared and respected and there to be married to the most glorious woman on earth. And it was in Grande Rivière, as Saint Rose was now called, that Dessalines's dear Aunt Victoria still resided. Her love was the only true home he had ever known. It

seemed proper to Dessalines that his nuptials to the pious, gentle Claire be performed in the church of his pious, gentle Aunt Toya.

After the wedding, he acknowledged the adulation of the citizens of the
town, but he did not tarry. Grande Rivière was in the North, and Dessalines
wanted to return to his own district to celebrate his new happiness.

On Thursday evening, October twenty-second, 1801, Dessalines and Claire
gathered with their friends and admirers to celebrate in Petite Rivière, the chief
market town of the fertile Artibonite. Even Toussaint interrupted his plans to
supervise the reorganization of the Spanish courts in Santo Domingo to attend
the fête.

A dinner and reception for Dessalines and his bride were held in the rectory,
but in the cool, clear evening, under the lights of the stars and sisal torches, the
party flowed out into the church square, where citizens of the town and workers from the neighboring habitations joined in the flood of wine and music and
in the toasts to the district commander and his lady. Dessalines, resplendent in
his best dress uniform, led his beautiful bride in the carbinier. The dance, with
its demand for stately, military-like bearing flattered the man, and with its flow
of seductive, rhythmic steps glorified the sensual beauty of the woman.
Dessalines, delighting in Claire's grace and his own elegance, danced until Claire,
hot and winded, begged for a reprieve. They stole from the crowd and walked,
his arm tightly around her, into the shadows of Crête-a-Pierrot, the fort crown-
ing a solitary hill rising to the town's east. Dessalines held Claire tightly and
kissed her with a joy he had never felt before. Above them, the shadowy ramparts of the fort hid Vega and the stars of Hercules from view.

Dessalines's idyll was short-lived. The general might create the appearance of
solitude, but there were those whose job it was to know at every moment where
he was. From the shadows where he stood with his arms around the beautiful
Claire, Dessalines saw the figure hurrying up the hill toward him.

"General," his adjutant addressed him with an air of urgency despite his
attempt to appear unhurried, "the Governor-General requires your presence."

Without hesitation, Dessalines stepped from Claire and moved quickly down
the hill.

"See to Madame Dessalines," he called back to his officer as he hurried
toward the town.

———————◆———————

Anacaona heard Moïse's call and slipped from the house and joined him. He greeted her warmly, but clearly he was distracted. On the ride to Bréda, he fell into a silence. He made love to her passionately that night, but said little.

The next morning, Moïse rose early. Anacaona prepared to return to Duclero, but Moïse stopped her. He explained that he had difficult work to do, but needed her to wait for him. He would return when he could.

Anacaona waited. He did not return until long after dark. He was tired and fell into an uneasy sleep. She sat by him watching his troubled breathing. She occasionally rubbed his temples lightly with her fingertips. The touching eased his discomfort without waking him.

In the morning, Anacaona asked him why he was troubled. He would not talk of it.

"Then I must go," she declared.

"Stay," Moïse begged.

"I am not a woman of pleasure," she said sternly. "If you do not share your soul with me, I do not share my body with you."

"It is best you do not know the work that I do," Moïse responded.

He left abruptly.

Through the window, Anacaona watched him talk earnestly in the corral with several men who waited there for him. They mounted, Moïse with them, and rode off in different directions.

Anacaona debated with herself for long minutes. Her pride was hurt. She allowed no man to treat her as a servant. She sent the groom to fetch her horse. She would return to Duclero. She might or might not accept Moïse's apology.

She mounted and started toward the Cape intending to cross the bridge at the mouth of the Haut-de-Cap River, but the river was low, and in her impatience she forded the river where she was. As her horse mounted the steep eastern bank of the river Anacaona saw before her a plume of smoke. She halted her horse and examined the horizon. In the east, in the south, in the west they rose, thin black plumes in the still air: plantations burning.

She spun her horse around and galloped back to Bréda. She would not let her hurt pride separate her from Moïse at such a time. It was, she knew, the uprising against Toussaint. The people were speaking.

That night she begged Moïse to give her an assignment.

"I can help," she urged. "Send me on errands. The people know that I speak for you."

"No," he said. "There are no messages from Moïse. I do not raise the people. The dam has broken of its own weight. It is the people who speak. I listen, and when they call me, I will answer, but not until the people have won their victory."

It was a dangerous game Moïse played. Anacaona knew that. But she did not challenge him.

That night they did not make love. While to the south of them in Petite Rivière Dessalines and Claire were celebrating their wedding, Moïse and Anacaona at Bréda talked of Moïse's dream. He told her of his parable of the jackals and lions.

"Men do not understand the jackals and lions," he explained. "The jackals seem lowly creatures, arguing and fighting among themselves. The lion, they say, is the king of the jungle, beautiful, proud and brave. But in truth, the lion is a leech. It waits for the jackals to kill, and then, with threats and intimidation, the lion chases off the jackals and eats its fill, leaving only scraps for the rightful owners of the dinner.

"The society of men is like the jackals and the lions," he continued earnestly. "The people are the jackals. Their leaders are the lions. The jackals have strength in their numbers, but they do not know their strength. They bow and scrape to the lions believing that the lions are like gods, believing that only the lions can rule. The lions preen themselves, stretch in the sun and accept the gifts of the jackals as their due.

"When the jackals understand that they have the power, that the lions would starve without them," Moïse went on, "then the jackals will rise up and throw out the lions. They will say, 'You may be a jackal with us, but you cannot be a lion above us.'

"Tonight, the people of Saint-Domingue are throwing over their rulers," Moïse explained. "The jackals are rising. I do not lead them. No man leads them. When their work is finished, I will join with them, but as another jackal, not as a lion."

Throughout the night Moïse and Anacaona talked of the new society to be, the society of true equals, of what it would be like, and how it would be defended.

———————◇———————

While Moïse waited to be called, Christophe reacted quickly and efficiently. He broke the revolt that night in the Cape with savage attacks upon the barricades, and in the morning led his troops against the well-armed field hands who approached the city in two columns, one from the south and one from the west. Christophe threw himself against each column in turn with such savagery that the rebels broke ranks and fled.

They fled into the guns and swords of Toussaint and Dessalines, who, alerted the night before, marched through the night to reach the Northern Plain.

Toussaint and his generals had a week of hard fighting to repress the rebellion. At Plaisance, Dessalines repressed it by killing a fourth of the city's population. Christophe was in open warfare with the garrison of Limbé under the command of the rebel, Colonel Flaville. Toussaint moved with equal vigor against Marmelade.

At Bréda, Moïse was heart-stricken at the news. He sent Anacaona back to Duclero and rode himself to inspect the damage.

Moïse rode alone across the plain. As best he could he avoided contact with forces on both sides. He felt the sickness of indecision in his stomach. He thought to declare openly for the rebels, to regroup them and lead them himself, but he knew they would be no match against the combined forces of Toussaint, Dessalines and Christophe.

There was no news that the rebellion had spread to the West or South.

Moïse was confused. He had expected Christophe to resist. Christophe's love for the Europeans was well known. But Moïse had expected Dessalines to honor the rebellion. Surely Dessalines resented the suzerainty of the whites under Toussaint.

Moïse knew the cause was lost. He contemplated joining with the next group of rebels he encountered and sacrificing his life with theirs. But he could not. When he was dead, who would speak for the people? He must live.

Moïse feared that he acted more from cowardice than idealism, but he was not prepared to die. He had not raised the rebellion. He had sympathized with it, but he had been careful not to lead it.

Moïse knew he must live, and to do that, he must keep the good will of Toussaint. He knew that he too long had avoided the messengers from Toussaint who searched for him.

Heartsick but resolved, Moïse rode to Marmalade in search of his uncle. Toussaint was not there, but the commander had orders from Toussaint for Moïse to move against the rebels at Dondon. Moïse gathered up fifty solders of

the Fifth Regiment, who had marched from Fort Liberté to Marmelade looking
for Toussaint's army, and proceeded with his orders.

The defenders of Dondon were confused to see Moïse against them.
Disheartened, they gave up, many fleeing for the mountains to the south. Moïse
moved vigorously against them, killing all he captured.

On Wednesday, October twenty-eighth, Toussaint called Moïse to Habitation
Hericourt, where they had met to plan the final campaign against Hédouville.
This time he found his uncle unforgiving.

Toussaint would hear no word of Moïse's innocence.

"I have done nothing, Uncle," Moïse insisted.

"I have heard them call your name. 'Moïse!' they shouted as they moved
against me," Toussaint retorted.

"They know I am sympathetic to their needs, but I did not lead them in rebellion against you," Moïse answered with a clear conscience.

"You have been most imprudent. You do not understand what you have
done." To this point in his encounter with Moïse, Toussaint was controlled, but
as he spoke, his temper exploded. "You have no confidence in my politics!"

"I have told you as much," Moïse replied. "The rebellion is from the people's
discontent, not from my agitation."

"You have broken my heart! You know the dangers we face," Toussaint continued. "You think that I want to enslave my people, I who freed them! I who
was a slave!"

Toussaint raved on about the hurt Moïse had caused him. Finally he grew
more controlled again.

"You force me to make a sacrifice that will break my heart," he said. He gestured impatiently for Moïse to leave him.

When Moïse was gone, Toussaint lamented, "When I sent you to Dondon,"
he cried to an empty room, "why did you not flee into the hills?"

Moïse did not know what to expect and was relieved when the next morning
he was directed by Toussaint to lead a force of the Governor-General's personal guard against the rebels at Port-de-Paix.

When he reached Port-de-Paix, Moïse was puzzled to find the city in peace.
His confusion was cleared when the commander of the city, Maurepas, arrested
him for treason and imprisoned him in the great fort.

CHAPTER 25
Trial and Execution

The areas of confinement in the great fort at Port-de-Paix are located beneath the walls. The prison cells are entered through removable iron grates at ground level. Prisoners either jump or are dropped the twelve feet to the floor. All food, water and communications are lowered through the single opening. Prisoners can leave only by being pulled from the cells by ropes lowered from above. It was in one of these cells that Moïse was imprisoned. He was permitted to occupy the cell alone.

The cell was small, less than eight feet square. There was no furniture, only a straw pallet. The walls were of rough stone. The floor was clay. Although the sun shone into the cell for a few hours only at noon, the temperature was sweltering. There was no circulation of air. When it rained, water ran in through the open grate and lay on the floor until it slowly drained or was evaporated by the heat. A careful prisoner dug holes in the floor to bury his feces. The rain unburied it.

Moïse had suffered many agonies in the struggle for freedom. He had been wounded a score of times. He had experienced the pain and trauma of having his eye gauged from his head in hand-to-hand combat. He had been near starvation. He had been near death from fever. As a slave he had been beaten a hundred times. He had worked the cane fields in shackles, his head encased in the tin mask the French invented to keep slaves from chewing the sugar cane. He had suffered pain and indignity most of his life. But he had never before experienced the exquisite mental anguish of languishing for days, confined in prison, unable to communicate with anyone, unable to speak to his uncle, unable to present a word in his own defense. Moïse understood the process. He had employed it against his enemies. He expected such treatment from an enemy, but not from Toussaint.

Moïse was not tortured physically. He was not beaten. He was not chained. He was not forced to sign a confession. He was ignored, forgotten. A thousand times he rehearsed his indignation in his mind. He spoke it aloud to the spiders who shared his cell.

Moïse began to accept the fact of his impending execution. No one spoke to him of it, but he knew Toussaint. It was no less than he, Moïse, would do if he believed that he had been betrayed. Moïse would have done it instantly, in the field. Toussaint moved cautiously, bolstering every act with the trappings of law.

Toussaint would have to move slowly against him, Moïse reasoned. He was too popular. Such an execution might again raise the people in revolt.

Moïse suddenly sat up on the pallet where he had been lying. Perhaps the rebellion was not over. Perhaps the people persisted and his execution would be the catalyst that moved them to success. The people loved and followed him, Moïse knew that. He saw their love for him in their eyes. He was a powerful leader. Perhaps that is why Toussaint arrested him, to keep him from the people. Toussaint was afraid of him. Moïse had known of his power since the defeat of Hédouville. If Toussaint had not intervened, he could have driven out the Frenchman without assistance. Yes. The people followed Moïse, and Toussaint knew it.

But was he guilty of treason? Moïse struggled for days with the question. He invented reason upon reason to deny his guilt: Toussaint was jealous. He had a suspicious nature. He looked for treason everywhere.

In the end, Moïse gave up the struggle. He could not deny the truth in his mind. He was guilty. He did not openly lead the revolt, but he encouraged it. He wanted it to succeed. How many times had he thought that Toussaint's time was over, that new leadership was needed? He remembered fantasies in which he protected Toussaint from the angry people and magnanimously retired him to Desachaux.

Moïse beat his fists on the rock wall. Fool! Fool! He was not guilty of treason. He was guilty of cowardice. The revolt had offered him his moment and he had lost it! He should have acted. He owed no less to the people, to himself...to Toussaint! He should have stamped out the first traces of sedition and cast his lot with Toussaint, or he should have seized the moment and snatched at his own destiny.

The people were right. Their grievances were just. They called for him. He failed them.

Moïse thought of his parable of the lions and jackals. He had not understood the power of the lions to terrify the jackals. If he had thrust himself to the front of the people he could have eased their fears. Then many who held back would have come forward. In numbers they would have had courage. They would have won.

The walls of the cell crushed him. He could not breathe. He stumbled into them when he tried to walk. He pounded the rocks. He shouted at the grated window.

"I am a fool! A fool!"

In the days that followed, Moïse grieved for his lost moment. He lay for long hours motionless on the pallet. Only his mind moved. It raced in a dozen directions simultaneously, repeating itself interminably.

Moïse contemplated escape. He would flee to the hills and mobilize the people. No. Those who had trusted in him, had called to him, were dead. They died waiting for him to act. There would be few with the courage to follow him now.

He would reach Toussaint, make him understand that he was not a traitor.

But Moïse knew the people were right. Toussaint was wrong. The land must be divided among the people. The whites must be driven out.

Moïse decided he should leave a testament for the people. He began to scratch his ideas in the clay floor. As he wrote he realized he was paraphrasing the words of Toussaint's Constitution, guaranteeing equal rights to all.

Moïse stopped writing. The words were not enough.

Then Moïse saw it. It was a question of property. The whites owned the property. The blacks in leadership—the lions—had acquired property through the Revolution. But the laborers, the soldiers, the fishermen—the jackals—had no means to acquire property. Either property must be equal or the right to property must be abolished. With unequal ownership of property there never could be equality before the law.

But there could never be equality of property. If property were equally divided, it soon would be concentrated again in the hands of the whites and those blacks who acted as whites. The whites understood the process of acquisition. The black laborer cared little for property and would lose it to the greedy.

Then there must be education for the blacks. Sonthonax had preached education. He required adults as well as children to learn to read and write. Toussaint had continued Sonthonax's policies and had employed the French to teach the blacks. Moïse believed in education. He, like Sonthonax, preached it to the people. But education, too, was a false promise of equality. The laborers saw that when they asked where was the school that taught the whites to cut cane. Education would continue the privilege of the whites and only equip the blacks to serve the whites more efficiently.

If there was to be equality, Moïse reasoned, there must be no property. The denial of the right of one man to own another was only the first step. The second, and equally essential step, was the denial of one man to own more than another. The French Revolution had foundered on the reef of property, and theirs was endangered by it. Toussaint had guaranteed the right to own property in the Constitution. Regardless of other freedoms, that one doomed the blacks. They would be free only when the right to own property was abolished.

Toussaint lost no time consolidating his control over the Northern Plain. On the fourth of November, he marched from Hericourt to the Cape, bringing with him forty prisoners of importance, men of military rank or civilian responsibility, who were suspected of leading the rebellion.

Toussaint commanded all citizens of the Cape to gather at the Place d'Arms. He had the troops of the First and Second Demi-Brigades formed in a square, and behind them a squadron of his personal guard. When all were assembled, three horse-drawn pieces of artillery were wheeled into the square, their cannoneers with matches at ready. Both civilians and soldiers stood uneasily, not certain of Toussaint's intentions, but fully aware that he might train the cannons upon all assembled.

Toussaint rode into the square on Bel-Argent. All could see his anger in his posture. Those close to him could see it in his eyes.

"Look at me!" he shouted, as he rode around the square, fixing the gaze of all whose eyes he commanded. "Am I the traitor General Moïse says I am? Am I the man who wants the death of his brothers? Do I want to drive you again into slavery, I who have felt the bite of the whip upon by own back? Do I want to climb to power on the bodies of my children? Who says I am a traitor?"

Toussaint waited for a reply. There was none.

"This day," Toussaint continued his voice loud and strident, "the guilty will be punished. None shall escape. Even my nephew, General Moïse, will not escape punishment for his treason. I would punish the guilty even if he were my own son!"

Toussaint saw in the assembled troops an officer whose name Christophe had given him, a man accused of treason by the informer Troisballes.

"You," Toussaint commanded, pointing to the man. "Step forward."

The man did so.

"You are a known traitor," Toussaint accused. "I condemn you to shoot yourself!"

An aide with Toussaint handed the officer a loaded, primed and cocked pistol. The officer placed the barrel to his head and pulled the trigger. The powder flashed and the man, his head blown open, crumbled dead on the ground before Toussaint.

Toussaint moved on, identifying other traitors, ordering each to shoot himself. Each accused man obeyed without hesitation.

The prisoners Toussaint had brought from Hericourt, including Colonel Flaville and the informer Troisballes, were led, chained, into the square. The three cannons were trained upon them. The soldiers facing the cannons, without waiting for orders, raced to the flanks. The cannoneers blew upon their matches to warm them and moved them to the touchholes of their pieces. The cannons fired in broken cadence and grapeshot cut into the prisoners. The men fell, many clawing in agony in the dust of the field.

Toussaint turned Bel-Argent away from the carnage and rode out of the Cape.

Moïse was not permitted to testify at his court-martial. It did not matter to him. The magistrate who conducted the trial was white. Moïse had nothing to say to him.

Moïse thought to attempt one speech, calling for the abolition of property, but chose not to. The speech would accomplish nothing. The officers of the court would not hear him. The people had no need to hear him. The people had taught him what was needed. In time they would find a leader who would have the courage to act when they called him

Moïse was surprised when the president of the court declared him innocent of treason, that there was insufficient evidence to convict him. Moïse was not surprised when, despite the ruling, he was returned to his cell.

Several days later, on Friday, November twentieth, Moïse was summoned once more before the court. This time his uncle sat in the seat of the president. Moïse tried to catch Toussaint's eyes, but the older man would not look at him.

"It is the verdict of this military tribunal," the clerk began when Moïse was in position before the tribunal, "that you did on and before September twenty-first, 1801, plan and lead a general insurrection of laborers in the Northern Plains of Saint-Domingue against the established government of the colony. For said action you are hereby convicted of treason against the government of France and are condemned to be executed by a military firing squad at dawn on the twenty-first day of November, in the year of the our Lord eighteen hundred and one, in the year of the Revolution, ten. May God have mercy on your soul."

Moïse, awakened before light by the Catholic chaplain, was startled at how well he had slept. He remembered hearing drums faintly at sunset through the small opening over his head. And then, what seemed to him only moments later, it was time to die.

Moïse agreed to final absolution, but in the middle of the blessing he regretted his weakness. The white priest praying to the white mother of a white god to keep his soul from a white hell brought Moïse no comfort. He yearned for the consolation of the drums that had echoed softly in his ears as he fell into sleep.

As Moïse stepped into the slight chill of the pre-dawn darkness he again heard the drums from Haut Aton south of the city. They must have beaten throughout the night. The thought passed his mind that the drums were signaling him that there was help in the mountains if he chose to escape.

Was escape possible? The thought tantalized. Why did the mind seek paths around the fact of death? He lived his life as a soldier, and he was prepared to die as a soldier. If he could have chosen his death it would been at another time and in another manner. Man always sought to delay the inevitable, but in the end it was Ghèdé's choice, not man's.

He marched between rows of musketeers toward the parade ground where the garrison was drawn up in formation to witness his execution.

Moïse was impatient for the dawn.

The thought would not leave his mind. The one moment he failed to act, failed clearly to choose, he had fallen. In his mind, Moïse was being executed not for treason, but for weakness.

The young lieutenant in command of the execution tied Moïse's hands behind the stake. To Moïse, having his hands tied felt right. The physical helplessness, the roughness of the cords cutting into his wrists, the awkward posture reaching behind the stake, helped him to clarify his role, helped him to sense the reality of life and death. Only at the moment of his death, the houngan taught, does man recognize his life.

As the light swelled rapidly, the drums stopped. Moïse knew that after the moment of his death they would begin again, beating the ceremony of his dèssounin, helping him in his passage. In the silence that followed the cessation of the drums, noises close at hand seemed to Moïse to come from a far distance. It was as if he stood on a mountain hearing sounds deep in the valley: the officer ordering the firing squad into position, the rattle and scrape of the muskets, the droning of the chaplain.

In the silence of his mind, Moïse remembered the ceremonies of Canzo—the initiation by fire—that he witnessed when he was a child. He remembered being passed the plate of food for the Marassa, the divine twins, ancestors to the loa. He remembered eating and being asked the ritual question, "Are you satisfied?"

He was born an animal. Through the voudoun he was reborn a man. Through the ceremony of reclamation he would have his third and final birth, into the life of the people, to live as long as the loa are honored and worshipped. Before his soul could experience the final birth he would first have to die as a man. That was the message of the drums that beat through the night in violation of Toussaint's laws. In a year and a day he would be recalled to the people.

Yes, Moïse was satisfied.

"Prepare...."

The officer's command broke the stillness that engulfed Moïse.

"Aim...."

Moïse saw the soldiers hesitate. The officer gripped his pistol nervously, uncertain for his own safety. Moïse felt a flush of power. He could stop the execution. Then he saw the terror in the eyes of the soldiers. He spoke to them in a quiet voice.

"Do not hesitate," he said. "If you fail in your duty, you will be shot, and others will take your places. You can not help me. I am dead. If not today, then tomorrow. Toussaint commands it. Fire, my friends, fire."

"Fire..." the officer commanded.

Moïse felt the savage blows crush into his chest. He spun backwards, uninhibited by the stake, into blackness.

At dawn, when they knew Moïse was no more in this life, the little band who had drummed and danced through the night on Haut Aton dispersed. There was no protection there from seeking soldiers.

One of those who kept watch through the night, a thin mulatto woman, walked higher into the hills, her eyes set on the heights before her. She acknowledged no greeting, no words of concern or comfort. She walked south, drawn to the heights, listening for the drums.

For the first time in her life Anacaona was happy she was barren. If she had given birth to children, she would this morning, like Media, have ripped out their hearts.

The pain in her chest matched the hurt in Anacaona's heart. It were as if the mountains she sought were piled upon her. She struggled for breath. When it came, it cut like a knife.

She could not stop walking. Although it was against Toussaint's laws for any to wander from his place of employment, no one stopped her. Those who saw her either turned from her in fear or thrust upon her gourds of water or bits of food for her nourishment. These from time to time she accepted, but as if in a trance, unaware of what she did.

In time, it became clear to her what she sought: the drums and the people who served them; the loa they worshiped; and the power, the power to destroy the demon who tortured and killed his children, who killed her lover, who killed Moïse.

In the months that followed, Anacaona found solace in the mountains of the Saddle. There, under the disciplined instruction of the maroon Lamour Derance, she learned of the deeper ways of the loa.

The proclamation had been prepared before Moïse's execution. At the prescribed hour, in accordance to Toussaint's instructions, it was read in every city and village, in every army garrison and on every habitation.

"General Moïse has been executed. He was a traitor to his people. He led an insurrection against the legal government of Saint-Domingue. By overthrowing that government he would have opened the way for anarchy and the resumption of slavery. Let his memory be erased from the list of the men brave and loyal who have won for France the freedom and peace of Saint-Domingue. He was a man of loose habits and moral degeneration. Let none mourn him."

Toussaint, alone, in darkness, raced his horse toward the Cape. He reigned in with brutal roughness before Pierre Baptiste's house, fell from the saddle, rolled onto the ground and lay there, his body jerking in tortured spasms, his uniform stained and twisted in disarray.

"Why do you betray me?" he shouted, his voice cracking in his throat. "Haven't I enemies enough? If you could have waited for this old man to die!"

Pierre Baptiste, awakened by the arrival of the horseman, was for a moment disoriented. When he recognized Toussaint's voice, he pulled himself up and felt around for the drinking gourd hanging from an upright of the hut.

"Moïse!" Toussaint shouted. "My children are only children. They are easily led astray!"

Baptiste was arrested in his actions by what he heard in Toussaint's voice.

"If those of us who are men do not stand," Toussaint continued in his delirium, "how will we endure?"

There was no mistaking the voice: thin, reedy, nasal. It is Ghèdé, thought Baptiste. He walked without hesitation to the cook fire behind the house, reached down and picked up a handful of cold ashes.

"You are my right arm.... I have lost my right arm," anguished Toussaint. His body shook violently. He gasped for breath between words. His actions were like those of a drowning man making desperate efforts to save himself. "How can I fight without my arms," he screamed.

Baptiste walked back through the house pausing only to find a partially filled bottle of rum tucked into a corner behind his bed. With the ashes and rum he continued to the front of the house and stooped before one of the uprights supporting the roof of the overhang of the entryway. He knelt before the post and

using the small pile of ashes from the fire drew on the ground around the post
the vèvè for Ghèdé. Working with a sureness undeterred by his blindness he
traced the pattern of an ornate altar topped with a cross, coffins on both sides
of the altar. From time to time he took a mouthful of rum and sprayed the clear
liquid through his teeth into the air, the mist falling onto the drawing and his
godson.

"Is there no one faithful to Toussaint?" Toussaint shouted. He tried to rise,
but his trembling legs would not support him. He fought against the enveloping
white darkness that moved from his forehead down across his eyes. But the
force was too much for him.

"Is there no one faithful to Toussaint?" he asked pitifully, his mind surrendering to the void stretching before him.

"Each man thinks to be faithful to what he loves, but ends being faithful to
what he fears," Pierre Baptiste answered, but he knew Toussaint's ears did not
hear him.

Pierre Baptiste could not see the change in his pupil, but he heard and sensed
that Toussaint had lost his struggle and had surrendered to the weight of the
divine rider pressing down upon his back and shoulders.

For weeks after Moïse's death, Toussaint and his officers combed the island,
identifying and killing enemies in every city, town, hamlet and habitation. Only
in the rough mountains of the South and center of the island, where the
maroons held their impregnable fortresses, was Toussaint's sword not felt.

Toussaint himself crisscrossed the island following the sounds of the forbidden drums or the anguish in his mind. With only a few soldiers able to keep his
pace, he raced without pattern or reason from habitation to habitation, beating
his horse unmercifully.

He jumped from his saddle and, half-running, half walking with stiff, irregular strides, rushed in among the laborers.

"Did you follow Moïse?" he demanded, his voice barking like a small dog.

If a laborer blanched or stuttered, terrified by the appearance of the wild man
in a general's uniform, Toussaint screamed, "Shoot him! Shoot him!"

And it was done.

"Shoot this one!"

And it was done.

"This one!"

And it was done.

"Why do you betray me?" he demanded of a man of thirty who never before had seen his benefactor.

"I do not betray you, my General," the man answered without hesitation and without fear.

"I say you betrayed me. Your eyes speak for you," Toussaint accused.

"I love Papa Toussaint."

"You betrayed me!"

"For Papa Toussaint to accuse me is for me to condemn myself. Shoot this one!" the man demanded.

"Shoot him!" Toussaint commanded.

And it was done.

Always it was done.

CHAPTER 26
Napoléon

Colonel Vincent arrived in Brest in early October. He had no difficulty inter-preting the activities he observed in the port. Transports and warships were being repaired and fitted in every available dock. Napoléon was preparing for a major naval expedition.

The carpenters and riggers to whom he spoke had their opinions. England was the consensus. "The little Corsican is going to make a Republican of King George," was the general opinion.

Vincent doubted it. The gossip in Philadelphia was that France and England were weary of war. Vincent doubted that the threat of a French invasion would encourage the English to make peace. Napoléon might be looking again at Egypt, but Vincent guessed the First Consul had had his fill of the desert.

It could only be Saint-Domingue, preparation for the confrontation that Toussaint had predicted. Vincent knew he would not be able to stop it. Even without Toussaint's Constitution to spur Napoléon, Vincent knew the First Consul would have to crack his whip over the island. Napoléon was not one to ride with a slack rein.

Vincent dreaded the task of giving Napoléon Toussaint's Constitution. It was a cowardly thought, but he hoped someone had preceded him to Paris with the news.

---------------◆---------------

Vincent took rooms in White's Hotel Philadelphie near the Church of the Little Fathers. He liked the hotel because Americans often frequented it, and he enjoyed their company.

He was tempted to walk to his audience with Napoléon. It was a short distance. He had been ordered to Napoléon's reception room at the Tuileries rather than to the Luxembourg Palace. Vincent enjoyed walking. In Saint-Domingue he preferred walking reasonable distances to the bother of horse or carriage. But he knew that was impossible in Paris. Even if he were not run over by the traffic, or drowned by the waste thrown from the houses, or trapped in the mud, upon his arrival he would hardly be in presentable form.

Vincent ordered a carriage. As the driver battled his way through the narrow, crowded streets the short distance from the Place des Victories past the Palais-Royal, across Rue Saint Honoré and on to Rue de Rivoli, Vincent wondered if the official residence of any other civilized country was surrounded by such filth and human misery. Every time he had reason to enter the center of Paris he understood the Bourbon's need to build Versailles to escape from the Louvre.

Vincent arrived at the Pavillon de Marsan earlier than he anticipated, and the weather being perfect, he decided to risk a short walk before confronting Bonaparte.

It seemed to Vincent that the density of mountebanks, street vendors and women of pleasure was much lighter in the area of the Place du Carrousel than he remembered. No doubt the Consulate was making efforts to win back the palace grounds from the people.

Rounding the Pavillon de Flore and entering Place de la Concorde, Vincent experienced a terrifying moment of déjà vue. He saw again the guillotine by the riverbank. Without thinking, he crossed himself. Vincent knew that the tolerance he had for the failings of the West Indian blacks was partly conditioned by the guillotine. The blacks of Saint-Domingue could be savage. He had seen them kill with alacrity, but from emotions he could understand: fear, hatred, revenge. But never had he seen them kill in the festive spirit that marked the executions at the guillotines in Paris.

Despite his walk Vincent was still early for his appointment and waited in the anteroom for some minutes. He spoke briefly to several men leaving Napoléon's reception room before he was admitted. They were former landholders in Saint-Domingue whom Vincent recognized. Because of his support of Toussaint and his organization of the plan for sharing the profits of the habitations, he knew they bore him little love. He also knew that if they had influence with the First

Consul whatever hope he might have had of softening Napoléon's resolve was lost.

Vincent was ushered into Napoléon's reception room. In it were a half dozen men scattered about the room engaged in official pursuits. Napoléon greeted Vincent standing on a low dais before a large window. Vincent was instructed to stand on the floor before him. The interview was conducted with both men standing.

Napoléon requested the document that Vincent had for him. Vincent handed him the printed copy of the Constitution Toussaint had given him. Napoléon took the pamphlet and turned toward the window for more light. He looked through the book quickly and handed it to a secretary. Vincent could not believe that the First Consul could have grasped the sense of the document in so short a time.

"It is clear," Napoléon began, "that Toussaint is sold to England. He wishes to cut Saint-Domingue adrift from her proper mother but to do it so as not to pay the penalty for treason."

"Forgive me, Consul," countered Vincent, "but that is not true. Toussaint is loyal to France and wishes to serve as your agent in Saint-Domingue."

"Colonel, you are a fool," Napoléon retorted impatiently. "Like a silly trout you have swallowed the silver and feathers of that gilded African. I tell you, sir, I shall not leave a French epaulet on the shoulders of a single nigger."

Vincent was startled by the vehemence of Bonaparte's reaction. He knew that he had no chance of influencing the Consul, but his sense of duty and his respect for Toussaint forced him to attempt the effort.

"Excellency," Vincent began with respect, "I fear you have been misadvised regarding the nature of the blacks of Saint-Domingue."

"Savages, sir," interrupted Napoléon. "They are savages from the jungle, sir."

"These savages, Excellency," Vincent persisted, "in the name of France defeated the best armies England could field."

"Yellow fever and their own command incompetence defeated the British!" Napoléon corrected. "You compare the British mercenaries with the Revolutionary army of the Republic of France?"

Vincent saw little difference to contemplate, but thought it politic not to challenge Bonaparte's opinion. He took another tack.

"There is danger in attacking Toussaint with force. If France sends a military expedition to the West Indies, the British will surely aid Toussaint."

"The British will not aid Toussaint," interrupted Napoléon. "They will not, sir!"

"I do not wish to contradict the First Consul," Vincent persisted, "but I fear they will."

"They will not!" Napoléon pounded his fist upon a small table near him to emphasize his point. "In the beginning the English had some inclination to oppose my expedition," he continued, "but I threatened to clothe Toussaint with unlimited powers and recognize the independence of the island."

Bonaparte, delighted with his own brilliance, paused for a moment to observe Vincent. He found his reward in the colonel's obvious confusion.

"Then, sir," he continued, "the British danced to another tune. Independence indeed! License for Toussaint to export his poison to the blacks of Jamaica and the Bahamas. Independence for Saint-Domingue means insurrection in the West Indies. Do you think that is in the interest of Britain?"

Napoléon paused for Vincent's response.

"No, your Excellency," Vincent replied when he realized that the question was not rhetorical. "It is in the interest of no one."

"Precisely! Rest assured," Napoléon continued, "Toussaint will receive no aid from England."

Vincent left the interview in a state of despair. Clearly Bonaparte was unapproachable on the subject. The preparations were far advanced for the expedition, and Addington was apparently in collusion with Napoléon.

Vincent knew Toussaint was a formidable force in Saint-Domingue. But if Napoléon made peace with England, and if the British did not harass his ships, and if he committed enough men and resources to the task, it was possible, no doubt, for him to defeat Toussaint. But at what cost and for what purpose? If only he could make the First Consul realize how many men he would lose in the attempt, and that if he won, what would be left would be of little value to anyone. Vincent had no doubt that the blacks would burn the island to the sea before surrendering and that those who survived would continue the battle from the mountains for generations.

Napoléon dismissed Vincent from further involvement in Saint-Domingue. Risking Napoléon's displeasure, Vincent wrote to the Ministry of Marine in an effort to stop Bonaparte. He described Toussaint's preparations against an invasion, the fortifications, the weapons and ammunition at his command, the strength and loyalty of the army, the skill of their soldiering and the determination of their resolve. He tried to describe the authority Toussaint exercised over the inhabitants, his intelligence and energy, the fanatical loyalty he inspired in the people.

Several days after sending the dispatch, Vincent had his answer. He was ordered by ship, at his earliest convenience, to France's new possession, the island of Elba, to inspect the island's defenses. His assignment was without termination date and without promotion.

Exile. For his efforts to save France from disaster he was to be lost where he would not again trouble the First Consul.

Before Napoléon's ships sailed for Saint-Domingue, Vincent sailed for Elba aboard the small naval packet "Alioth."

The "Alioth" was a two masted galley of two hundred and thirty tons, an old but able ship. During the morning hours it drifted with the tide and light winds past the islands guarding the port of Marseilles. By late afternoon, under a developing southerly wind, the ship rounded Cape Croisette and ran comfortably along the French coast on a close reach.

The warm, dry wind blowing from North Africa created nostalgia in Vincent for the trade winds of the Caribbean.

He felt that his circumstances called for feelings of outrage and bitterness, but he could not conjure them from his heart. He had been wronged many times. Napoléon was not the first. He had been imprisoned by the Jacobins and by Toussaint. In comparison, Napoléon's sentence of polite exile was of no consequence.

The thought of life on Elba brought Vincent no sadness. He had developed a fondness for island living and island dwellers. The simple life and gentle poverty of the mountainous little island off the coast of Tuscany was far to be desired to the crush and ambitions of Paris. His sadness was for his country, for the soldiers of all races who would lose their lives in Saint-Domingue.

Vincent was a soldier. The army was his life. He had declined even to marry. He had served the army of the Bourbons, the army of the Revolution and the army of the Republic. He understood war. He accepted the risks of death. But the coming massacre in Saint-Domingue saddened him because it would serve no purpose.

As the ship bore through the darkness, he stayed by the rail, listening to the splash of the hull cutting into the waves and the groan of the rigging as the

"Alioth" lifted her bow again and again from the embrace of the sea. So much of his life, Vincent thought, had been lived on ships, sailing on missions east and west. He looked forward to sedentary years on Elba.

Isaac and I had never met Napoléon. The several times Josephine received us at Malmaison, he was not present. It was, then, of great excitement to us when we received an invitation to attend him at the palace.

Three of us were invited, Isaac and I, and the college master, Abbé Coison. The Minister of Marine, Forfait, a tall, thin man of sallow complexion who never spoke more words than were needed for the occasion escorted us from the college to the palace.

Forfait escorted us into Napoléon's parlor and formerly introduced us. Napoléon received us accompanied only by Josephine and his secretary.

The meeting was short, but the First Consul was most cordial. He told us we were going home. He was sending us back to Saint-Domingue.

Both Isaac and I were delighted. We had long wished to see our family. The early excitement of living in Paris had worn thin and we had begun to find the city tiresome. I was the oldest of the contingent of students at the college and was most impatient with my cloistered life, and Isaac suffered from a never-ending homesickness.

Napoléon said he asked us to talk with him because he wanted us to take a letter from him to our father.

"When you arrive in your country," he instructed us, "you will explain to your father that the French government extends to him protection, glory and honor, and is sending to his country an army not to fight against him, but to make the enemies of France respect France."

Isaac and I were delighted with the trust Napoléon placed in us. In retrospect it is easy to see our naïveté, but at the time we were excited about seeing again our family, and we were flattered by Napoléon's attention.

The following evening Forfait entertained Father Coison, Isaac and me at an elaborate dinner. Many of the officers assigned to the expedition were there, including the commander, General Leclerc—Napoléon's brother-in-law—and General Rochambeau. The highlight of the dinner was the presentation to Isaac and me of our commissions in the army and elaborate uniforms, swords and side arms. As Isaac and I paraded and posed through the rest of the evening we felt a bursting pride for our mother and father to see us. We felt we were now men. Our school days were ended. We were ready to stand with our father as soldiers of France.

Napoléon had several sticky problems on his hands, and he saw a solution to them all in making his brother-in-law, Charles Victor Emmanuel Leclerc, commander of the expedition to Saint-Domingue. His solution, in his own mind, had the simplicity and symmetry of genius.

Bonaparte found his sister, Pauline, vain, superficial and exasperating, especially when she was in the midst of one of her all-consuming love affairs. But despite her faults and his irritations with her, he was genuinely fond of her.

As fond as Bonaparte was of Pauline, he was equally annoyed with her husband, Victor Leclerc. Leclerc was of good family, reasonably intelligent and fiercely loyal, but Napoléon found that success was turning his brother-in-law into a pompous bore. Besides, Leclerc was totally incapable of keeping his wife in check, and Pauline's indiscretions were becoming a source of embarrassment to the First Consul. It also annoyed Bonaparte that the wags of Paris found entertainment in referring to Leclerc as the "blonde Napoléon." The reputation was due to Leclerc's small stature and his bragging and posturing. Let him earn the reputation, reasoned Napoléon. Let the "blonde Napoléon" crush the "black Napoléon." In his heart he knew he would not be inconsolable if Leclerc failed to return. There was room for only one Napoléon in the world.

Napoléon also found that his plan to invade Saint-Domingue was meeting with resistance in his government. The ministers with responsibilities for the colonies were divided in their support. When Napoléon offered the command of the forces to the capable Bernadotte, the general refused.

"I would go with one frigate, negotiate with Toussaint and win more than your force will win," he declared.

But Napoléon was not to be stopped. He put Leclerc in command. Leclerc was no military genius, but he was competent and diligent. It would not take a military genius, Napoléon reasoned, to crush the blacks. The seasoned officers and men he was sending on the expedition were the best trained and equipped in the world. Toussaint and his rabble were no match for them. An adventure in the West Indies was the very thing to keep his soldiers sharp. He would need them at their best when war with England began again. And it would begin.

Napoléon needed some time to reorganize, but he knew his destiny was to unite all of Europe under the tricolor of France, and England would surely oppose a unified Europe.

Sending Leclerc would also provide Napoléon with the means of removing Pauline from the capital. A season in the tropics would provide her new worlds to conquer—half a world away from Paris. Bonaparte knew he would miss Pauline, but he needed the peace.

Napoléon wanted to be certain that Leclerc understood his mission. In a series of confidential letters and conversations, the First Consul made clear the tasks he wanted accomplished and the timetables for accomplishing them. He knew that he would need to provide the resolve for Leclerc, and it was infinitely easier to do it while they were both in Paris rather than trust to communications across the ocean.

"You must first establish yourself in all areas of the colony," Napoléon instructed. "Then promise Toussaint whatever you must to get his confidence. Instruct him to come to you to swear allegiance to the Republic. On that very day you are to arrest him and all his supporters and ship them to France!"

"And if he will not come to me?" Leclerc questioned.

"Then he and all his confederates are to be declared traitors," Napoléon replied irritably. "They are then to be hunted down like animals. Those captured must be shot within twenty-four hours."

In his Constitution of the Year VIII, and again in his Constitution of the Year X (the one that provided that he should be Consul for life), Napoléon had mention made of "special laws" for the colonies. These laws were not specified, but in Napoléon's mind they were clear: the reestablishment of slavery. But he was not prepared for public discussion of the issue until he had secured control of Saint-Domingue.

"When Toussaint and his henchmen have been deported or killed," Napoléon reminded Leclerc, "on that same day, all doubtful persons, of whatever color, are to be arrested, the population disarmed and the police and National Guard reorganized under your command. Then," Napoléon continued pointedly, "then we shall be ready to introduce the special laws for the colonies."

I was not aware of Napoléon's political intentions when I sailed with his army, nor did I know that his hatred of blacks was deeper than political. While I lived in Paris I had no suspicion of it. Those of us at the College de la Marche were isolated, but not ill-treated. I felt welcomed at my visits with Josephine, and was treated cordially by Napoléon the one time I met him. Only since have I learned of the depth of his feelings toward the black race.

"Equally important as defeating Toussaint," he instructed Leclerc, "is reestablishing not only the power, but the prestige of the white race. You must not tolerate any talk of the rights of blacks. Every white woman who has submitted herself to a black man, regardless of her rank or circumstances, is to be returned to Europe. And no one, male or female, who can not see the absolute intolerability of blacks shedding white blood, shall remain one instant longer than necessary on the island.

"And," he cautioned Leclerc, "there must be no talk of slavery until the island is safely in your hands.

Napoléon's army sailed for Saint-Domingue on December fourteenth, 1801. It sailed in a fleet too large to be contained in one or two ports. Ships sailed from Flushing, Le Havre, Brest, Lorient, Rochefort, Cadiz and Toulon.

One man who sailed with the fleet was more suspicious of Napoléon's intentions than was I.

Alexander Pétion, the hero of the defense of Jacmel, fled with Rigaud from Tiburon at the end of the War of Knives. He wished to get to France, but, like most of the mulattos who fled Saint-Domingue, he found the passage difficult. He arrived penniless in Aruba and had to sell his horse for food for himself and his companions. Because of his skill with artillery, he was enlisted in the civil war between the Dutch and English in Guadeloupe. Three months after fleeing Saint-Domingue, he managed to take passage for France, but a British man-of-war captured his ship. Pétion was taken to Portsmouth. Finally, on his parole, he embarked from Portsmouth for Paris on January twentieth, 1801.

In Paris he lodged in a modest apartment in Rue du Cloître-Sainte-Opportune. Seven months later, after many appeals, he secured a commission in the army, to serve at the discretion of the Minister of Marine.

Like the other fugitives in Paris from the War of Knives, Pétion welcomed the news of Napoléon's expedition and the opportunity it offered for revenge against Toussaint. But when Pétion received his sailing orders, his excitement was tempered by suspicion.

"I like it not," he complained to his old commander, André Rigaud. "All mulattos are to sail on one ship, the 'Vertue.'"

"It is a reasonable arrangement," Rigaud countered. "We go as a single brigade, old comrades who have served together. I prefer that to being scattered about."

"It is an ominous sign," Pétion insisted.

"There is no love for men of color in Bonaparte's army," Rigaud argued. "Why would you wish to be billeted with officers who despise you rather than with men who love and respect you?"

"A single ship can be dealt with as a single man," Pétion countered. "A hundred men scattered throughout a score of ships must be dealt with as a hundred men."

"You think, then," Rigaud asked, "that Bonaparte does not intend us to land in Saint-Domingue?"

"That is exactly what I think. There is a rumor...."

"I care not for rumors," Rigaud interrupted.

"There is a rumor," Pétion persisted, "that if Toussaint does not resist, we are to be sailed to a state of Islam and sold into slavery."

"Toussaint will resist." Rigaud spoke with the absolute confidence of experience.

"But if he does not?"

"Then it is good that we are in one ship. Napoléon will find it more difficult to subdue us all at once than to subdue us one by one."

Pétion was not free in his mind. In the past year he had learned that as a man of color he was no more welcomed in Napoléon's France than he had been as a student in the military college. He was equally unwelcome in Toussaint's Saint-Domingue. Pétion did not have Rigaud's faith that the expedition against Toussaint would change anything for the mulattos. But in Paris, at least, he reminded himself, even though he was poor, he was free.

"I would not be sold as a slave," Pétion confided with deep emotion to Rigaud.

"If I knew for certain that Bonaparte intended us for the Arabs, I would still sail," Rigaud insisted. "My home is Saint-Domingue and it is there that I shall live or die."

Pétion made no further arguments. He had witnessed Rigaud's histrionics before, and was in no mood for the general's courageous posturing.

On the fourteenth of December, 1801, Pétion leaned against the rail of the "Vertue" and watched the shore of France fade into the fog. He made no guess as to what death might be. But he often thought that the experience of dying was like drifting into the thick, quiet, cold fogs of the northern latitudes.

He wished the ship might strike a rock and let him drown in the gray silence, for every way he turned he saw a worse death. Pétion wanted to cling to the peace of the fog, to stop the ship, to go no farther.

CHAPTER 27
Leclerc Arrives

Duclero was in a state of deep melancholy. He could not sleep. He paid no attention to the needs of his plantation. He drank heavily each day and walked the rooms and corridors of his empty house each night. Since Anacaona's disappearance, Duclero found no joy in living. He saw no reason to remain any longer in Saint-Domingue, but his petitions to Toussaint for permission to return to France were unanswered.

It seemed incredible to Duclero that in such a short time Toussaint's promising government had turned to chaos. The civil war with the mulattos and the occupation of the former Spanish colony had been unfortunate, but it appeared that Toussaint had recovered from those debacles. The civil restrictions were stringent, but there was law and order and economic opportunities were once more flourishing. Duclero found American buyers for his coffee and sugar at the Cape.

Then the incidents with Moïse startled Duclero. The abortive revolt of the workers was unnerving, but the terror that followed was as frightening as that of the Jacobin uprising. There were reports of executions in all parts of the island, in areas unaffected by the rebels. Although he executed only blacks and mulattos, Toussaint deported many whites. The rumor was that he wanted to remove from the island all whites sympathetic to Napoléon Bonaparte.

The thing that puzzled Duclero the most was the execution of Moïse. He could not believe Toussaint's accusation that Moïse intended to kill all the whites on the island. Duclero understood black hatred of whites. He had seen it in the eyes of blacks many times, especially in the early days of the Revolution, before Toussaint's calming influence. But Duclero had never seen that hatred in Moïse. The few times he was with Moïse, Duclero looked for it. Because of Anacaona, Duclero expected Moïse to hate him. He had a deep fear that Anacaona would be the cause of his death, that when Moïse wanted her, he would not hesitate to kill for her. Duclero thought that he, of all men, should have seen hatred in Moïse, but he did not. He saw pride, disdain, but not hatred. Duclero could not believe Toussaint's accusation.

At one time, Duclero might have secretly rejoiced at Moïse's death, if it would have freed Anacaona. But he had lost Anacaona. She left the house two days before the uprising of the workers. She returned when the rebellion was repressed. Her body returned but not her spirit. She spoke to no one, ate little, and sat on the veranda looking always to the west. In her face was the same sad but beautiful resignation as in the face of the Virgin in Raphael's "The Beautiful Garden," a copy of which he had seen once in Paris.

When Duclero heard that Moïse was imprisoned, he understood Anacaona's suffering. He tried to assure her that Toussaint would not hurt his nephew, that in a few days he would release him. She heard nothing Duclero said to her. On November twentieth—Duclero remembered well the date—she disappeared. He had not seen her since. When Duclero heard that Moïse had been executed, he knew he would never see her again. He could find no news of her. She died with Moïse, Duclero decided, if not in body, then in spirit.

With the coming of the Christmas season, Duclero's melancholy became unbearable. He knew that if he did not escape from the island, he would kill himself.

Early in January, 1802, after a sleepless night, he ordered his horse saddled and before dawn started the long ride to Gonaïves to see the Governor-General.

When Duclero arrived at Toussaint's headquarters, he found the place in shambles. People were everywhere. Some seemed to have camped on the grounds and in the anteroom for days or even weeks. There were cook fires burning on the tile floors. Children ran about indiscriminately. He was struck by the resemblance of the people's behavior to that of birds before a hurricane.

He despaired at getting into the inner chamber to see Toussaint. Each time the door opened, there was a rush of people to enter. The guards held firmly against the press while an officer indicated the chosen ones.

Duclero wrote a few short sentences on the back of his card and bribed a guard to deliver it to the inner chamber. The wait was shorter than he feared. A few minutes after his messenger exited, the door opened and an officer called Duclero's name.

The situation was equally confused inside the reception room, but inside the milling crowds wore uniforms, the ornate, bizarre uniforms indulged in by Toussaint's officers. A cage of tropical birds, Duclero thought.

He was led to a far corner of the hall where Toussaint stood behind Hédouville's Louis Quatorze desk. An elderly laborer grasped the Governor-General's hand, attempting to kiss it, while two soldiers, somewhat roughly, pulled at the man.

"Thank you, Papa Toussaint. Thank you. God bless you, Papa Toussaint," the elderly man repeated over and over as he was led away.

As Duclero approached, Toussaint sank wearily into his chair. Although he did not appear to observe the planter's approach, the moment Duclero arrived at the desk Toussaint spoke in a low, intense voice.

"I have shown you my love and esteem. Why do you want to leave Saint-Domingue?"

Duclero was startled both by the manner in which Toussaint spoke and by his effusively friendly words. Duclero had several times spoken to the Governor-General at official functions and had observed him from the crowd at some of his remarkable public performances. The Frenchman's support of the black leader was an established fact in the white community, but he was not aware that Toussaint had any feelings toward him.

"Pressing needs of my family call me to Paris," Duclero lied.

The two men could hear each other above the din in the room only with intensive effort. The confusion around them forced each to study the other's face carefully when he spoke.

"You do not speak to me with candor," Toussaint accused.

Toussaint's eyes staring at him made Duclero uncomfortable. He wanted only to leave Saint-Domingue, not debate with its dictator. Duclero felt the heat rising in his neck and face.

"I wish to leave because I am white," Duclero was surprised to hear the words come from his mouth. He spoke, he realized, from his despair with no heed of the consequences. "And although I know the kindly feelings you have in the past showed the white planters," he continued, "I see that you have become now the angry chief of the blacks."

"You accuse me without justification."

Duclero was surprised by the sadness in Toussaint's response.

"I do not accuse you, Citizen Governor," Duclero continued more moderately, "but I know what I see. You deport the whites who look to the Paris to reestablish French authority here. You purchase tens of thousands of slaves from the English and American slavers to swell the black army. I find such actions argue poorly for the future of Saint-Domingue."

Toussaint was slow to reply. When he did, it was with great effort.

"France sends an army to destroy the island...to destroy me...to destroy the whites...."

"I do not believe that," Duclero answered imperatively. He did not want to argue with Toussaint. He wanted only to get a passport. But the confusion of the circumstances, the submissiveness of the little man before him, clouded his mind, and he found that he made statements that until the moment he spoke them he did not know how keenly he felt the emotions behind the words.

When Toussaint spoke again, his voice was so low that Duclero had to lean forward to hear him.

"You are determined to leave for France?"

"With your permission, I am."

"Then you must do Saint-Domingue a service." As he spoke, Toussaint's vigor returned. "Take letters for me to the First Consul. In them I will entreat him to listen to you. Tell him about me. Tell him how prosperous commerce and agriculture are here. Tell him what I have done here. I must be judged on what I have done."

Toussaint became more and more agitated.

"Twenty times I have written to Bonaparte. I have asked him to send back the old colonists, whites instructed in public administration, machinists, teachers, priests. He has never replied. Now that France is finally at peace with England, he sends against me an expedition, a great force armed for war."

"I cannot believe the First Consul means you harm," Duclero again lied. From his wife's letters he knew that Toussaint spoke the truth. Duclero realized that behind his great need to leave the island was his desire not to be in Saint-Domingue when Napoléon's forces arrived. Unless God in heaven intervened, the island would explode in the horrors of a race war. But Toussaint had himself to blame, for his vacillations, his weakness with Hédouville, his excessiveness with Moïse.

"It is true!" insisted Toussaint. "Every letter from Paris confirms it. The English speak it openly in Jamaica and laugh at Napoléon's folly. The expedition comes and in its ranks I see my enemies, people I deported to secure the peace of the island. Now they return to destroy me, to destroy the colony and to raise again the specter of slavery. You must reach France in time to make the First Consul change his mind," Toussaint implored.

Duclero wanted to flee. He did not want Toussaint's commission. He did not want to be caught between the hammer and the anvil. But he knew that above all he must have a passport.

"General," Duclero again lied, "I will do all I can for you in Paris."

Toussaint, sensing the planter's dissembling dismissed him with a wave of his hand.

"I will see that you have your passport," he promised without conviction.

Duclero bowed. As he turned to leave, Toussaint shouted after him. "No Frenchman can claim greater loyalty to France than I!"

Duclero was not certain that he had been dismissed. He paused, afraid to continue and unwilling to turn back.

"France has no right to take back the liberty she gave the blacks!" Toussaint shouted.

Duclero sensed that all activity in the room stopped, and that everyone stared at him.

"Our liberty is no longer in the hands of France!" Toussaint continued. "It is in our own. We shall defend it to the death! Bonaparte is the first man of Europe, but Toussaint is the first man of the West Indies!"

Duclero hurried out of the building and into the morning air, fearful for his safety.

Within a week Duclero received his passport and dispatches from Toussaint to Napoléon Bonaparte. Three days later Duclero secured passage to France. He packed only his personal effects for the journey.

On the day he left, Duclero rode away from the fertile plantation that had been his inheritance from his father and his grandfather before him, that had been the object of his life's endeavors. He left with no compensation for his property and no knowledge of its future. As he rode, he dared not look back. The pain of seeing again his house and lands was deeper than he could endure.

Duclero arrived in France long after Napoléon's fleet had sailed. He hid the dispatches in a secure place. He was afraid to destroy them, but felt that the interests of all, especially his, were served best by telling no one of their existence. He felt that his relations with the black ruler of Saint-Domingue were ended. He had no prescience of the role he still was to play.

Late in January, when Toussaint was visiting his brother in Santo Domingo City, he received news that French ships were anchored in the Bay of Samaná on the east coast of the island. He rode north from the city, across the Cordillera Mountains, across the swamps at the mouth of the Yuna River, to the cliffs of Cape Samaná to see for himself. There he saw six ships of the line and ten transports anchored in the calm waters of the bay. As he watched, he saw other ships appear on the horizon.

As he stood, transfixed by the sight, his body shivering despite the warmth of the sun, the ships grew larger and filled the ocean as far as he could see to the east, then the north and the south. There were men-of-war, transports, merchantmen, couriers, ships of all sizes and sail plans. Some drifted into the calm seas toward the fleet in the bay below him. Others headed along the north coast towards the ports to the west. A smaller squadron pointed south, toward Santo Domingo City. Never in his life had Toussaint seen so many ships. He found it difficult to believe the evidence of his eyes.

Toussaint turned to the men standing behind him—his aide-de-camp, the captains of his guard, his groom—and spoke to no one in particular.

"We shall all perish," he said. "All of France has come to overwhelm us." He spoke without apparent emotion, as if he were making a simple statement of fact.

In Cape François, Henri Christophe played a close game. To the best of his knowledge, Toussaint was in Santo Domingo City and the French fleet was at Samaná. He hoped the French would reach the Cape before Toussaint or instructions from Toussaint.

Over the years that he had served as military commander of the Cape, Christophe had labored hard to restore the city to its pre-Revolutionary grandeur. The church had been rebuilt, the streets repaired and landscaped, the old mansions restored and many more houses built. The Cape supported a flourishing theatre company and an orchestra. The city's prosperity was built on trade with the Americans: the export of agricultural products from the Northern Plain and the import of machinery, clothing, arms and ammunition. While the laborers in the interior of the colony languished under Toussaint's strict labor laws, planters, merchants and laborers at the Cape flourished under his renewed trade agreements.

Christophe anticipated that Toussaint would order him to resist the French. But Christophe wanted to welcome them in peace. He believed that Napoléon wanted only to renew the authority of the metropole over the colony. The problem was caused by Toussaint's Constitution. Christophe had warned Toussaint. Vincent had warned him. Toussaint had gone too far. Leclerc's expedition was the result. But Christophe felt there was still time to redress the mistake. He felt that if Leclerc were welcomed and received in peace, he, in turn, would respect the authority of the blacks in power.

Christophe was particularly bitter about the prospect of losing all that he had built at the Cape. His own house in the center of the town on Rue Royale was one of the most beautiful on the island, both in structure and furnishings. In it each Sunday he entertained the society of the city with music and feasting. At each festivity, he honored one of the beautiful young women of the Cape, mostly young white women, but occasionally brown or black.

There were factions in the city supporting all choices. The Cape's venerable black mayor, César Télèmaque, insisted that no resistance be offered. Télèmaque at one time had served in the Convention in Paris but had no understanding of the changes in France under Napoléon. Many of the citizens rose to Télèmaque's support. Others, white as well as black, urged Christophe to resist. They either feared their support of Toussaint condemned them in Napoléon's eyes, or they wanted independence for the colony.

Christophe let himself be swayed by Télèmaque and ordered the streets swept and the barracks and public buildings cleaned for the reception of the French. But he kept all of his options open and ordered the cannons of Fort Picolet primed and the buoys removed from the entrance to the harbor.

Toussaint raced after the French ships sailing the northern coast, trying always to keep them in sight. When the ships dropped their sails and anchored in a large bight of the shore east of Monte Cristi, close to the border between Santo Domingo and Saint-Domingue, Toussaint sat upon his horse on a bluff staring at the squadrons spread below him. The sight held him much as the hands of the houngan hypnotize the sacrificial animal.

Toussaint woke himself from his torpor sufficiently to send messengers to his brother in Santo Domingo City.

He sent two letters of instructions, one ordering Paul to resist the French and burn the city if he must, the other instructing him to receive the French in peace. Toussaint gave copies of both instructions to two messengers. They were ordered, if they were captured by French soldiers who may have already landed, to surrender the instructions for peace, but to deliver the message of resistance to Paul Louverture.

The messengers also were instructed to ride separately to better insure that one would get through to their destination. They ignored the instructions and chose for convenience to ride together. French soldiers who had landed outside of the walls of Santo Domingo City intercepted them. The French killed both messengers, discovered both sets of dispatches, and delivered the one to Paul instructing him to submit, and occupied the city without resistance.

Unaware of the fate of his messengers, Toussaint rode to the Cape and discovered its commander and citizens preparing to welcome the French.

"They are not to land," he instructed Christophe.

Toussaint did not stay at the Cape. He did not want Christophe to see how physically ill he had become.

While he chased the French ships westward, Toussaint neither ate nor slept. He tried, but his stomach rejected all food and his eyes would not close in sleep. By the time he reached the Cape, he was wracked by alternate attacks of sweating and shivering. His body trembled, his head ached almost beyond endurance, and his stomach retched up bile.

Toussaint attempted to ride to his headquarters at Gonaïves, but by the time he reached Ennery he could no longer hold to the saddle, and the pain in his head dimmed his eyes until he could barely see.

Alarmed for Toussaint's life, his aides took him to Desachaux, where Suzanne put him to bed and instructed that no one should know of his condition or his whereabouts. Suzanne had seen Toussaint struck by such illness before and knew he would recover. She worried not about the sickness, but that his enemies would find him in his weakened state and kill him.

At the Cape, Christophe knew he could with ease prevent the French from landing in the harbor. The entrance was narrow and the guns of the forts controlled the entrance. But he knew he could not prevent them from landing elsewhere on the island. He decided his best course of action was to delay. He would keep them at bay with diplomatic actions and wait for the press of events to decide his future course. He would do his best to keep all options open to him and jump to one side or the other only when he had no other choice.

The section of the fleet with which Isaac and I sailed left from Brest under the command of Fleet Admiral Latouche-Tréville. We tossed about horribly for a week in the winter seas of the Bay of Biscay waiting for other squadrons of the fleet to join us. Everyone aboard, except the heartiest of the sailors, was sick. We thought several times that we would be swamped by the waves. With the fleet still incomplete we finally started our journey west. The crossing was stormy and rough and took longer than I anticipated. It was a joy, then, to experience both calm weather and the sight of the land of my birth.

The lost elements of the fleet were waiting for us in Samaná Bay.

We sailed along the north coast of the island until we reached the boundary of the Spanish and French colonies. There we anchored and waited. At the time Isaac and I did not know the reason for the delay. We knew only that we were almost in sight of our destination, Cape François, and our long desired reunion with our family.

The delay was caused by command squabbles between Leclerc and Admiral Latouche-Tréville. After three days, we set sail again. Some of the ships left the fleet at Fort Liberté to land General Rochambeau and four thousand soldiers there. Other ships proceeded ahead of us to continue on west and south to Port-au-Prince with eight thousand troops under general Boudet. At noon on February first we lay to, a fleet of fourteen ships with four thousand soldiers four miles from the Cape. We could see that the harbor was crowded with merchant vessels.

The wind was favorable and Isaac and I did not understand why we did not sail into the harbor. Two hours after we hove to, we watched from the rail of the "Syrene" as a cutter and two frigates trimmed their sails and headed toward the port. As the vessels approached Fort Picolet we saw puffs of smoke rise from the fort. A few moments later we heard the muted crack of cannon fire. The frigates turned back, but the cutter continued through the harbor entrance and into the port.

The French cutter, staying close to the west bank of the harbor entrance to avoid the unmarked coral reefs to the east, pulled in at the first commercial dock, by the inner artillery battery.

Christophe immediately put the cutter and its crew under guard and dispatched a launch to Leclerc's flagship, "Ocean," with the message that he could not admit a warship to the harbor without Toussaint's instructions and that he had sent a messenger to inform the Governor-General that Leclerc had arrived.

The launch returned from the "Ocean" with a courier and landed, as Christophe had instructed, at Fort Picolet. When Christophe reached the fort, he found an arrogant white officer waiting for him.

Lieutenant Lebrun handed Christophe a letter from Leclerc warning Christophe that the French general would accept no excuses, that French troops were already ashore at Fort Liberté, Port-au-Prince and Santo Domingo City, and that if Leclerc were not allowed to land peacefully, if the forts and coastal batteries at Cape François were not handed over to him, he would land at daybreak with fifteen thousand men and take the city. Lebrun cautioned that despite the good opinion that Leclerc had of Christophe because of his former accomplishments, he would hold Christophe responsible for the consequences of any conflict.

With effort, Christophe held his temper. He had become unaccustomed to being treated with disrespect. He did not want to sacrifice his city, but he also was not prepared for a return of white arrogance.

As Lebrun and Christophe rode to Government House, Lebrun let drop along the road copies of Napoléon's proclamation promising peace and brotherhood to men of all colors who rallied to Leclerc. On the ride Lebrun whispered to Christophe that Leclerc was prepared to bestow great honors on him. Christophe looked in amazement at the thin-faced white man. Christophe needed no one to bestow honors upon him. He had won in battle more honor than Leclerc would ever know.

While Christophe prepared his reply to Leclerc, he had Lebrun entertained—alone—in the most sumptuous manner, served dinner on silver plates by four liveried waiters and housed for the night in the most luxurious of curtained rooms. He wanted the white officer to understand that the black generals of Saint-Domingue were not ignorant savages.

In his reply to Leclerc, Christophe explained that he had sent his aide-de-camp to find Toussaint, and that until he had further orders, he could not receive the French commander. He warned that if Leclerc used force, Christophe would meet force with force. If Leclerc won, when he entered the city he would find it a heap of ashes. Christophe added that he did not desire Leclerc's good will if it was to be won at the cost of acting against his orders.

Christophe sent a launch to the "Ocean" with his reply, but he received no answer that day because the wind rose and forced the French ships to sail away from the port.

Citizens opposed to resisting the French found copies of Napoléon's proclamation dropped by Lebrun and took them to Télèmaque who had them posted in the city and read in the Place d'Arms. Later in the afternoon, rumors circulated in the city that the senior artillery officer of the forts, a white man named Guilmond, had ordered torches prepared for the burning of the city. With an aroused citizenry behind him, Télèmaque led a deputation that night to Government House to try to persuade Christophe to summit to Leclerc.

Christophe was not happy with the run of events. He did not want to burn his beautiful city, but he also was disturbed with the treatment he had received from Lebrun. It aroused deep suspicions in him. What Christophe wanted was time. When Télèmaque begged permission to lead a delegation to Leclerc to request a forty-eight hour reprieve from any belligerent action, Christophe readily agreed.

Although it was past midnight, Télèmaque went to the house of Tobias Lear, the American agent at the Cape, to ask him to join the peace delegation. Télèmaque hoped that Lear, representing the foreign community in the city, would add weight to the appeal. Lear, who had spent the day warning the many Americans in the Cape to be prepared to flee in the morning on the thirty-five American merchant ships anchored in the harbor, readily agreed.

The next day the wind kept the fleet away from the port until two in the afternoon. When the delegation, with Lebrun, sailed out to the "Ocean," Leclerc received them curtly and dismissed them with the admonition that he would begin the invasion one-half hour after their boat reached the dock, unless Christophe acquiesced to his demands.

Télèmaque and Lear returned to Christophe and begged him to open the port. Christophe refused.

"I do not know that the ships are French," Christophe insisted. "I see Spanish and Dutch flags on some of the vessels."

Télèmaque was not persuaded by such sophistry. He gathered a large group of citizens, including women and children, in the park before Government House where they waited to hear the guns from the ships. Télèmaque begged Christophe to consider the safety of the women and children.

Despite all pleas, Christophe held firmly. "I follow Toussaint, as should you," Christophe told him. "We owe our liberty to Toussaint, and I will not summit without his orders."

The frightened citizens waited for the fighting to begin. When Leclerc's half-hour was up, they waited. When the rapid nightfall of the tropics came, they still waited. Leclerc had not followed his threat, the city was still secure, and Christophe was still in command.

That night, no one slept, waiting for the guns to fire.

Leclerc had hoped to frighten Christophe by exaggerating the size of the French forces before the Cape, but he had failed. He had no intention of launching a direct assault on the city. He did not want it razed, and he did not want to lose soldiers needlessly. If Christophe resisted, Leclerc planned to attack the Cape from the land.

Rochambeau was under orders to march from Fort Liberté to the Cape after he had secured the smaller port. He was to attack the city from the east. Leclerc planned to land a force to the west of the city and coordinate his attack with Rochambeau's while his ships cannonaded the city's forts.

Leclerc sent landing parties ashore to find fishermen willing to pilot his ships into the shallow Bay of Acul, west of the Cape. His soldier found no one willing to admit that he knew any of the waters of the coast.

To add to his miseries, when Leclerc ordered his ships to sail west for a night landing on the coast beyond Morne Haut du Cap, the wind died and they were becalmed for the night.

The next morning, when the wind came up again, Leclerc decided to sail to Port Margo, twenty miles west, where he knew he had water enough to land.

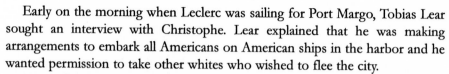

Early on the morning when Leclerc was sailing for Port Margo, Tobias Lear sought an interview with Christophe. Lear explained that he was making arrangements to embark all Americans on American ships in the harbor and he wanted permission to take other whites who wished to flee the city.

"No," Christophe commanded. "You may take Americans and other foreign nationals, but no Frenchmen!"

The racial tensions engendered in the city by Leclerc's arrival infuriated Christophe. If black Frenchmen were threatened by Leclerc, then white Frenchmen would not escape from the danger.

Although Christophe would not let the white French flee with the Americans, he saw no reason for civilians to be hurt if Leclerc attacked. He gave orders for all non-combatants to evacuate the city and to move into Morne Haut du Cap where they would be in less danger. Christophe also mustered all military units, other than those assigned to the forts, in the Place d'Arms where he ordered every man to swear allegiance to Toussaint—under penalty of death.

Shortly after noon, news reached Christophe that pushed him instantly into action. The French general Rochambeau had landed his forces on the shore of the Bay of Mancenille east of Fort Liberté, slipped between the aptly named River of the Massacre and the Lagoon of the Oxen and attacked Fort Liberté from the south. After Rochambeau over-ran the weakly defended forts on the land side of the port, the ships supporting him sailed into the Bay of Fort Liberté, crushing with heavy broadsides the batteries guarding the entrance. Then, with a coordinated attack from land and sea, the French gained entry into the main fort. When the city fell, Rochambeau put to death all of its black defenders.

Christophe's indecision was ended. He realized that Rochambeau must be marching for the Cape from the east and that forces landed by Leclerc in the hours Christophe had delayed would be coming from the west. Christophe ordered all white refugees ashore from the American ships, ordered the buildings of the Cape prepared for burning, and called laborers in from the neighboring plantations to help with the task of razing the city.

Throughout the afternoon, soldiers and laborers poured tar and other tinder on the houses. Télèmaque, desperate to stop the conflagration, instructed the inhabitants to collect water to douse the flames. Christophe ordered Télèmaque and the rest of the city council from the city and posted sentries to prevent house owners from interfering with the preparations. By late afternoon most non-combatants had accepted the inevitable and had fled.

At six that evening, a French ship of the line attempted to run past Fort Picolet. The fort fired a warning shot across the ship's bow. The ship answered with a broadside into the fort.

When he heard the firing, Christophe rushed to his own house in which barrels of tar had been poured, seized a lance that had been tipped with flaming hemp, and threw it into the open door. It was the signal. Squads of soldiers and laborers scattered throughout the city to predetermined posts and torched the mansions, stables and public buildings.

On the "Syrene," Isaac and I knew nothing of the negotiations for the city. We knew only that our homecoming was delayed three days as the ships were blown away from the port and tacked back, and that boats went between the "Ocean" and the Cape. When we saw the city go up in flames, we were dismayed. All night we watched as the contours of the fire changed, flaring up in one section of the city and then another. We said little to each other, but both of us felt a fear we had not before experienced. We knew General Leclerc would be furious, and we did not want our father punished.

On the "Ocean," Pauline Bonaparte Leclerc also stood by the rail and watched the city burn. She cried through the night. The voyage had been terrible for her. She had been sick for the month of the crossing, suffering from nausea and excruciatingly painful headaches. She was exhausted from the sea. She longed with her whole soul to be ashore again. She had heard from the Saint-Domingue exiles in Paris how beautiful Cape François was. Leclerc had promised her a house by the water where she could establish a salon, become the center of society and bring a new level of culture to the colony. She planned to collect exotic animals and birds to make a zoo which she would take back with her to Paris to delight Napoléon.

But now it was all gone. The black savages had destroyed her city. She wished now she had not brought her little son Dermide with her. He was only four, an impressionable age. She was glad he was asleep and had missed the horrible sight of the city burning. It would have frightened him terribly.

"Why? Why? Why?" she repeated over and over.

On the "Vertue," Pétion and Rigaud watched the Cape burn.

"Now, at least," Pétion suggested, "we have escaped the Arab slavers of Madagascar."

CHAPTER 28
Reunion

Leclerc met with little opposition in his short march from Port Margot. He encountered groups of armed laborers, but they appeared confused and leaderless, and at Leclerc's bidding they disbursed. As he approached the Cape he was attacked by a band of soldiers which included in their ranks blacks, whites and mulattos. These Leclerc fought off with little loss.

At the Cape, Leclerc was dismayed. He had not witnessed the city's destruction and was shocked at what he found. Not fifty of the two thousand houses were still standing, and few of those standing had escaped damage. In the hill above the city people wandered in despair. A few had returned and begun to poke about in the ashes.

It was late afternoon before the cautious Comte Louis-Thomas Villaret-Joyeuse, commander of the northern squadron of the fleet, brought his ships into the harbor. Despite the fact that Tobias Lear sailed to the "Ocean" and assured the admiral that the forts defending the city had been abandoned, Villaret-Joyeuse would not attempt the passage past their guns until he knew that the Cape was safely in the hands of Leclerc.

Pauline wanted to stay aboard the "Ocean." She, who got seasick in a bathtub, could not believe that she wanted to stay on a ship. But she did. It was only with the greatest effort and her desire not to disappoint Victor that she consented to disembark.

Leclerc greeted his wife at the government pier when she arrived in the lighter. She was beautiful in her bright dress, her shoulders bared, a lacy parasol held over her head to protect her white skin from the sun, the handsome little Dermide beside her. Despite her cheerful smile when she greeted him, Leclerc could see that Pauline had been crying.

"I have a surprise for you," he said cheerfully as he helped her from the boat and embraced her briefly.

"I hope it is a happy surprise," she replied as she looked about at the still smoking ruins.

Leclerc drove his wife and son along the quay, away from the main destruction of the city. A kilometer north of the government dock he had the carriage stopped before the gate of a villa set back from the shore between two arms of the protecting hills. It was habitation Bailly, the house occupied by Hédouville when he was at the Cape. Because of its isolation and because its owner was Toussaint Louverture, the house had been spared from the fire.

"You can move in immediately," Leclerc assured Pauline. "In a few days we will have it as good as new."

Pauline cried with relief. She had her house by the water. It would soon become an oasis for the poor planters who had lost their homes to black vengeance. She would cheer them. She would give parties that would bring back their joy. She would vanquish their worries. Soon their biggest concern, she thought with a laugh of delight, would be getting invitations to dinner with General Leclerc and his charming wife, the beautiful sister of the First Consul.

Dessalines was enjoying life with Claire in their new palace in Saint Marc when he heard that the French fleet was at Samaná. Concerned that he had received no orders from Toussaint and distrustful of Christophe's intentions at the Cape, Dessalines rode north with his honor guard and a brigade of his best troops.

Before he left Saint Marc he gave orders that the French were to be resisted at all the ports of the West: Gonaïves, Saint Marc, Arcahaie and Port-au-Prince. And if the French fought their away ashore, the cities were to be burned.

On the morning of February third—the day that Christophe burned the Cape—while Dessalines was in the North, the French general Jean Boudet arrived with his army in the harbor of Port-au-Prince.

Boudet sent two couriers ashore, with copies of Napoléon's proclamation of peace, to arrange for the landing of the French soldiers. General Agé, the white commander of the Port-au-Prince district, received the envoys courteously.

Toussaint had appointed Agé as the commander of the district over Dessalines's objection. Agé had proved himself an able administrator as Toussaint's chief-of-staff, but Dessalines distrusted all whites. In anticipation of the coming war with Napoléon and to frustrate any treachery by Agé, Dessalines had Colonel Louis Lamartiniere appointed as commander of the city's defenses.

When Boudet's envoys met with Agé, Lamartiniere burst into the room and, over Agé's objection, took the envoys hostage.

Lamartiniere was a small, thin, hotheaded man of thirty years who by all appearances was white. He was the illegitimate son of a white father and a sacra-tras—a quadroon—mother. Lamartiniere's father owned a sugar plantation and refinery near Léogane. He had recognized his mulatto son, but left his property to his legitimate, white son.

Lamartiniere chose the profession of his paternal grandfather, that of a soldier, and enlisted under Rigaud. When the English were driven out, Lamartiniere drove out his half-brother as well and took possession of the family lands.

Lamartiniere shared Rigaud's hatred of whites. He despised their arrogant superiority. He despised being defined by the percent of white blood that flowed thorough his veins. He found himself spiritually bound to his mother's black ancestors, whom he did not know. When Rigaud fled the island, Lamartiniere gladly accepted Dessalines's offer of clemency and enlisted under the black general.

Lamartiniere was fully aware of the role France played in inflaming the hatred between the mulattos and blacks. More clearly than did Rigaud he understood Hédouville's role in fermenting the War of Knives. Lamartiniere had no great love of Toussaint, but his hatred of the French was greater. Above all he wanted independence for Saint-Domingue and saw Toussaint as the best agent to that end.

After Lamartiniere's intrusion, Agé, Lamartiniere and the other officers of the city argued through the night. Most believed Napoléon's promises, but Lamartiniere did not. He demanded obedience to Dessalines' orders. As the argument continued, Lamartiniere became more heated. He commanded that they burn the city immediately and kill all the whites. Lamartiniere's followers persuaded him from his drastic course, but they could not control his anger.

"If one French soldier lands without the permission of Toussaint Louverture," Lamartiniere threatened, "I will fire three shots of cannon in alarm. The alarm will be repeated across the island from hill to hill. It will be the signal to burn everything and kill all the whites."

Lamartiniere spoke from passion. He knew that the plan he described did not exist. But he believed it would happen. He believed that the blacks and many of the mulattos on the island shared his hatred of whites and would respond spontaneously to his signal.

Agé, fearful of Lamartiniere's temper, chose moderation, and sent his own envoy to Boudet advising that he could not agree to the French soldiers landing until he had orders from Toussaint.

The next day, Lamartiniere moved quickly to seize full control of the city. He placed black officers he trusted in command of the fortifications. When he heard that the soldiers were not permitted to draw ammunition for their muskets and cannons, Lamartiniere rushed to the armory and confronted the white commander of the arsenal.

"Citizen Lacombe," he instructed, "in the name of Toussaint Louverture, the only constitutional authority in this colony, I demand that you open the armory."

Lacombe refused, on the orders of General Agé.

Lamartiniere saw white soldiers and armed citizens of the city approaching the armory and knew that his small guard would be overwhelmed by numbers.

He drew his saber in one hand and his pistol in the other.

"Give me the keys, you miserable colon," Lamartiniere threatened Lacombe "or I will kill you."

When Lacombe hesitated, Lamartiniere shot him through the head.

Lamartiniere rushed from the armory and down Rue de Conty the three blocks west to Government House. The soldiers and citizens that had begun to gather dispersed rather than face his rage.

Lamartiniere burst into Borgella's office.

Every citizen not locked behind his own door," Lamartiniere directed, "will be arrested."

He exited without further comment and issued orders for arms and ammunition to be drawn for the defense of the city and for all citizens in the streets to be arrested on sight.

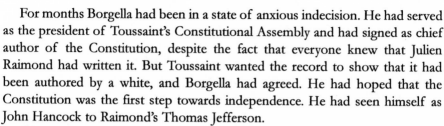

For months Borgella had been in a state of anxious indecision. He had served as the president of Toussaint's Constitutional Assembly and had signed as chief author of the Constitution, despite the fact that everyone knew that Julien Raimond had written it. But Toussaint wanted the record to show that it had been authored by a white, and Borgella had agreed. He had hoped that the Constitution was the first step towards independence. He had seen himself as John Hancock to Raimond's Thomas Jefferson.

When Toussaint did not declare the island's independence, and when Moïse and the black laborers of the North revolted, Borgella had second thoughts about his name being on the document. And now that Raimond had died—peacefully in his bed, Borgella remembered a little enviously—he was the only author left for Napoléon to hang.

When Lamartiniere took command of the city, Borgella felt relieved. He did not want the city destroyed again, but at least the decision was not his. He published Lamartiniere's order to the citizens and then went home to his own house and his frightened wife and locked his doors.

The French general Boudet was not happy that his envoys were held hostage. During the day he had reports of the confusion in the city and of the conflict between the whites and the blacks.

Jean Boudet was a handsome man of thirty-three. He was experienced in the wars of the West Indies having led the victorious French forces against the British in Guadeloupe, Grenada, Saint Lucia and Saint Vincent. He was among the favored officers who accompanied Napoléon to the Council of Five Hundred at Saint Cloud to complete the Revolution of Eighteen Brumaire. And Boudet won everlasting honor when he took the place of the dying Desaix and led the charge at Marengo that turned sure defeat for Napoléon into his greatest victory.

Boudet believed Napoléon's assurances of respect for men of all races in Saint-Domingue. He believed because as a true son of the Revolution he felt none of the hatred that Rochambeau and other ex-Royalist Saint-Domingue veterans had for the blacks.

Boudet could not understand the resistance to his landing. He posed no danger for those who were prepared to swear fidelity to France. He could only conclude that those who resisted him were traitors.

In the middle of the morning after Lamartiniere took command of the city, Boudet landed his army on Point Lamentin, the projection of land that formed the southwestern arm of the harbor.

By noon Boudet, with six thousand soldiers, was at Fort Bizoton, a league west of Port-au-Prince on the road from Léogane. He sent an emissary to the commander of the fort with the plea, in the name of France, to submit peacefully. He promised that there would be no changes in the colony and that all officers and soldiers would be maintained in their grades. Then Boudet addressed his own soldiers arrayed before the fort and exhorted them, if the defenders refused to surrender, to take the fort and kill all who resisted.

Some of the defenders believed Boudet's promise, and rushed from the fort. They were greeted by the French with shouts of welcome and were embraced as brothers. The rest of the defenders, seeing the greeting, also submitted.

Lamartiniere was enraged when he heard of the loss of Fort Bizoton. He ordered the whites he arrested for being in the city streets marched north, and the cavalry and Toussaint's honor guard stationed in Port-au-Prince to dismount and fight with him on foot at Fort Léogane, a low redoubt that guarded the west entrance of the city.

Boudet, as he approached Fort Léogane, again sent an emissary to request that the defenders surrender.

Colonel d'Henin, the emissary, approached the fort on foot and requested to speak with the commander. Lamartiniere appeared on the fort's battlements.

"We should not fight," d'Henin insisted. "We are French. We are brothers." He threw his sword to the ground behind him and asked to come into the fort and talk to the soldiers.

"No!" responded Lamartiniere.

Boudet, impatient with Lamartiniere, ordered his soldiers forward, bayonets fixed, as a show of force. The defenders from Fort Bizoton argued with the French soldiers to wait, to talk with Lamartiniere. Boudet continued forward.

Lamartiniere replied with a volley of musket fire into the advancing soldiers. D'Henin was wounded. The French returned the fire.

A quandary marked the battles between Leclerc and Toussaint's forces. Both sides fought under the tricolor to the cries of "Long live liberty! Long live the Republic!" The soldiers were confusion as to why they were opposed to each other. They were all children of the same Revolution, fighting under the same banner for the same principles.

The defenders of Fort Léogane fought ferociously and inflicted terrible casualties on Boudet's troops, but the weight of numbers and the guns of the French ships in the harbor won the day. Lamartiniere and his soldiers retreated to the National Fort in the heights behind the city, beyond the range of the ship's guns. There they held until nightfall.

In the darkness they slipped from the fort into the plain of the Cul-de-Sac. There, in revenge for the loss of the city, Lamartiniere ordered the white prisoners shot.

Boudet brought peace and confidence to the citizens of Port-au-Prince. He treated white, black and brown with dignity. All wounded soldiers, those that came with him from France and those loyal to Toussaint, were treated with equal care at the military hospital.

Boudet requested that Bishop Lecun—the same churchman who served Toussaint in welcoming back the whites after the defeat of the English—hold a mass of celebration of peace in the cathedral. There Lecun blessed the children of all races and gave thanks to God and Boudet for the city's deliverance from the despotism of the monster, Toussaint Louverture.

Pacification was going well for Boudet. Soon after he secured Port-au-Prince he received word that Toussaint's commanders of the South, on the news of Boudet's great success, had joined the French without resistance.

Then, on February ninth, Boudet heard ominous news. Dessalines was in the plain of the Cul-du-Sac.

Dessalines found Lamartiniere at Croix-des-Bouquets.

"It is because of Toussaint!" Dessalines shouted.

He could not eat. He swept the food from the table with one angry gesture. He got up and stamped out of the house onto the great porch. Lamartiniere followed him.

On the porch, Dessalines stared at the slope of hills concealing from his view the buildings of Port-au-Prince three leagues to the southwest.

"Damn Toussaint!" he shouted. He ripped off his tunic and shirt, throwing them from him, and stood naked from the waist up, the whip scars glistening in the sweat of his chest and back. Then he remembered something, retrieved his tunic and from a pocket extracted a silver snuffbox, and threw the tunic away again. Lamartiniere, gnawing on half a chicken he brought from the table with him, leaned against the doorjamb and watched his friend and commander.

Dessalines flipped open his snuff box, took a large pinch of powdered tobacco between his thumb and forefinger, held it to his nose and sniffed strongly with one nostril and then the other. He sneezed loudly, closed the snuffbox, put it into a trouser pocket, and sat down on the porch steps. The ritual calmed somewhat his anger.

Lamartiniere sat beside Dessalines and offered him a drink from the wine bottle he carried from the table. Dessalines took the bottle gratefully, drank deeply and returned it to Lamartiniere.

"Where is Toussaint?" Lamartiniere asked.

"I don't know," Dessalines answered.

"Has he surrendered to the whites?" Lamartiniere asked.

"No!" Dessalines answered sharply. "I don't know," he said a moment later. "Damn him!" he roared a moment later.

"They have all surrendered," Lamartiniere complained. "Without resisting! They ask to have the chains put on again! Laplume. Your cousin Dommage. Toussaint's brother. Nobody has any sense."

"It is Toussaint's fault," Dessalines accused. "With one mouth he tells them the French come to enslave them again. With the other he tells them that we need the whites and we should trust them. He gives the commanders no orders. They don't know what to do."

"What are we going to do?" Lamartiniere asked.

Dessalines looked at him in disbelief. "Do? We are going to purge the whites from this island. We will burn everything. We will surround them with fire and drive them into the sea."

Before they parted, Dessalines and Lamartiniere began the destruction of the Cul-du-Sac by burning the village of Croix-des-Bouquets.

While Lamartiniere harassed the French at Port-au-Prince, Dessalines marched boldly through the Cul-du-Sac, across the mountains east of the city and into the South, drawing Boudet's army after him.

Dessalines was exhilarated by the forced march through the mountains. When other men gasped for breath in the thin air, he felt buoyant and invigorated.

The cool air against his skin, the sharp pull in his chest, the throbbing in his legs, persuaded him of his superiority over lesser beings. While others succumbed to their pain, he pushed always ahead, daring, threatening, cajoling the others to stay with him.

Dessalines felt a oneness with the mountains such as he imagined sailors must feel with the sea. He picked his way confidently, sensing the profitable paths, seldom needing to retrace his steps. It was in the mountains that Dessalines first found freedom as a runaway slave. It was Dessalines' skills as a mountain scout that first brought him to the attention of Toussaint, and it was into the protection of the mountains that Dessalines now retreated to wage his war on the whites.

As he moved south, Dessalines destroyed everything he passed. He burned the houses and the crops. He put all whites to the sword and left their bodies heaped in piles, unburied, where the French soldiers who pursued him would find them.

Dessalines hoped his presence in the South would draw to him the blacks who had submitted and now fought under Boudet. But his hope was frustrated. The residents of the South remembered too well the War of Knives, only two years past. They remembered the purge that followed the war, when mulattos loyal to Rigaud and blacks loyal to the loa were cut down like sugar cane.

The slave owners of Saint-Domingue had attempted to destroy the strong African ties of their slaves by breaking up families and tribal groupings. But the blacks never lost their sense of loyalty. Where there were no chieftains or tribal elders to guide them, they turned to the houngans or the military commanders for leadership. When a man gave his loyalty to a leader, that loyalty was not easily changed. If a man changed his loyalty, his guilt was assuaged only by the passion of his commitment to his new leader.

The black generals who had submitted to Boudet clung steadfastly to their new allegiances, supported by their pride and by the assurances of the French that Toussaint, Dessalines, Christophe and the others who resisted would have to follow their example and submit to Napoléon's rule.

Those who followed the black generals accepted the allegiances of their leaders, with some exceptions. Some saw in Dessalines or Toussaint the great houngan whom the loa had chosen as the leader of leaders. These rallied to Dessalines. Others, fearful both of the promises of the French and the persecutions of Dessalines, chose a third path, the path of the loa. They, like Anacaona, followed the sounds of the drums into the high mountains.

Lamour Derance knew that his enemy, the persecutor of the faithful, was in the South, within striking distance of his armed maroons, and Derance knew that Dessalines' army was tired from its running battle with the French.

But before Derance could act, he had to persuade the elders of the nation, those who argued for caution, who argued that the faithful should not risk placing themselves between warring factions. When he convinced them that the hopes of peace lay with Dessalines' defeat, the loa had to be summoned to aid the faithful in their efforts.

By the time all preparations were made, Dessalines was gone. With a speed that amazed Derance, his enemy had moved his army north again, into the plain of the Cul-du-Sac, leaving a frustrated French army to limp exhausted back into Port-au-Prince.

Dessalines was furious.

"I could not shake the French," he complained to Lamartiniere. "Boudet is a bulldog. And the traitor Laplume moves slowly but carries a fine net."

Dessalines was concerned about Claire. He had left her at Saint Marc. The French had not yet occupied the city, but with the South, Port-au-Prince and the Cape firmly in their hands, they would now move against Toussaint in the West.

As Dessalines moved north, Boudet once again marched from Port-au-Prince in pursuit. South of Arcahaie the armies met. The artillery of the French and the fervor of the blacks proved a bloody match. Neither side could advance, and neither side would retreat. Boudet swung the balance by bringing up his ships from Port-au-Prince and raking the road with the naval guns.

Dessalines and Lamartiniere sat talking, heedless of the crackling musket fire to the south and the naval rockets bursting around them.

Dessalines bit into the sweet, gelatinous flesh of the ripe star apple he held in his left hand and casually spit the seeds onto the ground. "No," he explained, drawing with the stick in his right hand in the red clay of the road. "We only begin an engagement. Then we withdraw and reset our line here, well beyond the artillery range. We engage their infantry and hold." He sucked at the silver pulp and black-red flesh of the small fruit. "They will move the cannon to here," he continued, marking the spot with his stick. "We will let them fire long enough to heat their guns, and then we withdraw again to here." He licked at the juice running down his fingers.

"And the ships?" questioned Lamartiniere.

"When the French are moving, the ships dare not fire until they are certain of our position. The more often we move, the less effective the ships will be."

For two days Dessalines retreated north, burning Arcahaie and the smaller villages on the coast as he passed and killing all whites who had imprudently remained in the area. When he finally broke off engagement with the French and slipped into Saint Marc, the French were too exhausted to follow.

In Saint Marc, he sent Claire and the other of his soldiers' families living in the city to Petite Rivière, up the Artibonite River, deep into the center of the island. Dessalines knew that the Artibonite was where the blacks would make their last stand before retreating into the mountains and to the lives of maroons.

When the families were gone, Dessalines systematically set about executing all whites left in the city. Then he had fires kindled on the parade ground and all the buildings of the city dowsed with tar and filled with straw, dry grass, palm leaves, sugar cane, underbrush, guncotton and every other tinder available.

At nightfall, Dessalines assembled the citizens and soldiers on the parade ground.

"Comrades," Dessalines addressed his followers, the light of the fires glowing from the gold trim of his uniform and flashing red against his face, his many shadows snapping and jerking across the parade ground like flags beating in a silent wind. "We can not hold Saint Marc. Let each man make a proper gift of his house to the French. A gift of ashes! Let each man follow Dessalines and burn his own house!"

Dessalines snatched from a prepared pile a short stick wrapped at one end with dried grass and tallow. He thrust the brand into one of the fires and strode into the dark holding the blazing torch over his head. Soon the city was filled with flickering torches trailing away from the parade ground in all directions into every street and alley. While Dessalines was still walking a thousand fires lighted the night sky.

When Dessalines reached his palace, he did not hesitate. He broke into a run through the gate, across the garden, into the main hall and up the grand stairs. He walked briskly from room to room igniting the piles of straw and grass strewn about. Then he went down the stairs and through the great rooms on the first floor. When he walked out of the building and back into the street, Dessalines did not look back at the flames leaping from the windows and lapping at the walls of his wedding gift to Claire. He walked quickly back to the parade ground to organize the evacuation of the city.

Throughout the rest of the night, the survivors of the city, herded by the protecting soldiers, streamed east and then southeast along the Artibonite river toward Petite Rivière. They crossed the river at the bridge near the town of Artibonite. While he waited for the heavy wagons to cross, Dessalines stepped away from the glare of the torches and looked back at the fires of Saint Marc glowing against the western blackness of the pre-dawn sky.

It was, Dessalines decided, his sacrifice to Ogoun Fai Saint Jacques. May the old warrior be pleased with the gift and bless his namesake, Jean-Jacques Dessalines, with victory over his enemies.

In late afternoon, Boudet marched into the still smoking cinders of Saint Marc, all that was left of what was once the third largest city in Saint-Domingue.

Dessalines, after escorting the civilians safely to Petite Rivière, left that garrison city under the command of Lamartiniere. Dessalines then made a large show of marching his army north to join Toussaint and Christophe, but then, by night, circled Petite Rivière and followed the Artibonite to Mirebalais, where he turned south across the mountains, again toward Port-au-Prince.

The day that the French ships sailed into the harbor of the Cape, Isaac and I thought we would soon be ashore. Despite the violence with which Leclerc was greeted, we still hoped we would soon see our father and mother. We were greatly disappointed when we were transferred from the "Syrene" to the smaller ship the "Jean Jacques," and remained on board, anchored in the harbor. Leclerc explained that we would be more comfortable and safer on the ship than in the ruins of the city. We requested to go to Bréda near the city, but Leclerc did not answer our request.

While we were confined in the harbor, Isaac sought, as was his want, solace through religion, and he and Father Coison spent many hours in prayer. I contemplated jumping ship and swimming ashore, but because I did not know what was happening beyond the Cape, I checked my impatience and waited.

On the afternoon of February seventh, the fourth day of our confinement, we were summoned to see Leclerc. He received us in a tent erected in the Place de Montarcher that now served as his command headquarters. He explained that through an unfortunate misunderstanding our father had resisted the landing of the French troops.

"Most of the island receives us in peace," he explained. "Only your father and a few of his officers resist. I could crush them, but we have not come to make war. We have come in peace. You could serve France, the citizens of Saint-Domingue and your father if you would take to him the messages of peace the First Consul sends and urge your father to trust in my good will."

We readily agreed to the task, and I requested that we be allowed to leave immediately.

"But is nearly dark," Leclerc replied. "Get a good night's rest before your journey," he urged.

"We will not sleep," I answered for both Isaac and me.

Leclerc gave into my entreaties, and at eleven in the evening, with a small detachment of soldiers to accompany us through the French held areas, we left the Cape.

Even in the darkness we could see the results of Christophe's retreat. We passed by plantations devastated by fire. In some the embers still smoldered. With the light that came with the dawn we saw the extent of the destruction.

Because of Father Coison's age, we traveled slowly. By evening we reached the end of Leclerc's authority. We spent the night in the house used as command headquarters by general Edmé-Etienne Borne Desfourneaux.

Desfourneaux was an old hand in Saint-Domingue, having served under Laveaux against the English. Our father had written of his praises and we looked forward to meeting him, but he did not see us. His adjutant, Colonel Dampierre, who treated us with great respect, saw to our needs.

We left the camp at dawn, now only three of us. The French escort dared not accompany us further. Isaac and I assuaged Father Coison's anxieties with assurances that we knew well the country through which we rode and that he was safe with us. No one would harm the sons of Toussaint Louverture.

The land we rode through was rich in vegetation, untouched as yet by the new war.

Early in our journey we were greeted in the villages by the curious. When Isaac and I identified ourselves and explained our mission, the people cheered us on. The word of our arrival spread before us and the villages prepared celebrations. Our striking appearance in the rich uniforms Napoléon had given us impressed the people with the importance of our mission. They greeted us with

shouts of joy and displays of the French tricolor. Toussaint's sons were home
from France.

"We go to see our father," we told the crowds. "We bring assurances from
Napoléon that there will be no war. We bring the promise of peace and liberty,"
we told them.

They believed us. We were Toussaint's sons, dressed as French officers, speaking Parisian French without a trace of Creole. We believed ourselves.

Our excitement at seeing Desachaux again was almost unbearable. We galloped our horses the last few miles, leaving poor Coison far behind. The news
of our arrival preceded us, and our mother waited for us on the porch. When
she saw us she rushed across the lawn to greet us. Isaac and I leaped from our
saddles and threw ourselves into her arms.

We were surrounded by our family: our mother and our little brother Jean,
now a strapping boy of twelve whom we had not seen since he was seven; and
others whom we knew only through letters, Rose, an orphan Toussaint brought
home from the war, now a beautiful young lady of thirteen; and our cousins
Louise Chancy and Victorine Thusac—the daughters of Toussaint's sister
Genevieve.

We kissed. We hugged. We cried. We laughed. Everyone spoke at once. No
one listened. I lifted Rose from her feet and embraced her as if I had known her
all my life. Isaac would not let go of mother's hand. Mother marveled at our
good health and handsome appearances. Isaac and I bathed in the love we had
missed during our years in France.

Before we reached Desachaux, Toussaint had recovered sufficiently from his
illness to return to his headquarters in Gonaïves. Mother assured us that he had
been notified of our arrival. We waited impatiently for his return. At nine that
evening we heard the sounds of many horses approaching in the darkness.
Mother ordered the servants to light torches and we rushed to the porch of the
house to greet father.

My first impression was one of wonder at the size and display of the retinue
accompanying him. My memory of father was of him in humbler surroundings.
I had in France gotten used to the idea that he had become a man of great
importance, but the images in my mind had not spanned the changes in his fortune from simple officer to Governor-General of the colony.

Despite the press of men and uniforms and the dimness of the light I recognized father at once. Isaac and I waved and shouted at him like two young

schoolboys and ran to his horse. He sat for a moment looking down at us. It was as if he searched our faces to assure himself that it was truly us.

I was surprised at the restraint he showed as he dismounted and greeted us. I felt a little uncertain of his feelings, but Isaac rushed into his arms, yelling and pounding him in delight. Toussaint responded energetically, and in a moment he was hugging me as well and marveling at how much we had grown.

"Look, Suzanne," he shouted at mother who had remained on the porch. "See what men they have become."

The three of us walked arm and arm to the house. I was surprised at how small Toussaint seemed to me. I am several inches taller that Isaac, but Toussaint was smaller than both of us. I had not realized how much we had grown in the past five years. Father also seemed thinner to me.

In the torchlight and excitement at seeing him I had a poor sense of father's appearance, but when we reached the house and the brightness of the oil lamps, I was startled at the extent he had aged. His shoulders were bent as if he carried a weight on them. His eyes were tired and the edges of his mouth were lined. It was, I knew, the other side of the balance sheet from the pomp that marked his arrival.

We talked late into the evening. In the excitement, each of us found the opportunity and the audience for a recital of the events of the years of separation. We forgot the suffering of Saint-Domingue in the joy of our reunion.

As our happiness began to succumb to exhaustion, Father Coison stepped forward and reminded us of our mission.

"Excellency," he addressed Toussaint, "your sons bring you a gift to you from the First Consul."

Coison directed Isaac to fetch from our luggage the package Leclerc had given us.

"Excellency," Coison continued as we waited for Isaac to return, "the First Consul greets you as one victorious general to another. The love he bore the sons he sends through them to the noble father and requests that you extent to his representatives in Saint-Domingue the same courtesies he showed to yours in Paris."

Coison droned on, weaving a tapestry of flattery with his carefully balanced conceits.

"Enough!" Toussaint commanded when Isaac returned with the package.

"I believe Napoléon wants peace," Isaac declared in defense of Coison as he handed the package to Toussaint. Isaac explained that we had talked to Napoléon in his palace and that he had spoken of his admiration for Toussaint.

Toussaint, as he unwrapped the package, seemed not to hear Isaac. Under the heavy wrapping was a gold box. Inside the box, nestled in a lining of white silk, was a rolled parchment upon which lay a replica of the Great Seal of State.

The change in Toussaint was startling. It were as if he shivered from sudden exposure to chill mountain air. For two years he had begged Bonaparte to write to him. Now it came, too late and weighted with deception.

Toussaint unrolled the parchment and read it. It seemed to me he glanced at it only.

He spoke to Coison calmly and politely.

"Thank you for bringing to me my sons," he said. "If Leclerc wishes peace, let him stop the progress of his army."

Toussaint rose from his chair.

"I will write more in a letter you can take to General Leclerc tomorrow," he said, and then nodding politely to his family and the officers gathered in the room, he exited to his study.

CHAPTER 29
At War with France

Toussaint arose at four a.m. and left for his headquarters in Gonaïves before the rest of us were awake. In Gonaïves, as was his custom always, he attended mass at the break of dawn. At Desachaux Abbé Coison, Isaac and I waited for the dispatches for Leclerc. While we waited, mother put us to work packing the valuables in the house, including father's collection of gems.

"I will not have the French take from us everything we have worked for," she explained.

Later that day she accompanied the carriage with the valuables to Gonaïves to be put with others, the state treasuries from Ennery, Gonaïves, Saint Marc and Arcahaie, and the personal valuables of Dessalines and others of Toussaint's officers in the West, for shipment to Petite Rivière and into the Cahos Mountains for burial and safe keeping until the times were safer.

I have heard since that the valuables were hauled on mules accompanied by four hundred Spaniards from Santo Domingo, and that after the valuables were buried, the Spaniards were killed to keep secret the location. I do not believe this. Toussaint would not put so great a value on riches. Besides, the location was a poorly kept secret. Within a month General Rochambeau found the treasure and moved it to Port-au-Prince.

On the morning of our third day at Desachaux, Father Grenville, our brother Jean's tutor, arrived from Gonaïves with Toussaint's dispatches for Leclerc. Grenville, Coison, Isaac and I left at once for the Cape.

We arrived at Cape François after midnight and were taken immediately to Leclerc's command headquarters where we waited. Leclerc had given orders that he was to be called when we returned, no matter the hour.

In his letter to the Captain-General, Toussaint asked only that all fighting cease before any negotiations could proceed. He explained that he was returning his sons to Leclerc as proof that he had no desire to make war, but he would not accept Leclerc's gift of his sons in exchange for the subjugation of the blacks. Toussaint's response to Leclerc was reasoned. Leclerc's response to Toussaint was not.

"Lecture to me, does he?" Leclerc complained angrily after he read the letter. "For his treason let him be treated as a traitor!"

In a state of passion Leclerc withdrew from us. We were directed to rooms in the partially restored Government House where we waited further instructions.

While we waited, Isaac slept fitfully on the floor. I slept not at all. I puzzled over Leclerc's anger. Only much later did I learn that he had lost many men in the early fighting and was concerned about his ability to control Toussaint if he had to do it by arms.

Shortly after dawn we were called once more to Leclerc's tent.

"I have prepared a final appeal to your father," he informed us. "In it I call upon him to present himself to me here, at Cape François, within four days. If he does, I will accept his oath of loyalty to France and will appoint him my second in command. If he does not, I will declare him and all his lieutenants traitors to France and declare that they are outside of the law.

"I want to make certain that you understand what is in this letter," he continued, looking at Isaac and me, "so that you may persuade your father of the sincerity of my intentions. If he obeys he will be forgiven. If he does not, he will be hunted and killed.

"Toussaint should realize that I am capable of acting on my threat," Leclerc continued. "France has restored its rightful authority in Santo Domingo, in Port-au-Prince and in all of the South. I hold Fort Liberté and the Cape and most of the Northern Plain. In the Northwest even now I am moving against Port-de-Paix and have ships blockading the Môle. Toussaint holds only the West, and I can crush him there whenever I chose."

Isaac and I left immediately for Desachaux. Grenville and Coison remained at the Cape. They argued to return with us, and Isaac did not wish to part from Father Coison, but I insisted that they remain behind. They both were exhausted.

I feared continued exertion would endanger their health. They were men of advanced years, scholarly men, not physically able to sustain days of riding and nights without sleep.

On the ride, Isaac and I agreed that that we must persuade Toussaint to obey Leclerc. It was the only way to keep peace. When we reached Desachaux, we were surprised by the coldness with which Toussaint received us. He met us on the porch. His face was hard. He made no effort to embrace us, and when I reached to embrace him in greeting, he withdrew from me and waved me to silence.

Without leaving the porch, he read, silently, the dispatch we handed him.

"Do you know what the Captain-General has written to me?" he asked after he had finished reading.

"Yes, sir," I replied.

"I will not obey him," he declared in a calm voice that did not conceal the emotions I sensed within him.

"Father, you must obey!" Isaac cried. In great alarm he pleaded with Toussaint, arguing that only obedience could save his life and save many from needlessly dying. Isaac swore by the Holy Mother that Leclerc was an honest man whose word could be trusted.

Father silenced Isaac's torrent of words by reaching out for him and pulling him into his arms. Isaac burst into tears and held tightly to his father, his head resting on the shorter man's shoulder.

After a moment, Toussaint gestured for me to come to him. When I did, he reached out and drew me into the embrace with Isaac. I found that I could not keep the tears from my own eyes.

After a few minutes, Toussaint released us. We could see that he, too, was crying.

He turned from us for a moment, to compose himself. Then he gestured for us to walk with him across the lawn. He indicated that everyone else, his guards and even mother, was to remain at the house.

As we walked, he told us how greatly he loved us, each of us equally.

"I can see," he said, "that you have grown into men of whom I can be proud. I can see, also, that you are Frenchmen. I am proud of that. I know that you love your country, as I do. I cannot tell you what you should do, but I know what I must do. I must make war against Leclerc...."

Isaac interrupted him. "No, father! Then you are a traitor to France!"

"I am no traitor!" Toussaint replied angrily.

Toussaint and Isaac each tried to control his feelings. After a few moments Toussaint spoke again, quietly.

"I do not make war against France," he explained. "I make war against Leclerc only."

"Leclerc is France in Saint-Domingue," Isaac insisted.

"He is not!" Toussaint retorted. "France has a Constitution and Saint-Domingue has a Constitution. Leclerc violates both. It is he who brings soldiers and guns to an island at peace. It is he who brings with him enemies to our liberty: Rigaud, Rochambeau, Pétion, men whom I have deported for their crimes against our government. It is Leclerc who marches with an army now to destroy me and to enslave again the blacks."

"That is not so, father!" Isaac retorted angrily.

To my surprise, Toussaint answered Isaac softly.

"I love you, Isaac," he said. "You may oppose me, but I shall love you always. But I fear you do not understand these men as I do. I see how Leclerc treats us when we have power. I fear to think how he will treat us when we are powerless."

Our walk took us in a long arc around the house. When we reached again the porch where the others waited, Toussaint announced to Suzanne that Isaac and I would rest for the night and leave in the morning with his answer to Leclerc.

Toussaint left shortly after for Gonaïves. Although I could see that mother was displeased with father's announcement she said nothing. I was greatly discomforted for the rest of the afternoon and evening, retired early to bed, but could not sleep.

Throughout the night I wrestled with my decision. In my mind I needed to believe Leclerc's promises, but in my heart I needed to believe my father. I was in an agony of turmoil. I feared that Toussaint had no chance of defeating Leclerc in battle. I did not wish to die needlessly in a hopeless and errant cause. I was angry at my father's stubbornness. When I considered that Toussaint might be right, a wave of deep fear encompassed me. It seemed inconceivable to me that Napoléon would create such an elaborate charade just to enslave again the blacks. I argued to myself that the people of France would not permit it. Then I recalled little happenings that grew in my mind into an avalanche of remembered looks, gestures, slights, experiences that overwhelmed me with the certainty that Toussaint was right. But even if France reestablished slavery, I argued to myself, they would not make me a slave. I was an educated Frenchman. But I knew as I made my arguments that I engaged in self-delusion. The Revolution had changed laws only, not the hearts of men. If the laws were changed again, the age-old bigotries still intact in the European mind would emerge to embrace the change.

Just before dawn, I found peace in my decision. I knew Toussaint saw clearly Leclerc's and Napoléon's intentions, and I knew that even if I had absolute knowledge that I could live out my life in France in peace and liberty, I would chose to fight and die beside my father rather than see one black again shackled in slavery.

My mind at peace, I got up from my bed, dressed quickly and walked out to the porch. The household was already stirring. The grooms were looking to the horses. The cooks were busy in the kitchen. Shortly after dawn Toussaint and his attendants rode in from Gonaïves. I greeted him as he dismounted.

"I am staying with you," I said without preamble. "Someone else must take your answer to Leclerc."

For a moment Toussaint was startled. Then he embraced me and kissed me on the cheek. "You are my son in truth," he said.

I felt that my heart would break with pride.

"Does Isaac stay, also?" he asked.

I buried the anger I felt at his question. "I do not know," I answered. "I have not talked with him since yesterday."

At breakfast Toussaint asked Isaac if he were still determined to return to the Cape. Isaac was surprised at the question. He looked at me in some confusion.

"I am staying with father," I told him.

Toussaint sensed the anxiety my response created in Isaac.

"You are of course free to return, and you go with my love," Toussaint reassured him.

I saw the anger in Isaac's eyes. I knew he felt that I had betrayed him, betrayed the agreement we had reached on the ride from the Cape. We had often in our lives been at odds, but our battles were few because as the elder, I felt it my responsibility to care for him. I bowed always to his needs. This time I did not let his anger affect me. I feared only that he would change his mind and remain also with Toussaint.

"I am going back! I am no traitor!" I was relieved to hear Isaac answer. He addressed the accusation in his words to me, not Toussaint.

"It is settled then," Toussaint replied. He spoke as if he were agreeing to a routine matter of business such as the price of a foal. "You will take my answer with you to the Captain-General."

Through all the conversation mother said nothing. She sat as if she did not hear. Her silence surprised me.

After breakfast, Isaac prepared for the ride to the Cape. Toussaint assigned two officers to accompany him and gave a copy of the letter to Leclerc to each officer in case the party was attacked.

By eight o'clock Isaac was prepared to leave. He had no sooner mounted his horse than he dismounted and embraced again mother, then me and finally father.

"Come with me, please," he pleaded with Toussaint as they held each other.

"Where the stream divides, each must follow its own course," Toussaint replied.

Isaac mounted again, but before he was firmly in the saddle, mother stepped forward and took the reins from the groom.

"Ride on," she commanded the officers with Isaac. "Isaac stays with me."

"No!" exclaimed Isaac. He pulled at the reins and spurred the horse, but Suzanne was not intimidated by the confused beast. She held tightly to the reins with her right hand and with her left slapped at the hunches of the mounts of the officers with Isaac.

"Yah!" she shouted. "Ride on!" she repeated.

The startled officers let their horses have their heads and galloped from the house. Isaac struggled to free his horse from Suzanne's restraint.

"It is my choice!" he shouted over and over. "Father says it is my choice!"

"I say you are staying with me," Suzanne replied.

Isaac did not have the strength to resist his mother. He leaped from the saddle and ran into the house in a fury of tears and anger. Toussaint and I waited outside for the grooms to bring our horses for the ride to Gonaïves.

Isaac stayed with mother until we were all sent to France. He did not return to the Cape nor did he join Toussaint and me in the war. I have never spoken to him since of the incident. I feel too strongly his humiliation. In the years since, he has had on occasion the need to remind me, as he has all his life, that he was the natural son. I have restrained from making the obvious reply. We both know the truth. That is enough.

In Gonaïves, Toussaint assembled the soldiers of the garrison and of his personal guard. He sat upon Bel-Argent in the middle of them and told them of the battles to come.

"Only our Constitution guarantees our liberty," he told them, "and General Leclerc comes to overthrow the Constitution. We must fight once more for our freedom."

The soldiers swore to fight by him to the death.

He then called me to his side and before the assembled troops appointed me to the grade of commander and gave me the command of a battalion of his personal guard. With great pride I swore to follow him to the death.

I was pleased that Toussaint gave me a command. I had neither experience nor training as a soldier. But I had faith in my courage, my intelligence and my loyalty. In my heart I was prepared. I had feared that Toussaint would give me a position on his personal staff. I was grateful and pleased that he saw in me the ability to lead men.

In the mountains southeast of Port-au-Prince, Lamour Derance donned his red jacket and met once more with the elders of his nation. The scouts had brought two pieces of information which he believed were providential.

André Rigaud had returned with Napoléon's forces. Derance had little respect for Rigaud, but Beauvais had served Rigaud, and Derance served Beauvais. Derance was certain that Beauvais was dead, but out of respect for his old benefactor, Derance felt that he now owed alliance to Rigaud.

The scouts also reported that while Boudet looked for Dessalines in the Artibonite, Dessalines had slipped away and was now marching toward the lightly guarded Port-au-Prince.

The elders readily agreed with Derance. Out of loyalty to Beauvais they must warn the garrison at Port-au-Prince.

Pamphile de Lacroix, the ranking French officer at Port-au-Prince, was confused by the ragtag band of blacks who appeared before the walls of the Saint Joseph Battery. From what he and his captain of the guard could understand through the heavy Creole dialect of the intruders, they had come to warn the city of an attack from Dessalines. Lacroix suspected treachery, but sent for Borgella and other citizens of the city to help him fathom the situation.

Borgella assured Lacroix that the elderly man in the British uniform could be trusted.

"He is a maroon, a free black," Borgella explained, "who has an abiding hatred for Dessalines."

Lacroix called a conference of his officers, and with the urging of Borgella and other citizens, agreed to follow Derance's instructions.

Dessalines was stunned by the news. "A thousand men lost," he mourned. His advance guard had fallen into an ambuscade at the Fond Diable, where the road from Mirebalais to the Cul-de-Sac runs by high cliffs. When he heard that Lamour Derance had set the ambush, Dessalines's mood became murderous.

Dessalines continued on his march to Port-au-Prince, but he knew his plan to take the city by surprise had failed. Warned by Derance, the French were alerted, and Boudet was in full march from Saint Marc to reinforce the city's defenders.

Dessalines spent the next days and nights in frustration. He did not have the force to attack the city, now prepared to repulse him, and he could not draw Boudet from the city to engage him in the field. In his angry efforts to punish the whites, Dessalines crisscrossed the Cul-de-Sac burning the habitations that had survived Lamartiniere's ravaging. He also worked at recruiting black laborers to his army, but even here he met frustration as most of them fled to the French for protection from him.

At the Cape, Leclerc was pleased at the beginnings of his conquest. "Many of those who envied my command in Paris would be defeated here," he wrote to Napoléon. "I shall prove to France that you have made a good choice."

But he could not hide from himself nor from the First Consul his alarm at how difficult things were in Saint-Domingue. He complained about his losses of soldiers: "Calculate on a considerable waste of life in this country," he wrote to Napoléon. He complained about the destruction of property: "The burning of the Cape and the districts through which the rebels have retired deprives me of all resources," he wrote. He complained about the merchants with whom he had to trade: "The traders at the Cape are all agents of the Americans and the Americans are of all Jews, the most Jewish."

The American traders at the Cape angered Leclerc more than the black rebels. The Americans were white and should have been thankful to the French for keeping the Caribbean from becoming an African bastion.

Leclerc found that some American ship captain claimed every piece of merchandise in the city, every bolt of cloth, every barrel of flour, every keg of nails. When Leclerc tried to purchase anything, the Americans jumped their prices, competing, it seemed, to see who could gauge him the deepest.

When he discovered that some of the American ships in the harbor secretly carried munitions for trade with the rebels, Leclerc had had enough. He took what he wanted from the Americans and jailed the captains who complained.

When Tobias Lear demanded that they be treated according to the law, Leclerc's answer was short and swift.

"They are all thieving Arabs," Leclerc told him, "and don't deserve the protection of the law."

When Lear protested, Leclerc gave him a week to leave the island.

Faced with such treatment, American merchants stopped calling at the Cape and Leclerc had to depend solely on France for his supplies.

By the middle of February Leclerc had passed Napoléon's deadline for the pacification of the island. But with the arrival of reinforcements and supplies from France, Leclerc was finally prepared to move against Toussaint. On February seventeenth, he issued a proclamation promising liberty to all who submitted to him, and declaring Toussaint, Christophe, Dessalines and all who followed them outlaws.

Leclerc's plan of attack was Napoléonic in design. Rochambeau was to march from Fort Liberté (which he had restored to its pre-Revolutionary name of Fort Dauphin) turning Toussaint's right flank and opening the way into the Artibonite from Santo Domingo. Humbert was to keep Maurepas bottled up in Port-de-Paix. Hardy was to push Christophe south into the arms of Rochambeau. Leclerc was to march on Toussaint from the north and Boudet was to march north from Port-au-Prince and hit Toussaint from the south. With his superior numbers and the skill and courage of his soldiers—veterans of Napoléon's European wars—Leclerc anticipated an early victory.

CHAPTER 30
Ravine-à-Couleuvres

As a battalion commander in Toussaint's guard, I was able to observe my father on many occasions during the Three Months' War against Leclerc. I was sometimes troubled by what I saw.

The first task that Toussaint faced was to check the flow of defections. Leclerc promised amnesty and continuation in grade to all who came to the French. He painted the conflict as between, on one side, the legal government of France restoring its authority in the colony, and on the other, rebels attempting to establish an independent black state. He called for all to return to the forgiving bosom of their mother country. Those who returned were treated with respect and given positions in the French army. Many wrote to their friends and relatives in the rebellion forces describing their treatment by Leclerc and urging the others to follow them.

By the time I joined Toussaint, he had in his army less than half the number he had before Leclerc landed. The only commanders still loyal to him were Maurepas who held the Northwest and the besieged Port-de-Paix, Christophe who fought in the mountains south of the Cape, and Dessalines who harassed Boudet at Port-au-Prince. Toussaint himself held Gonaïves and the surrounding area.

The defections continued because Toussaint was not able to make the people see Leclerc's real intent. In his efforts to arouse the workers, Toussaint did not move with the vigor and decisiveness that he was want. He found himself paralyzed by the memories of past mistakes. On several occasions he confessed to me his litany of omissions: if he had acted more vigorously before the French arrived; if he had removed the white officers from high commands; if he had listened to Dessalines and put Lamartiniere in command of Port-au-Prince; if he had been precise in his instructions to the port commanders.

But of all Toussaint's regrets, the one that struck him hardest was the loss of Moïse. I saw it in his behavior to me. On several occasions he inadvertently called me Moïse. It wasn't that he mistook me for Moïse. He knew who I was. But "Moïse" came to his lips before "Placide" when he looked at me.

On one occasion I rode behind him on a trail circling west of Plaisance. I fell behind and Toussaint waited at a break in the trail for me to catch up with him. When I arrived, I was startled at the expression on his face. When I asked him if he were well, he turned and rode on. It seemed to me that he wept. Mars Plaisir, Toussaint's personal servant who was with us, later told me he thought Toussaint expected Moïse to appear.

I worried that my father might be losing his mind, but Mars assured me that Toussaint was well. He needed time to accept the crushing defeats he had suffered and to find the resolve to do battle once again.

Mars told me how great the lose of Moïse was to Toussaint. It was Moïse who held for him the people of the North, the center of Toussaint's power. They were now scattered and confused. Toussaint must go to them himself and raise them against Leclerc, but in going to them he carried two stigmata that alienated the people from him, his execution of Moïse and his suppression of the African rites.

In both of these, Mars assured me, Toussaint did what he had to do. Moïse had betrayed Toussaint when most he had need of him, Mars insisted, and even today the voudoun houngan sent malicious spirits upon him. "He is only free of them when he is in church," Mars explained. "Be patient with him," the gentle old man advised. "Toussaint knows what he must do to bring the people to him again. He knows that nodding the head will not break the neck."

One evidence I had of my father's mental confusion was a conversation we had regarding Thomas Jefferson.

"I have written to Jefferson," he told me one night when neither of us could sleep. "He will send us help."

I did not feel that I should contradict my father. He had, no doubt, information which I did not, but I found his expectations of Jefferson surprising. I knew that in Paris Jefferson's election to the presidency of the United States was applauded. They looked to him to improve relations between the two countries, to correct the cool neutrality that Adams had taken in the war between France and England. Jefferson was heralded as an admirer of Napoléon.

"Why do you think Jefferson will help us? What has he to gain?" I asked, not to be argumentative, but to improve my awareness of politics.

"Jefferson has a great deal to gain," Toussaint assured me. "I offer him the means to advance himself both morally and politically."

I could not understand Toussaint's hopes in Jefferson. "The only interest America could have in us," I insisted, "is trade or a ready source of slaves. If the British are successful in their efforts to abolish the slave trade in Africa, then the American slavers would appreciate having a source of blacks to exploit this close to their shores."

"But Jefferson does not support slavery," Toussaint explained. "He is embarrassed by it. The man who wrote the American Declaration of Independence could never be at ease with slavery, and I offer him a way out of his dilemma before the blacks of North America rise up in bloody retribution as we did here."

I wasn't sure whether Toussaint was inspired or confused. "What do you offer him?" was all I could ask.

"I offer him the means to free his country of the horrors of slavery while satisfying the greed of the slaveholders."

"How?"

"By trading land for their slaves."

"What land?" I asked in bewilderment.

"Louisiana."

"Louisiana?" I asked. "But we don't have Louisiana to give him."

"Yes we do," Toussaint assured me.

"Louisiana belongs to Spain," I argued.

"The King of Spain is Bonaparte's lackey," Toussaint answered as if that made everything clear.

When he saw that I could not follow his reasoning, Toussaint, checking first to see that no one overheard us, beckoned me to move closer to him so that he could talk in a quiet voice.

"The secret," he said, "is to understand the larger forces at work in the world. If I had not understood the larger forces I could not have gotten trade with the English and Americans without being eaten by them."

"But Louisiana?" I asked.

"The reason Napoléon wants us enslaved again," Toussaint patiently explained, "is to establish a base and build an army to invade Louisiana and the Floridas, and I have written to Jefferson warning him of Napoléon's plans."

I was confused by what Toussaint was telling me, but I felt I did not know enough to challenge his contentions.

"Don't you see," he continued, "if Jefferson sent his slaves here to help us defeat the French, then he serves himself in many ways. He has solved his slave problem. He stops Napoléon here, preventing him from occupying Louisiana, and he needs only then to move a small militia into Louisiana and the Floridas to take them from Napoléon and use the land there to compensate the slave holders for their losses."

"But if Jefferson wanted to attack Louisiana why would he need to help us first? Why would he not just take the territories?" I asked.

"We give him the moral reasons for his actions. The sentiment for abolition is strong in America. The question that slows them is what to do with the blacks when they are free. Free blacks from Saint-Domingue fought for American freedom in their war against England. Now they can send free blacks to us to fight for our liberty against France. To protect the Americans—black Americans—fighting here, Jefferson would be justified in keeping the French from Louisiana, and in taking Louisiana he could compensate the slave holders who released their slaves to fight in Saint-Domingue. When Saint-Domingue is free and independent, the two republics, the white one in the north and the black one in the south, could between them defend the new world forever from the encroachments of Europe. We would live in peace, one with the other, because there would be no issue of color between us."

"You wrote this to Jefferson?" I asked.

"Yes," Toussaint responded.

"Has he answered you?" I asked.

"Not yet," Toussaint answered. "But with the French holding Port-au-Prince and the Cape, it is difficult for his letters to reach me."

I was startled by the power of my father's vision but dismayed that he put his hopes in its fruition. I knew that the blacks of Saint-Domingue had only themselves to depend upon. I knew, also, that we were divided and uncertain. And I feared that Toussaint no longer had the will to unite and lead us.

My fears were soon allayed. When the battle was pressed upon Toussaint and his family was threatened, he sprang free of his malaise and was again, for a time, the vigorous leader of his people.

Toussaint had instructed Christophe to avoid confrontation with Leclerc's army but rather to hit and run in guerrilla fashion, as Dessalines fought in the South. Toussaint did not want his forces further depleted by major engagements before he could rebuild and plan his strategy. Christophe, angry at the loss of the Cape, ignored Toussaint's instructions and engaged in a series of confrontation with Hardy. Christophe avoided disaster by effectively withdrawing each time Hardy attacked. But with each retreat he drew closer to Ennery, the nearest town to Desachaux, and to Gonaïves, Toussaint's last stronghold. Rochambeau, meeting with no resistance in the east, was marching west to encircle Christophe and block his retreat.

On Saturday, February twentieth, a heavy rain stopped all fighting. Despite the short reprieve, Toussaint found himself in a desperate position. Christophe could not hold Ennery. Rochambeau was threatening to take Gonaïves, and Boudet had left Port-au-Prince and was moving toward Saint Marc to block Toussaint's retreat to the south. Toussaint knew that he must stop Rochambeau long enough to allow Christophe to escape and to secure his own retreat.

Toussaint had only his honor guard reinforced with a few hundred field laborers to stop Rochambeau and three thousand of Napoléon's veterans. Toussaint chose to confront Rochambeau at Ravine-à-Couleuvres.

Ravine-à-Couleuvres is a narrow, seasonal streambed, usually dry, that forms the eastern end of the pass through the Black Mountains from Saint-Michel to the coastal plain near Gonaïves. Because of the recent rain, a shallow stream of water ran through the gully.

On Tuesday, February twenty-third, after two days of maneuvering the two forces were in position.

On the night of the eve of the battle, I accompanied Toussaint and two laborers familiar with the area in a reconnaissance of the enemy. Toussaint wanted information on Rochambeau's deployment, but more importantly he wanted to make contact with the blacks who marched with Rochambeau, to persuade them of their folly in trusting the French.

We waited until after the moon had set, and in the darkness of the night penetrated Rochambeau's outer picket line. But one of the laborers scouting for us stumbled into an outpost and was shot and killed. The noise alerted the camp. Toussaint, the other scout and I lay noiselessly in the underbrush waiting for the opportunity to slip back to our own lines.

While we hid a few fathoms from his tent, Rochambeau met with his company officers to plan the morning's battle. All the faces were white. None of the rehabilitated black officers held positions of command under Rochambeau.

Donatien Marie Joseph de Vimeur, Viscomte de Rochambeau, was the son of Jean Baptiste Donatien Rochambeau, the commander of the French auxiliaries in the American War of Independence, where the son served under the father.

A Royalist, the elder Rochambeau served as a marshal of France under Louis XVI and barely escaped the guillotine. The son fared better in the Revolution, primarily because of his friendship with the Marquis de Lafayette, with whom he shared equalitarian sentiments. In 1796, Rochambeau was sent to Saint-Domingue as a military commander to serve equally in authority—as was the practice of the Jacobins—with the political commander, Sonthonax. When Rochambeau objected to the rising wealth and dominance of the black generals, especially Toussaint, Sonthonax dismissed him from command and shipped him back to Paris. Rochambeau felt that with his experience in Saint-Domingue he should have been selected by Napoléon to head the expedition. He waited now only for Leclerc to falter.

After Rochambeau had checked the readiness of his officers, he reminded them that in the morning they faced Toussaint Louverture, a man none of them should take lightly as an opponent.

"He is an able, I might say inspired, leader," Rochambeau cautioned, "but he is devoid of Christian virtues and the compassion's of a civilized gentleman. He would spare you no mercy. You should spare him none. Alert your men that if they are captured, they can expect to be executed in the most horrible manner. They must fight accordingly and give no quarter."

Rochambeau reminded his officers of their recent history, of their victories in Egypt, Austria and Italy. "We have not come three thousand miles to be defeated by slaves. We who were victorious at the Tiber, at the Nile and the Rhine will not fall at the Artibonite!"

Rochambeau had his servants serve his officers glasses of wine and then raised his in a toast. "Gentlemen, I give you Ravine-à-Couleuvres. May it stand in history as an echo of Marengo—where the French army met the enemy and won the war. To Ravine-à-Couleuvres and victory!"

"Ravine-à-Couleuvres and victory!" the officers enthusiastically echoed the toast. Others followed. To France. To Napoléon. To Rochambeau.

———————◆———————

We escaped back to our lines only under the noise of the pre-dawn stirring of the French soldiers preparing for battle. Toussaint was bitterly disappointed that he had not been able to contact any of the blacks. He wished to avoid firing upon his own people.

In the hour before first light, Toussaint rode energetically from unit to unit assigning them to their stations. He placed his small cavalry behind a concealing bluff on the road to Mare Louise where they could fall upon the flank of the French when they emerged from the ravine. His infantry he concealed behind trees and other barriers on the sides of the ravine. From his observations of Rochambeau's preparations, Toussaint expected him to march his army in file through the gully.

As he moved among his soldiers, Toussaint exhorted them to courage.

"I know how weary of war you are," he told them. "Like you, I, too, am weary, but we must stand firm before our enemy. They are men who know neither faith nor trust. They promise you liberty, but they intend your slavery. They refuse to recognize you as obedient children. If you are not their slaves, they call you rebels."

Toussaint spoke to the soldiers of their victories against slave masters and foreign invaders. To many he spoke of shared moments in the field.

He described the fruits of their efforts, "a land of slavery purified by fire evolving more beautifully under liberty. Your enemy will not succeed in snatching from you the victories of your struggles," he promised. "If you are faithful, your enemies' bones will be scattered among these mountains and tossed about by the waves of the sea. Liberty will forever reign in Saint-Domingue over their forgotten tombs."

As Toussaint's soldiers took up their posts, the native drums sounded, calling them to courage. I looked to Toussaint to see his response. He made none. As Mars had promised, Toussaint knew when to nod his head.

When the short twilight was gone and the morning sun was hidden only by the Black Mountains in the east, Rochambeau's soldiers, held in step by the beat of the military drums, marched in a column of four toward Toussaint's ambush. The contrast in sounds—the drums of Dahomey and the drums of de Brienne—was symptomatic of the estrangement that drove Frenchmen against Frenchmen. As one who had walked in both worlds but now, in ways of the soul, was alienated from both, I felt a profound sadness.

———————————✧———————————

The battle of Ravine-à-Couleuvres was my first taste of armed combat. Although my experience is limited, I can not imagine a battle more ferociously fought. Neither side had artillery and Rochambeau had no cavalry. After the initial exchange of gunfire, the combat was hand to hand with knife, club and sword, soldiers standing cheek by jowl within the confines of the narrow gully. Toussaint's position gave him an early advantage, but Rochambeau's superior numbers evened the contest.

Never before, nor since, did I witness my father in such a state. He was as one possessed. He was everywhere: now slashing at the enemy; now cajoling his soldiers; now driving them. When his cavalry was slow to attack, he struck at its commander, Monpoint, with his baton.

But his soldiers fought. I fought as I had not believed myself capable. Repeatedly I regrouped my battalion and charged with them into the mêlée. The wounded and dead, black and white, fell around me, but I felt myself immortal. I knew I would not fall because to do so would have displeased Toussaint.

In the middle of the morning, Toussaint received word that Suzanne, Isaac and the rest of our family had fled from Desachaux before the advance of Hardy.

"There is not time for them," I heard him complain. He instructed that they be put on the road to Esther, a league south of the fighting, where the Esther River is bridged.

By noon, those who still fought had barely the physical strength to strike at one another. By mutual exhaustion the two forces withdrew, leaving over six hundred dead lying in the water and boscage of the gully.

Each side declared itself victor. Toussaint left the field to Rochambeau, but he gained time to burn Gonaïves and to allow Christophe to slip away from Hardy.

Before Toussaint burned Gonaïves, he evacuated the civilians of all races. He also released the thirty prisoners he had taken at Ravine-à-Couleuvres. He sent them back to their companions.

"Tell those who fight against us," he instructed the prisoners, "that they do us a grievous injustice. We are countrymen. We should not be at war with one another. You have been told," he reminded them, "that we would torture and kill you. But you see that we treat you with kindness."

Whatever lessons of humanity Toussaint wanted to convey by his mercy were lost in the horrors of the atrocities that started with Leclerc's arrival and continued for ten months. What began in February as executions grew by November into ecstasies of exotic tortures. The drive for annihilation was powered on one side by Dessalines' conviction that no white person should remain alive on the island, and on the other side by Napoléon's instructions that all blacks who did not submit to his authority, and ultimately slavery, should be put to the sword. The practice of both armies was no prisoners. The cauldron of cruelty in which all boiled, effected all, and rare indeed was the individual who displayed mercy to his enemy.

Such an individual was my father. Toussaint's treatment of the prisoners at Ravine-à-Couleuvres was typical of his concerns for the suffering of all. I know of his treatment of the followers of Rigaud after the War of Knives and of his treatment of the voudoun houngan. I wrote honestly of those events. But in the Three Months' War, when I was with him almost daily, I saw his concern for the safety of civilians of all races, and his compassion for the suffering of soldiers, both his own and French prisoners. I saw him in anger execute old slave owners who flocked to support Napoléon's army, but he treated with mercy the common soldiers of all races who fell into his hands. Never did I see him engage even once in a wanton act of cruelty or torture.

At the end of February, Toussaint's military position worsened. Maurepas, weakened by the desertion of subordinates, defected to the French, placing the entire Northwest in Leclerc's control. Boudet was in Saint Marc and Leclerc was in Gonaïves.

To escape from Rochambeau's pursuit, Toussaint laid before him a curtain of soldiers who drew him north again, toward the Cape. While Rochambeau chased the illusion, Toussaint moved his main force up the Artibonite River to Petite Rivière. Toussaint had a plan for the defeat of Leclerc for which he needed Dessalines.

CHAPTER 31
Crête-a-Pierrot

At the center of Toussaint's plan to defeat Leclerc was Fort Crête-a-Pierrot, located half a league southeast of Petite Rivière. When Toussaint reached Petite Rivière he found Dessalines in the processes of dismantling the fort to keep it from the French and to take the cannon into the Cahos Mountains. Toussaint stopped the destruction of the fort and met with Dessalines, Lamartiniere and other officers from Dessalines' command to present to them his plan. The plan was daring, and its only chance of success lay with the courage of Dessalines and the men who served under him.

Toussaint was convinced that Leclerc was desperate for a decisive victory. He had to have one to mollify Napoléon's impatience and to keep the colonial troops in his army from growing restless. Toussaint proposed to draw Leclerc into a trap, baiting it with Crête-a-Pierrot. Toussaint wanted Dessalines to strengthen the fort, supply it against siege, and then tempt Leclerc to the bait. When Dessalines drew Leclerc into the center of the colony, away from his supply points, Toussaint and Christophe would disrupt the flow of supplies, raise up the laborers, and fall upon Leclerc from the rear and crush him.

At the meeting, Dessalines and his officers accepted their assignment. They pledged their loyalty to Toussaint and their vow to fight with him to the death.

Toussaint was visibly moved by their commitment. His emotions showed in his voice as he spoke.

"With such courage we can not fail," he promised. "You are my children, all my children. You, Lamartiniere, with your skin as white as white, but with the knowledge of the blackness flowing with the Negro blood in your veins; and you, Dessalines, my guide, my right arm, with your skin as black as mine, I entrust to you this post. I know you will defend it to your deaths. Each hour you hold brings us an hour closer to victory."

I heard the pledges Dessalines and his officers made, and I saw how deeply they moved Toussaint, but I saw something else, as well, something Toussaint did not see or did not want to see. I saw the look of impatience in Dessalines' eyes, the patronizing glance he shared with Lamartiniere. This was the first time I had met Dessalines, and I did not trust him.

When Toussaint and I left the meeting, I told him of my concerns. I asked if it were not unreasonable to ask men to risk almost certain death to give Toussaint a few days of time.

"They will hold! They will hold to the death!" Toussaint answered me impatiently.

Time proved us both correct.

Crête-a-Pierrot was a small fort, unimpressive in its setting. It was located on a small hill, eighty-five meters high, in the flood plain between the Artibonite and Esther Rivers. It overlooked the Artibonite on the south and west and the city of Petite Rivière on the northwest. The Esther River lay a league to the north across the fertile plain. To the east and southeast the rugged Cahos Mountains blocked the rising sun.

The fort itself was old and since the withdrawal of the English, much neglected. It was rectangular, less than seventy-five meters long. The walls were low, but built with an overhanging parapet to discourage scaling. At the four corners the parapet widened into squares to provide footing for the dozen or so eight and twelve pound cannons with which the fort was armed. The courtyard of the fort was dirt and contained a small stone building that served as the magazine, and near the magazine, a well for water. Crête-a-Pierrot offered small protection and meager quarters for the twelve hundred men and women who endured within it twenty days of siege and bombardment.

Dessalines divided his men into four companies. The largest, under the command of Lamartiniere, dug a ditch six feet deep, eight feet wide, surrounding the fort within easy musket range, about one hundred meters. The dirt from the digging was scattered out from the ditch, away from the fort. Every possible crevice which could conceal a man, with the exception of the ditch, was leveled for hundreds of yards in all directions. All underbrush and trees were removed.

The one direction from which the fort was vulnerable to attack was from the southeast. Here the hill fell gradually from the top for one hundred and fifty meters, and then sharply beyond that. The break in the hill provided protection to attackers. To protect that flank, Dessalines had Lamartiniere supervise the building of a redoubt—an earthen mound protecting a cave—at the break of the hill.

Lamartiniere requested and was granted command of the force defending the redoubt.

The second of Dessalines' companies foraged the area for food. Soon they had great heaps of mangos, melons, bananas, star apples and limes piled in the fort yard. In the corners of the yard, pigs and chickens were crowded into small pens. A guard was posted at the well. Dessalines shared Toussaint's fear of poisoning.

The third of Dessalines' four companies looked to the reconditioning of the fort and its cannons.

The fourth, directed by Dessalines himself, retrieved weapons and ammunition from the mountain caches where they earlier had been hidden.

By the fourth of March the preparations were completed, and just in time. The French general Debelle was sweeping the Artibonite Valley, moving toward Verrettes—two leagues up river from Petite Rivière—where he was to meet Boudet coming north from Port-au-Prince.

Dessalines, with a small detachment of soldiers, marched to meet Debelle. When the two met, Dessalines retreated toward Crête-a-Pierrot and Debelle pursued closely after. When the two forces were in sight of the fort, Dessalines' soldiers broke into a full run. The French raced after them in the effort to catch them before they reached the safety of the fort.

Just as it seemed Debelle's soldiers would overtake Dessalines', the blacks disappeared into the ground and the French were met with a withering barrage of cannon and musket fire from the fort. The French forces were devastated. Over four hundred were killed in the first volley. Debelle and his second in command were wounded.

The French withdrew beyond musket range. Dessalines' soldiers climbed out of the ditch and returned to the fort, elated at their success. Debelle deployed his remaining troops in a defensive ring and sent for reinforcements.

Only under cover of darkness were the French able to retrieve their dead. Debelle gave thanks to God that the savages did not press an attack on his weakened forces.

The second French commander to arrive before Crête-a-Pierrot was Boudet, coming from Verrettes where he was to have met Debelle. He brought with him three thousand soldiers and artillery. As senior officer in the field he took command. He encircled the fort to prevent its occupants from escaping and sent an officer, under the flag of truce, to discuss with the rebels the terms of surrender.

When the officer started toward the fort, Dessalines grabbed a torch from one of the cannoneers and held it close to a barrel of gunpowder.

"If one Frenchman puts foot in here," he declared, "I will blow us to hell."

The soldiers in the fort cheered, and, as one, shouted, "We die for liberty!"

They shot Boudet's messenger before he reached the fort.

Boudet, disgusted by the barbarity of the blacks, prepared to lay siege to the fort until its inhabitants cried for terms or starved to death. He changed his plans, however, when he received orders from Leclerc to attack the fort at once.

Leclerc held all of Saint-Domingue except for Crête-a-Pierrot, but he was not secure in his position. His loses in men were staggering. He did not want the First Consul to know how many had fallen in battle, and wrote to the Minister of Marine that many had succumbed to illness, a lie that, in the months to come, would become self-fulfilling. Everywhere in the colony the retreating rebels destroyed agriculture. With no trade with the Americans or British, and Napoléon unwilling or unable to supply him from France, Leclerc did not know how he would equip and feed his army.

Except at Crête-a-Pierrot, the black army was invisible. They struck by surprise and disappeared before Leclerc could pursue them, and they struck again where he least expected them. Christophe dragged a cannon even into the hills behind the Cape, bombarded the city, and disappeared—with his cannon—before the French could find him.

Leclerc was far behind the schedule that Napoléon had given him for reorganizing the colony. Dispatches came from the Minister of Marine inquiring as to his progress. The letters were from the Minister, but Leclerc detected the barbs of his brother-in-law behind the impatient language. He cursed the damnable winds and currents that brought reminders of Napoléon's displeasure to him within what seemed days but delayed his own pleas for assistance for weeks and months.

But Leclerc's biggest worry was Pauline. She was unhappy. The Cape was too depressing for her. She could not bear the filthy condition of the razed houses nor tolerate the confinement to her house and gardens. Christophe's cannonading of the city was the final outrage.

Leclerc suggested that she return to France until he could complete his work in Saint-Domingue.

She refused.

"Unless I can have a hundred thousand francs to buy a carriage, I can not possibly live in Paris," she pouted. "Caroline has a carriage. Joachim gave her a carriage. I will not be humiliated by my sister."

Leclerc did not have a hundred thousand francs to give her. He intended to get rich from the mahogany trees on the island of Gonave, but he could not look to his interests there until he had subjugated the blacks.

To pacify Pauline, he sent her by ship to the more secure Port-au-Prince, and he marched to command the army before Crête-a-Pierrot.

Boudet was uncomfortable with Leclerc's orders to attack Crête-a-Pierrot, but he obeyed. He elected to attack first the redoubt. With that in French hands, he reasoned, he could mass a hidden force in the draw and launch from there an attack against the fort itself.

When the French moved against the redoubt, Lamartiniere directed a perfunctory defense. As the French approached, he and his small force withdrew from the outpost and ran toward the fort. Boudet led his soldiers in hot pursuit. When Lamartiniere and his men reached the ditch, they jumped in and the soldiers in the fort opened fire. For the second time the French were caught in a murderous concentration of cannon and musket shot. The French broke and ran, leaving several hundred dead behind. Boudet was wounded.

When the firing from the fort ceased on command, Lamartiniere and his men scrambled from the ditch, fell on the retreating French and easily regained the outpost.

As Boudet's troops staggered back to their positions, Leclerc arrived with reinforcements. Leclerc sent the wounded Boudet to the infirmary and prepared to lead an immediate assault on the fort himself. To avoid being lured into the traps in which Debelle and Boudet fell, Leclerc ordered a full frontal attack.

Confident that Toussaint was within the fort and that a victory at Crête-a-Pierrot would end the rebellion, Leclerc sent six thousand soldiers against the fort's twelve hundred defenders.

The French advanced upon the fort in good order, their drums beating the time of the march. Behind the infantry, the artillerymen drove their gun carriages and caissons to closer range, whipped their horses about and quickly prepared to fire.

Dessalines ordered his sharp shooters to fire at the cannoneers, but the range was too great and few of the artillerymen fell.

Dessalines held his general fire until the first wave of French infantry was almost to the ditch. The first barrage from the fort cut deeply into the blue line. Several hundred fell.

The French took the blow and kept advancing. The soldiers in the fort, reloading, could not maintain an unbroken fire. The French artillery had found the range and crumbled several of the firing parapets.

The French advanced in disciplined order until they reached the ditch. The soldiers readily jumped into the ditch, but when they attempted to climb out, they presented static targets to the musketeers in the fort.

The French began to waiver. Those behind hesitated when the witnessed the difficulties the first wave had negotiating the ditch.

When Dessalines saw the French hesitate, he whistled for the attack. The defenders burst from the fort, some carrying planks of wood.

The French were caught by surprise. Those between the fort and the ditch and those still in the ditch fell easily before the charging rebels. With the aid of the planks, Dessalines' soldiers crossed the ditch and engaged Leclerc's main force.

At the initial charge of the blacks, the French fell back and regrouped. Leclerc recognized that his forces outnumbered his attackers and ordered a counterattack with bayonets. With sword drawn he rushed forward to lead the counterattack himself.

As soon as the French started forward, the blacks turned and fled. When they reached the ditch, instead of recrossing it on the planks, they leaped into it. The pursuing French were hit with a cannon and musket barrage from the fort. The French attack broke. Leclerc and his chief of staff, Dugua, were hit. Leclerc was wounded, Dugua killed. The French turned and fled.

In the afternoon's engagement, Leclerc lost eight hundred, Dessalines less than a hundred.

Leclerc was furious with himself for his stupidity. He was a child to have fallen for such tricks. But the damage was done. In the several attempts on the fort, the French had lost more than a thousand dead and twice as many seriously wounded. And for what? They were no closer to dislodging the rebels now than they had been when Debelle first approached the fort. Leclerc had no choice but to hold in siege position and wait for reinforcements.

The delay of siege rankled at Leclerc. He was desperate for victory. His wounds were superficial, but the pain in his soul was deep. When news reached him that Toussaint was in the North, burning and attacking with little opposition, and not at Crête-a-Pierrot as Leclerc had surmised, the French commander retired to his bed and refused to see anyone for two days.

Early in the French siege, Dessalines slipped men in and out of the fort by night. The few that were caught were executed, but most avoided capture. The nightly messengers allowed Dessalines to direct the laborers in the area in guerrilla action against Leclerc. While the French besieged the fort, the laborers besieged the French.

The French were no more comfortable in their fortified camps than the blacks were in Crête-a-Pierrot. By day, the French endured—in heavy uniforms and inadequate shade—the heat that even in March was oppressive to men unacclimated to the tropics. By night, their sleep was destroyed by the guerrilla raids and the drums sounding always from the mountains and from the fort.

The blacks loved music, and when they were not engaged in the dances of the African rites, they sang and danced the songs of their secular celebrations. The voudoun music annoyed and confused the French soldiers, but they were more disturbed by the Revolutionary songs—"The Marseillaise" and "Ca Ira"—that Toussaint's band, which was among the defenders of the fort, played and the others sang. The French enlisted men at first were angered, convinced that the rebels sang the songs to mock them.

But the white soldiers saw the flags that flew, day and night, from the four corners of the fort—the revolutionary tricolor of the Republic of France. They heard the stories told by the blacks who fought beside them, the blacks who had defected to Leclerc. They told of how they sang the songs of the Revolution in remembrance of their liberation from slavery, of how, before the Convention in Paris abolished slavery, Sonthonax—the honest white father—freed them and dispatched teachers throughout the island to teach them to read and write, of how the songs of the Revolution were for many their first lessons in freedom.

The anger of many of the white soldiers changed. For whose freedom did they fight, they wondered. For the freedom of the merchants of Bordeaux to make money, many decided.

The Polish regiment refused to execute any more prisoners.

At one of the nightly ceremonies in the fort a singular event occurred. A houngan, digging into dark rites half forgotten in an attempt to call new allies to their aid, invoked Mounanchou Ogoun. Mounanchou was a devilish soldier of the Master of the Crossroads—a fierce loa of the ancient Pétro family. Mounanchou had powers of malevolent magic and partook as much of the nature of the evil bacalou as of the benevolent loa. He was a man-goat child born in the period before the loa gave the gift of voudoun to the great King Akadja, in the period before history when men bred with she-goats and women bred with he-goats. The vèvè for Mounanchou was a man with three horns.

The rituals for Mounanchou were shrouded in deep mysteries. They were performed quickly so that the observers had no opportunity to learn their details. It was not wise for the uninitiated to invoke so powerful a force as Mounanchou.

The ceremony was short. The drums beat in broken, erratic rhythms. The dancers moved against the beat. Mounanchou did not appear.

In the French camp, the unusual drum rhythms awakened many soldiers. The whites cursed the savages for disturbing their sleep and soon fell asleep again when the short rites ended. The blacks serving with the French crossed themselves and sought strong talismans from the initiated among them.

The morning after the ceremony to Mounanchou Ogoun, Dessalines addressed his soldiers. He, too, had been awaken by the rites. Since the fall of Port-au-Prince he made no effort to suppress the drums. A people in rebellion needed the gods at their sides. But in his wakefulness he decided to tell his comrades of the decision he had reached at Croix-des-Bouquets when he cursed Toussaint for his vacillation. He wanted them to know for what they died.

As Dessalines spoke, the French began again their daily bombardment of the fort. The cannon balls smashed into the rock walls and into the courtyard. The fort's defenders had learned where best to stand to avoid the deadly missiles.

"Take courage!" Dessalines shouted above the din. "Take courage! I promise you that although the French may appear to overwhelm us, they will soon all fall and die like flies...."

A murmur began among several of the listening soldiers.

"Take courage," Dessalines continued. "You will see that when the French are few, we will beat them. They will try to occupy the country, but they will find only ashes."

The murmur spread and became louder. "Ogoun...Ogoun...."

"They will die," continued Dessalines, apparently unaware of the cause of the growing excitement before him. "And those who do not die will be driven out, then I, Dessalines...."

There was no question, now. Every man saw it. Dessalines' voice was deeper, his body taller. His face twisted into a cruel grin. Ogoun! Mounanchou Ogoun had come!

"Then I, Dessalines, will make you free! There will be no more whites among us!"

The excitement in the soldiers rose. The drummers reached for their instruments and began to beat the Mounanchou rhythms. The houngans began the low chants.

"Listen, comrades..." Dessalines-Mounanchou Ogoun continued, his voice like a cannon, his face like a death's head, "If you hear that Dessalines has surrendered to the French, then in your hearts you should smile. If he surrenders to them a hundred times, it will be to deceive them a hundred times. Take courage. He will make you a free people!"

That night, Dessalines slipped through the French lines and into the mountains to lead the laborers in their attacks on Leclerc. He promised the faithful in the fort that he would raise the siege.

Before there were sufficient French outside the fort to close the holes through which the rebels passed, many who were outside came in to be with the defenders. Among them were wives who chose to die with their husbands rather than live without them. Marie-Jeanne Lamartiniere was one. She joined her husband in the redoubt.

One night, before the moon rose, she slipped into the outpost with those bringing supplies from the fort. For a moment Lamartiniere thought he was dreaming, but he knew he was awake when he wrapped his arms around her thin body and pulled her to him in an uninhibited embrace. Both of them wept without restraint. For a few moments neither could speak in words, only joyous sounds crying from deep in their throats. Lamartiniere pulled his wife's face to his and kissed her violently on the lips, crushing her mouth. She pulled herself tightly to him, rejoicing in the pain of his roughness.

The other soldiers in the redoubt sat quietly watching the shadowy figures of their commander and his woman. When finally Lamartiniere and Marie-Jeanne broke from their embrace and began laughing and touching each other like small children, several of the other soldiers could no longer restrain themselves. They crowded around the couple and began to press Marie-Jeanne with questions.

"My wife, Sarah. She was at Gonaïves. Is she safe?" one asked.

"Are you Jules Besse?"

"Yes, lady. Is my Sarah safe?"

"She is at Saint Raphael with Madame Louverture."

"Thank you, lady. Thank you," Besse said gratefully. "May the blessed Erzulie bring you children of beauty."

Others pressed Marie-Jeanne for information of loved ones. When she was uncertain, she spoke words of encouragement and hope. When she recognized a name of someone she knew to be dead, she made no effort to conceal the fact. When she knew for certain the ceremony of dèssounin, of the separation of body and soul, had been performed, she identified as best she could the time and elaborateness of the rite.

When all the questions were answered, the soldiers grew silent and retreated into their private worlds of joy or sadness. Lamartiniere released the few for whom Marie-Jeanne was certain of the death of loved ones but uncertain of the performance of the dèssounin, and allowed them, if they chose, to make their way out through the French lines. Lamartiniere knew that if the dead were not properly released from their bodies and their souls released from the loa, the loa would turn their dissatisfaction upon the deceased's family, and he knew a man could not fight for the political freedom of others when he feared for the spiritual safety of his family.

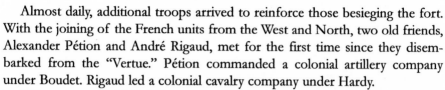

Almost daily, additional troops arrived to reinforce those besieging the fort. With the joining of the French units from the West and North, two old friends, Alexander Pétion and André Rigaud, met for the first time since they disembarked from the "Vertue." Pétion commanded a colonial artillery company under Boudet. Rigaud led a colonial cavalry company under Hardy.

"We are expendable," Pétion complained when he and Rigaud found a few moments to talk alone.

"No more than every soldier is expendable," Rigaud replied.

"At each engagement," Pétion explained, "my company is thrown into the battle first and held there the longest."

"You are honored for your valor and dependability."

"Your irony is not amusing," rejoined Pétion.

"I do not speak ironically," Rigaud insisted. "The only way the mulattos will prosper in Napoléon's new order is by proving their value. Rejoice that you visibly display your courage daily, and pray for victories," Rigaud instructed, remembering the disdain with which Napoléon greeted him after his defeat by Toussaint. "Courage in defeat brings no glory," he continued. "For my part, I shall be conspicuous in my loyalty and daring, for the honor of France."

Pétion found his old commander's fanaticism disturbing. Rigaud was, Pétion thought, like a provincial actor, filled with the passion of the words but unaware of the meaning of story in which he acted.

Leclerc grew increasingly impatient with the siege. The guerrilla actions of the rebels outside of the fort were taking a heavy toll in both men and morale. But he was determined, despite his losses, to win a crushing victory at Crête-a-Pierrot. He needed something to report to Napoléon.

By March twenty-first, the seventeenth day of the siege, Leclerc had secured sufficient guns, powder and shot to initiate a massive artillery barrage. He was determined to continue the cannonade night and day until Crête-a-Pierrot was reduced to rubble.

Dessalines was furious as he watched the cannonade from the Cahos, far above Petite Rivière. Where was Toussaint? The defenders of the fort had bought Toussaint two and a half weeks of time, but still he did not come with the forces to sweep down upon the French and destroy them. Dessalines sent messengers to Toussaint begging him to come.

During March, I rode with my father on his sweep of the North. His initial army of one thousand grew in number each day, but not as he hoped. Many, when they knew he was near, came to him. But many others fled from him because always before him rode the specter of Moïse.

Dessalines' call for help reached Toussaint while we attacked Fort Bedourete at Plaisance. There we encountered the soldiers of the Ninth Brigade who had defected with Maurepas. Toussaint called to them and I think they would have come, but the white soldiers with them fired on us and drove us back. During the battle, the messenger from Dessalines arrived and rode into the fray to hand Toussaint his dispatch. As he did, the young officer was hit and killed.

Toussaint, although with fewer troops than he had hoped and the North still not secured, rushed to Dessalines' aide. But we arrived after the issue was settled.

On the night of March twenty-second, Lamartiniere, with Marie-Jeanne and the other one hundred and fifty defenders, withdrew from the redoubt to the fort where there was better protection from the cannon shot. They knew there would be no more infantry attacks until the fort had been reduced to dust.

Lamartiniere had no need to urge his soldiers to hold fast to their promise to defend to the death the fort, for none thought to break his oath to Dessalines and Toussaint.

On March twenty-fourth, the third day of the bombardment and the twentieth day of the siege, an elderly black couple wandered into the French camp. The man appeared to be blind. Only the whites of his eyes were visible. The old lady appeared to be deaf. The soldiers taunted and tormented them, but one was suspicious and took the couple to General Lacroix, the officer who had followed Derance in preventing Dessalines from attacking Port-au-Prince.

Under Lacroix's questioning the elderly couple appeared to be senile. They had no sense of time or place. They denied ever hearing of Dessalines or Toussaint. Reluctantly, Lacroix agreed to the use of force to make them answer sensibly. Soldiers kicked and beat them. The couple lay on the ground and sobbed and wept in pain.

Lacroix, sickened at the sight, ordered the two to be released. When told to go, they lay still, not understanding the order. Soldiers dug at them with bayonets and threatened to shoot them if they did not move on.

As if dazed and lost, the couple staggered away from the French and toward Crête-a-Pierrot. Soldiers yelled at them to go in a different direction. They appeared not to hear or not to understand. A soldier fired at their feet to warn them. They broke into a run toward the fort. The surprised soldiers were several moments reacting. By the time the French had their wits about them, the couple was almost to the fort. In the firing that followed, the old woman was hit and fell. The old man stopped, but as he started for her, she waved at him to continue. He ran again through the fire toward the fort.

"Break out! Break out!" he yelled as he ran. "Dessalines orders you to break out. Abandon Crête-a-Pierrot!"

When he reached the fort, he was pulled in by helping hands through a break in the crumbling walls. After he had delivered his instructions to Lamartiniere, he wanted to return to his wife to aid her, but the soldiers restrained him. Under darkness, Lamartiniere sent out a party to find her. She was dead.

Lamartiniere's plan for escape was simple. They would fight their way through the French cordon. That night the garrison abandoned the fort and attacked the French sector commanded by Lacroix. It was well known to all—rebel and French—that Lacroix was losing heart in the war and was capable of foolish mistakes.

Leclerc moved reinforcements quickly to aid Lacroix, but as soon as the battle was engaged, the blacks broke contact and hit the sector commanded by Rochambeau.

Rochambeau was stunned. He had felt invincible to attack. His forces, overconfident and unprepared, collapsed like ripe sugar cane before the fanatical rush of the blacks. Rochambeau himself fled to save his life.

Lamartiniere escaped with seven hundred of the original twelve hundred defenders of Crête-a-Pierrot. Leclerc, with twenty thousand troops, white, black and mulatto at his disposal, lost over two thousand dead and many more wounded. Several of his key officers were wounded. His chief-of-staff was killed. The captured fort offered nothing of value.

Leclerc begged his officers to moderate their casualty reports.

CHAPTER 32
Capitulation

Leclerc's capture of Crête-a-Pierrot was a hollow victory. Although Toussaint and his partisans were isolated in the mountains, Leclerc was no closer to controlling the colony. He was still dependent on the black troops in his army, and he was learning the same lessons about the mulattos that Sonthonax and Toussaint learned before him: they might swear allegiance to France, but in the South they operated as if they were independent.

Leclerc was under pressure. Napoléon was impatient. He wanted rebel leaders arrested and sent to France. Leclerc dared not deport any of Toussaint's lieutenants serving in the French army for fear of demoralizing the rest and sending them flocking back to Toussaint.

In an impatient and desperate move to appease Napoléon and at the same time weaken the mulatto oligarchy, Leclerc struck at Rigaud.

Rigaud met with Leclerc at Saint Marc, where Leclerc was temporarily headquartered. Rigaud wanted permission to take his wife to Les Cayes on the south coast. Leclerc indicated that he was sailing to the South and invited Rigaud and his wife to accompany him.

Rigaud gratefully accepted. He and his wife were rowed to the "Cornelie" where they was delighted to greet a number of mulatto friends who had just arrived on the frigates "Indienne" and "Creole" from Cuba, where they had fled after the War of Knives. Rigaud was surprised, however, to discover that Leclerc was not on the "Cornelie," but on another frigate, the "Guerriere." His confusion was soon cleared when the captain of the "Cornelie," accompanied by armed marines, informed Rigaud and the others that they were under arrest.

Rigaud threw his sword overboard in disgust.

The "Cornelie" sailed first to the Cape. The prisoners were allowed to collect from the city any possessions they had there, but none of it reached the ship. The sailors stole everything of value before it could be off-loaded from the lighters. For the long journey to France, the prisoners had only the clothes and comforts that concerned friends at the Cape smuggled to them before the ship sailed. In France, Rigaud and the other men were imprisoned.

Leclerc's action against Rigaud strengthened Pétion's conviction of the dangers the mulattos faced. He was prepared to break from the French, but the others, because of the bitterness left from the War of Knives, followed Leclerc for revenge against Toussaint. Pétion knew the real enemy was Napoléon.

Lamour Derance waited no longer. When he heard of Rigaud's arrest, he broke immediately from Leclerc. He did not join with Toussaint or Dessalines. His hatred of them was stronger than his fear of the French. Derance and his maroons left Port-au-Prince and returned to the mountains, at war with the world.

After the loss of Crête-a-Pierrot, Toussaint designed a new plan of battle. From the natural fortress provided by the Black and Cahos mountains, he planned to strike at the French in three directions. Dessalines would move south to Verrettes, cutting in half the French forces in the Artibonite, and then move down river and retake Crête-a-Pierrot. Christophe would engage Hardy in the Northern Plain, and Toussaint would strike west against Rochambeau in Gonaïves and Saint Marc. Leclerc would be isolated at the Cape.

During the later days of March, deep in the Cahos mountains, Toussaint waited for the rains. He waited for the sickness to come upon the French, and he waited for the flooding rivers to make the roads impassable. Then he would attack his weakened enemy.

There was hardship in the camp. In addition to the few thousand soldiers, poorly equipped, were thousands of refugees. With us were the wives and families of many of the soldiers, including Toussaint's family and Dessalines' wife. The tents were crowded and the meals were scant.

The solitude of the mountains, the majesty of the pine and palm covered peaks lost in the gathering clouds, was both comforting and frightening; comforting in the protection the mountains promised, but frightening in the imprisonment they threatened. I remembered with dread the old proverb, "Deye mon ge mon": beyond the mountains, more mountains. Our only escape was through miles of rock strewn paths along the crumbling edges of steep gorges. At noon, the sun, untempered by the sea breezes, burned mercilessly. At night, the chill cut into bodies unprotected by blankets. And the rains, when the came, soaked bodies unprotected by cloaks.

When we camped, Toussaint's tent, the tricolor flying from its peak, was erected in the center of a clearing. The other tents were spread out from it, and on the outside of the camp armed guards stood always at the ready.

There was a sadness in the camp for the losses we had suffered and for the privations we saw before us. But no one felt greater sadness than Toussaint.

On a day before the offensive began, someone brought to Toussaint two French officers, chief of brigade Sabès and naval lieutenant Guimont. Before the battle for Port-au-Prince, Boudet had sent them as emissaries to Agé. They were the officers Lamartiniere took hostage when he took command of the defense of the city. By some miracle they had escaped execution when Lamartiniere fled. The officer who brought the Frenchmen to Toussaint wanted to know what he should do with them.

Toussaint ordered them freed. In return, he asked them to deliver to Boudet in Port-au-Prince a message to Napoléon. After the document was written, he had it read to the officers so that they would understand the nature of their task.

Toussaint begged Boudet to forward to Napoléon a plea for peace. In his plea, Toussaint assured the First Consul of his loyalty to France, and asked that Leclerc be withdrawn from the island and that Napoléon send someone else who better understood Saint-Domingue and respected its citizens.

The French officers agreed to take the messages, but Sabès argued that Toussaint was wrong to accuse Leclerc of bringing war. If Toussaint had only submitted to Leclerc's legitimate demands, he insisted, there would be no war and no suffering.

Toussaint was incensed at Sabès' words. He rose in a fury defending his loyalty to France. He had rescued the colony from the British and the Spanish! His efforts had kept Saint-Domingue for the French!

I saw my father grow sick from his anger. He burned as if from fever. His heart beat convulsively. His eyes rolled into his head. I was terrified for his condition, but I dared not embarrass him before the other officers. Finally, Mars Plaisir helped him into his tent, put him to bed and sat beside him throughout the night

On April fifth, reinforcements for Leclerc from France arrived at the Cape, twenty-five hundred soldiers, inexperienced and unequipped for battle, who thought they were being sent to a loyal French colony for garrison duty. However unprepared the reinforcements were, with their arrival Leclerc was ready to begin another assault against the rebels. He intended to root them out, one by one if necessary, from their mountain fastness.

But something else arrived in April. The seasonal rains began, the rain that brought with it the yellow fever, an annoyance to the blacks, but a deadly scourge to the Europeans.

The epidemic that struck the French troops in 1802 was more severe and lasted longer than any other in the history of the island. The Europeans continued to be infected not only through the summer, but also throughout the fall and winter, on through the spring, into the summer fever season of the next year.

Yellow fever is often fatal to those who contract it, but as often it is not. And those who survive it once are never sick with it again. But the sickness suffered by Leclerc's army was singularly deadly. Few survived, and many that did were struck again.

At the time I was little aware of the exceptional nature of the epidemic. Toussaint had predicted the sickness of the French and as a soldier I welcomed the destruction of the enemy. Only later did Mars Plaisir explain to me that the natural miasmas of the steamy summer heat were augmented by a deliberate war of poison.

The French were served by blacks. The blacks cooked their meals, washed their clothes and nursed their sick. Poison had long been the best weapon slaves had to strike back at cruel masters. In the beginning, the war of poison was sporadic. But as the blacks understood with certainty that Napoléon threatened them with slavery, the war intensified. Poison, administered secretly during the time of wide spread natural illness, was a weapon against which the French had no defense.

With the coming of the April rains, Toussaint began his offensive. Its success was staggering in its quickness. Within weeks, the French, weakened by illness and helpless against the coordinated onslaught, fell back into the fortified cities. There they nursed their sick and wounded, despairing of mustering enough men to defend against the next attack.

Leclerc was desperate. His first priority was to prevent Christophe from capturing the Cape. He urged old acquaintances of Christophe, both black and white, to write to him, to persuade him that he was misled by Toussaint and that he would serve himself well by bringing his soldiers over to the support of the French. Christophe was offered money and the means for him and his family to leave the colony if he wished to escape retaliation from the other rebels.

"You will have a great fortune," he was told, "and you can live in comfort under the protection of France in any country you wish."

Christophe informed Toussaint that he had offers of peace from Leclerc. Toussaint gave Christophe permission to explore the offers, but ordered Christophe to show him all correspondence and to make no agreements without his approval.

Christophe could neither read nor write. He was dependent on his secretaries for all correspondence. Toussaint made certain that the secretaries were properly instructed as to Christophe's answers. Above all, they were instructed, Leclerc must present proof that Napoléon's special laws for the colonies guaranteed the blacks' freedom.

In one of his letters, Leclerc requested that Christophe help him in capturing Toussaint. At that point, Toussaint thought to break off further negotiations, but relented, and had Christophe respond angrily that such action would be treacherous and he, Christophe, would never betray his superior and friend.

At Leclerc's request General Hardy wrote to Christophe. Hardy was most persuasive in describing his own sacrifices for twelve years in the cause of liberty. He would never consent, Hardy wrote, to see slavery restored. Hardy personally guaranteed Christophe's safety if he would meet with Leclerc.

On the ninth day after the correspondence began, on Sunday, April twenty-fifth, at 11:00 a.m., Christophe met Leclerc at Bréda. Satisfied with Leclerc's assurances, Christophe surrendered to him all of his fortified positions around the Cape, disbanded the thousands of field hands who served with his army, and placed himself at the command of General Hardy.

When he heard of Christophe's surrender, Toussaint was dismayed.

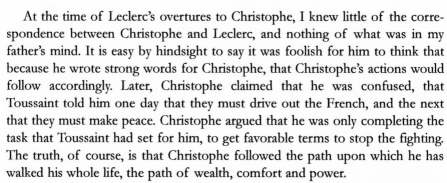

At the time of Leclerc's overtures to Christophe, I knew little of the correspondence between Christophe and Leclerc, and nothing of what was in my father's mind. It is easy by hindsight to say it was foolish for him to think that because he wrote strong words for Christophe, that Christophe's actions would follow accordingly. Later, Christophe claimed that he was confused, that Toussaint told him one day that they must drive out the French, and the next that they must make peace. Christophe argued that he was only completing the task that Toussaint had set for him, to get favorable terms to stop the fighting. The truth, of course, is that Christophe followed the path upon which he has walked his whole life, the path of wealth, comfort and power.

But the larger question is, why did Toussaint, when he had Leclerc defeated, feel the necessity to negotiate? In light of the consequences of Christophe's actions, it was a poor decision. I have thought much about the matter since. I have pondered it with Mars Plaisir, with my mother, and with others who had insight into Toussaint's mind.

My father was a complicated person. Like Caesar and like Napoléon, there are few men who had his breadth of vision.

Always before, Toussaint had succeeded with his tactic of fighting to the point of victory and then negotiating a peace which secured his interests and left his enemy an honorable retreat. Sometimes, as with Laveaux and Maitland, he was able to gain the support of his defeated foe. But that was before he encountered an enemy as implacable as Napoléon.

Also, Toussaint had a great fear of crushing the French. He desired independence, but he also feared it. He feared for the safety of a small, black nation vulnerably set in the middle of a sea of belligerent white nations.

And Toussaint was tired. In April he had news of the Treaty of Amiens: Napoléon was free of his war with England. Saint-Domingue was again divided. The mulattos were again in power in the South. The economic and military base Toussaint had built before Leclerc's invasion was destroyed. My father was fifty-six years old. For ten years he had led a people in revolution, eight of those years at war. He had been wounded sixteen times. He suffered repeatedly from headaches, bouts of nausea and debilitating nightmares. Those who did not trust or understand him had vilified him, and those he had served had deserted him. I think he now despaired of enduring again the pains of rebuilding all that he had built before.

Two conversations of later years stand strongest in my memory now as I write. In our confinement in Agen my mother spoke often of Toussaint's wish to have been spared the tasks that fell to him. He had been content as a slave at Bréda. Through his skills he had won a comfortable life for himself and his family.

"If God had let the black man sleep for another generation," he said often to Suzanne, "I could have lived my life in peace." He saw clearly the suffering of his fellow slaves, my mother told me, but he never understood why God had chosen him to lead them out of their bondage.

The second conversation I remember was with Mars Plaisir. We both knew Toussaint as a man of intelligence, faith and compassion. But it was Mars' opinion that twice in Toussaint's life he suffered from madness. Each time it took a different form, but each time it separated him from his mind.

The first was after he had beaten Rigaud.

"It was the first time," Mars said, "that he showed no mercy for a defeated enemy."

Mars described my father then as a man whose head was disconnected from his body. "He was a man always blessed by God," Mars added, "but for a time he forgot that the crowing of the cock did not make the sun rise."

At about the time that he was recovering from the first madness—Mars puts that as after the writing of his Constitution—Toussaint was struck by a second and more terrible madness from which he never fully recovered. It struck after the execution of Moïse.

"I begged him to have compassion on his nephew," Mars explained, "but Toussaint felt Moïse's betrayal so strongly he could not think."

Toussaint knew that Napoléon was the mortal enemy of the blacks. But Toussaint had no heart to continue the fight. After his surrender to Leclerc, Toussaint talked of waiting for the French to be further ravaged by fever, and then he would call to the people to throw out Leclerc. But to me his plans seemed as gossamer as his hopes that Jefferson would send down armies of freed slaves from the United States to aid us. Toussaint's last great stand was at Ravine-à-Couleuvres. He had heart for no more.

When he heard of Christophe's surrender, Toussaint rode south to Fort Marchand on the north side of the entrance to the Artibonite Valley.

Dessalines was sick with dysentery at Fort Marchand. It was with great effort that Claire kept him in bed. She allowed no messengers to disturb his rest, not even Toussaint's. Dessalines knew nothing of Christophe's negotiations with Leclerc and was surprised when Toussaint arrived with news of Christophe's surrender.

Dessalines was furious. He dragged himself from his bed and, to Claire's consternation, ordered his valet to dress him in his uniform and give him his sword. He was prepared to ride immediately to punish Christophe.

Toussaint tried to calm Dessalines, arguing that the matter was now out of their hands.

"Treason!" Dessalines shouted. "And you were wrong to let him write to the French!"

When Dessalines was calmer, he asked Toussaint how they should proceed without Christophe. Toussaint replied that he had received, just before he left Desachaux, a letter from Leclerc offering to the other black generals still in the field the same terms he had given to Christophe.

"You are going to accept?" Dessalines asked in disbelief.

"Yes," Toussaint answered.

Long into the night Dessalines argued with Toussaint. He argued that the blacks were ready to rise up in a general insurrection, but they would not if Toussaint withdrew. He argued that only Toussaint had the power to lead all of the blacks.

Toussaint was not persuaded. He promised Dessalines that he would win from Leclerc amnesty for everyone. Dessalines answered that he was interested in war, not amnesty. They parted in anger.

After another week of exchanges of letters with Leclerc establishing the terms of submission, late in the afternoon of Thursday, May sixth, Toussaint rode into the Cape.

Toussaint had accepted the protection of General Hardy and wished to ride with him alone to meet with Leclerc, but we of his guard would not allow him to. All of his dragoons, four hundred of us, rode with him.

His coming to the city had not been announced, and his appearance caused turmoil. Citizens rushed to the streets to see him pass. Some, mostly white merchants and shopkeepers, taunted him in his weakness. But the blacks and most of the whites greeted him with praise, strewing flowers in his path, grateful that the fighting was over.

Of his distracters, Toussaint said to General Hardy, "Soon they will have reason to regret my passing."

The other officers and I drew up the dragoons in smart order, sabers drawn, in Government Square. Before Toussaint acknowledged the officials in front of Government House waiting to greet him, he reviewed his guard. We could see the sadness in his eyes as he passed us.

The French officers escorted Toussaint into the recently restored Government House to await the arrival of Leclerc, who was dinning on board a ship in the harbor to escape the heat of the city.

When Leclerc arrived, out of breath from rushing, he saluted Toussaint smartly.

"General! In the name of France I welcome you," Leclerc said.

Toussaint returned his salute but made no reply.

Leclerc stepped forward and embraced Toussaint in the fraternal manner of the Revolution.

"You are most welcome, sir, to Cape François," Leclerc continued.

Toussaint did not return the embrace.

"General Leclerc," Toussaint replied formally, "at your bidding I have come."

"We are honored at your presence," Leclerc answered.

Leclerc took Toussaint into his private study.

"You have no need for so many guards," Leclerc said lightly, attempting to reassure Toussaint of his safety.

"If I were to bid them leave," Toussaint responded acidly, "they would not obey me."

Leclerc was not pleased that he had to make terms with the man he was sent to imprison, and he was less pleased with what he considered Toussaint's surly manner, but he wished to keep matters civil and began the process of the formal submission by praising Toussaint for his attention to the government of Saint-Domingue before Napoléon was able to send a new administration.

Toussaint, well aware of Leclerc hypocrisy, was cold in his response. He stated bluntly that he blamed Leclerc for the fighting, for the death of thousands and the destruction of most of the colony.

Leclerc wanted to avoid arguing with Toussaint. He was not comfortable in his presence and wanted the surrender settled as quickly as possible.

"But it is all past, now," Leclerc insisted. "Let us put the past behind us," he urged. But Toussaint would not be assuaged.

After their discussion, and Toussaint had signed a statement recognizing Napoléon's authority in the island, Leclerc, as he had promised to do, offered Toussaint the post of Lieutenant Governor, second only to himself. Toussaint refused, without explanation.

Leclerc escorted Toussaint into the reception hall where many of the black officers who had submitted earlier to the French were waiting. They greeted Toussaint enthusiastically, relieved that they were no longer fighting against him. Among the officers was Toussaint's brother, Paul. Paul attempted to embrace Toussaint, but Toussaint drew back.

"Stop," he said. "You do not conduct yourself properly. I am here to meet with the Captain-General, not for an unseemly display of affection."

Paul was hurt by Toussaint's rejection, but Toussaint, as yet unaware of the substitution of his orders to Paul, had been hurt by his brother's summary surrender.

Leclerc begged Toussaint to stay another day to allow the city time to prepare a proper celebration for the coming of peace. Reluctantly, Toussaint agreed.

Throughout the next day the city celebrated. The cannons in the forts and on the ships were fired in salute. Rockets were fired from the Morne Haut-du-Cap behind the city. Government Square was strewn with flowers, and throughout the day there were games and dances. That night, Leclerc hosted a dinner for the notables of the area. At the head of the table he and Pauline sat with Toussaint and Suzanne.

Toussaint refused to eat at the dinner until Leclerc implored him, for the sake of his health, to have something. In an elaborate show of precaution, Toussaint cut the sides from a small wheel of cheese and ate only the heart and poured himself a glass of water from Leclerc's carafe.

After dinner, Toussaint with Suzanne left the Cape as quickly as possible. They rode to Habitation Hericourt on the road to Ennery where they spent the night as the guests of the French general Fressinet, who had served with Toussaint earlier in the government of Toussaint's friend Etienne Laveaux.

The next day Toussaint and Suzanne rode to Desachaux.

———————————◆———————————

Among Leclerc's officers and their wives at the Cape, Toussaint was the subject of politely concealed derision. His diminutive body lost in the ornate uniform he wore, and what they called his clown-like face with its protruding jaw and wide-set, bulging eyes were in themselves objects of humor. But his appearance was made more ridiculous by recent gossip in circulation at the Cape.

The gossip averred that General Boudet had recently discovered in Port-au-Prince a trunk with a false bottom. In the secret compartment were letters and mementos from prominent white women in the colony testifying to their amours with Toussaint.

The story alleged that Boudet, because of Napoléon's condemnation of white women who had submitted themselves to black men, burned the contents of the trunk to protect the women. Before he burned it, however, he showed the contents to General Lacroix for confirmation of his decision. General Lacroix, the story continued, in confidence shared the story with Pauline Leclerc, who shared it with all of Saint-Domingue. Many claimed that Lacroix named names, but that Pauline, out of compassion for the poor women, refused to identify them.

When I first heard the story some years later, I rejected it out of hand as absurd and malicious. But in the years since my father's death, it has become such common gossip in France that I feel compelled to comment on it.

The story is difficult for me to believe because of what I know of my father's character. Also, because of his feelings for the inhabitants of Port-au-Prince and the little time he spent there, I can think of no reason why he would conceal in that place anything he wished to keep secret. But even with such doubts, I might give the story more credence if I could trace it to Boudet himself. Although he was put in a position of enmity to Toussaint, Boudet was a man of honor. But the story is attributed to Lacroix and Pauline Leclerc. The first is a man of indifferent honesty and the latter is a woman of no honor.

Over the years, however, I have had other thoughts on the matter. It is my opinion that all men of power draw to them women who wish to honor them with their favors. I see no reason why that should not have been as true of Toussaint as it was of Napoléon, as true of a black man as of a white. In perspective to Toussaint's accomplishments, such failings, if true, are of no consequence. The ultimate irony is that the source of the story is Pauline Leclerc, whose life in Saint-Domingue was consumed by her indiscretions with men of all colors.

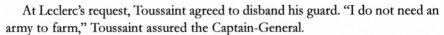

At Leclerc's request, Toussaint agreed to disband his guard. "I do not need an army to farm," Toussaint assured the Captain-General.

Shortly after Toussaint's return to Desachaux, he rode out for the last review of his soldiers, mounted on Bel-Argent. French soldiers had stolen his beautiful silver when they over-ran Desachaux, but General Hardy returned the horse to him.

The units of Toussaint's personal guard were drawn up in a large field near Gonaïves. In the ranks of the soldiers, tears ran down the cheeks of men who had endured undauntedly the bitter wars against the Spanish and English, the bloody struggle for Jacmel, the courageous stand at Ravine-à-Couleuvres and the valiant defense of Crête-a-Pierrot.

Toussaint rode among them, greeting them by name, returning their embraces. Then he rode to a mound before them to speak.

"There is a new order in Saint-Domingue," he said. "There is a new order in France, and we are part of France. France gave us our liberty, and we must look to France to preserve it.

"We have brought together here diverse peoples," Toussaint told the soldiers, "and made them one. We have set an example for all the world to see and follow. I leave you now," he continued, but was drowned out in cries of "No! Do not leave us!"

"I must. I must," Toussaint replied when there was order. "But if Saint-Domingue calls me again," he promised, "I will answer, for you are my children."

"Vivat Toussaint!" the men shouted. "Papa Toussaint! Papa Toussaint!"

I shouted as loud as any of the soldiers and cried as deeply. I felt the loss they all felt. And I felt the same fear for the future.

After the review, Toussaint rode back to Desachaux. I stayed at Gonaïves for several hours to say goodbye to my soldiers. Then I rode to Desachaux to be with my father.

Many of the officers and men in Toussaint's guard followed my example. They came to Desachaux and asked for work as field hands on the plantation. Toussaint tried to send them away, but they would not listen to him. Although he said nothing of it, I knew he felt safer with them there.

Several days after Toussaint's visit to the Cape, Dessalines rode there to submit. He arrived unannounced and with his personal guard.

The reaction of the city was markedly different. When the citizens heard that Dessalines was at the Cape, they rushed to the streets and prostrated themselves before him in fear.

Leclerc met him at Government House. The French commander was relieved that Dessalines was docile in manner even though his face was distorted in unsuppressed anger. Leclerc had wanted to destroy Dessalines while he was isolated, but Toussaint had refused to submit unless Dessalines was included in the general amnesty.

Dessalines refused to sign the order of submission.

"I have served France for ten years," he said. "My actions speak my allegiance."

"You must show that you come in peace," Leclerc insisted.

"If I came in war," Dessalines responded, "the Cape would be in flames and you would be in your grave."

Leclerc did not press matters further and, in accordance with his agreement with Toussaint, appointed Dessalines commander of Saint Marc. Leclerc was of mixed feelings when Dessalines accepted. He was happy to have the black general and his soldiers out of the Cape, but he was not pleased with the thought of the black tiger of Saint-Domingue in command of his home district, sitting on the road between the Cape and Port-au-Prince. But for Leclerc, the main business was won. Toussaint was disarmed. He resolved to domesticate Dessalines with flattery and rewards.

In Saint-Domingue, Leclerc twisted and wriggled, accommodated and prevaricated to preserve his dwindling army and maintain some semblance of French rule. In France, Napoléon fumed. Despite his brother-in-law's pleas not to let one whisper of slavery reach Saint-Domingue, Napoléon, impatient for his new-world empire, moved to establish his new laws. What if Saint-Domingue and Guadeloupe were still too unsettled for the new order, the smaller islands were ready.

The merchants and legislators from the maritime provinces flooded Napoléon with pleas and petitions. It was a tenant of faith in the maritime provinces that only the reintroduction of slavery and the reestablishment of the old discriminations against mulattos could preserve France's economic interests in the Caribbean. The English had maintained their slave empire and flourished. The French had foolishly abandoned theirs and wallowed in disasters.

On Thursday, May twentieth, two weeks after Toussaint dismissed his guard and retired to Desachaux, in Paris, Napoléon's Minister of the Colonies presented to the Legislature a bill to rescind the act of abolition. The Tribunat had proposed the measure, and under Napoléon's Constitution of the Year VIII, it was now presented to the Legislature of three hundred to be voted on without discussion.

Observing that afternoon was Henri Grégoire, one of the architects of abolition and now a senator in Napoléon's government, one of eighty men who had the power to appoint the members of the Tribunat and the Legislature and to annul unconstitutional acts of the Legislature.

As Grégoire listened to Minister Briux's presentation, he remembered vividly the day, eight years earlier, when he hurried to the Convention at the Tuileries in anticipation of the great moment when slavery would be ended. It had been a cold morning, but in his excitement he had not felt the wind whipping at him, the rain cutting at his face. What a contrast to his walk today, he thought, without topcoat, the sun warming his face, the gentle breeze pregnant with spring. On a day bursting with the evidence of the grace of heaven he had come to hear a plea to return one half of God's creatures to hell on earth.

"France is a bastion of liberty in a world of monarchies," Briux told the Legislature. "As a free people we are proud of our freedom. In an act of unparalleled charity we shared that freedom with the wretched Negroes of the West Indies.

"But what have been the fruits of abolition?" Briux asked. "You know them all too well. Terror, bloodshed, rape and torture," he answered. "Such are not the acts of freemen. They are the acts of savages.

"There are those who would shout 'shame' at my remarks," Briux continued. "But I ask, where does the guilt lie? With France who offered the handshake of fraternity to the Negroes, or with the slaves who turned upon their benefactors?

"There are those who accuse me of wishing ill to those poor savages," continued Briux in a conciliatory tone. "I deny the accusations.

"Citizens," Briux asked, "what alternatives do we have? We can sit in terror and watch our Republic and her people tortured and murdered. As a man of blood, that is a choice I cannot accept. We can wage a war of annihilation against the Negro and drive him out of the Caribbean. As a man of conscience, that is a choice I must reject.

"What choice have we," Briux concluded, "but to restore the one institution which brought peace and order to the land and protection and guidance to the Negro, who, like an unruly child, can prosper only under stern discipline?"

Grégoire did not wait for the vote. As he pushed his way into the outer corridor, he passed the First Consul.

"Senator," Napoléon called to Grégoire, "are you not staying for the vote?"

"I have no doubt of its outcome," Grégoire responded.

"How do you view the matter?" Napoléon asked.

Grégoire stopped and looked down at the shorter man.

"One does not need eyes to see that the legislators are white," Grégoire answered. "If God in his gracious wisdom were this moment to change their color, I have no doubt the result would be different."

The vote was two hundred and eleven in favor, sixty opposed, to restoring slavery in Martinique, Tobago and Saint Lucia. Within a month, the governor of Guadeloupe would take it upon himself to restore slavery there. Only in Saint-Domingue were the blacks still free.

Leclerc's problems did not stop with the submission of Toussaint and his chief generals. The black resistance continued, led by lesser officers and maroon chieftains. The resistance was not organized. Each band of rebels fought independently, often in conflict with each other as well as the French. The situation was much as it had been in 1791 when the slaves first revolted, before Toussaint emerged to mold them into a cohesive army.

Leclerc used the black generals, Christophe and Dessalines included, to suppress the rebels. The generals were efficient in their efforts, but the revolt was too widespread and too spontaneous to be crushed.

Leclerc accused Toussaint of fomenting and secretly leading the insurrection. Toussaint denied it. His only interest was farming, he informed Leclerc.

My father took no active part in the continuing rebellion. He was aware of the fighting, but he gave no orders. No leaders came to him for advice or support. His position was much as it had been with Hédouville. "If Leclerc wants to govern, then let Leclerc govern." Now, however, there was no Moïse around whom the blacks could rally, and the leaders they had followed before, now hunted them.

One month after he surrendered to Leclerc at the Cape, Toussaint received a letter from the commanding officer of the Gonaïves district, General Jean-Baptiste Brunet. Toussaint had written to Brunet complaining that French soldiers in Ennery were stealing from his plantation. Brunet invited Toussaint to his headquarters to discuss the problem. Brunet assured Toussaint of his respect and on his word of honor promised to protect his person. Brunet, declaring his interest in meeting Madame Louverture, offered to send his carriage so that she could accompany Toussaint if she wished.

Suzanne chose not to ride with Toussaint. She had no interest in meeting the Frenchman.

Although we did not know it at the time, on the afternoon of Monday, June seventh, 1802, we, his family, said goodbye to Toussaint for the last time.

He rode to Gonaïves with two former officers now employed on his plantations. They reached Brunet's headquarters at Habitation Georges at eight in the evening.

Toussaint was ushered into Brunet's study. The French general greeted Toussaint cordially, and then excused himself for a moment. When Brunet left the room, another French officer, Leclerc's aide-de-camp Major Ferrari, at the head of a squad of soldiers, bayonets at the ready, burst into the room.

Toussaint drew his sword to defend himself, but Major Ferrari walked up to him, his own sword lowered.

"General," Ferrari addressed Toussaint. "Put up your sword. I am under orders to arrest you, not to harm you."

Toussaint was sick with fury, but he saw the futility of resisting and dropped his sword. For a second time he submitted to Leclerc, but this time he was accorded no dignity. His arms were bound, and he was put in a carriage and driven to Gonaïves.

In Gonaïves he was taken to the office of the port commander who was smoking a cigar. Toussaint complained that the smell of the smoke made him ill. The port commander laughed.

"Good," he said, blowing the smoke toward Toussaint. "I am pleased to see you suffer."

The port commander took Toussaint to the quay to board a lighter. Toussaint complained that he was subject to seasickness and did not want to travel by boat. The French soldiers guarding him forced him roughly into the boat.

"Good bye, Papa Toussaint," they taunted. "Have a good journey."

Toussaint was rowed to the frigate "Creole," which was moored in the bay outside of the shallow harbor of the city. Behind him in the city he could hear the soldiers celebrating. After dark, when the ship weighed anchor and drifted out with the tide, he still could hear the soldiers singing and laughing.

Shortly after Toussaint left Desachaux for Gonaïves, a troop of French soldiers arrived under the command of Major Pesquidou, the district commander in Ennery. With them was Naval Lieutenant Guimont. I knew both of the officers. Lieutenant Guimont was one of the two prisoners whom Toussaint spared after Crête-a-Pierrot and sent to Boudet with his appeals for peace.

I greeted Pesquidou and Guimont from the porch of the house, but was met in turn with a show of bayonets and pistols. Within minutes my mother, my brothers Isaac and Jean, my cousins Louise and Victorine, and several former officers of Toussaint's who were in the house, and I, were arrested. After binding our hands the soldiers ransacked the house, stealing whatever they wanted and wantonly destroying what they did not take.

The officers who were arrested were taken to Ennery. The rest of us, Toussaint's family with Justine, Suzanne's, servant, and Mars Plaisir, Toussaint's valet, who were not arrested but insisted on accompanying us, were driven to Gonaïves. In the darkness of the night we were rowed to the frigate "Guerriere." We had no idea what was to happen to us and we had no idea what had happened to Toussaint.

On board the "Creole," Toussaint did not know that his family had been arrested. He demanded of Ferrari to see Leclerc. Ferrari assured Toussaint that the "Creole" was bound for the Cape and Toussaint would meet with the Captain-General there.

Toussaint was convinced that when he reached the Cape, matters would soon be righted. He had no doubt that Christophe, who Leclerc reappointed to his old office of commander of Cape François, would put a stop to this injustice. And if Christophe hesitated, Dessalines, when he had word of Toussaint's arrest, would march for the Cape. The news that Dessalines's army was in the Northern

Plain would put fear in Christophe and Leclerc, and they would soon release Toussaint. This was the mistake, Toussaint decided, that would give him the authority to dismiss Leclerc and send him back to France.

But Toussaint was out of touch with the new politics of Saint-Domingue. Leclerc dared not move against Toussaint without the compliance of Dessalines and Christophe.

At the end of May, Leclerc confided to Christophe his belief that the continuing unrest in the colony was fomented secretly by Toussaint. Christophe agreed and assured Leclerc that there would be no peace on the island as long as Toussaint was free to incite rebellion.

Emboldened by Christophe's concurrence, Leclerc wrote to Dessalines of his concerns about Toussaint. Dessalines responded that he had no doubt that Toussaint was at the heart of the continuing resistance and accused him of authoring the recent defection to the rebels of the Red Jackets, an elite cavalry regiment.

Leclerc pressed Dessalines for advice.

"Deport Toussaint to France," Dessalines wrote. "Only with him gone will there be peace in Saint-Domingue."

Leclerc thanked Dessalines and presented him with a brace of pistols, a ceremonial sword and eight hundred piasters of gold in appreciation for his support of the government.

Why did Christophe and Dessalines turn against Toussaint? It is a question I have wrestled with for many years.

Christophe, I think, was embarrassed by his weakness in surrendering to Leclerc. Although no friend of slavery, he was happy with the wealth and position he had through Leclerc and did not want to sacrifice his comforts. Christophe feared more the probability that Toussaint would begin again the fighting than he did the possibility that the French would take from him his liberty.

Dessalines's motivation was much different. He was angry that Toussaint had surrendered. Dessalines had not forgotten the promise he made at Crête-a-Pierrot to lead Saint-Domingue to independence. As long as Toussaint held the people's hearts and was unwilling to let go the hold the whites had on him, Dessalines knew the people would not follow him in driving out the whites. Toussaint had to go.

Why then, did Dessalines serve Leclerc in hunting down and destroying the blacks still in revolt? As much as Dessalines wanted independence, he was afraid to grasp for it. Toussaint's thoughts still filled Dessalines' head. Even when Toussaint was gone from the island, Toussaint's thoughts filled his head. Dessalines killed all who still followed Toussaint in the effort to kill the thoughts. Even when he broke from the French with the absolute knowledge that Napoléon demanded his death, Dessalines was not able to hold to his own thoughts. Only when he heard that Toussaint was dead, was Dessalines finally free.

The "Creole" was three days in reaching the Cape. It had to beat against a steady wind and moderate seas along the north coast. Toussaint was sick for the entire trip.

When the ship was safely in the harbor at Cape François, Toussaint demanded to be taken to Leclerc. Instead he was rowed to the merchant ship "Heros." He was not allowed to set foot on land nor see anyone except the sailors who rowed the boat and the marines who guarded him. When he boarded the "Heros," the captain, a civilian officer named Savary, met him with a guard who placed chains on Toussaint's wrists and ankles.

"Why do you do this to me?" Toussaint asked.

"I am under orders to sail you to France," Savary replied.

"You do not need to chain me," Toussaint complained.

"It would be my life if you escaped," Savary replied.

"It is of no consequence," Toussaint replied. "Those who wish to overthrow the Revolution in Saint-Domingue by imprisoning me will fail. In felling me you cut down only the trunk of the tree of liberty. The tree still lives, for its roots are deep and strong."

Toussaint was locked in the brig in the bow of the boat, where the tossing of the sea was most violently felt. He was not allowed on deck for the entire trip.

We boarded the "Heros" from the "Guerriere" after Toussaint and were at sea several days before a sailor told us Toussaint was also aboard. We were not allowed to visit with him, but Mars Plaisir badgered the captain until he was given access to Toussaint. Savary relented because of Toussaint's illness. The captain was afraid he might die and was relieved to have a nurse for him.

On July twelfth, 1802, after an exceptionally fast and reasonably gentle crossing, the "Heros" docked at Brest on the west coast of France. Toussaint was sick
every minute of the journey.

On arrival, Toussaint was confined to the fortress at Brest. The commander
permitted Mars Plaisir to accompany him but would let no one in the family see
him. The rest of us were put aboard another ship, the "Naiade," where we waited for several weeks. Then the "Naiade" sailed south to Bayonne where
Suzanne, Isaac, Louise, Victorine and Justine were put ashore. I was sailed north
again to Belle île where, after being stripped of my rank in the French army, I
was confined to prison. I was held there for more than a year before I was
allowed to join my mother, brothers and cousins in what has become our permanent place of confinement, Agen.

After a week of confusion, Toussaint's jailers were ordered by Napoléon to
transfer Toussaint to the prison at Fort de Joux. Napoléon feared the British
might attempt to free him and wanted him confined far from the sea. Toussaint
was allowed to take Mars Plaisir with him.

They were driven in a closed carriage, forbidden to communicate with anyone outside. The area through which they first traveled, west and south of Brest,
was in disorder from Royalist inspired revolts only recently suppressed. Bands of
Royalist sympathizers still roamed the countryside.

The soldiers who guarded the carriage were veterans of other such clandes-
tine journeys and had been chosen for their discipline and their loyalty to
Napoléon. They did not know the identity of their prisoner. They knew only
that if they were attacked, they were to kill him before he could be freed.

At the border of each military district, the carriage and its guards were met
by the local commandant and a detachment of cavalry and escorted to the next
district.

Several times the caravan sighted bands of Royalists and formed into a defensive posture until the dangers passed.

Toussaint left Brest on July twenty-third. He reached Besançon, high in the
French Alps, at one-thirty in the afternoon on August twenty-second. He had
ridden for a month in a closed carriage in the summer heat a distance of two
hundred and forty leagues. Whenever he was allowed from the carriage to sleep
or eat, he was accompanied every minute by guards. He wore the same uniform
he wore when he was arrested three months earlier. He had no other clothes to
wear. He was sick from the ordeal of the ocean crossing and weakened by the
deprivations of the journey across France.

That evening he slept in an inn in Besançon. The next morning he was delivered to the prison at Fort de Joux and was locked in a cell where he was confined for the rest of his life.

CHAPTER 33
Haïti

The events in Saint-Domingue after my father's arrest and deportation are only incidentally relevant to his fate in France, but I feel the need to give an account of those events at least to the extent that they involve the people who have been prominent in this narrative.

After he deported Toussaint, Leclerc was buoyed in his efforts to pacify the colony. He had the black generals under his power. "I am the master of their wills," he wrote Napoléon.

Leclerc was ready for the last task before he could implement Napoléon's new laws: disarm the people. The colony was an armed camp. The maroons in the mountains were armed. The black soldiers and cultivators released from the army carried with them their guns. The weaponry of years of war was scattered throughout the island.

Leclerc instructed Dessalines, Christophe and the other generals to collect from the civilians all their arms and ammunition. But before Leclerc's orders could be implemented, an incident occurred at the Cape which rendered them useless.

In early July, the ship "Cockarde" anchored briefly in the harbor to refill its water casks. It had sailed from Guadeloupe with bad water and a hold filled with slaves destined for sale in the Bahamas. The slaves were the leaders of the black resistance to slavery in Guadeloupe. The black stevedores loading the water casks made contact with the slaves chained in the hold.

By the time the "Cockarde" weighed anchor, the news had spread throughout the colony: the slavers were in Guadeloupe; they were coming to Saint-Domingue. Resistance to Leclerc stiffened everywhere. As fast as arms were collected in one village, they were stolen from the barracks in the next. As soon as one area was pacified, insurrection broke out in another.

From his sanctuary deep in the Saddle, Lamour watched Dessalines, Christophe, Pétion and the other generals, black and brown, send their soldiers through the land, gathering up weapons and ammunition.

"It is the day the kind white father, Sonthonax, warned us of," he told the council of elders. "He told us that if we wish to keep our freedom, we must use our arms on the day the white authorities ask us for them."

When the news of the "Cockarde" reached the deep mountains, Derance knew that Sonthonax had been right.

The story was the same in a hundred camps and villages. The maroons, who had defended their freedom for generations, were prepared to defend it again. The more recently affranchised, the political children of Papa Toussaint, joined with them. It did not matter what the old generals said or did. The people would die rather than submit again to the chains and whips of the whites.

Leaders rose up among them: the old maroons, like Derance; officers who had followed Toussaint but would not follow his generals into service under Leclerc; and always the houngan, the priests who called the loa to strengthen their worshipers and give them courage.

The unifying force, the thread that knit together this disparate and despairing people was the drum. The drums sent warnings of attacks and assurances of divine aid. The drums comforted and inflamed. The drums buoyed the people and terrified the enemy. The drums replaced politics and strategy with rage. There would be no slavery, the drums said. There would be only death.

The French losses to fever and poison grew worse in the heat of August. Leclerc ordered the bodies buried in common graves to conceal the number. Reinforcements from France did not arrive fast enough to replace the dying. In August, Generals Hardy and Debelle died of the fever. Leclerc begged Napoléon to let him return to France. Napoléon told him to complete his mission first.

Leclerc moved with Pauline to the island of Tortuga, two leagues off the north coast of Saint-Domingue. The land was high there and a sea breeze blew away the infecting vapors. Pauline, who moved back to the Cape from Port-au-Prince, had grown restless at the Cape, complaining of the heat, the signs of sickness and the never-ending drums. The move to Tortuga also isolated her where her flagrant amours with his officers would not embarrass Leclerc.

By September, Pétion was ready to break from the French, but he knew he could not stand alone. He began cautiously to build an alliance of officers prepared to join him. It was dangerous work. If Leclerc knew his intentions, he would be a hunted man.

Pétion found the South intransigent, but the mulattos in the North and West were ready to follow him. They hesitated out of fear of the black generals, not the French.

Pétion could not believe that Dessalines was inexorably sold to Leclerc. At great risk he called to the black general to join him.

Dessalines was difficult, but he made no threat to betray Pétion.

"I have no love for you," Dessalines told him. "I would have killed you at Jacmel if I had had my way, and you would have killed me at Crête-a-Pierrot if you had had yours."

"And I have no love for you," Pétion replied. "I do not propose a marriage, only an agreement to survive."

Pétion and Dessalines parted unreconciled.

Shortly after, Dessalines was ordered by Leclerc to hunt down Charles Belair—Toussaint's nephew—and his wife who had defected to the rebels. He found Belair at Vallieres near Gonaïves. Dessalines offered to negotiate. When Belair appeared, Dessalines arrested him. Belair's wife agreed to surrender when Dessalines promised to plead to Leclerc for leniency. Dessalines was angered when Leclerc executed both of them.

"How many more?" Pétion asked Dessalines. "How many more good men will you hunt down before you begin to feel the rope around your own neck?"

Dessalines continued the deadly errands Leclerc assigned him, but he stopped turning over confiscated weapons to the French. He hid them for the future.

Dessalines knew in his heart that the time would come when he must break from Leclerc. He had not forgotten his pledge to make Saint-Domingue independent. But he did not trust Pétion. He did not trust the black rebels who had remained faithful to Toussaint. He did not trust the maroons who had sworn his death for the murder of the houngan. He did not trust Christophe wallowing in his comforts at the Cape. Dessalines stood alone, and was not prepared to take on the world.

But the death of Belair's wife angered him. He knew when his usefulness to Leclerc was over he would be hunted. For that he was prepared. But the thought of Claire standing before a firing squad or hanging from the gibbet filled his mind with blood.

The incident that drove Dessalines from Leclerc and into an uneasy alliance with Pétion was the death of another officer and his wife.

Lamartiniere was unhappy when Dessalines submitted to Leclerc. But Lamartiniere was a good soldier, a courageous soldier. He endured the insults from the citizens of Port-au-Prince when he was assigned to the Third Colonial Regiment there. He followed faithfully Dessalines' orders to hunt down and kill the insurgents, but he did not like the task. He heard Dessalines' warnings that the time was not ripe for the destruction of the whites, but Lamartiniere saw no evidence of the times changing.

He avoided confrontation with the rebels as often as he sought it. He let prisoners go. He contemplating joining the rebels himself, but he knew without the generals, without Dessalines, Christophe, Pétion and the others, there was no hope of victory. He held his tongue and waited.

Lamartiniere feared treachery from both the French, whom he hated, and the insurgents, whom he persecuted. He always slept with a loaded and primed pistol by his side.

Early in October, Lamartiniere knew he could not continue the battle against his heart and conscience. He broke from his campaign against the rebels in the mountains above Arcahaie and returned to the city. It was his intent to take Marie-Jeanne to a place where she would be safe, and then to throw his lot with those who opposed Leclerc, even if in doing so he incurred Dessalines' wrath.

Lamartiniere and Marie-Jeanne were asleep when the men burst in upon them. Lamartiniere had time to grab his pistol, but it misfired. No one answered their cries for help.

There were seven attackers, white Frenchmen clumsily disguised as black laborers, their faces smeared with burnt cork. Four of them grabbed Lamartiniere. They tied his hands behind him and bound him to a bedpost, a garrote around his neck.

The other three held Marie-Jeanne to the bed. Until Lamartiniere had been secured the three could not subdue her, despite their blows to her face and body. When all seven were free, four of them held her, one by each limb, a fifth ripped the torn night clothes from her body, a sixth dropped his trousers to rape her.

Lamartiniere, choking more from the fury rising in his throat than from the garrote, screamed, "Let her go! You have me!"

"Your turn will come, white nigger," one of the attackers answered him.

The soldier entered Marie-Jeanne with deliberate brutality, pulling her hair with both hands. The only sounds she made were low groans in her throat. With a sudden movement she wrenched free her right hand and racked her fingers down the side of his face, ripping out his left eye. Screaming, he rolled on the floor, blood flowing from between his fingers pressed against his face.

"If I had a knife," were the only words she spoke.

After they had secured her again, the soldier who had ripped off her clothes prepared to take his place upon her. But the wounded soldier shoved the other aside and, before anyone could move to stop him, plunged his knife into her vagina.

Her body jerked in giant spasms, but the only sound she made was the groaning in her throat.

The soldier who had been denied his pleasure attacked the other. In the confusion the two victims were forgotten. Marie-Jeanne's body curled into a tight ball. It was rhythmically wracked by spasms. With each movement, the red-brown stain on the mattress grew larger. Lamartiniere jerked at his bonds. The cords cut into his wrists. He could feel the blood flow down his hands.

One of the soldiers detached himself from the argument, turned to Marie-Jeanne, pulled up sharply on her hair and plunged his knife into her throat, once, twice, three times. With a release of air her body lay still as a second stain spread across the bed.

One of the soldiers turned to Lamartiniere. "The son-of-a-bitch is cutting his wrists," he warned.

"Not before I've had my fun," said the soldier who had been denied his turn on Marie-Jeanne.

When someone pulled down his trousers Lamartiniere pressed his neck against the garrote desperately grasping for unconsciousness.

"He's choking himself. Don't let him choke himself."

Someone released the garrote.

"Give it to me."

One of the soldiers slipped the thin cord around their victim's testicles.

Lamartiniere lost all strength in his legs. His body hug from a single point of pain. The scream started in his groin and burst from his throat, shattering his brain. Nothing after that was unbearable. He slipped into a stupor filled with the disoriented images of Marie-Jeanne.

When they shoved the fleshy objects down his throat, Lamartiniere drowned in his own vomit.

With Pétion and Dessalines in the field against him, Leclerc's position grew weaker daily. He could no longer stay in Tortuga. His presence was demanded at the Cape. Despite the new dangers, Pauline insisted on accompanying her husband. They moved into new quarters in Government House and Pauline busied herself decorating her apartment and collecting the animals for her zoo she intended to take with her back to France.

By the middle of October, Pétion was master of the Northern Plain and stood ready to attack the Cape. Leclerc ordered all the blacks in the city to be taken into custody and imprisoned on ships in the harbor. He feared they would rise up in support of Pétion when the battle began.

The attempt to imprison all the blacks fell from the force of its own weight. Many fled. Others resisted. Eventually there was no space left on the ships, and the arresting soldiers had to abandon their efforts in order to prepare for battle against Pétion. But before the plan was abandoned, more than a thousand blacks had been arrested.

Among those imprisoned was my maternal grandfather—Toussaint's old tutor—Pierre Baptiste; and my aunt and cousins, the wife and children of Toussaint's brother, Paul.

When the soldiers swept through the district in which Pierre Baptiste lived, he refused to flee.

"I am too old," he told those who pleaded with him to go.

"We will help you," they argued.

"I will burden you, and you will be caught. Save yourselves," the old man urged. "I have no fear of the French."

Pierre Baptiste made no effort to resist the soldiers when they arrested him. He explained to his captors that he was blind and apologized for causing them difficulties. Around him he heard the crush of musket butts against flesh and bone. He heard the curses of the beaters and the cries of the beaten, but he was treated without cruelty.

As he sat on the still deck of the ship, the sun burning down on his uncovered head, Pierre Baptiste drifted into dreams of his past. He saw his wife come to him as she had as a young girl, before she grew heavy with the cares of age, before her mind left her to wander absently about, before Ghèdé slipped her soul away silently one night while both of them slept.

Pierre Baptiste was at peace with himself and his fate. He had lived a full life. He had known joy and suffering. He had seen birth and death. He had served the loa faithfully, and they had blessed him with knowledge and wisdom beyond that of most men. He had served his neighbors, and they had respected him.

What have I to gain by clinging stubbornly to my weary body, he thought. He had completed a stage of his journey. To start the next his soul had to be freed from its imprisonment, and only the process of death could do that.

When Pierre Baptiste heard the sounds of the shots and the blows falling sickeningly on unprotected heads, when he heard the screams and curses of the victims of Leclerc's fears, he sat quietly waiting for his turn. As he sensed the sailors approaching him, Pierre Baptiste had a sudden realization that for the past ten years he had been a free man. For ten long years he had not carried chains on his legs or felt the sting of the whip on his shoulders or back.

Pierre Baptiste smiled as the belaying pin smashed into his head. He was still conscious when he hit the water. He made no effort to fight the cool womb that surrounded him and pulled the last of the air from his lungs. He followed eagerly his divine guide into the depths of the abysmal waters where he would rest for a year and a day before entering the next stage of his journey.

My aunt and cousins also died that day, drowned in the harbor. My uncle, Paul Louverture, was not in the city and lived for several months longer. An officer loyal to Toussaint who objected to Paul's plea that they all support Dessalines as the Captain-General of the rebellion beheaded him.

On the day that Pétion attacked the Cape, Leclerc directed Pauline to take refuge on one of the naval ships in the harbor.

Pauline refused. "I am the sister of Napoléon and a Bonaparte," she informed the aide-de-camp who came for her, "I am not afraid."

The aide-de-camp, following Leclerc's orders, informed her that he was to use force to make her go if he must. She refused to leave her chair. The officer ordered four soldiers to pick up the chair and carry her to the dock. Another soldier carried her son on his shoulders. Another held Pauline's parasol over her head as they walked.

Pauline laughed at the silly parade they made. "We are like mummers at the playhouse," she explained.

When the soldiers were putting the chair and its occupant into a lighter to row her to the ship, word came that Pétion had been repulsed, and the danger was over.

"See!" Pauline exclaimed. "I told you there was no need for me to go on board a ship!"

Leclerc repulsed Pétion's attack on the Cape, but found himself evermore isolated from the rest of the colony. He retired to his bed, too sick to dictate reports to France of his recent losses.

Leclerc fell into the pattern of avoiding people. He refused audiences, except for Pauline, whom he wanted always with him. The only other person he wanted to see was Christophe. Christophe was the last of the black generals still loyal to France, and his presence gave some comfort to Leclerc.

Leclerc sent for Christophe, often two or three times a day, to praise him for his loyalty.

"I will make you my second in command," Leclerc promised Christophe. "I will see that France rewards you with wealth and honor."

Christophe dreaded the thought of returning to the mountains and the ordeal of guerrilla warfare. He knew he could not hope to stay indefinitely at the Cape. He knew also that the earlier he joined the rebels the stronger his future position with them would be. He simply could not tear himself away from the pleasures of the city. As much as he despised Leclerc's hypocrisy, he enjoyed the honors the French conferred on him. Finally, though, even Christophe realized that the French position in Saint-Domingue was bankrupt.

"I have riches and honor enough," Christophe replied to a startled Leclerc when the latter began once more to heap upon the black general promises of future rewards. "I shame myself in staying here," Christophe continued. "Tomorrow I shall be with Pétion and Dessalines."

That day Christophe marched his troops openly from the city. No one attempted to stop him.

After Christophe defected, Leclerc fell even deeper into his sickness. The drums from the Morne Haut-du-Cap kept him from sleeping. Even when they were silent, he heard them in the pounding in his ears, as a sailor hears the ocean when he is far inland.

Day and night Leclerc thought only of death as he watched what he came to see as Saint-Domingue's funeral pyre, the glow of flames by night and the haze of smoke by day that marked the fires consuming the houses, fields and forests of the island.

Pauline was frightened by her husband's illness. She visited him each day, but she could not stay long because his suffering brought her anxiety. In the evening she continued her dinners and parties. She considered it her duty to keep up the spirits of what was now a besieged city, open only by sea. But nothing, not the music, not the wine, not the perfume of the tropical flowers laid in giant sprays along the dinner table, could mask the stench of death flowing from the city hospital.

On Monday morning, November first, 1802, Leclerc appeared to rally from his sickness. He sat up in bed and attempted to prepare a summary report for the Minister of Marine, but he could not force himself to commit the figures to paper—twenty-four thousand French soldiers dead, eight thousand hospitalized, two thousand, many walking corpses, left to hold the island for France.

Leclerc lay back in exhaustion. He could not stop a great pain of grief from swelling up in his chest. Despite his efforts to hold his decorum, he burst into tears. In ten months, what had he done? Sacrificed the flower of the French army. Lit the fuse to a race war of uncompromising ferocity.

Leclerc knew he was dying. He knew also that he was all that prevented Saint-Domingue from becoming in its fire and blood the altar to the Holocaust foreseen by the divines. Then Rochambeau and Dessalines would stand face to face unhampered by any inhibition of civilization.

We deserve a better fate, Leclerc mourned to himself. I deserve a better fate, he corrected himself. The blacks deserve better. France deserves better.

That night Leclerc complained of the drums. Pauline, who had come to mark the deathwatch with him, ordered the shutters closed.

He complained of the heat when they were closed. "I burn. I burn, Pauline, I burn," he moaned and shoved away the bedclothes.

She had the shutters opened again and had the servant bathe him with cold water.

"The fires, they never stop burning," Leclerc lamented.

"Lie still, Victor," Pauline begged.

"Day and night I see the fires," he groaned.

The windows of the room opened onto the city and the harbor beyond. Pauline knew he could see no fires from where he lay, but to humor him she again had the shutters closed.

"No!" Leclerc ordered. "I must have air. I can not breathe."

Pauline indicated for the servant to leave the shutters open.

"Will the drums never stop!" he complained. "I cannot sleep with those drums!"

Pauline was frightened by the wildness in her husband's eyes, and sent the servant to fetch the doctor.

"No, is too late for the doctor," cried Leclerc. "Send for the priest."

Pauline did not know what to do. She wanted to hold her husband, but she was afraid to because of the fever and because she could not touch someone dying. She stood as close to Leclerc as she dared without touching him.

"I will be in hell tonight," he said in a frightened voice.

"Hush, Victor," she answered, wishing the priest would hurry.

"I will burn forever."

When the priest arrived, Leclerc was dead.

Leclerc's body was prepared to be shipped home to France for his funeral. The body was embalmed and placed in a lead casket. Pauline had his heart put into a lead vase which she personally sealed in a golden urn. She had inscribed on the urn: "Pauline Bonaparte, married to General Leclerc on the fourteenth of June, 1797, has enclosed her love with her husband's heart. She shared his perils and his glory."

On November tenth, eight days after his death, she and their son sailed with his body on the captured English frigate "Swiftsure." The grieving family landed in Toulon on New Year's Day, 1803.

Rochambeau welcomed his promotion to command of the French forces. Leclerc had too long dallied with the rebels. His use of persuasion and tricks had only delayed the inevitable. The rebels had only two choices, slavery or death, and Rochambeau intended to enforce those choices if it meant killing every black and mulatto man, woman and child on the island.

Rochambeau had a special hatred of the mulattos. Even though the blacks might struggle to resist the natural order of things, their fate was clear. They were destined to serve the whites. But the mulattos persisted in the belief that the white blood flowing in their veins compensated for the black blood. They considered themselves the allies of the whites in the struggle against the blacks and sought to deny their origins in slavery. Rochambeau was determined that before he left Saint-Domingue the natural order would be restored, and there would be no discussion on the island of the rights of blacks or mulattos.

Rochambeau wrote to the Minister of Marine and promised full compliance to Napoléon's instructions. He requested reinforcements to replace the men Leclerc had squandered. He needed fifteen thousand soldiers immediately, ten thousand more by the first of the year, and ten thousand more by spring.

When the first reinforcements arrived, ones originally requested by Leclerc, Rochambeau launched a major offensive against Dessalines, Pétion, Christophe and their allies. Throughout the months of November and December of 1802 the island groaned under a blood bath such as it had not experienced in its four hundred-year history of suffering.

Rochambeau executed five hundred prisoners at the Cape and buried them in a common grave.

Dessalines hanged five hundred French soldiers in the hills behind the Cape where the city's inhabitants could see their swinging bodies.

Rochambeau imported from Cuba fifteen hundred dogs trained to hunt blacks. On the day the dogs arrived, the French held a special celebration. The fête was held on the grounds of the former convent of the Jesuits. The women dressed in their brightest finery and carried parasols for protection from the sun. Priests blessed the occasion and offered prayers for the dogs' success. Rochambeau arrived to martial music, accompanied by his personal staff.

Several young black men were tied to stakes in the center of an improvised arena.

"Do not be concerned," Rochambeau reassured the squeamish among the spectators. "Negroes do not feel pain as we do," he explained. "They can contract their muscles with so much force, they can make themselves insensible to pain."

Rochambeau ordered the dogs released. The dogs approached the victims cautiously and refused to attack them. Rochambeau's chief-of-staff jumped into the arena and split open the belly of one of the blacks—his own servant whom he had given to Rochambeau for the occasion. The dogs leaped at the wounded man and devoured him. The French watching applauded and the band played.

Dessalines retaliated, torture for torture, atrocity for atrocity.

The bays and harbors of the North were so filled with the dead that the inhabitants refused to eat fish caught near the shore.

The event that drove Borgella, the mayor of Port-au-Prince, from the island occurred in his city in January. Rochambeau, buoyed by new reinforcements from France, went to Port-au-Prince to open his war of attrition against the mulattos.

The French commander invited the leading citizens to a ball. At midnight he called for the dancing to stop and divided the mulatto women from their husbands for the entertainment. After some minutes the women were led into a room adjoining the ballroom. The second room was lit by a single lamp and was hung in black draperies decorated with white skulls. In the corners of the room stood wooden coffins. From behind the draperies came the sounds of a funeral dirge.

The macabre setting disconcerted the mulatto women, but they found reassurance in the continuing gaiety of their host and his friends. At Rochambeau's urging, the women approached the coffins. As they began reluctantly to raise the lids—and before their eyes were filled with the sight of their husbands' mutilated corpses lying in the coffins and their ears filled with the sounds of their own screams—Rochambeau announced with undisguised pleasure: "Thank you, ladies. You have assisted at the funeral services of your husbands."

In the winter and spring of 1803, Rochambeau's campaign against the mulattos filled the South with agonies paralleling those of the North. By March the South was in full rebellion.

Despite his campaigns of terror, Rochambeau could not strike the deathblow to the resistance. Whether or not Napoléon would have sent him enough troops for him to have succeeded in annihilating every rebel on the island, we will never know. The matter was decided by England.

On April twenty-fifth, 1803, England withdrew its diplomatic representative from France in preparation for war.

On May third, Napoléon sold Louisiana to the United States.

On May sixteenth, England and France were again at war. There were no more reinforcements for Rochambeau.

On May eighteenth, Dessalines called for a conference at Arcahaie of the leaders of the war against the French. There he presented the armies with a new flag. They would no longer fight under the tricolor of Revolutionary France. Their flag had two colors only, blue and red.

"The flag of independence," Dessalines declared. "There is no white in it as there shall be no whites on this island. Above, the blue of honor, as the blue sky is above us. Below, the red of courage, the red of fire, the red of the blood of patriots which soaks our land. And across our banner shall be inscribed our faith: 'Liberty or Death!'"

One prominent leader who did not attend the conference at Arcahaie was Lamour Derance. He refused to submit to Dessalines' leadership. For his insolence, Dessalines imprisoned and then executed him.

By the middle of November, 1803, Rochambeau was beaten. He held only the Cape and he could not hold it for long.

On November sixteenth, a torrential rainfall kept Dessalines from overrunning the forts guarding the city from the land.

On November seventeenth, Rochambeau contacted the British naval squadron blockading the Cape and asked for clear passage to France or a neutral country. The British commander, Captain Loring, refused. If Rochambeau evacuated the city, it would be to a British prison.

Rochambeau expected compassion from the English. As Europeans they should have been appalled at the threat of blacks massacring whites. But the British commander remained adamant.

Rochambeau sued to Dessalines for peace terms.

"Leave or die," Dessalines answered.

Rochambeau hoped to slip past the British fleet. On November twenty-fifth, when a squall hit the coast and blew the British ships off station, he embarked eight thousand of his soldiers and their families—all who were well enough to travel—into twenty ships. But the wind kept his fleet pinned in the harbor.

On November thirtieth, Dessalines, tired of waiting for Rochambeau to leave, occupied the forts of the city and threatened to blow the French ships from the water.

Rochambeau appealed to Dessalines for mercy for the French wounded and sick still in the city hospitals. Dessalines agreed.

Loring, seeing the blue and red flag flying from Fort Picolet, sent a dispatch boat to investigate. Rochambeau gratefully surrendered to the English officer, struck his colors and sailed from the Cape to a British prison, where he stayed until he was exchanged in 1811. He was killed in 1813 in the battle of Leipzig.

After Rochambeau's departure, Dessalines' systematically burned every inch of the Cape. The sick and wounded French soldiers were consumed in the flames.

On the last day of December in 1803, the leaders of the island met at Gonaïves for the final reading of the Declaration of Independence of their new nation.

"We are Saint-Domingue no more," Dessalines announced, "but Haïti, the second free nation in the new world and the first black one."

The British agent, Hugh Cathcart, who had often urged Toussaint to declare independence, attended the meeting at Gonaïves. He sought to revive British trade. Dessalines agreed, but only if the English agreed to sell him guns and ammunition. Cathcart demanded that the weapons not be used against whites.

Early in 1804, Dessalines used his new arms in a bloody purge of the whites still living on the island.

CHAPTER 34
Death and Dishonor

The cell in which Toussaint was confined in the prison at Fort de Joux was on the ground floor. It was four meters square with an arching stone roof, thick stone walls, one door, one barred window, a fireplace, one chair, a table, one candle and a pallet of straw. Mars Plaisir slept in another room and visited Toussaint only when permitted by the jailer, Jean-Louis Baille. André Rigaud was for a time imprisoned in a cell near Toussaint, but Napoléon allowed no communication between the two enemies.

When he was put in the cell, Toussaint was stripped of the uniform he had worn since his arrest and was given dirty prison clothes to wear, torn rags which irritated his skin and provided little protection from the dampness of the stones and cool mountain nights. The clothes and the straw sleeping pallet were lice infected. Toussaint was allowed to keep his watch, two letters from his wife and pen and paper.

In September, Napoléon's aide-de-camp, Marie François Auguste Louis Caffarelli, a thin, mustached, aristocratic, soft-spoken man of thirty-six years, visited Toussaint. Caffarelli wore an expensively tailored uniform of a major general and carried in his cuff a perfumed handkerchief which he periodically pulled out and waved beneath his nose to relieve himself of the smells of the prison.

"If you cooperate with me, I can make your life considerably easier," he told Toussaint. "The First Consul is interested in your well-being."

"If Bonaparte is concerned with my well-being," Toussaint answered, "why does he not respond to my letters? I have written him a dozen times. Why am I not allowed to see my family? Why am I never allowed to see the sky or smell the fresh air?"

"You forget you are a prisoner," Caffarelli replied.

"I do not forget," Toussaint answered sharply.

Caffarelli's visits continued throughout the fall. He wanted Toussaint to confess he had acted treasonably when he was Governor-General of Saint-Domingue, and he wanted to know where Toussaint buried his treasure.

Toussaint grew weary of denying again and again his guilt. To escape Caffarelli's patient attack, he sat huddled by the fireplace, the vermin ridden blanket wrapped tightly around his shoulders.

In October, Caffarelli brought him a second blanket.

"The First Consul is concerned for your health," Caffarelli explained. "He asked me to bring you this."

Toussaint took the blanket and added it to the other one covering his trembling body.

"I need handkerchiefs," he complained. "I have asked for them repeatedly. They are denied me."

Caffarelli made no response. He waited patiently for Toussaint to finish coughing. When Toussaint finally got control of his body, coughed the phlegm from his lungs and cleared his nose so that he could breathe without gasping, Caffarelli resumed his questioning.

"I have with me the recent letter you dictated for the First Consul. It does not answer our questions."

"I do not lie," Toussaint responded.

"Do you deny that you were planning with the British to overthrow the Republic in Saint-Domingue and set up an independent state with you as its head?" Caffarelli persisted.

"I have always been loyal to the Republic," Toussaint answered without emotion. "My only wish is that the Republic did not chose to reward me so harshly."

"You need only to cooperate with the First Consul in clarifying some questions and you will see your family again," Caffarelli promised.

"Napoléon will never let me see them," Toussaint replied wearily.

"Where did you bury your treasure?" Caffarelli asked.

Toussaint made no reply. Caffarelli waited several minutes and then patiently repeated the question.

"I didn't bury it," Toussaint replied wearily. "I had none."

"You had soldiers of your personal guard bury your treasure and then you executed them, did you not?"

"No."

"Do you have bank accounts in the United States?"

"No."

"In Britain?"

"No."

"In Jamaica?"

"No."

"You do," Caffarelli insisted.

Toussaint turned from his tormentor and curled himself into a ball in the corner of the cell by the hearth. He refused to answer any more questions. To drown out all sounds other than its rhythmic ticking, he held his watch tightly to his ear.

Caffarelli rose and left.

When he was alone, Toussaint spoke, too softly even for his own ears to hear above the ticking of the watch.

"I have lost many things, all more precious than money."

Baille entered the cell, gathered up Toussaint's candle, pen and writing paper, crossed to the huddled form and pulled the watch from his unresisting hand.

"I am sorry, General," Baille said awkwardly, "but I must."

When Baille exited from the cell he tried to close the heavy door quietly.

With the sharp snap of the latch falling, Toussaint's eyes opened. In the silence that followed he could not close them.

Mars Plaisir was released from the prison at the end of October. He did not want to leave Toussaint, but Baille would not let him stay.

Soon after his release, Mars understood the reason. Napoléon did not believe Toussaint's denials of hidden wealth. Mars was to be sent back to Saint-Domingue to lead the French to the treasure. Mars did not know what tortures the French were prepared to inflict upon him to produce what he knew did not exist, but he was saved from the ordeal by the deteriorating military position of the French and was never sent back to the island.

When he was released from prison, Mars dedicated himself to working for Toussaint's release, or, if that were impossible, to the improvement of the conditions of his imprisonment.

Mars contacted members of the Society of the Friends of the Negro, men who early supported abolition and were vocal in their admiration of Toussaint. Mars received some money, enough to cover his immediate expenses, and much sympathy, but, as Abbé Grégoire predicted when Mars called upon him, no means of touching the sympathy of the French people or of reaching Napoléon Bonaparte.

In his efforts to secure help from former friends of Toussaint now living in France, Mars called upon Louis Duclero.

Duclero did not recognize Mars Plaisir's name, but the sentence neatly lettered on his card brought Duclero anxiety. His mind jumped with misgivings to the dispatches from Toussaint to Napoléon that he had hidden. He reluctantly agreed to see the caller.

Mars, in his quiet, intense way described for Duclero the inhuman conditions of Toussaint's imprisonment.

"But what can I do?" Duclero complained with a gesture of helplessness.

"You are a man of some means. Perhaps if you appealed to the First Consul...." Mars' voice trailed off, leaving the sentence incomplete.

"I have no influence with Napoléon. There must be others, more able," Duclero insisted. "Senator Grégoire, for instance."

"I have spoken to all of the Friends of the Negro, Abbé Grégoire included. None...." Again Mars could not complete his thought. He sat, his eyes moist, starring helplessly at the table.

"I'll do what I can." Duclero promised.

After Mars left, Duclero had no idea why he had agreed to help. More importantly, he had no idea what to do.

For several weeks he did nothing. But he could not erase from his mind the small, elderly mulatto gentleman quietly begging for help. Nor could Duclero erase from his mind the images Mars had painted of Toussaint's suffering in prison. Finally, more from the need to purge his conscience than from any illusions that he could effect any changes, Duclero sought an audience with the Minister of Justice, André Joseph Abrimal. Duclero had heard only praise for the good Abrimal and hoped that his compassion might be equal to his integrity.

Duclero's appointment was for 10:00 a.m. He sat in the austere reception hall of the Palace of Justice for an hour. When he inquired as to the reason for the delay, he was told that the Minister was unexpectedly detained.

"Shall I wait or return later?"

"Monsieur must chose as he wishes."

"May I return at ten tomorrow?"

"I am certain his Excellency will be accessible at that hour."

The next day, Duclero returned at ten and again sat. His inquiries brought polite evasions. This time he elected to wait. Finally, at three he was informed, with apologies, that the Minister had left at two.

For two weeks Duclero returned each working day at ten and waited for the Minister to see him. His persistence was met with apologies and evasions. Duclero knew that Abrimal had no intentions of seeing him, but the situation angered him, and he refused to surrender.

Finally, when he arrived one morning promptly at ten, a deputy-secretary ushered him to one corner of the reception room. "Surely, Monsieur, you must realize that the Minister will not see you?" he said.

"He has not informed me of the fact."

"Then allow me to inform you. He will not meet with you."

"Why does the a Minister of the Republic refuse to meet with one of its citizens?"

"Monsieur Duclero, let us not play with one another. The Minister knows the purpose of your visit."

"I informed him of my purpose when I requested an audience."

"He does not wish to speak to you or to anyone on the subject."

"I insist on my right to see him," Duclero persisted.

The deputy-secretary led him deeper into the recesses of the empty hall. "Citizen Duclero, I appeal to your good sense. You must realize the reason for the Minister's reluctance."

"No, Citizen Deputy," Duclero answered formally, "I do not."

The deputy-secretary frowned as if in some pain and waited several moments before replying.

"For God's sake," he finally blurted out of frustration. "You must realize that the First Consul has no intention of responding to your petition."

"That is the purpose of my visit," Duclero persisted, "to persuade Minister Abrimal to persuade Bonaparte to change his mind!"

"The Minister will not speak to the First Consul on the matter," the deputy continued, appealing to Duclero for reason. "General Bonaparte has specifically forbidden the name of the man to whom we refer to be spoken in his presence."

The deputy-secretary was for a moment shaken by his indiscretion, but he quickly gained control of himself.

"To save you from more embarrassment, Citizen Duclero," he continued, "I have said to you more than I should. If you refer to anything I have said, I will, of course, deny having said it."

The deputy-secretary turned to leave. From a polite distance he turned back to Duclero. "You are free, of course," he said in a formal voice, "to call upon the Minister at your convenience. Hopefully, sometime he will be able to see you." He continued in a more intimate voice. "If you wish to make a foolish spectacle of yourself each day waiting, that is, of course, your choice." He turned again and walked briskly away.

As Duclero rode home, he contemplated returning each day to the Ministry until he won an audience. Before he reached home, his gentler nature prevailed, and he abandoned the project as a waste of time.

For several weeks Duclero brooded on his inadequacy to aid Toussaint. Mars Plaisir called several times for appointments, but Duclero avoided him. Finally he wrote him a brief note in which he described his efforts in Toussaint's behalf and declared his inability to do more. Mars replied with a polite note of appreciation. In it he gave the names and addresses of others working for Toussaint's welfare, urging Duclero to consider joining his efforts with theirs. Mars included in the note the address of Toussaint's family.

Duclero put Mars' letter aside, but he could not get his mind off the matter. Finally, he decided that the one constructive thing he might do is visit Madame Louverture and express to her his concern, and that of the well-intentioned people of France, for her and her family's misfortunes. He thought it might comfort her to know that many in France thought highly of her husband and were working to bring some relief to the conditions of his imprisonment. Through an old school friend in the Ministry of the Interior, Duclero secured permission to visit with her.

Although he was well aware of his political impotence, on the long journey south Duclero took some solace in his efforts to be humanitarian. He knew his small act of kindness would not correct the abuses of justice, but it might make the endurance of injustice more bearable

Justine ushered Duclero in to see Suzanne. Suzanne was seated on a plain, sturdy rocking chair. The afternoon sun flooded through the uncurtained window and engulfed her. She sat motionless, staring into the light, her hands folded lightly in her lap. She was dressed in a simple frock, clean and neat. She wore neither jewelry nor lace.

Duclero approached her quietly. He stood for several moments a few feet from her waiting for her to acknowledge his presence. When she didn't, he spoke hesitantly.

"Madame Louverture?"

She turned her head toward him, looked at him, and, showing no interest in him at all, turned her gaze again to the setting sun.

"Madame Louverture.... I am Louis Duclero."

She made no sign of having heard him. He waited a moment and then continued.

"I knew and respected your husband when he was Governor-General of Saint-Domingue.... I have come to pay my respects to his wife and family. And to express to you my outrage at the way he has been mistreated by my government."

Suzanne made no response. She continued to stare out of the window.

"I want you to know that there are thousands of Frenchmen who share my sentiments. We want you to know that we do not intend to rest until this injustice has been righted."

Suzanne turned again to look at him. Her eyes focused on his for a moment. He thought she was about to speak, but she turned her attention again to the window and the setting sun beyond it.

Duclero thought to speak again, decided against it, turned and left the room.

The experience unnerved Duclero. He had meant to perform a kindness. For his efforts he felt stupid and impotent. He returned immediately to Paris and decided to let the course of history flow on without further help from him.

In his cell in Fort du Joux, Toussaint felt a crushing loneliness. His chest felt as if it would crack from the pressure pushing upon it. Now that Mars had been taken from him and even Caffarelli visited him no more, the only persons he saw were Baille and the guards who came with Baille to bring his food and occasionally empty the stinking ordure from his pot.

As winter deepened, Toussaint huddled under his rotting blankets. His body shivered without pause in the bitter cold. For months the sun failed to enter his cell. The room was lit only by the reflection of the gray sky and the uneven glow of the small fire Baille allowed him. In the drafty cell the fire warmed only to the edge of the hearth.

Toussaint knew he was dying, but Baille allowed him no doctor. When Toussaint implored, Baille told him it would be useless to bring a doctor.

"The doctor could not treat you," Baille explained. "He knows nothing about the physiology of Negroes."

Baille continued to send his reports to the Minister of Justice. When he could report no word of Toussaint's hidden fortune, he was instructed, on the pretext that the prisoner might be suicidal, to watch him day and night and to report everything he said.

"Mostly," Baille wrote in response, "the prisoner murmurs to himself, 'Give me fire. I freeze.'"

In March, the sun again visited the cell briefly each day, touching the stones high above Toussaint's reach. He held to the light as an omen that he would survive the cold.

The fever burning in his brain took him back to Saint-Domingue. In his mind it seemed that wherever he walked his fever set fire to the grass. The flames consumed the fields and trees, even the mountains and rivers, but they could not stanch the bone shattering cold that wracked his body.

Toussaint reached in his mind for Suzanne's warm body to draw from him the cold. When she held him, he could hear in her heart the drums that no longer sounded in his.

In his delirium, it was not Suzanne who held him, but Mary, the Queen of Heaven. She wrapped him in her rough cloak and fed him from her black breasts.

When she warmed him and eased the pains in his chest and belly, Toussaint recognized her.

"Nananbuluku!" he cried. "Mother."

On Thursday, April seventh, 1803, Toussaint sat on his one chair, his body pressed to the tepid bricks of the fireplace, his face arched upward to the splash of spring sunlight above him on the wall. He did not respond when Baille called to him. The jailer opened the cell door and discovered that the prisoner was dead.

CHAPTER 35
The Abysmal Waters

At midnight on Sunday, April eighth, 1804, on the Morne Chapelet south of Desachaux, a year and a day after Toussaint's death, a ceremony was conducted to recall his soul into the life of the people.

Despite Henri Christophe's claims that he was sponsoring the ceremony because Toussaint's close relatives were either dead or in France, the houngan knew that the general hoped to increase his political strength through Toussaint. Christophe and Dessalines had quarreled, and Christophe sought to call the great father to his aid.

The houngan recognized the precariousness of his position. Dessalines had outlawed the voudoun and would not forgive anyone helping Christophe increase his power. For the sake of the deceased and the well being of the community, the houngan could not deny a request for the rites of reclamation, but he demanded compensation appropriate to the dangers.

The night was threatening. In the northeast, great black clouds boiled up against the lighter blackness of the night, blocking the stars from view. Dry lightning lit the clouds, dancing in rhythms echoing those of the ceremony.

The houngan erected a small tent of white sheets at one end of a clearing, and, set back in the trees on the far side of the clearing, a hounfor of freshly cut branches. The sheets of the tent hung motionless in the still air as the houngan and his entourage, dressed in traditional white robes, made their slow walk from the hounfor to the tent. A single hounsis followed the priest, carrying upon her head a red earthen jar—the govi in which Toussaint's soul was to be captured.

Behind the hounsis came the la-place, the houngan's chief assistant, with a whip in his hand to ward off any wandering spirit who might seek to claim the govi for himself. They were attended by six functionaries whose immediate task was to place straw mats in front of the hounsis to keep her bare feet from touching the earth. If given the opportunity, invisibles would mount from the earth through her bare feet to take possession of the govi and deny it to Toussaint.

When the procession reached the tent, the houngan entered. The hounsis lay upon the mats before the entrance, the jar still upon her head, its mouth facing the tent. The lesser assistants spread a sheet over her, hiding her and the govi from view. The la-place stood beside her, whip in hand.

Inside the tent, the houngan lit a candle and began to chant and shake his sacred rattle and bell. The drummers and singers outside the tent echoed his rhythms.

The sounds of the drums carried far. All who heard them understood the nature of their mission. The people gathered in the small circle hoped that Papa Toussaint would be compliant, for if the struggle were long, there would be time for those who wished to prevent the ceremony to discover its location.

In attendance at the ceremony was the mulatto woman, Anacaona. When she heard that Toussaint had died, she marked carefully in her mind the date of his death and made her way to the area of Desachaux in time for the calling of his soul.

For the two years since Moïse's death, she had lived with the maroons of the Saddle. They remembered her mother and received her back as one of their own.

From Lamour Derance, Anacaona learned much. She was an apt pupil and moved quickly through the stages of priesthood. Her experience of the mysteries went deeper than she imagined possible. The land received her offerings with special love, for in her, she discovered, flowed the blood of a civilization at the edge of extinction. Through her it breathed for a moment longer.

The white slavers brought to Saint-Domingue Africans from many tribes, but for the safety of the whites, scattered them throughout the island. The slave owners did not want members of a single tribe concentrated in a single area. The slaves, alone among strangers, discovered that those from other tribes worshipped similar gods. In time the Rada gods of the Dahomean Empire predominated.

The gods of Dahomey were hospitable and gracious, but they were no match for Yahweh, the European jealous god of vengeance.

In the inner reaches of the island, hidden in the protecting mountains, a tiny remnant of Arawaks and Caribs, refugees from earlier enslavement and genocide in the name of the European's male-god-in-three-persons, waited and prayed. When the maroons, refugees from the second enslavement, fled into the mountains, they found a nation of gods waiting for them, cruel gods, hungry for worshipers, gods made crafty from earlier encounters with Yahweh.

It was these gods who spoke to Anacaona, daughter of Anacaona, descendant of Anacaona, Carib, martyred queen of the Xaraguas, who welcomed the Europeans with songs of love and was rewarded by them with death from a gibbet.

The houngan in the tent, his candle casting distorted shadows on the white sheet, chanted for many minutes with no response, his words seldom comprehensible to the celebrants without. Occasionally they heard the name of Légba or Ghèdé, and entreaties to Toussaint to appear. The houngan sometimes pleaded, sometimes begged, sometimes commanded, but to no avail. It was clear to all that Toussaint's gros-bon-ange would be difficult to persuade.

Finally, softly, as if from a far distance, and then louder, another voice was heard from the tent. At first the voice made gasping sounds, as a drowning man might make. Gradually the voice became distinct.

"Who calls me? Who forces me from my rest?"

Christophe recognized Toussaint's voice, and respected the anger in it. Christophe's first impulse was to flee, but he knew he was protected by the ceremony.

"It is I, my General," Christophe answered.

"Why do you call me? Why do you not let me sleep?"

"Your time of rest is over. You must return to your people."

"Go away!" Toussaint thundered. "Leave me in peace!"

The storm in the northeast echoed Toussaint's anger as the wind broke the still air and whipped through the clearing in small, sharp vortexes, ripping at the branches of the surrounding trees and the hounfor and shaking the sheets of the tent. The houngan's voice, still chanting, became choked, as if someone had him by the throat.

"Please, my General," pleaded Christophe. "It is for your sake we call you back, so that your immortality may be preserved."

"You lie! You care nothing for me!"

The wind whipped up swirls of dust. The hounsis, clinging to the govi, trembled in fear.

"Peace, my General," pleaded Christophe.

The wind whipped the dust into the faces of the celebrants, stinging their eyes.

"Go home!" Toussaint's voice screamed. "Leave me in peace."

"We cannot, my General," replied Christophe, his voice revealing his fear. "The loa would punish us if we fail to call so great a man. Have compassion on us, Papa Toussaint. What we do we do in obedience to God."

"I will not return."

For a few moments nothing was heard of Toussaint's voice. The only sounds were the drums, the chanting, the bell and the click of the asson. The wind grew still. Many began to fear that Toussaint had escaped back into the abysmal waters. Then, quietly at first, then louder, came the sound of weeping.

"Why do you cry?" Anacaona asked the question.

There was no answer to her question.

"Why do you weep?" she asked again. "Your children come to you in love. Does their love bring you pain?"

"You come in fear, not love." Toussaint's voice was still angry, but he was gentler with Anacaona than he had been with Christophe.

"We come in love," several of the celebrants insisted.

"You call to me from fear," Toussaint accused, "fear of what the loa will do to you if you abandon me in death as you abandoned me in life."

"No! No! Papa Toussaint!" cried many of the celebrants. "We loved you! We did not abandon you! We followed you always."

"It was Dessalines who betrayed you," accused Christophe.

"Silence!" shouted Toussaint. "I say you all betrayed me and continue to betray me!"

"Perhaps," corrected Anacaona, "it was you who betrayed your children."

A bolt of lightning struck near the clearing. The thunder from it momentarily eclipsed the drums. In the pause that followed the wind rose sharply, hitting from the northwest. Everyone could feel the rain in the darkness behind the wind.

"You have angered him," an elderly man chided Anacaona.

"Don't drive him away," others begged her.

"Be gentle with him, Mambo," instructed the old man.

"Call him back and apologize," others begged Anacaona.

"Your children call you back, Papa Toussaint," Anacaona called into the darkness beyond the dim glow of the candles reflected on the white sheets of the tent.

Her entreaty was answered only by the sounds of the ceremony and the low hiss of the approaching rain.

"Apologize," the elderly man quietly urged her.

"I call you back," continued Anacaona obediently, "contrite at heart for any offense I might have given you."

The wind stirred again, but gently and for a moment only. The sounds of the coming storm ebbed.

"I have suffered enough in my mortal body." Toussaint's voice came from the stirring of the wind. "I would not suffer forever in my immortal spirit."

"But the suffering is over, my General," Christophe interjected. "The French are gone and we are free. We call you to rejoice with us in our freedom."

"You lie!" A bolt of lightning struck again, but some distance away, and less threatening than before. "You do not call me to rejoice in peace," Toussaint continued. "You call me to give you the courage to murder Dessalines."

Christophe was stunned by the accusation. "But Dessalines is a tyrant!" he defended himself. "He takes away our liberty. He restores the tortures of slavery!"

Toussaint's voice groaned, as if from the pain of great sorrow. "I have seen too much of killing and dying. I will not return to more." His voice faded into the retreating storm. The heaviness in the air lightened. The celebrants felt his presence withdrawing from them.

"Don't desert us!" cried an old woman.

"We need you," cried another.

"Come back, Papa. Come back," the old man called. "We love you."

There was no answer.

"Call him," the old man instructed Anacaona. "I know he hears you."

"Does Papa Toussaint not love his children?" Anacaona asked.

His voice came again from the tent, very quiet, as if from a long distance away. "Their hands are covered with blood!"

"Are not yours?" Anacaona asked.

"Gently, Mambo," the old man urged.

"Are not yours?" she asked again.

Toussaint began to weep, as he had when he first appeared.

"Are not yours?" Anacaona asked a third time, unrestrained by the sounds of his suffering.

"I did what I had to," he replied.

"Do not they?" she asked.

"No!" Toussaint cried, his voice growing stronger. "I did what I did to keep them free. They are free, but they transgress still. They drive the loa from them as they drive me from them."

The celebrants were heart stricken by his accusation. Some wept. Some answered in anger. Some beat their chests in remorse. All insisted on their unbroken loyalty to Toussaint and to the loa.

Toussaint shouted them to silence.

"I say you drive me from you as you drive the loa from you. All of you!" He continued against their declarations of innocence. "The priests do not serve the loa. They look only to their own benefit. The rich wish only to purchase the blessings of God. The poor follow the bacalou, each stealing from his neighbor. In the end, when the loa are driven away, each will stand alone, distrustful of the others, afraid of the void before them. The fires that consume this island will burn until they engulf all the world."

"Is there no way to redemption for us?" asked the old man.

"There is none!" Toussaint declared. "Even now you arm against the innocent and follow Dessalines to the slaughter. The blood of the innocent calls for retribution!"

"Like the blood of Moïse," Anacaona accused.

"Mambo!" shouted the old man in alarm.

The others cried out against her, begging her to be quiet.

The storm which appeared to have passed to the north burst upon the clearing in a squall line. The wind knocked the tent to the ground, and the rain beat against the celebrants and soaked the drums. For a few moments everyone's concern was for his own safety and for the protection of the instruments of the rites. The attendants of the houngan looked to his safety and that of the hounsis. The drummers looked to the drums. The celebrants sought protection under trees and cloaks.

The force of the storm passed in a few minutes. Within a half an hour the rain ceased and the houngan began to put back the battered pieces of the ritual.

The celebrants were deeply disturbed by the course of events, and found in Toussaint's accusations and the interruption of the storm, signs of dire consequences. Many argued for abandoning the ceremony, and some left. But most stayed, persuaded by Christophe and the houngan that despite the dangers, the ceremony must be completed.

"We must call him back," the houngan argued. "It is the nature of those in the abysmal waters to resist. Like infants, they cry against the pain of birth. We conspire against them, against the living and against those not yet born when we fail in the responsibilities of the retirer d'en bas de l'eau. When one soul is lost," he explained, "all souls are lost. Like seeds from a ripped sack, each will fall away until where once there was promise of harvest for all, there will be scattered shoots, food only for birds and mice."

Some argued to have Anacaona driven from the ceremony.

"She angers him," an old woman argued.

The houngan recognized the power Anacaona had over Toussaint's spirit, and although he wished her influence on him was less disturbing, he knew he would not return if she were gone.

When the storm had passed, the houngan began again the ritual procession to the restructured tent. This time Toussaint's spirit was more compliant. Within a few minutes it appeared.

"Who are you who torments me?" the voice asked from the tent.

"He speaks to you," the old man prompted Anacaona when she was slow to respond.

"You know me," she answered.

"I do not," Toussaint replied.

"I am Anacaona, the barren."

"Why do you torment me? Was it not enough that I carried you in life? Must you pull at me now in death? Let me go."

"You are mistaken," Anacaona corrected him. "You did not carry me. I walk upright. And I let you go. Return to your watery sleep, and may your spirit find the peace of annihilation."

The other celebrants were dismayed. Many shouted at her in anger. Others argued that their warnings should have been heeded and she should have been driven from the circle.

"Do not listen to her," shouted an old woman.

"If you desert us, there will be no one to protect us from Dessalines," cried a man.

"We will find our way by ourselves," replied Anacaona.

"Call him back," commanded Christophe. "Do not drive him away again!"

"You can play this game no longer," the old man instructed her. "You dare not defy the loa."

"Come back," called Anacaona, her voice revealing a sense of resignation. "Your children will not let you sleep. They call to you to obey the loa."

The wind, which had grown gentle with the passing of the storm, rose once more, but died again as if exhausted from the effort.

"No!" Toussaint's voice answered from the stillness.

"You must," answered Anacaona. "I would let you sleep, but the choice is not mine, nor is it yours. It is the fate ordained for all of us by Nananbuluku, the giver of all life."

"No!" answered Toussaint.

"We cannot disobey the all powerful ones."

"They have no power over me," Toussaint declared.

For a few minutes Toussaint's voice was silent. The only sounds were those of the houngan and the drummers and the distant thunder from the storm now far to the southwest.

Toussaint began a third time to weep, this time quietly, as if from weariness.

"Weep," comforted Anacaona. "We weep with you. We weep for the sorrows you see. But as those who died in the middle passage returned to endure with their children centuries of slavery, so those who have lived to glimpse the promise of freedom must return to suffer with their children the pain of tyranny and incessant killing. But the wheel turns, endlessly turns. What you see may be the end. When the loa are neglected and each man turns against his brother, the wheel may stop. But it may turn again. We may live yet to see crimes expiated, victims appeased, murderers punished. We may die in despair and live to see the rise of the good father who will lead his children in recalling the loa. Weep, for to live is to suffer. But struggle no more. What is ordained is ordained. Today the loa are respected. The rites are properly performed. The people call. You must obey."

The houngan cried out in pain, calling for his la-place to assist him. The younger man rushed with his whip to the houngan's aid. The sounds of a struggle came from the tent. Suddenly the hounsis jumped up, trembled and then shook violently. The houngan and the la-place rushed from the tent, pushed her to the mats again and covered her again with the sheet. When she was again covered, the govi shook and rolled rapidly from side to side. Then it was still.

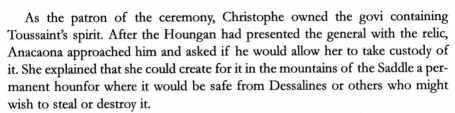

As the patron of the ceremony, Christophe owned the govi containing Toussaint's spirit. After the Houngan had presented the general with the relic, Anacaona approached him and asked if he would allow her to take custody of it. She explained that she could create for it in the mountains of the Saddle a permanent hounfor where it would be safe from Dessalines or others who might wish to steal or destroy it.

Christophe had some trepidation about giving up the govi, but he also feared the consequences of possessing it. When Anacaona assured him that in giving the jar to her he did not surrender the power he had earned in sponsoring Toussaint's recall, Christophe relented and allowed her to take it.

For three days and nights Anacaona carried her burden south through the Cahos and Black Mountains. She crossed the Artibonite at La Chappelle and followed the River Degiacie deep into the mountains the locals call Terrible. With much effort she reached and climbed the steep path beside the great falls in which dwells Simbi of the lesser waters.

There, in the darkness of the night, by the stream running from the springs to the falls, she put down the govi and sat beside it waiting for the dawn. The roar of the falls thundered in her ears. The coolness from the water rushing past first refreshed her from her climb and then, before dawn, chilled her through the light dress she wore.

With the first light of day, Anacaona rose, picked up again the govi and pushed as close to the top of the falls as she could, working her way past the burned trunks of the trees that lined the stream. Few pilgrims came to the top of the falls. Simbi dwells in the mists and pools at the bottom.

When she was as close to the falls as she could climb, Anacaona placed the govi in the stream and with a stick pushed it out into the current. For a moment the jar caught on some rocks, but the water pulled it free and spun it over the crest. From where she stood Anacaona could not see with her eyes what happened, but in her mind she saw the govi disappear beneath the crush of water and fall to the rocks below, shattering to bits.

Anacaona felt dizzy. She felt herself falling into the stream, but she held to the trunk of a tree and would not let herself go. In the darkness of the night she knew she could not have resisted the forces she had let loose, but in the light of the dawning sun she had the strength to hold on.

She had chosen carefully the place in which she released again Toussaint's soul. Simbi was a crossroads god who would escort Toussaint back to the abysmal waters, but not by way of his cousin, Agwé. Anacaona had witnessed in the storm the power in Toussaint's spirit. If Agwé of the ocean adopted Toussaint, Toussaint's power would truly be horrible to behold. Anacaona did not want to strengthen Toussaint. She wanted to send him to oblivion.

She sat, exhausted, by the stream until the sun was overhead. Then she rose and climbed down the rocky path. When she reached the bottom of the falls, she felt no malignant forces there. Simbi was not angered.

The revenge she had sworn the morning of Moïse's death was done, but she was of two minds concerning her actions. In sending Toussaint back into the abysmal waters, she had only fulfilled his own wishes.

She had before her, now, one more task: revenge for the murder of Lamour Derance. There would be no ambivalence in the fall of Dessalines.

The morning after the ceremony to recall Toussaint's soul, Christophe rode recklessly down the mountain, his horse stumbling on rocks and roots. Wet branches lashed at his face and body. He slashed at his mount with spurs and crop, heedless of the dangers before and around him. He would win. He had won. He had brought Toussaint's gros-bon-ange into his ramasser, into his sphere of power. Dessalines would fall. Dessalines must fall.

Christophe sensed the loa riding behind him, and he spurred his struggling mount to greater speed. He knew that soon one of the loa would mount him. Ogoun or Ghèdé or Papa Légba. Christophe never had been possessed by the gods. But now that he was destined to win, to rule, one would possess him.

Memories of Toussaint's fears and forbodings swirled through Christophe's brain. They were of no consequence, he told himself. Did not every soul struggle against the call to return?

Christophe felt the loa closing upon him. He whipped at his horse unmercifully. He wanted the power. He wanted to be mounted. Then why did he flee from his engagement with the all powerful ones?

He thought of the young mambo, Anacaona, who had commanded the resisting spirit of Toussaint. Christophe should not have let her go. He would send for her. She would summon the loa for him. She would intercede for him. She would help him bear the weight of the divine horsemen.

As Christophe pursued his dangerous race down the broken mountain path, his mind a convolution of fears and desires, the waning moon inched upward in the eastern sky. Before he reached the road at the bottom of the mountain the sun burst above the horizon. Its burning light erased the tiny crescent. Christophe felt an unaccustomed chill in the wind as it dried the rain and the sweat from his face and clothes.

BIBLIOGRAPHICAL NOTES

Papa Toussaint is a novel. The story involves historical characters and the sequence of events is to a great extent accurate, but the story has been imaginatively augmented. I chose to explore some events while ignoring others. I added descriptions, dialogue, motivations and interpretations. Two major characters are entirely fictional: the French planter Louis Duclero and the mulatto woman Anacaona. Louis Lamartiniere and his wife Marie-Jeanne were killed by the French but not in the manner depicted. Another of Toussaint's generals and his wife, whose stories I did not develop in the novel, suffered the fate described. I attributed the death to Lamartiniere and Marie-Jeanne for dramatic effect.

While the central themes of the novel – the three Rs of racism, revolution and religion – are as compelling today as they were two centuries ago, Toussaint's experiences are far removed from those of a white man living in the United States in the last half of the twentieth century. It was only through Placide that I could begin to approach the material. Placide was a boundary person living between cultures, uncertain of his identity. As such he gave me a point-of-view through which I could risk being wrong in my judgments of events. Isaac, Toussaint's natural son, wrote an account of his father's life. Placide, Toussaint's adopted son, did not. Until someone else speaks for him, *Papa Toussaint* will have to stand as Placide's testament.

In the research for the novel *Papa Toussaint* I drew on hundreds of sources of varying political points-of-view and levels of scholarship. Following is a brief outline of those which I found the most helpful.

MAJOR SOURCES

I am most indebted to three historians. Two are Haïtian, Thomas Madiou and H. Pauleus Sannon. The third is West Indian, C. L. R. James.

Madiou wrote his three volume *Histoire d'Haïti* in 1847 and had access to contemporary Haïtian newspapers and other documents which have since been destroyed.

Pauleus Sannon wrote his three volume *Histoire de Toussaint-Louverture* in 1933 and drew upon documents in the French archives which were not available to Madiou.

James wrote *The Black Jacobins* in 1938 and revised it in 1963. In my opinon, it is the best history of the period in English.

OTHER HAITIAN AUTHORS

Other Haitian authors which I found helpful are:

Alfred Nemours, *Histoire de la Captivité et de la Mort de Toussaint Louverture* and *Histoire de la Famille et de la Descendance de Toussaint Louverture.*

Joseph Saint-Remy, *Pétion et Haïti.*

Timoleon C. Brutus, *L'Homme d'Airain* (biography of Dessalines)

Gerard M. Laurent, *Toussaint Louverture, a Travers sa Correspondance, (1784-1798)*

Roland I. Perusse, *Historical Dictionary of Haïti.*

FRANCE

The "tide of official histories" that flowed after the "arrogant Bonaparte" are prodigious, indeed, as are the books recording the events of the French Revolution. It is impossible to narrow the choices, but five books I had at hand were:

Alfred Cobban, *A History fo France, Vol 1.*

E. J. Hobsbawn, *The Age of Revolution, 1789-1848.*

Will and Ariel Durant, *The Age of Napoleon.*

Margaret Laing, *Josephine & Napoleon.*

Len Ortzen, *Imperial Venus, the Story of Pauline Bonaparte-Borghese.*

UNITED STATES

Useful sources in exploring the involvement of the United States with Toussaint include:

The National Archives Diplomatic Relations files.

R. W. Logan, *Diplomatic Relations of the United States with Haïti, 1776-1891.*

Henry Adams, *History of the United States.*

GREAT BRITAIN

I spent several enjoyable weeks researching in the British Public Records Office. I found there many original documents, including Toussaint and Maitland's secret trade covenant and a copy of Toussaint's Constitution.

GEOGRAPHY

In the British Public Records Office I found also many late eighteenth century maps of Hispaniola, including large scale maps of most of the cities of Saint-Domingue.

I found also very useful:

Moreau de Saint-Mery, *Description Topographique, Physique, Civile, Politique et Historical de la Partie Française de l'Isle Saint-Domingue and Topographical* and *Political Description of the Spanish Part of the Island of Saint-Doming.*

M. E. Descourtilz, *Voyage d'un Naturaliste en Haïti, 1799-1803*.

With the approval of the Haïtian government I was able to secure U.S. National Defense 1:50,000 scale maps of Haïti. For place names I depended on the United States Board on Geographic Names Gazetteers for Haïti and the Dominican Republic.

Also, I visited—two centuries after the fact—many of the locations of the novel in Haïti, the Dominican Republic and France.

VOUDOUN

The books that were the most helpful were:

Maya Deren, *Divine Horsemen, Voodoo Gods of Haïti*.

Alfred Metraux, *Voodoo in Haïti*.

Harold Curlander, *The Drum and the Hoe, Life and Lore of the Haïtian People* and *Haïti Singing*.

Karen Brown, *The Vèvè of Haïtian Vodou: a Structural Analysis of Visual Imagery* (unpublished doctoral dissertation, Temple University).

MISCELLANEOUS

Two other sources which I found useful, although I reject their points-of-view, are:

Hubert Cole, *Christophe, King of Haïti*.
Thomas O. Ott, *The Haïtian Revolution, 1789-1804*.

MAP OF HISPANIOLA

Cristi

•Saint Yago

Central Mountains

Samana Bay

Santo Domingo

Sierra Prieta   •Santo Domingo City

Bahoruco